"KAGAN HAS PROVEN HIMSELF
A MASTER OF ADVENTURE."
—CLIVE CUSSLER

On-screen, Bonetti got up from his seat, looked out the observation slit for a moment, then raced back to the camera. His face was white and his voice was stitched with hysteria. "The beam is killing the trees around the southeast perimeter," he gasped. "I've never seen anything like it. All the leaves are dropping off and the trunks are exploding like bombs. The sap must be boiling." His voice became a hoarse whisper. "Mike. There are farms out there. A lot of people . . ."

Sunstroke

A family in New Mexico were the first victims.
Then a young couple in Florida.
The environment was destroyed,
every living thing ravaged by intense heat.

The government tried to cover it up.

Now, it is too late.

SUNSTROKE

DAVID KAGAN

DIAMOND BOOKS, NEW YORK

This book is a Diamond original edition, and has never been previously published.

SUNSTROKE

A Diamond Book / published by arrangement with the author

PRINTING HISTORY
Diamond edition / February 1993

ISBN: 1-55773-854-8

Diamond Books are published by The Berkley Publishing Group, 200 Madison Avenue, New York, New York 10016.
The name "DIAMOND" and its logo are trademarks belonging to Charter Communications, Inc.

PRINTED IN THE UNITED STATES OF AMERICA

10 9 8 7 6 5 4 3 2 1

To Nancy Love

Acknowledgments *

I would like to express my sincere gratitude to the individuals and organizations who contributed to this project. These include Christopher C. Craft, Jr., director of the Johnson Space Center in Houston; John P. Schaefer of the University of Arizona, who is chairman of the Solar Power Satellite Advisory Panel; Michael Riches of the U.S. Department of Energy; Wayne Jones, Lockheed Corporation; Ray A. Williamson, director of the Solar Power Satellite Project; Simon V. Manson, National Aeronautics and Space Administration; A.R. Thompson, National Radio Astronomy Observatory; and Dr. Peter Glaser of the A.D. Little engineering firm, the man who proposed the concept.

Special thanks to John Talbot, Senior Editor of the Berkley Publishing Group, for contributing an ingenious element to the book, and for making it all possible.

—D.K.

Preface *

This novel is based on the true-life $19.5 million alternative energy proposal prepared by NASA and the Department of Energy entitled *Solar Power Satellites* that is currently under review by the United States Congress.

—D.K.

The sun began to climb the heavens,
    And with new rays
Smote the surrounding fields.
                    —Homer, *Iliad*

September 10
The First Day *

Chapter 1 *

JIM ROBERTS OPENED a can of Budweiser and settled back on the worn sofa to watch the governor's speech. What had the newspaper headlines said? Something about the governor explaining the big light that'd been in the sky for the past few nights. It was somehow tied to the new power plant three miles up the road. The speech was supposed to last fifteen minutes and afterward there was that new cop show. He took a long gulp of beer. The kids were doing their homework and it was nice and quiet. It was going to be a great night for watching TV and drinking cold beer and just plain relaxing.

Jim was a stocky man of medium height in his early thirties, wearing a white T-shirt and blue jeans. He turned the volume up when the politician's familiar face appeared on the screen.

"A special good evening to the residents of Albuquerque, New Mexico. Tonight, I would like to tell you about that bright new addition to the night sky and how it will benefit your community. As some of you already know, that spectacular light is actually an enormous satellite locked in orbit over Albuquerque."

"You hear that, Sharon?" yelled Jim.

An indistinct reply came from the kitchen.

". . . and because the satellite is in geosynchronous orbit high above the earth, it is bathed in perpetual sunshine. Right now, even though night has fallen down here, this solar satellite is collecting sunlight and converting it to microwaves, the same type of energy your microwave oven uses to cook dinner. These microwaves are beamed to the experimental solar power plant just outside Albuquerque, where they are changed into electricity."

The television camera pulled back to show the governor standing inside an elaborate control room.

"I'm talking to you"—he stretched out his arms—"from the very heart of the solar power plant. At this very moment, all of

Albuquerque's energy needs are being supplied by free power from space. Without burning one barrel of oil or using nuclear fission to—''

And then the sound went dead. The governor's image shrank to a blue spot and vanished. Simultaneously the lights in the house went out.

''Hey!'' cried Sharon. ''What happened to the power? Better check the circuit breaker.''

The TV set was dark and silent and there wasn't a light on in the house. It also seemed oddly quiet: the soft hum from the dishwasher and the air conditioner was missing.

Jim got up too abruptly and hit his shin against the sharp edge of the coffee table. He winced from the pain and massaged his sore leg. He could barely make out the ghostly figure of his wife standing in the doorway. ''Why don't you light some candles, so I can see where I'm going?''

''Right, boss.'' Sharon knew the house so well that she moved in the dark with the confidence of a blind person in familiar surroundings. She took the utility candles from the French chest in the dining room and went to the kitchen for matches.

She had just lit a candle and was letting wax drip in the bottom of a saucer to hold it upright when three boys came boiling out of a distant bedroom and raced into the living room. Eleven-year-old Eric was in the lead, followed by Tom, nine, and Jeff, five. All three were towheads and slightly small for their ages.

''Hey, Mom and Dad!'' yelled Eric. ''The lights don't work.''

''I'm scared,'' announced Jeff.

''That's because you're a big baby,'' accused Tom.

''I am *not*.''

''Knock it off, you guys,'' ordered Jim.

Sharon took the burning candle into the living room and placed it on the coffee table. The glow illuminated her chin and her full lips, and brought out the golden highlights in her hair. The flickering candlelight cast shadows on the wall that twisted and shifted. The boys huddled around the dim but cheerful glow.

Jim went over to a nearby window and peered outside. ''I'll be damned,'' he said. All of the other farmhouses on the outskirts of Albuquerque were dark, too. He glanced accusingly at the new satellite, huge and bright, shining like a lamp high in the cloudless sky. What the hell happened to all that free power from space?

''What's wrong?'' asked Sharon.

"There isn't a light on in the whole valley," he replied. "That new power plant must have screwed up."

"Oh, no!" she exclaimed. "We've got two weeks' worth of steaks and chops in the freezer."

Jim shrugged. "There's nothing we can do about it but wait for the 'lectricity to come back on."

He looked at his digital watch. It was 7:05 P.M. The power had been off four minutes.

The three boys began to roughhouse, rolling around on the floor and bumping against the sofa. Their loud, raucous giggling was incessant and irritating.

"Look, kids," said Jim heavily. "Your mom's upset. How about taking it easy tonight?"

"Sure, Dad." Eric stood up and began making menacing shadows on the wall with his hands, first a bird of prey, then a horned devil. Jeff was fascinated by them at first, then quickly became frightened and started to cry.

"Come on, guys," groaned Jim. "Settle down."

At Red Desert Farm, where Jim worked during the day, he often referred to his sons as "my wild animals" and told his foreman how it was a full-time job taming them. It wasn't that he didn't love the boys. There were just some nights when he felt like auctioning them off.

"Maybe there's something on the radio," suggested Sharon.

Jim got up and went to the kitchen, felt along the counter for their battery-powered Sony, found it, and tuned in a Santa Fe station. For an instant soft music filled the air. Then suddenly the music was drowned out in static that rose sharply in pitch to a grating, animallike screech. He furiously turned the dial but the radio still produced the same shrieking static. He became exasperated and switched it off.

"This is just too goddamned much," he said in a hoarse whisper. "First no 'lectricity and now the radio is shot to hell."

Sharon joined him in the kitchen. "What's wrong with the radio?"

"I don't know," he snapped.

"It worked fine this morning."

Jim felt on edge, nervous. "God, I sure could use a cigarette," he muttered.

Sharon frowned. "After the hell we went through when you quit?"

Jim sighed. "You're right," he said with resignation. "I'll settle for another Bud."

He had just grabbed a can of beer from the refrigerator and was about to open it when their dog began barking ferociously outside the house. The barks came in rapid succession and were followed by a frantic howl.

"What's got into Red?" asked Jim.

"He's never howled like that before," said Sharon.

Jim set the can down on the counter. "I'm going outside and see what's bugging him."

Jim went to the hall closet, groped around inside, and found the heavy-duty flashlight. He snapped it on and illuminated his way to the front door, opened it, and stepped out onto the wooden porch.

The barking and howling continued unabated. He extended his arm, as if aiming a pistol, and swept the bright thin spear from his flashlight across the front lawn. The probing beam struck the dark shape of the big Irish setter standing at the edge of the lawn near the road. Its features were a mask of black shadow, its haunches wound tight, ready to spring into a run.

"Red!" called Jim. "What is it, boy?"

The setter ignored him. Its attention was riveted to the field of barley that was on the other side of the road. The vast field of short, thick grain stretched off to the invisible horizon in a clean unbroken pattern. The dog noisily sniffed the air, then bolted in one smooth, easy motion, loping across the road, and disappearing into the barley field.

Jim heard the dog thrashing through the stiff stalks as he illuminated the outer fringes of the field with his flashlight. "Red!" he yelled. "Come back here." But there was no sign of the dog.

A sudden gust of warm wind blew in from the field and touched his face. He smelled something: a strong odor that was carried by the wind. It smelled like steaming hot cereal.

Then he heard the crackling sound.

It came from deep within the field. The image of corn kernels popping came to mind. He squinted into the distance, squeezing his expression into a tight, fierce grimace, as if making a fist of his face. But he only saw the endless stalks of grain.

The front door of the house opened and Sharon and the children appeared on the porch. "Where's Red?" Sharon asked.

"He heard a noise and shot off like a rocket into the barley field," replied Jim.

"I hear something, too," said Sharon. "A funny popping sound."

"It smells like Malt-O-Meal out here," said Eric.

A soul-wrenching cry of animal pain suddenly pierced the night. Over and over again the animal cried out in short, sharp yelps that grew in depth and intensity.

"My God, Jim," said Sharon in a small voice. "That sounds like Red."

"Yeah." Jim instinctively drew Sharon close to him.

The boys were wide-eyed, their mouths open.

They heard the rustling of grain stalks and Jim shot his light at the field. The stalks parted and a limping, black shape slowly staggered out. It made soft whimpering noises.

"It's Red!" yelled Tom. "Something's wrong with him. He's hurt."

The dog painfully crept forward, dragged itself across the dirt road, and then collapsed on the front lawn near the mailbox. A gurgling sound issued from its throat and it lay very still.

Before Jim could act, the three boys raced to the still form and huddled around it. A child's scream, thin and high, echoed throughout the valley.

Sharon ran to Jeff and held the sobbing boy in her arms. "It's all right," she murmured. "It's all right." Jeff looked away from the dog's body and screamed again. The boy threw his face convulsively against his mother's stomach, while a few feet away Jim squatted down and inspected the body of the dog. Eric and Tom stood back and gagged.

Impulsively Jim reached down and touched the dog. It felt very hot and he quickly withdrew his hand. A sickening, sweet odor of partially boiled meat reached his nostrils. He shined his flashlight back and forth across the dead animal. "Jesus, sweet Jesus."

The dog's body was bloated, misshapen. Its snout was a mass of huge blisters. The eyes were glazed over with a gray film and they protruded grotesquely from their sockets. Something faint and gauzy was captured in the flashlight beam: thin wisps of steam were rising from the carcass.

The crackling sound from the barley field grew louder.

Jim stood up. He felt weak, shaken.

Eric moved close to him. "What happened to Red, Dad?" The boy's voice was barely audible over the noise from the field.

Jim slowly shook his head. He had no idea what had killed the dog.

Without warning the crackling became a chattering roar, resembling the sound of automatic weapons firing. The smell of cooked cereal was now overpowering.

Jim swung his light at the stalks of barley near the road. Something was happening to the ears of ripe grain growing at the top of the stalks. He stared in disbelief. The kernels of grain were exploding like billions of little firecrackers, hurtling clouds of fragments into the air. The spent stalks began writhing and swaying in an undulating motion, like seaweed moving in an underwater current. Then they shriveled, split apart, and fell in crazy patterns, as if an invisible herd of cattle had trampled them to the ground. The entire field lay shredded and flattened.

The sight stunned each member of the Roberts family into frozen positions: Jim held the flashlight in a firm grip, his arm extended; Sharon had her arms around Jeff, whose eyes were wide, his face pale; Eric stood rigid, his mouth gaping; Tom had covered his face with his hands and was peering through the gaps between his fingers.

The leafy dandelion weeds growing on the shoulder of the road quickly withered and dried up.

Eric frantically rubbed his arms. "Mom, I feel funny."

Jim felt his body tingle as though a net were slowly tightening around him. The hairs on his body tickled and stood erect from his skin. A tic pulled at the corner of his eye. He began to feel hot and his clothes became damp with perspiration.

"It's getting hot out here!" Sharon cried in a trembling voice. She quickly undid the top buttons of her blouse.

Steam began rising from the lawn around them and the blades of grass curled. The yellow marigold flowers bordering the driveway wilted, then shriveled.

Jim was frightened like no other time in his life. "Get inside the house," he shouted. "Hurry!"

Sharon picked up Jeff bodily and ran with him toward the house. Eric and Tom bolted ahead of them. Jim was in the rear, illuminating their way.

Eric raced up the porch steps, threw the door open, and ran inside, with Tom at his heels. Burdened by the weight of her youngest son, Sharon stumbled on the top step. Jim caught her in time but dropped the flashlight on the porch. It went out, clattered down the steps, and rolled onto the lawn. He left it and helped his wife into the house. Perspiration streamed down his face and he had difficulty breathing. He slammed the door shut and locked it. He felt light-headed and sluggish.

The candle Sharon had lit earlier had gone out and the house was dark. It was steadily growing hotter inside.

Panic-stricken, the family stumbled over chairs and tables as they rushed to the living room. With her breath coming out in rasping sounds, Sharon collapsed onto the sofa with Jeff in her arms, while Tom and Eric slumped down onto the floor. Their clothes were soaked with sweat and clung to their skin.

"Mom, I'm so hot," cried Tom.

Jim fumbled around blindly for the telephone that was perched on an end table. He found it and snatched up the receiver. But before he could dial 911, a high-pitched screeching sound shrieked into his ear. He threw the receiver down in disgust and despair.

"Jim," gasped Sharon. "What's happening to us?"

The heat was now incredibly intense, seeming to come in waves. Jim tore off his sopped T-shirt and threw it, then clawed at his jeans and briefs and pulled them down to his ankles. He kicked furiously and his tennis shoes and jeans flew off. But it didn't help. The skin on his arms and the back of his hands felt like he had brushed them against the burners on an electric stove. His face felt puffy, swollen. He heard a strange clicking sound that seemed to be more in his head than outside it. He had the insane thought that they were all going to die. Then it came to him. "The *bathtub*," he shouted. If they could make it to the bathtub and submerge in cold water they would survive the heat.

After he helped Sharon up he quickly undressed her, then yanked the three boys to their feet and stripped them down. He slung Jeff over his shoulder. "*Come on, come on,*" he yelled. "We've got to make it to the bathtub!"

Recalling the path to the bathroom, he started to his right! Weaving under the weight of his son, he tripped on a magazine rack and a footstool and became disoriented. He recovered his bearing and staggered down the hall, breathing raggedly, with the others close behind. His face was blistering, his eyelids and lips swelling. Thick mucus began dribbling from his nostrils. He coughed deeply and tasted blood. He turned a corner and felt the slippery tile floor beneath his feet. They had made it.

He gently lowered Jeff into the bathtub and, after propping him up to a sitting position, plugged the drain and twisted frantically at the faucet until cold water gushed out. He helped Sharon into the rapidly filling tub, while behind them Tom and Eric fought briefly,

David Kagan

without shame, for space in the tub. Eric won and jumped into the water first, then Tom shoved his way in. Jim activated the shower head and squeezed in between them, letting the water run down his blistered face and chest. He forced himself to believe that everything was going to be all right.

The clicking sound inside his head became a metronome steadily beating away. Bright splotches spread before his eyes. He was now blind. Dizziness overwhelmed him. He slowly slumped down onto the soft, struggling bodies beneath him. He heard Sharon utter a strangled cry of pain and felt bodies wildly thrashing about. He tried to get up but couldn't.

Then the water turned scalding and the bathroom echoed with screams of agony.

The water in the tub soon came to a boil and the screaming died and the thrashing stopped. As his bodily fluids heated and swelled his tissues, Jim slowly curled up into a ball. A moment passed and he no longer felt the heat or the pain.

His last thought was that he would never see his boys grow up.

Chapter 2 *

THE CATASTROPHIC CHAIN of events that culminated in the death of the Roberts family had begun earlier that night, in the cold loneliness of space 22,300 miles above the earth.

At precisely seven P.M. the experimental solar satellite designated SOLSAT X-1 was sweeping through the airless void at a speed of seven thousand miles per hour. This velocity matched the earth's rate of rotation, and as a result the satellite hung apparently motionless over Albuquerque, New Mexico. The ten-thousand-ton spacecraft consisted of a long cylindrical module with two huge solar-paneled wings extending outward, creating the illusion of a great bird poised for flight. But SOLSAT X-1 was dormant, inoperative, waiting to be summoned by its ground-based controllers.

Then electronic voices whispered into its parabolic communications antenna and the giant orbiting station immediately came to life, ready to harness the incomprehensible power of the sun.

With its on-board systems now fully activated, the satellite began converting the incident sunlight into electricity. Like blood flowing through arteries, raw electrical current surged into the hundreds of klystron converter tubes inside the shielded microwave transmitter, an octagon-shaped projection mounted at the rim of the satellite's forward end. First the klystron tubes became suffused with a pale orange luminescence. Then tenuous shapes moved across their surfaces and in their depths. The shapes coalesced into shifting bars of light and shadow, then formed spoked patterns that started to rotate. The wheels of light spun faster and faster as the klystron tubes miraculously transformed electricity into microwave radiation. Simultaneously, the slotted waveguides on the underside of the microwave transmitter discharged an invisible, coherent beam of high-intensity microwaves at the planet below.

In one-eighth of a second the tightly focused beam leaped from the satellite to the earth, aimed unerringly at the solar power plant on the outskirts of Albuquerque, where it was instantly changed back into electricity and funneled into the utility power grid. Countless homes, hospitals, restaurants, traffic signals, and streetlights were now running on energy from space. SOLSAT X-1 was utilizing the inexhaustible power of the sun to run the entire city of Albuquerque with unlimited electricity.

What occurred over the next sixty seconds was unseen by the human eye, unheard by the human ear, and unobserved by ground-based radar systems.

The intruder had begun its attack.

A black metallic sphere barely ten feet in diameter was rapidly ascending from a lower orbit. An observer, if he were present, could make out the small daggers of flame stabbing the darkness around the sphere as the attitudinal-control thrusters made fine adjustments to its trajectory. It was now on a collision course with SOLSAT X-1.

With a velocity exceeding 15,000 miles per hour, seven times faster than a high-powered rifle bullet, the intruder was a projectile hurtling through the void. Its specially formulated opaque surface and spherical shape rendered the intruder virtually invisible to optical and radio frequency wavelengths. Even the NORAD network of high-resolution radar installations scattered across the North American continent was unable to completely detect it.

SOLSAT X-1 was unaware of the intruder's presence: its complex array of sensors was fully engaged in monitoring the atmospheric attenuation, thermal ionospheric heating, and the electromagnetic interference created by the passage of the microwave beam through the earth's atmosphere.

The intruder was now less than a mile from the orbiting station. In another moment, the two celestial bodies would be drawn together by the relentless laws of orbital mechanics. The small compact sphere was aimed directly at the octagon-shaped microwave transmitter. Although the intruder was a tiny slug of metal compared to the immense solar satellite, incredibly powerful kinetic energy lay coiled within it.

A fraction of a second later there was a sudden, dazzling explosion of light as the intruder silently impacted at meteoric speed. The energy released was equivalent to a low-yield nuclear detonation. The intruder was instantly vaporized into a cloud of incandescent gas. Its suicidal mission was now complete. But instead of disabling its target as intended, the collision unleashed a destructive force upon an unsuspecting world on a scale that was unprecedented in all of history.

Shuddering violently from the force of the explosion, SOLSAT X-1 broke away from its geosynchronous orbital lock and began drifting. It was seriously damaged. The circuitry inside its command computer had been jolted, altering the pathways of electricity. The original programming was now jumbled. The fuel and oxidizer lines to the course-correction thrusters were ruptured, rendering the small rockets useless. However, the damage to the microwave transmitter housing was infinitely more important, its consequences far-reaching. The housing had been fractured, exposing the klystron converter tubes to the unfiltered, fiery rays of the sun.

Within moments the solar heat fused the phase-control circuitry at the base of the klystron tube assembly, making it impossible for ground controllers to disperse the microwave transmission beam. The heat sensors inside the housing were incapable of issuing a sufficient warning; their soldered connections had been jarred loose by the collision.

As it wandered from its orbital position, SOLSAT X-1 continued to transmit its shaft of intense microwaves to earth. But now the beam was slowly veering away from its precisely designated path and was no longer focusing on the ground-based receiving station.

Far below, inside the large, windowless central control room deep within the U.S. Department of Energy's experimental solar power plant, the lights suddenly flickered and went out. When they flared on a moment later, the group of men monitoring the signals from the solar satellite spoke in loud voices, gazed at their viewing screens, and furiously scribbled cryptic notes.

Mike Doheny quickly leaned forward in his seat at the main control console to study a readout. The glowing green numbers running in reverse sequence across his console screen told him the plant was now barely producing a trickle of electricity. He could hear the distant whine from the emergency generators as they struggled to supply power to the building. He realized with a sickening feeling that something had just gone horribly wrong with the Solar Satellite Project.

At forty-one, Doheny was accustomed to crises. By training he was an aerospace engineer with a degree from Caltech and a background in satellite design and construction for Rockwell and later Nore Space Industries. In his middle thirties he had shifted to management, which led to his present position as project director.

Doheny looked up from the readout and turned to the thin, young technician with auburn hair who manned the nearby microwave systems console. "Give me a full status report, Phillips."

Phillips's hands flashed over his console, ordering a stream of telemetry from the microwave transmitter aboard the solar satellite.

As he waited for the technician to analyze the data, Doheny checked the time. It was 7:02 P.M. One minute had elapsed since the plant first began losing power.

He glanced around the huge control room. A dozen men in white lab coats sat at long rows of consoles, staring intently at a bewildering display of video screens, numerical readouts, and computer terminals. The screens were alive with bright rotating and shifting forms and green linear motion. Doheny was vaguely aware of the murmuring spectators clustered together in a corner of the room.

Among the onlookers was the governor of New Mexico, a short, broad-faced man wearing an immaculate light blue suit. He was obviously outraged at having his televised speech interrupted by the power failure. Standing beside him were Deputy Energy Secretary Howard Averson, and Everett Nore, president and chairman of Nore Space Industries, the solar satellite's manufacturer. Averson looked startled and confused, while Nore's face was icy, noncommittal. The three men were surrounded by a knot of stunned reporters and their entourage of cameramen and assistants. The small crowd was assembled in front of a mural depicting a stylized satellite catching the sun's rays and directing a conical orange beam at a distant earth.

Doheny could hear the governor asking in an angry voice, "What the hell is going on?"

"Just a fluctuation, Governor," replied Nore, an imposing man in his early fifties with grayish brown hair. "The plant will be up to full power again in a few minutes and you'll be back on the air."

Doheny turned away but he felt their eyes on him. They were depending on him to bring the plant up to its maximum generating capacity. He was acutely aware that each passing minute added greatly to their political embarrassment.

Then Phillips began calling out the incoming data on his console readouts. "Incident sunlight conversion proceeding at optimal thirty-nine percent efficiency rate. Klystron power amplifiers are in a normal phasing mode. The microwave transmitter is operating at a reference frequency of two point four-five gigahertz."

Phillips paused to study a ghostly infrared image of New Mexico on a display screen. This false-color image was produced by the infrared radiometer device aboard the solar satellite. The radiometer measured the heat generated by the microwave beam as it passed through the gaseous layers of the atmosphere. A bright fiery spot of light in the center of the screen represented the beam's focal point. Phillips could determine the beam intensity by running a computerized optical scan of the color tones composing the image. He pressed several keys, then glanced at the series of numbers flitting across the bottom of the infrared display.

"Ionospheric heating corresponds to an average beam intensity of nine hundred kilowatts. Atmospheric attenuation is within acceptable limits." He looked up from his console. "All satellite power systems are functioning perfectly, sir."

Doheny frowned. According to Phillips's status report the satellite was in good shape. It was efficiently converting sunlight to microwaves and beaming them down to the plant. The ground-based rectenna must have malfunctioned, he thought.

He pressed a button marked "Video, Rectenna Site," then glanced up at the TV screen above his console. After a momentary blur of static the screen cleared and he was looking at an overhead view of the huge receiving antenna located one-quarter mile away from the main building. The circular grid of wire mesh was three thousand feet in diameter and contained billions of dipoles tuned to the satellite's microwave frequency. The rectenna was illuminated by floodlights and, onscreen, it resembled a lake covered with a thin coating of ice. The resemblance was enhanced by the hundreds of full-grown eucalyptus trees planted around the site for aesthetic reasons. The entire installation was monitored by the rectenna substation, a small bunker located at the southern perimeter of the sprawling grid.

Doheny saw that only a portion of the rectenna was glowing with the eerie bluish purple radiance produced by the conversion of microwaves into electricity. The power transmission lines stretching from the rectenna to Albuquerque were undoubtedly dead.

He touched the button for the rectenna substation and the scene on his screen shifted to the interior of a long, narrow room packed with electronic equipment. From floor to ceiling dozens of monitors and LEDs flickered and glowed. The technicians in the room didn't notice the red light on the camera; they were far too intent on their tasks.

Doheny leaned toward the intercom. "What's the situation over there, Bonetti?"

On-screen a harried man in the foreground looked startled for a moment, then realized the room was on camera. "Not good, Mike," he said with frustration in his voice. "Power output is down to fourteen percent and still dropping. Our readouts here show only a fraction of the dipoles are registering a microwave signal. We ran a check on every critical system in the grid and nothing turned up. There isn't anything wrong at our end. That satellite up there must have developed some kind of glitch."

"Run a subprogram against your readout boards," ordered Doheny. "I'll check back with you later."

"You heard the man," Bonetti said to the other technicians inside the substation.

Doheny felt oddly bitter. They thought they had eliminated the possibility of human error by entrusting all the safeguards to a computer. But somewhere an inexpensive relay may have fused itself shut. Or a two-bit resistor had burned out. Or a slice of silicon had been jolted enough to break its integrated circuit connections. Or possibly some obscure inspector in an electronics firm had suffered from a morning hangover and overlooked a defective piece of circuitry.

But that was not the case.

The voice of the main computer broke in, its tone unemotional and mechanical. "Satellite orbital deviation has occurred. Phase-control sequence has begun. Microwave transmission beam is being defocused."

The computer must have erred, thought Doheny. The satellite couldn't be adrift. He turned to a bearded heavyset engineer with a receding hairline who sat at the satellite guidance console. "Give me a positional report, Jenkins."

Jenkins hunched over his console and activated a high-frequency radar scan by punching a numerical code on his keyboard. A fuzzy, green image representing the satellite's position instantly appeared on the scope in front of him. He twisted knobs and set dials to resolve it. Within seconds the green blip was sharp and clear. But it was not centered between the cross lines. Jenkins stared at it for a moment, then studied a blinking readout.

"Orbital SATLOCK had definitely been broken," he announced. There was a trace of excitement in his voice. "My HF scan shows the satellite has drifted point zero zero two eight degrees from geosynchronous position."

Doheny quickly got up from his seat and raced to the satellite guidance console. He was tall and strongly built, with broad shoulders and dark brown hair. There were lines in his face and streaks of gray in his sideburns. He crouched over Jenkins's console and examined the image on the radar scope.

Jenkins nervously glanced up at Doheny. "I don't know how the hell it happened, Mike."

Doheny was stunned. This wasn't a simulated test; the impossible had actually taken place. The solar satellite was no longer locked in orbit above the plant. He thought quickly. "Compute a firing sequence for the attitudinal-control thrusters, Jenkins. We'll try nudging that bird back into place."

The murmur of background conversation from the onlookers in the corner of the room started up again. They had faith in him, Doheny thought wryly. But he was worried. It didn't feel right.

"Has something happened to the satellite, Mr. Nore?" asked the reporter from CBS.

"A temporary malfunction. It'll be cleared up very soon."

"I sure hope you're right, Everett," the governor said stiffly. "My political career and your company's future are riding on the success of this plant."

"Has the microwave beam been turned off?" asked the tall, slender woman from Cable News Service.

"The computer has defocused the power beam to a harmless level," answered Nore. "As a purely precautionary measure."

Phillips suddenly half rose from his seat at the microwave systems console and stared with disbelief at the display in front of him. He shouted in a loud voice that had a thin note of fear running through it. "We're still getting a strong microwave signal from the satellite! The beam hasn't been defocused. It's still at full power!"

Doheny's stomach knotted. The computerized fail-safe mechanisms had broken down. "Override the computer, Phillips. Send an RF cutoff signal directly to the satellite's transmitter. *Shut off that beam.*"

Doheny ran to the main control console and hit the red klaxon alarm button; a scream went up from the score of klaxon horns scattered around the plant. Then he thumbed the intercom switch to PA and his amplified voice suddenly reverberated throughout the complex.

"This is the director speaking. All first- and second-floor personnel are ordered to descend to the basement level immediately. Everyone is ordered to stay inside the plant. Do *not* leave the building for any reason. I repeat. Do *not* leave the building."

Phillips's face turned ashen when he studied his console readout. "It's not responding to the cutoff signal," he yelled, his voice cracking.

Doheny's mind immediately filled with radio frequency schematics and emergency procedures. "Boost RF frequencies to three hundred thirty megahertz. Transmit a one-second pulse."

The technician's hands swept over the panel, deftly making dial adjustments and furiously punching the keyboard.

Doheny heard tinny, muffled obscenities coming from his console loudspeaker. Something was going on inside the rectenna substation bunker. He glanced up at the video screen and saw Bonetti gesturing wildly, flailing his arms and pointing to indicators. He leaned toward the intercom. "Doheny here, Bonetti. What's going on over there?"

Bonetti's voice was high pitched, excited. "Our radiation counters are going wild. That satellite is flooding us with microwaves. We're being exposed to over six hundred milliwatts per square centimeter." Rivulets of perspiration began streaming down his face. "It's getting like an oven in here. For God's sake, shut that thing off, Mike!"

Doheny felt his heart lurch. The microwave beam had veered away from the rectenna grid and was striking the substation bunker. It was no longer just a matter of a multibillion-dollar plant and five thousand megawatts. Now, for the first time, the crisis was assuming a human dimension.

He turned to the bearded engineer at the guidance console. "Fire those thrusters, Jenkins."

Suddenly a steady, urgent beeping sound echoed through the control room. Red warning lights were flashing on every console.

Jenkins looked up from his keyboard. His forehead had developed an oily sheen. "We've got a LORCON on all frequencies!" he shouted.

For an instant there was silence in the control room, except for the clicking of relays, the whining from the generators, and the incessant beeping sound. Doheny was frozen at his console, his mind racing.

And then there was an outburst from the spectators in the corner of the room. A swirl of questions and vague answers and the smell of the biggest news story in decades.

"What happened?" asked the governor. "What's a LOR-CON?"

"Loss of radio control," replied Nore tightly. "The satellite won't respond to ground-based radio commands."

"Will they be able to shut off the microwave transmitter, Everett?" asked Deputy Energy Secretary Averson.

"Of course. Within the next few minutes."

"Do you mean to tell us that satellite is *moving* and you can't turn its microwave beam off?" asked NBC. "This project is in big trouble, isn't it?"

"Like I said, it's just a temporary malfunction. We'll be back on stream in the morning."

"The hell you will," murmured NBC. "The public is going to demand a full-scale investigation."

"How come the director ordered everyone to stay inside?" asked ABC.

"Just a precaution—"

"Were the critics right?" asked CBS. "Has the microwave beam been turned into a death ray that's out of control?"

Doheny cut in. "Get those people out of here!" he bellowed. "We've got an emergency."

Then he turned to Phillips and said, "Transmit that cutoff signal continuously. There's a chance the LORCON will clear and the signal will get through." It was a remote possibility, he thought, but they've got to be prepared for any contingency, no matter what the odds.

He said to Jenkins, "Compute a thruster firing sequence that will tilt the satellite forty-five degrees on its axis. That angle will direct the microwave beam away from earth and shoot it into space. Activate thrusters the instant the LORCON clears."

Doheny swore quietly. There was nothing more they could do, he thought bitterly, but wait.

Behind him, he could hear the reporters protesting loudly as Nore quickly and efficiently ushered them out of the control room and into the corridor. Within moments the only spectator left was the governor: he had firmly insisted on staying to evaluate the

crisis. He stood motionless in the corner, his expression midway
between shock and concern.

At the communications console near the front of the control
room, a sandy-haired technician listened to a report coming in
over his headset. He spoke briefly into his mouthpiece, then
glanced at Doheny. "Sir, Albuquerque Grid Central just reported
they're having problems compensating for our loss. Their computers switched in the spinning reserve but a sudden current surge
blew out the primary lines. They want to know if we'll be back in
the grid tonight?"

"Not very damn likely, Larsen," snapped Doheny.

He reached for the intercom switch. "Bonetti, any change in the
microwave intensity?"

Static suddenly screeched from the loudspeaker and Bonetti's
voice faded in and out. ". . . eight hundred fifty milliwatts and
rising. Can't take much more. . . ." Then the speaker died.

Doheny fought down a wave of panic when he glanced up at the
screen and saw the video image from the substation bunker rapidly
deteriorate into shifting lines of static. The microwaves were now
interfering with all communications. He had a final glimpse of
Bonetti hunched over his readout board before the image dissolved
into snow.

He knew the substation was lined with half-inch-thick lead
shielding. This was more than adequate protection against the
low-level microwave leakage expected during normal operation of
the rectenna. But now, as a result of some unforeseen catastrophic malfunction, the bunker was being subjected to an onslaught
of microwaves five hundred times more intense than residual
leakage.

The technicians inside the bunker had only one chance, Doheny
thought desperately, but it was a tenuous one. Their survival
depended on which section of the power beam was sweeping over
them. Microwave radiation levels at the beam's edge were considerably less than at the center. There was a possibility the lead
shielding would protect the men if the outer region of the beam
was passing over them. However, they would still experience
some heating of their bodily tissues and perhaps require hospital-
ization. But they had no chance at all if the beam's center struck
the bunker. The power levels at the center were in excess of 100
kilowatts per square meter. This intensity was capable of bringing
cold water to a boil in an instant. Or flash-cooking a human
being.

He spun around to face Jenkins and saw that the engineer had finished his computations. "Positional report, Jenkins."

Jenkins's hands moved swiftly over his console. After examining his digital readout he said, "Satellite has now drifted point zero zero three two degrees from geosynchronous position." He turned to Doheny, his face strained. "What about Bonetti and his crew, Mike? Do they have a chance?"

"Only if the central portion of the beam bypasses them," replied Doheny in a worried voice. He hoped to God it would. He had known Martin Bonetti since their days at Rockwell. Four years ago he had recommended Bonetti to the personnel selection board for the Solar Satellite Project. The two men had worked together on the Ionospheric Heating Test conducted at the Seward radio telescope observatory in Alaska. They had used the huge 1,000-foot Seward dish to heat the ionosphere with high-intensity radar to simulate the effects of the satellite's microwave beam on the atmosphere. Bonetti was married and had five children. A beautiful family.

Doheny looked up at the stop clocks mounted on the front wall of the control room. The special timing clocks had automatically cut in when the rectenna power levels had first dropped. Three minutes and seventeen seconds had elapsed. During that time the satellite had drifted .0032 degrees. He did some quick mental calculations and determined that the microwave beam was traveling at a rate of about fifteen feet per second. It should veer away from the substation at any moment now, he thought.

The loudspeaker suddenly sputtered back to life and the image on the video screen rapidly resolved into Bonetti's face. "Substation to Control," he said in a jagged voice.

Relief swept over Doheny as he lunged for the intercom. "Bonetti—thank God!"

On-screen, Bonetti wiped his face with a huge handkerchief. His hair was wet and plastered to his scalp. He was breathing heavily. "That was too close, Mike. *Too goddamn close.*" In the background, four badly shaken technicians were mopping their faces and drinking from paper cups. Their unbuttoned shirts were soaked with sweat.

They look like they've been through a war, thought Doheny. "Are you and your men all right, Bonetti?"

"Yeah, I think so." Bonetti peered at his readout board. "Intensity is down to one hundred milliwatts per square centimeter and dropping." He paused, then said, "That's it. The dials have just gone to zero. We're in the clear.'' He sighed, then looked into the camera. "We were lucky, really lucky. According to the indicators, only the fringe of the beam hit us.''

"Listen, Bonetti,'' Doheny said with concern. "I'm sending a medic team down there to examine you as soon as it's safe for them to go outside.''

Bonetti's eyes were wide and glistening. "I can't believe it. For a few moments there I thought we were going to be—''

Bonetti's voice was drowned out by frantic shouting coming from within the substation bunker. Doheny saw that the other technicians were huddled around a small window slit at the back of the bunker. They were yelling and gesturing to Bonetti.

On-screen, Bonetti got up from his seat and squeezed between the others. He looked out the observation slit for a moment, then raced back to the camera. His face was white and his voice was stitched with hysteria. "The beam is killing the trees around the southeast perimeter,'' he gasped. "I've never seen anything like it. All the leaves are dropping off and the trunks are exploding like bombs. The sap must be boiling.'' His voice became a hoarse whisper. "Mike. That beam is over a half mile in diameter. You'd better find some way to shut it off, fast. It's traveling to the southeast. There are farms out there. A lot of people . . .''

Doheny slowly sank back into his console seat. He looked away from Bonetti's pleading face on the screen and stared numbly at the red warning lights flashing dutifully on his console. He broke out in a cold sweat and could feel himself shaking.

The emergency in the substation bunker had distracted him from the overall scope of the crisis. He suddenly realized that the possibilities in terms of human life were staggering. Dozens of farms lay within a five-mile radius of the plant. Albuquerque was just eight miles to the southeast. A city with a population of more than three hundred thousand people. And that was where the beam was now headed.

Those people aren't inside shielded concrete bunkers, he thought grimly. They're in their homes, probably having dinner. Or in the streets. They might even be out in their front yards watching the satellite.

Doheny felt the skin tighten on the back of his neck. His hands firmly gripped the edge of the console until his knuckles turned white. He didn't want their deaths on his conscience.

Chapter 3 *

AT 7:05 P.M. the microwave beam from the solar satellite was traveling across the New Mexico desert at a speed of fifteen feet per second. It would reach Albuquerque in less than forty-five minutes.

Doheny summoned the governor to his console and briefed him on the situation. Afterward he urged the governor to use the console phone to call the Civil Defense authorities in Albuquerque and order them to begin evacuating the city.

The governor was both angry and frustrated. "If we start sounding off the air raid sirens there's going to be one hell of a panic. There aren't enough police to direct the entire population and it'll take hours to mobilize the National Guard. Without supervision, thousands of people could be killed."

"Governor," said Doheny firmly, "thousands *will* die when the microwave beam reaches the city."

The governor took a deep breath. The vein in his forehead was very pronounced. He looked accusingly at Doheny. "You people assured me the plant was ready to go on stream tonight," he exploded. "You claimed all the tests were successful, that everything was safe." He balled his fists. "My God, how could you have fucked up like this?"

Doheny made an effort to stifle the anger and resentment rapidly building up inside him, then got up from his seat. He towered over the politician. A part of him sympathized with the governor who had been suddenly thrust into a technological nightmare. He gestured to the phone and said, without rancor, "I suggest you start the evacuation at once."

The governor shook his head slowly. "I absolutely refuse. It would be insane to even try."

Doheny turned away, then strode briskly to Phillips's console and glanced at the ghostly negative image on the infrared screen.

Although the solar satellite was now drifting aimlessly in space, its infrared radiometer device continued to transmit a God's-eye thermal view of New Mexico to the control room. Doheny was aware that the radiometer had the capability of detecting a closed factory at night from the residual heat emitted by the building. At maximum resolution it could even sense the fading heat from a single soldier's footprint in a jungle.

Doheny studied the bright spot at the center of the screen for a moment, then said, "Increase IR resolution to four-hundredths microns, Phillips." This setting would provide a useful overview of the terrain, similar to what an aircraft might see through an infrared sensor at ten thousand feet.

The technician punched a button and slowly turned a vernier dial. Instantly the screen dissolved into a montage of swirling computer-generated colors. When the image reassembled it had infinitely more detail than before. Phillips looked at it and gasped. A cluster of reddish dots had appeared at the top of the screen and, at the center, there was now a large white disk.

Doheny stared at the screen. He knew the reddish dots, which varied in size and intensity, were the infrared signatures of farmhouses and agricultural buildings slowly radiating their stored heat to the night air. They belonged to one of the grain farms southeast of the plant. Red Desert Farm. The white disk was the intense focal point of the microwave beam striking the earth's surface.

Doheny felt his mind become completely oblivious to everything but the image on the screen. He perceived only one thing. The distance between the disk and the nearest red dot was diminishing before his eyes.

The control room engineers and technicians began to crowd around the IR display. They stared, mesmerized, at the image on the screen. Then they all saw it at once.

Without warning the white disk blossomed in size and brightened to sunburst intensity. At the rear of the enlarged disk, a small luminous appendage started to grow, like the tail of a comet as it approached the sun.

Doheny felt nausea rise in his stomach. "The grain," he said quietly.

"What?" asked Jenkins without looking away from the screen.

"The beam has reached the fields," said Doheny grimly. "It's heating up the grain."

"Christ," someone muttered.

The red dot closest to the white disk was small, slightly diffused. A house. Beads of sweat broke out on Doheny's forehead. He had to try to warn the people inside. He snatched up Phillips's console phone, got the operator, and ordered her to phone Red Desert Farm. As he waited he glanced at the screen. The microwave beam's focal point was slowly spreading across it like a cancerous growth.

An agonizing moment later the operator came back on the line. "I'm sorry, sir, but I can't get through. I'm getting nothing but static."

Doheny felt a surge of real fear. He realized the microwaves must be jamming the telephone lines between them and the farm. "Keep trying," he told the operator urgently. For an instant his mind frantically searched for some way to warn the farmhouse residents. Then he gave it up. Time had run out.

On-screen, the distance between the fiery white disk and the house was closing rapidly. There were only seconds left.

Jenkins turned to Doheny. "Mike, maybe nobody's home. The house might be deserted."

Doheny stared at the screen with a fierce intensity. He had to know for certain. "Increase resolution to eight-hundredths microns," he said in a low voice.

Phillips turned the vernier dial to the maximum resolution setting. When the screen cleared, the grainy, reddish outline of a house leaped up at them. It was easily distinguishable despite the strange shadings and inverted tone values. Everyone's attention was riveted to the five shimmering, pink spectral figures standing near it.

"Jesus," breathed Jenkins.

Doheny's eyes were fixed intently on the images. His head ached from the helpless anguish of watching five people who were about to die. Judging from the varying sizes of the figures, it was a family. Parents and three children. Doheny felt his body sag.

Writhing tendrils of brightness snaked toward the spectral figures as the fringe of the beam approached. With frightening speed the tentacles seemed to tighten around each person, as if trying to constrict the life out of them. The lethal microwave radiation was invisible to the people on the screen, but their bodies could sense it. They bolted toward the house just shortly before the fiery heart of the beam swept over it. The family inside was being flooded with high-intensity microwaves. No one could possibly survive the deadly onslaught.

Jenkins uttered a sound. It was low, guttural, agonized. A growl of despair.

Doheny looked away from the hellish scene and put his hand over his eyes. The image of those people running for their lives was cauterized on his brain. His teeth clenched together and the muscles at the back of his jaw became hard and tight.

They had just watched the satellite claim its first victims.

Chapter 4 ✳

SOLSAT X-1 MOVED silently through the black void, effort-lessly converting sunlight into microwaves and beaming them down to the earth below. Its infrared sensors were scanning the beam's track across the farmland on the outskirts of Albuquerque. The thermal heat pattern radiating from the grain fields was as clear and unmistakable as a single line of footprints over an expanse of virgin snow.

Electronic voices were screaming incessantly into its parabolic antenna dish, desperately ordering it to shut down. But the damaged satellite was unable to respond to the urgent ground-based commands. Instead SOLSAT X-1 continued to carry out the unalterable instructions deeply ingrained within its command computer. Because its circuits had been jolted from the collision, the programming had become confused. The subroutine ordering it to supply the earth with an unbroken microwave transmission beam was now controlling the satellite. Other subroutines contain-ing different instructions lurked within its memory, ready to surface at random. Once engaged, these other sets of commands would order the satellite to perform a series of tests whose nature was known only to a handful of U.S. Department of Defense personnel. But these tests would be conducted out of sequence, and not under anyone's control.

Meanwhile the satellite's solar-powered wings were steadily converting the fierce rays of the sun into a continuous stream of electrical current. The process of transforming electricity into high-intensity microwaves lit up the klystron tubes with spinning wheels of bright orange light. The tubes were made of transparent quartz crystal and contained resonating oscillator circuits sur-rounded by coils of coolant lines.

To a casual observer it would seem as if the klystron tubes were functioning perfectly and would continue to do so indefinitely. But the encounter with the intruder had fractured the housing for the microwave transmitter, and intense solar radiation was pouring in through the wide, jagged crack. Minutes passed and the temperature inside the housing rose to an intolerable level.

The klystron tubes were beginning to overheat.

The tube nearest the crack dimmed and its spinning wheels of light disassembled into stationary bars of burned amber and shadow. A moment later the entire tube darkened. One by one, like candles in a candelabrum being extinguished, a dozen neighboring klystron tubes overheated and winked out, reducing the total power output of the microwave transmitter by 3 percent.

The satellite's sensors registered the sudden power drop. Its command computer transmitted probing electrified impulses to the millions of relays, switches, and sensing devices located throughout its hull. In a fraction of a second it traced the problem to the klystron converter tube assembly. Thirteen tubes had overheated and shut down. SOLSAT X-1 automatically tried reactivating the dead tubes by pumping additional coolant into them. It sent a single impulse to the turbopumps connected to the coolant storage tanks located deep within the bowels of its immense hull. The tanks contained 75,000 gallons of frigid liquid nitrogen. But the icy fluid would never reach the klystron converter tube assembly: the collision had severely jarred the turbopumps, releasing a minute amount of liquid nitrogen, which caused the air trapped in the valves to condense into water. The moisture quickly froze into a block of ice around the valves, preventing them from opening. The intense cold emanating from the liquid nitrogen tanks kept the ice frozen solid.

Each of SOLSAT X-1's attempts to open the stuck valves met with dismal failure. Again and again it sent a pulsed electrical signal to the tanks but they stubbornly remained closed. In the meantime more klystron tubes started overheating.

The satellite's command computer tapped into an emergency procedure buried in its memory bank. It began rerouting reserve current to the dead tubes in a final, desperate attempt to resuscitate them.

The control room doors snapped open and Everett Nore walked in. He was desperate to know the status of the microwave beam and, having just been through a harrowing interrogation by the half dozen reporters in the corridor, he needed a respite from their incisive questioning. A cold, sick feeling swept over him when he

saw the red LORCON lights flashing on all the consoles. The
satellite was still out of control.

He silently approached the group huddled around the IR screen,
then paused, sensing something had happened and confirming it
with one look at Doheny's face—taut, gray with shock. The other
engineers were staring in horror at the glowing infrared image.

On-screen, the unmistakable, reddish thermal outline of a house
suddenly emerged from the beam's dazzling focal point. Nore
stared numbly at it, his hands at his sides. He felt his fingertips
shaking against his trousers. He slowly turned to Doheny and, in
a hoarse voice, asked, "Was there anyone inside, Mike?"

Doheny spun around, his eyes glittering like small pools of
agony. "Five people," he said savagely. "I couldn't warn them
because of interference from that goddamned beam. Does that
answer your question?"

Nore suddenly felt weak and breathless. A deep, horribly
intense wave of guilt came over him. Of all the men inside the
control room, he was the only one who was fully aware of the
carefully concealed primary purpose behind the solar satellite. He
longed for the bottle of whiskey in his office. He stared at the fiery
white disk on the screen, a tic in his cheek working furiously.

Suddenly, with no prior warning, the disk wavered, faded to a
faint blur, then abruptly vanished.

For a moment the men gathered around the screen were too
stunned to react or speak.

Then a strange humming came from the microwave systems
console. It flashed red and dimmed out. Phillips hastily looked
down at the readouts and blinked. "Power levels are at zero. The
satellite's microwave transmitter has shut down."

"Thank God," muttered Doheny.

A relief so intense it was almost a physical presence completely
enveloped the room. There was a chorus of sighs as everyone let
their breath out at once.

Nore felt the tension drain out of him. He glanced at his watch.
It was 7:30 P.M. The microwave beam had swept across the New
Mexico desert for almost a half hour. He was debating whether to
make his report to Washington now or wait until they had
accumulated more data when he saw the governor walking briskly
toward them.

"Have you figured out how to stop that thing yet?" the
governor asked angrily.

"Governor," said Doheny, "the microwave beam has just shut down."

The politician let out a long sigh, then speared Doheny with cold eyes. "This never should have happened. You've endangered hundreds of thousands of lives. You're not only grossly incompetent, but you've acted with criminal negligence."

Nore sensed Doheny was ready to explode, that the anger and horrible frustration he had experienced during the last half hour were now boiling unchecked to the surface, an erupting volcano about to spew its emotional lava. He looked from one to the other, and said hurriedly, "Mike, Governor, I think we—"

"Just a minute, Everett," snapped Doheny. "Listen, Governor, this isn't the time for petty politics," he snarled. "You can save your accusations and recriminations for the next election. No, let me finish. Something completely unforeseen happened to that satellite up there which caused it to malfunction. There was no way we could have predicted it. I tried to stop it in time, but I failed." His voice lost its acid tone. "Five people were killed."

The anger slowly drained from the governor. He turned pale and the muscles in his jaw slackened. "Five persons died? Are you certain?"

Doheny stared levelly at him and nodded. There was a haunted look in his eyes.

The governor lowered his head and kneaded his knuckles. "There'll be a congressional investigation," he mumbled.

"We'll all get our chance on the stand, if that's what you mean," Doheny said sharply. "But right now you'd better phone Kirtland Air Force Base and have them dispatch a CBR detachment in a helicopter out to the plant."

The governor looked up. "CBR detachment?"

"Chemical-biological-radiological emergency medical team," Doheny explained. "We've had some casualties inside the substation bunker. The crew was briefly exposed to high-intensity microwaves and I want them checked out by specialists. Kirtland is a special weapons center, they'll have a CBR team on hand. We'll need the helicopter for an aerial survey of the microwave beam's path." He paused, then said in a quiet voice, "And that farmhouse will have to be searched."

"I'll call them now," said the governor brusquely. He rushed to the main control console and grabbed the phone.

Doheny turned to Nore. "I think we should begin reducing every scrap of telemetry from the satellite. I'll have the Central

Computer Room team scan all the tapes for any anomaly, anything at all out of the ordinary that could give us a clue to what went wrong." Then he spoke over the intercom to the computer room.

As he walked toward the exit doors Nore glanced at the weary men hunched over the rows of consoles. They'll never forget this night, he mused wryly. And neither will he.

Outside in the corridor Nore was immediately besieged by the knot of anxious reporters who had been waiting to hear the latest developments. A television crew with lights and a shotgun microphone closed in on him. The harsh illumination made him blink.

"Is the microwave beam still headed away from the plant, Mr. Nore?" asked CBS.

Nore took a deep breath and faced the cameras. "No, the microwave transmitter aboard the satellite has just been shut down."

A clamor of voices rose from the small crowd in the corridor. The announcement came as a surprise.

"Mr. Nore, can you tell us how far the beam traveled before it was shut off?" asked the woman reporter from Cable News Service. She was in her late twenties, tall, with bluish green eyes, fair skin, and long blond hair pulled back and clasped with a barrette. A visitor's badge pinned to the lapel of her severe businesslike suit identified her as Diane Bradford.

"I really can't answer your question, Ms. Bradford," Nore protested. "I'm just an observer here." He tried maneuvering through the group but his path was immediately blocked.

"Is there a possibility the microwave beam struck any of the farms surrounding the plant?" asked NBC.

Nore waved aside the question. "Ladies and gentlemen, please. A detailed press statement will be issued within the hour. I'm certain it will answer all of your questions."

The smell of evasion permeated the air.

"Just a moment, Mr. Nore," persisted Diane Bradford. "You can spare that much. Was the microwave beam at full intensity before it turned off?"

"No comment," replied Nore curtly as he pushed his way past the reporters. He approached one of the security guards stationed in the corridor and ordered him to escort the newsmen and TV crews to the VIP lounge. Then he spun on his heels and strode in the opposite direction down the corridor.

Upon entering his office Nore went straight to his lavatory, splashed cold water on his face, and wiped it dry. Afterward he sat down heavily at his desk.

Nore was a man of strong liquor, hurried jet flights, phone calls, rumpled suits, technical conferences, and harried secretaries. He had always admired Bill Lear of the Learjet Corporation and succeeded in emulating Lear's flamboyant style. Nore personally ran his own aerospace company with a firm hand, and even regularly piloted his private business jet. It was presently parked on an airstrip outside the plant.

He had thrown all of his physical and intellectual powers against problems and obstacles, and his record of successes had been unbroken. His personal efforts had put Nore Space Industries at the leading edge of the highly competitive aerospace industry. He lived and breathed for NSI. His wife once said—just as a joke, for she loved and admired him—that she would have divorced him long ago but that he was never home long enough to discuss the subject.

Now it was all over. His satellite had just burned five people to death. It was only a matter of time before the news leaked out. Intellectually, Nore knew and accepted what was going to happen: the public outcry, his personal crucifixion in the newspapers and on television, the endless investigations, the lawsuits. It would be the end of everything. He also realized it hadn't hit him yet emotionally.

He felt weary, limp with fatigue. The emergency inside the control room and his dealings with the press had drained him. His throat suddenly felt very dry. He needed a drink badly. He unlocked the top left-hand drawer of his desk and pulled it open. A bottle of Scotch and a cut-glass tumbler lay inside. Nore stared at the amber liquid for a moment, then, feeling self-consciously resolute, slammed the drawer shut and locked it. "Not tonight," he said aloud. He had procrastinated long enough. It was time to make the call.

He looked at the squat and innocuous red scrambler phone perched on his desk. There was no dial to turn and no buttons to push. All he had to do was remove the receiver from its cradle and the connection would be made instantly. Nore had not been told exactly who would answer at the other end; he only knew that the phone was connected directly to an emergency switchboard at the Pentagon via a special Defense Department fiber-optic trunk line. He had been instructed to use the hot line only if a "first-order event" occurred at the plant. This was the official designation for any malfunction of the solar satellite system that inflicted either personal injury or property damage upon the civilian sector.

He sucked in his breath and picked up the receiver. No one answered. Instead, the phone hooted with a siren-blast urgency. After a moment the noise stopped and an authoritative voice said, "Please state your name, code, and message."

"Everett J. Nore, Code Sunstroke. I have confirmatory data that a first-order event has taken place at SOLSAT X-One Control."

"Please stand by," said the voice.

Nore grimaced, blew out his breath, and waited. It was going to be a long night.

Chapter 5 *

IN THE BRIGHTLY lit utilitarian office of the National Military Command Center within the labyrinth of the Pentagon, Major Thomas A. Linden was at his desk casually leafing through a stack of reports. Linden was serving as control officer for the skeleton night staff, a duty he begrudgingly performed once a month.

Evenings were uneventful and unexciting. To Linden it seemed as if nothing important ever happened at night. He took advantage of the long hours to review his organization's monthly budget justification reports prepared for the Senate Finance Committee. It was an unpleasant but necessary chore.

Tonight, Linden was halfway through the pile of gray folders when his phone rang. Someone at the switchboard made a mistake, he thought. No one ever calls the NMCC after hours.

He picked up the phone. "Major Linden."

"Sir, this is Lieutenant McNally in Communications. I have a Code Sunstroke call from a Mr. Everett J. Nore at SOLSAT X-One Control in New Mexico. He has confirmation that a first-order event has taken place. He's standing by."

Linden was instantly alert. As one of the ranking NMCC duty officers he had received a full briefing on Project Sunstroke. He knew that Nore was the civilian observer appointed by the President to monitor activities at the SOLSAT X-1 plant. "Put his call through, Lieutenant." His voice was flat and imperative.

A moment later Nore was on the line recounting the disastrous events that occurred shortly after the solar satellite became operational. The major listened intently, asked several incisive questions, and took notes.

When he hung up, Linden knew exactly what he had to do next. Keeping his face carefully expressionless, he grabbed his notebook, got up from his desk, and started toward a steel door at the rear of the cavernous office. He moved quickly but without haste.

The door was labeled Emergency Communications. Major Linden placed his right hand flat against a dark plastic square mounted on the wall next to the door.

The steel door slid open to reveal a small soundproof room. As soon as Linden stepped inside, the door closed behind him. He walked over to a special computer console and sat down on the single swivel chair before it. His hands were moist with perspiration.

He knew this particular Pentagon computer was tied into EMCON, the Emergency Military Communications Network of restricted fiber-optic lines and telephone cables that spiderwebbed the nation. In the event of a national emergency the computer could instantly connect Linden with every major government office and defense installation in the country simultaneously.

He leaned forward and tapped in his personal access identifier and the code designator. The computer then selected the highest-level names and organizations associated with the code and displayed them on the console screen.

```
TOP SECRET
CODE    DESIGNATOR:    SUNSTROKE
  SDS 099781 554032
ALERT STATUS ACCORDED TO:
KENDALL,  JAMES  W,  PRESIDENT,
  UNITED STATES
FITZPATRICK, HUGH L, SECRETARY,
  DEFENSE DEPARTMENT
THOMPSON, WILLIS P, LT GEN, US
  ARMY, CHAIRMAN, JCS
STRATTON, DEAN M, LT GEN, USAF,
  SPACE DEFENSE COMMAND
ABRAMS,  WALTER  D,  MAJ  GEN,
  USAF, KIRTLAND AFB
```

After consulting his notes, Linden started typing out the urgent message he would send to the indicated officials. The text of his message appeared on the screen directly below the list of names. When he was finished he jammed a finger against a large green button at the top of the keyboard. The word *transmit* was engraved on it. As he pressed it a sense of relief swept over him. He was now transferring the unwanted burden of responsibility to his superiors.

Moving at the speed of light through the nation's gigantic nervous system of restricted underground trunk lines and telephone cables, Major Linden's message flashed to the video-teletype terminals inside the offices of the men designated to receive it.

Across the Potomac River, President James William Kendall was in his private study at the White House, reading the evening edition of the *Washington Post*. For the first time in months he was completely alone inside the spacious presidential living quarters. His lovely wife, Caroline, was downtown dedicating the new Grosvenor Hall of Modern Art, while his two children—James, Jr., and Michelle—were away at school.

Kendall was making use of these quiet moments by personally sampling the press's reaction to the start-up of the solar satellite. His ornate wooden desk, a gift from the President of France, was covered with the editorial sections from a dozen newspapers. Tonight's assortment gave him a pretty clear idea of the mood of the country, and for the most part, it was a fairly positive one. He was pleased to note the letters in the *Post* were running two-to-one in favor of the satellite. Not bad, he thought, grinning broadly. The public relations people at the Energy Department did a good job.

But Kendall's smile of satisfaction faded when he suddenly heard a staccato rapping on the door to his study. He got up from his desk and moved toward the door with a springy walk, the stride of an athletic person who pursued tennis and skiing with equal fervor. He was of medium height but his commanding presence made him appear taller. Despite the fact that he was in his early fifties, his boyish good looks and youthful exuberance prompted senior members of the Senate to refer to him as "our young president." After running his hand over his unruly dark hair in a futile effort to tame it, Kendall opened the door.

One glance at the nervous Army Signal Corps sergeant standing at attention in the doorway told the President this was not a routine interruption of his evening. "Yes, Sergeant?"

The young man snapped off a salute, his face blushing. "I'm sorry to disturb you, sir, but we just received an EMCON message from the teletype downstairs." He handed Kendall a special sealed printout marked TOP SECRET.

Kendall quickly dismissed the Army sergeant and then closed

the door. In the six years of his presidency he had never received an EMCON message before. But he knew that it signaled the advent of a major crisis. In the privacy of his study he tore open the printout and began reading the urgent message.

```
TOP SECRET
CODE  DESIGNATOR:  SUNSTROKE
  SDS 099781  554032
PRIORITY 1-1-A MESSAGE AS FOLLOWS
AT 2118 HOURS EST THIS P.M. A
FIRST ORDER EVENT TOOK PLACE 4.8
KILOMETERS SOUTHEAST OF SOLSAT
X-1 CONTROL SITE. CASUALTIES: FIVE
CIVILIANS ASSUMED DEAD FROM
LETHAL  MICROWAVE  RADIATION
EXPOSURE. PRESENTLY ONLY THE
CONTROL ROOM PERSONNEL AND
THE GOVERNOR OF NEW MEXICO ARE
AWARE OF THE DEATHS. TRACKING
RADAR HAS CONFIRMED AN ORBITAL
DEVIATION OF SATELLITE. TELEME-
TRY INDICATED A SIMULTANEOUS
FAILURE OF ON-BOARD MICROWAVE
PHASE-CONTROL DEVICE. SUBSE-
QUENT LORCON PREVENTED RECEP-
TION OF ALL RADIO COMMANDS.
PROBABLE CAUSES UNDETERMINED
AT THIS TIME. SATELLITE MICROWAVE
TRANSMITTER SHUT DOWN AT 2130
HOURS  EST.  PROJECT  DIRECTOR
MICHAEL DOHENY INSTRUCTED GOV-
ERNOR WALKER TO REQUEST A CBR
MEDICAL TEAM AND AIR RECON-
NAISSANCE CRAFT FROM KIRTLAND.
MESSAGE BASED ON REPORT FROM
NORE, EVERETT J, CIVILIAN OB-
SERVER, NSI, SOLSAT X-1 CONTROL.
PRIMARY  AUTHORITY:  LINDEN,
THOMAS A, MAJ, USAF, NMCC
END MESSAGE.
```

Kendall reacted to the shattering news with a characteristic, forced calm. When he finished reading the classified printout he

went back over it to study several passages. Then he carefully
folded the strip of flimsy paper and slipped it into the breast pocket
of his light gray suit. He frowned and became lost in thought.
What was it Disraeli once said? "What we anticipate seldom
happens; what we least expect generally occurs."

President Kendall was not a profound man, but he was
intelligent and shrewd. Some years ago, when his father died, he
had realized, without effort, that nothing in life surprised him any
longer. It was a useful, liberating revelation. It sharpened his sense
of humor and gave him a feeling that in religious men passes for
virtue. Because of this unique attitude the majority of voters saw
him as a deep, philosophical man who could regard his personal
tragedies and triumphs with a certain equanimity. But unfortunately he saw himself growing callous, unfeeling.

Scowling deeply, with hardened gray eyes that seemed not to
see but to peer back into his thoughts, he looked around the room.
There were Eisenhower's flags, Kennedy's chair, Monroe's ornate
divan. Visible reminders of the presidency, of the power of the
office he now held. In his heart and in his mind Kendall knew
he would do anything to keep it.

He vowed to resolve this Sunstroke crisis as soon as possible.
Somehow he would manage to conceal the deaths caused by
tonight's satellite malfunction. There was no other alternative. He
had to prevent a congressional investigation of Project Sunstroke at all costs. The future of his administration and the security
of the United States were at stake.

He walked to his desk and phoned Jack Conley, his assistant for
national security affairs. Conley was a former army brigadier
general who now occupied the corner office at the West Wing of
the White House. "Jack, we've got a problem," said the President
in a nasal, New England–accented voice. He briefly outlined the
EMCON message to his stunned adviser. Afterward he directed
Conley to call an emergency meeting, in strictest secrecy, to be
held a half hour from that moment, inside the National Security
Council conference room at the White House. While Conley took
notes, the President dictated who should be there: Defense
Secretary Hugh Fitzpatrick, General Willis Thompson, chairman
of the Joint Chiefs of Staff, Energy Secretary Donald Addeo, FBI
director Harold Sorensen, and of course, Conley himself. Kendall
wanted a press blackout on this evening's meeting and gave
express orders that the four visitors were to arrive at the back gate.
He also told Conley to set up a direct video link with General Dean

Stratton at the Space Defense Command Headquarters deep within Cheyenne Mountain, Colorado, and with General Walter Abrams at Kirtland Air Force Base in New Mexico. When he hung up, the President immediately made a list of the matters to be discussed.

Then he left his desk and stood by the French window and waited. The evening was serene, the fountain playing steadily on the south lawn, the traffic sparse and leisurely. Very few people were traveling down Constitution Avenue, for Washington, unlike Paris or London, has a tendency to retreat into itself after dusk.

As he gazed trancelike at the peaceful scene, Kendall's thoughts drifted to another secret meeting that had taken place nearly six years ago, shortly after he assumed office. It was attended by the same men he had summoned tonight. At that time, they had gathered in the Blue Room at the White House on a cold, wintry night to discuss Project Sunstroke, a classified document advocating the transformation of the then newly proposed solar satellite into a viable, space-based weapons system.

Now, as Kendall stood alone before the tall window overlooking the south lawn, he bitterly regretted his decision to implement Project Sunstroke. But then he realized he was viewing the situation through hindsight, an exercise in futility. He shifted his focus to the problems that lay ahead. Kendall meant to control events, not to be swept along by them.

He took the elevator down to the first floor and walked briskly along the bright corridor to the West Wing of the White House. He met General Thompson and Harold Sorensen at the entrance to the National Security Council conference room. After greetings were exchanged the three men went into the Crisis Room.

Jack Conley was standing at the far side of the room, speaking softly to a technician sitting at a communications console. The large-screen television displays on the wall above them suddenly sprang to life. Conley turned around when the President and the others entered. He was a tall, physically fit man in his late forties, all bone and muscle. "Sir, the video link with Cheyenne Mountain and Kirtland is ready."

"Thanks, Jack," said Kendall as he motioned Thompson and Sorensen to the oval conference table in the center of the room. He took his place in one of the ocher-colored chairs ringing the table.

Outwardly, the conference room seemed as unimpressive and unimaginative a place as the boardroom of some faceless corporation. Yet it was here that thermonuclear Armageddon had been envisioned during the Cuban missile crisis; that the decisions which sent a half million young Americans to fight and die in Southeast Asia had been debated; where the orders to invade Grenada and attack Libya had been issued; and where the strategies for the Panama invasion and the war against Iraq had been mapped out.

The bland appearance of the room was deceptive. At the touch of a button a set of curtains swept aside to reveal an electronic map board. A drawer containing a secure telephone was beside each chair at the table. Most important were the banks of communication consoles and their television screens on the far wall. This equipment linked the room and the White House to every vital nerve center of the U.S. government: the Pentagon, the State Department, the CIA, the Space Defense Command, NORAD, the National Security Agency, and the Strategic Air Command. A call originating from this conference room could be dispatched to any U.S. military base in the world.

The door opened and Defense Secretary Hugh Fitzpatrick and Energy Secretary Donald Addeo walked in. Fitzpatrick was nearly sixty, gaunt, with a bush of wiry gray hair, and dressed in an immaculate blue pinstripe suit. Addeo was short and bald, with a ruddy face and freckles, wearing a rumpled tweed sports jacket. The President waved both of them over to the table.

Then Conley swiftly ushered the technicians and aides from the conference room. Afterward he sat down next to Kendall and gestured to the two brightly lit television screens on the back wall. Each one displayed the enlarged image of an air force officer in uniform. "General Stratton and General Abrams are now on-screen, sir," he announced.

The President gave an intense, steady look to each of his advisers. "I want to thank you for being here tonight," he said in the studied, mannered tone he liked to employ for dramatic effect. "You all know the reason why I've called this meeting." The men on the TV screens and those around him slowly nodded. "Our primary task tonight is to decide the course of action we should take regarding the first-order event which occurred near the solar power plant a short time ago. But first, I want to know what the hell happened to our satellite up there." He reached into his coat pocket, took out the EMCON printout, unfolded it, and glanced up at General Dean Stratton's televised image. "Dean?"

Stratton frowned. His on-screen image was unimpressive. He was soft faced, bespectacled, hardly the appearance one would expect of a man in his position. "Sir, the satellite has drifted away from its geosynchronous position over the SOLSAT X-One Control site. NORAD radar stations have confirmed this. We expect to obtain the satellite's new orbital parameters very shortly.''

The President tapped the printout with his index finger. ''And what the devil is a LORCON?''

''A term indicating loss of radio control, sir,'' replied Stratton smoothly. ''All main satellite power systems failed to respond to ground-based commands. This explains why the control room team was unable to defocus the beam when the satellite began drifting. Apparently the automatic defocusing sequence was not activated.''

''Do you know what caused these, ah, problems?'' asked the President in an impatient tone.

''A number of factors could have brought about these conditions, sir,'' said Stratton. ''Component failure due to launch vibrations, undetected defects, or even a random collision with orbital debris.'' He shrugged slightly. ''Until all telemetry has been evaluated we can only make assumptions.''

''I see,'' said the President. He made a notation on his scratch pad. ''Now, I'd like a brief rundown on the first-order event itself.'' He looked searchingly at General Walter Abrams's image on the other large-screen television display. ''Walt,'' he asked, ''what have you got on this?''

Abrams had a long, narrow face with pale blue, coldly observant eyes, heavy brow, and sparse sandy hair. He exuded the self-assurance that comes with years of command. ''Sir, our tracking station here at Kirtland monitored the progress of the satellite's microwave beam as it left the rectenna. Their infrared scanners reported a level-four reading when the beam passed over a farmhouse. There is no doubt that the people inside were killed. The beam traveled approximately eight kilometers before it shut down. Shortly afterward we received a request from SOLSAT X-One Control to dispatch a CBR medical team in a helicopter to the plant site. Three of their rectenna substation technicians received a high dose of microwave radiation.''

''Has the medical team been sent out yet?'' asked the President.

''No, sir. At this moment their equipment and supplies are being loaded aboard an air-recon craft.''

''Sir,'' said General Stratton, ''I'd like to make a suggestion. At the risk of sounding callous, what we have here is an excellent opportunity to study the lethal effects of the microwave beam on human subjects." The room grew very quiet. Stratton continued. "These unfortunate deaths can give us precise data on the actual combat capability of the Sunstroke satellite. An overflight of the irradiated area would also give us invaluable knowledge of the beam's effect on terrestrial agriculture. This could open up a whole new dimension of warfare involving the destruction of an enemy nation's food productivity. We must bear in mind that once the satellite's malfunction is rectified, we still have a viable space weapons system."

The President drummed the tabletop with his fingertips. "Thank you, Dean," he said dryly. "But our main concern right now is to keep those fatalities from the press." He sighed. "It seems our original idea of having an official plant dedication ceremony almost backfired on us, gentlemen." He shot an angry look at Energy Secretary Donald Addeo, the one who had proposed the dedication ploy to cover up the military aspect of the plant. "Fortunately our civilian observer over there is certain the TV reporters are in the dark about the casualties. I'd like to keep it that way, for obvious reasons. How can we do it?"

"Mr. President, I think the problem can be solved fairly easily," said Harold Sorensen. The FBI director was a small man clad in a light gray suit, with dark hair and large protuberant eyes, at once mournful and derisive. He lit a cigarette and inhaled deeply while everyone hung attendant on his words. "General Stratton is interested in studying the bodies for scientific and military reasons. Well, it seems to me if we had General Abrams's helicopter pick up the bodies and take them to a lab for study, there wouldn't be any physical evidence of civilian casualties. With your permission I could send a field team from the Albuquerque bureau office out to the site tonight to sanitize the farmhouse—strip the place, make it seem deserted. They could smooth it over with the local authorities."

Kendall suddenly felt very uneasy. There was a knot in his stomach. He knew they were treading on dangerous ground now. Christ, he thought, they didn't want a Watergate on their hands. But Sorensen's suggestion did make cold, logical sense. He cupped his chin with his right hand and contemplated the ramifications.

Hugh Fitzpatrick, the defense secretary, twisted in his chair to face the President. He was cross, outspoken, and at the same time a knowledgeable lawyer. "All ethical considerations aside, I think Harold's plan might work." His face became wrinkled in thought.

"But what are we going to do about the plant personnel and the governor of New Mexico? They're aware of everything. The casualties, the extent of the malfunction."

"That's true, Fitz," replied the President. He kneaded the bridge of his nose. "A lot of people know too damn much." He clenched his fist in angry frustration. "Why the hell did that satellite have to go crazy up there tonight? *Why?*"

General Willis Thompson, chairman of the Joint Chiefs, shifted uneasily in his seat. He had a strong jaw and high cheekbones with salt-and-pepper hair combed neatly in a side part. His army uniform, four stars glinting on each shoulder, clung to his big frame. "Mr. President," he began, "in my opinion we cannot rule out the possibility that the satellite was sabotaged, either in orbit or on the ground. It may be advisable at this time to place the entire SOLSAT X-One facility under direct military control. Fort Union is the nearest army post. I recommend dispatching a company of soldiers to the facility to secure the premises and to detain all personnel until a complete investigation of the malfunction has been concluded."

"Do you mean lock up the plant with everyone inside?" asked President Kendall incredulously.

"Yes, sir," replied General Thompson firmly. "There may be enemy operatives among the plant personnel."

Energy Secretary Donald Addeo slowly shook his head. He turned to General Thompson. "Locking up those people might be the correct military procedure, General, but it would cause more trouble for us in the long run. They'll start screaming bloody murder to the media. No. We can't risk anything like that. Your idea is out of the question."

The little wrinkles about Thompson's eyes tightened. He glared at Addeo. "As I see it, the main difficulty will be with those television reporters and the governor. They wouldn't have been there if you hadn't insisted on a dedication ceremony, which, I might add, has certainly magnified our problems out of proportion."

Addeo's face and the top of his head reddened. "Now, wait a minute, General. We all agreed that—"

The President rapped the table with his knuckles. "Gentlemen, we're wandering. Let's stick to the main issue at hand."

FBI Director Sorensen stubbed out his cigarette in an ornate crystal ashtray decorated with the presidential seal. "Incarcerating the plant employees and the TV reporters would have certain advantages, Mr. President.''

"Such as?''

Sorensen stared levelly at the President. "First, and most importantly, it would give us the time we need to completely eliminate all evidence of the first-order event. Secondly, it would make it easy for us to instigate a press blackout at the plant. Then we could feed the media a statement, through the project director's office, detailing a very minor malfunction that shut the plant down temporarily. If no one is able to contradict the statement, then it becomes fact.''

Sorensen was barking his plans like a top sergeant. No one moved to interrupt him and he plunged on.

"Thirdly, a covert military takeover would simplify a sabotage inquiry. All of the employees would be easily accessible for interrogation. Finally, locking the gates over there would keep out any investigative reporters—or congressmen, for that matter—who might be interested in digging up a little dirt to help promote their careers. The soldiers' presence could be explained away as an additional security measure to prevent terrorist attacks.''

The President slipped down in his chair, his thumbs hooked beneath his chin with his fingers pressed against the sides of his nose. He smiled faintly when the FBI director stopped talking. "Well, Harold,'' he said, "that's quite a list. I'll have to admit you've presented an excellent case for locking up the plant.''

Hugh Fitzpatrick cleared his throat. "I'm in full agreement with Harold's reasons for commandeering the plant. And I have one more to add to his list. If news of those deaths leaked out, then our good friend Senator Phil Hutchins and his Senate Finance Committee would have ample reason to investigate the Solar Satellite Project. If Hutchins poked deeply enough he'd find out about Sunstroke and our little creative accounting. You can be sure he'd make use of the information to hang each of us, especially you, Mr. President. Don't forget, the military nature of the satellite is a direct violation of the ABM Treaty we've got with the Russians.''

"I haven't forgotten, Fitz,'' snapped the President. He closed his eyes. For a long moment, he pondered everything they had discussed so far. He felt as if he were caught in a trap from which, in spite of all the power of his office, there seemed to be no honorable escape. To Kendall, it seemed that one cover-up automatically led to another, then another, and so on, each one precariously balanced against the other, like dominoes waiting for the final catastrophic push.

"Jack," he said to his national security assistant, "do you have any recommendations?"

Jack Conley crossed his long legs and laid the palms of his hands flat against the tabletop. "Well, sir, it goes without saying the most important thing is to hold this as close as possible. And that means bringing in the military. You're also going to have to maintain the facade of a normal existence. That's the best way to keep the press off the track."

"All right, then," said the President forcefully. "This is what we will do. I want the solar power plant sealed up and put under military control immediately. All plant personnel and TV reporters will be held there until we learn the exact cause of the malfunction. My office will contact the governor of New Mexico. I understand he's running for the Senate next year. An endorsement from me will cinch his election. He'll cooperate with us. And maybe I can have the FCC exert a little pressure on the heads of the TV networks to keep those reporters over there in line."

He leaned forward and folded his hands, letting his glance travel over his advisers ranged around the table, then the military men on the television displays. "I don't think I need remind any of you about the implications of what we're discussing here tonight. If word somehow gets out, every one of you damn well better be prepared to lie, stonewall, and deny this whole thing right into the ground."

On-screen, a uniformed officer handed General Abrams a note. "Sir," interrupted Abrams, "we've just received a follow-up communication from SOLSAT X-One Control. Project Director Michael Doheny wishes to participate in the overflight of the irradiated area. Doheny says he knows the exact location of the farmhouse."

"I think it's time Doheny was filled in on Sunstroke," suggested Energy Secretary Donald Addeo. "I've met with him a few times. He's a brilliant engineer. Solid, reliable. We can use somebody like that on our side right now."

Kendall contemplated the proposal. He knew Doheny had never been briefed on the military applications of the project. They had believed his lack of knowledge in the matter would add a ring of authenticity to his press statements proclaiming the satellite was only intended to generate electricity. But now they would need his complete cooperation in order to resolve the crisis. And that would necessitate informing him about Project Sunstroke. He nodded to Addeo. "We'll brief Doheny, then put him in charge of investigating the satellite malfunction. I'll send word to Everett Nore."

He turned to General Thompson, chairman of the JCS. "Will, contact Fort Union and order them to dispatch a company of soldiers to the plant under a search-and-seizure directive. Instruct them to bring adequate provisions for themselves and for the plant personnel to last at least a week. Their orders are to completely seal up the plant."

Thompson nodded and reached for the secure telephone in the drawer beside him.

Kendall glanced at the TV screen displaying the two air force generals. "Dean," he said to General Stratton, "which government facility is best equipped to . . . ah . . . study the civilian fatalities?"

"I recommend the Air Force Scientific Laboratory in Richmond, Virginia, sir," responded Stratton without hesitation.

"Very well," said Kendall. He looked at General Abrams's televised image. "Walt, I want you to send your helicopter to the plant. Have your men follow Doheny's instructions. But when they locate the civilian casualties, I want the bodies taken to Kirtland, then airlifted to that lab in Richmond. Put a project-cleared man in charge of the operation."

Abrams acknowledged the presidential directive and disappeared from the screen.

The President leaned back in his chair. His shoulders and neck felt tight. He hoped to God they were doing the right thing.

Chapter 6 *

AT 8:35 P.M. that night, Mike Doheny walked quickly across the solar power plant's front parking lot toward the waiting Skyguard FH-2 helicopter, its blades cutting cleanly through the warm, dry air. The blast from the rotors whipped his jacket and touseled his hair. The copilot helped him climb inside, then slipped into his cockpit seat.

The pilot glanced back at Doheny and asked, ''Your instructions, sir?''

''We'll fly to the rectenna site first,'' Doheny replied as he fastened his seat belt. ''It's just a quarter mile to the south. We've got some casualties inside a concrete bunker there. Three men received a high dose of microwave radiation.''

The pilot faced his instrument panel and felt for the four antitorque pedals on the floor with his feet. After nodding to the copilot, who was now on radio, he gripped the collective, a two-foot stick protruding from the left side of his panel, and pushed it forward. The large, squat aircraft trembled, hovered for a second, and began slowly turning as he corrected the torque. Then they were airborne, rising swiftly into the black sky. The pilot flicked a switch and the searchlight mounted on the helicopter's belly suddenly flooded the ground below with its harsh illumination.

Doheny glanced out the window and saw the roof of the plant's main building sweep beneath them. Then he peered around the cramped compartment, his eyes not yet adjusted to the dimly lit interior. There were nine other passengers: six CBR medics, two airmen, and a commissioned air force officer who sat across from him.

''Mr. Doheny,'' said the officer crisply as he stuck out his hand, ''I'm Colonel Douglas Harriman.'' He was in his late thirties, lean but firmly built, with thick blond hair and a carefully trimmed

mustache. There was none of the puffiness about the jowls that
some peacetime officers acquire. "I recognized you from the
newspaper photos," he added. "Your plant has received a lot of
press the last couple of days."

Doheny shook hands and said, "We'll be getting a lot more
publicity after tonight, I'm afraid."

Harriman studied him for a moment and Doheny got the
impression he was being carefully evaluated. "I'm sorry about
your problem," stated the colonel in a professionally smooth tone.
"The governor gave our base a quick rundown, but I'd like to hear
it from you. Off the record, of course. Exactly what happened?"

Doheny thought he detected the standard contempt of the
military for the civilian sector in the colonel's voice. He decided
to ignore it and briefly recounted the tragic events of the past hour.

Harriman listened intently. Afterward he shook his head. "Too
bad about those farm people," he muttered. "But it was lucky that
your satellite shut down when it did. If it had hit Albuquerque
there would be hell to pay."

Doheny nodded, then leaned close to the window and looked
out. They were approaching the rectenna, a circular metallic grid
three thousand feet in diameter, lit up by mercury-vapor lights. As
they flew over the sprawling structure, its mirrorlike sheen
reflected the helicopter's glaring searchlight back at them, forcing
Doheny to shield his eyes. He instructed the pilot to land near the
substation bunker, a lone blockhouse situated just outside the
rectenna's southern periphery.

Harriman shifted in his seat. "We can drop off two of the CBR
medics at the bunker and then begin our overflight of the
microwave track," he suggested. "Your substation crew will be in
good hands. We don't like to admit it, but the air force has
extensive experience in treating microwave radar technicians who
have been inadvertently exposed to a pulse at close range."

Doheny agreed to Harriman's proposal. When they touched
down, two of the medics reached into the cargo hold and grabbed
four brown cases containing their portable diagnostic equipment.
They left the helicopter and disappeared inside the substation
bunker.

Harriman signaled the pilot to lift off. The helicopter tilted and
made a rapid ascent. When they were hovering at twenty-five
hundred feet Harriman ordered the copilot to fire a salvo of
phosphorus flares.

Doheny felt a sharp jolt and caught a glimpse of ten orange

streaks arcing through the night. Seconds later the flares ignited and ten blazing, white-hot miniature suns lit up the sky, bathing the terrain below in an unearthly, glaring light.

The crew and passengers were stunned. In the eerie, sinister illumination they saw a huge scar several miles long stretching across the land. When the microwave beam veered away from the rectenna, it had swept over scrub land and grain fields, creating a half-mile-wide swath of shredded, flattened vegetation. The swath sliced through the terrain in a southeast direction toward Albuquerque, then disappeared in the darkness beyond the range of the flares.

Doheny turned away from the window and shut his eyes. He had built the solar satellite to harness the power of the sun to provide unlimited electricity, he thought bitterly, but instead it had only brought death and destruction. He suddenly remembered the pointed accusation made by one of the reporters inside the control room. He had been accused of unleashing a death ray against the residents of New Mexico. Now as he flew over the devastated land below, Doheny realized that was exactly what he had done.

The flares had almost exhausted their phosphorus charges and were burning low, becoming dim and subdued. Soon they were nothing but embers glowing in the night.

The copilot's headset crackled and a message murmured into his ear. He turned to Doheny. "Sir, I just intercepted a message from Albuquerque Grid Central," he announced. "Electricity will be restored to the city and outlying areas in the next minute or so."

A moment later clusters of lights flickered on across the dark landscape.

Then Harriman barked a series of orders to the cockpit crew and the helicopter sank suddenly, like a stone, toward the ground. In another instant they were flying barely twenty feet over the microwave track, with their searchlight blazing. The copilot activated the fore and aft cameras, which greedily captured the onrushing scene on tape.

Doheny looked down at the bizarre, unreal landscape. The ground was heavily matted with dead vegetation, nothing green, just grays, browns, and blacks. Mesquite and creosote shrubs had become torn and twisted branches and shards of bark coated with glistening sap. Tall, withered husks rose above the ravaged land—the remains of the majestic saguaro cacti that had thrived in the region. He leaned closer to the window and saw that the ground was littered with little furry mounds. Rabbits and pack rats had been caught in the microwave beam while out foraging for food.

The cockpit radar suddenly detected a low hill directly ahead and the pilot shoved the collective forward. The helicopter shook violently, tilted upward, and climbed. When they cleared the hill the copilot glanced back, his eyes bright. "Farmland coming up."

They were still low, only one hundred feet above the ground, and for a moment Doheny could see nothing but a seemingly endless stretch of barley stalks, split and denuded of grain. Then, up ahead, a house with lights shining in the windows, casting yellow glimmers across a dark landscape.

An acute sickening feeling came over Doheny. This was the farmhouse he had seen on the infrared screen in the control room. "That's the house, Colonel," he said in a low voice.

Harriman leaned forward. "Circle the structure. I want a good look at it."

The helicopter banked sharply and the crew and passengers looked down at a trim, neat farmhouse set back a short distance from the dirt road. It had a large wooden front porch, ornamental shutters, and a shingled roof dominated by a brick chimney with an enormous television mast fastened to it. Behind the house stood a small garage with a basketball backboard and hoop mounted above the door. A family's modest dream home.

Doheny desperately wanted to see something moving, some sign of life. But the only movement he saw was the stirring of sand and dust and bits of withered vegetation by the down blast from the rotor blades.

The pilot maneuvered the aircraft over the dirt road and gently set it down, raising a heavy cloud of dust. The air force personnel carried out their assigned tasks quickly and efficiently. Heavy-duty flashlights, medical kits, stretchers, and tools were broken out of the cargo hold. Then the hatch was tugged open and everyone got out.

It was an unusually warm night for early September. Doheny took off his coat and noticed a faint shadow on the ground mimicking his movements. He glanced up at the cloudless sky and saw a huge light brighter than the planet Venus, drifting slowly, almost imperceptibly, high in the eastern sky above Albuquerque. The solar satellite was moving farther away from the plant, traveling in a new, undetermined orbit. He wondered if it would become a derelict spacecraft, mute and unresponsive, forever circling the earth. Then he focused his attention on the activity around him.

A CBR medic named Vinson was handing out white gauze masks. He was young, with bristly, close-cropped dark hair and an easy smile.

"Why the masks?" Doheny asked.

"Sanitation mainly, sir," answered Vinson. "And sensitivity next. If there are any bodies inside, the stench will be pretty bad."

Harriman clipped a transceiver to his belt and turned to Doheny. "No need for you to accompany us. You can wait here with the air crew. We'll search the house and give you a complete report afterward."

Doheny shook his head. "No, I'm going with you."

Harriman gave him a questioning look. "Ever smell burned flesh?"

Doheny felt a disturbing sense of unrest as he recalled a carefully buried memory. "Yes, Colonel, I have. We had a bad accident a couple years ago." Images began crowding his mind. He had to make an effort to dispel them. "Two men died when an attitudinal-control thruster exploded. I still dream about it." He regretted mentioning the accident to Colonel Harriman. He felt as if he had betrayed a part of himself.

Harriman pointed to the farmhouse. "This could be a lot worse than normal burn victims," he said grimly. "If I were you I'd stay behind."

Doheny stared levelly at him. "Colonel, we tried to warn them before the microwave beam hit—but the interference was too strong. There was nothing I could do." He felt a sudden wave of anguish. "I have to go with you. I owe them at least that much."

Shining their flashlights before them the men walked slowly, deliberately, toward the farmhouse. They spotted a mailbox on the edge of the front lawn, near the road. The nameplate said THE J. ROBERTS FAMILY. Stretched out dead on the matted grass beneath the mailbox was a large dog with reddish fur. An Irish setter. Its swollen, misshapen body lay in a pool of brownish liquid.

Two medics cracked open a tan case and took out a special body bag; the interior was lined with a strange, yellow honeycomb insulation. After donning rubber gloves they lifted the dog— Doheny noticed they were careful to keep the oozing fluids off their clothes—and placed it inside the bag. The group moved on.

Harriman ordered a red-haired young airman named Rankin to

go out back and inspect the garage. Rankin acknowledged the order and disappeared into the darkness.

Doheny followed the others up the wooden steps to the front porch. They did not creak. Looking in a front window, he could see all the way to the rear of the house, past the silhouettes of furniture.

The front door was locked from the inside. Harriman stepped back and nodded to the swarthy, solidly built airman carrying a halligan tool, a long heavy bar hooked at one end, canted at the other. The airman caught a doorjamb with the hooked end and pushed hard. The jamb split with a cracking sound and the door flung open. Suddenly they heard harsh, aggravated voices coming from inside. They entered slowly, cautiously.

The television set in the corner of the living room was blaring. There was a police show in progress. An undercover cop was pistol-whipping an obvious drug dealer. It looked real.

Doheny stood in the entry and glanced around the room. A magazine rack had been knocked over and glossy sports magazines were scattered across the carpet. Tables, chairs, and a footstool were upturned. Clothes were strewn over the sofa and floor. They were heavily stained with perspiration. A phone lay on the floor, its receiver off the hook. There were no bodies in sight.

When the microwaves struck, the family had panicked in the dark, stripped off their clothes, and fled. Doheny felt a glimmer of hope. Could they have sought shelter in a storm cellar? If it was deep enough they could still be alive. Then a sickening odor penetrated his gauze mask and invaded his nostrils. It resembled the smell of rotting potatoes. They didn't make it, he realized grimly.

The rescue party quickly dispersed and the grisly search began.

USAF Medical Corpsman Gerald Vinson walked through a narrow hallway leading from the living room to the rear of the Robertses' house. Vinson was twenty-one years old. He had enlisted in the air force immediately after graduating from high school and, when his tour of duty was up, he reenlisted and spent a year at the Armed Forces Radiological Institute. This training, plus six months' experience with the CBR unit at Kirtland, had officially qualified him for tonight's special mission. But it didn't emotionally prepare him for what he would find.

As he walked down the hall he noticed the carpet was sopped. He saw a pool of water steadily growing on the floor near the bathroom entrance. The door was wide open and the light was on. He heard the sound of running water in the bathtub. The sickening stench that permeated the house was now very strong. He peered inside. The tile floor was submerged in an inch of water. The sink, a towel rack, and the toilet were visible from where he stood, but the bathtub alcove was hidden from view. He had a dread premonition of what lay inside it.

He steeled himself and went in holding his breath, his boots splashing through the water. When he reached the alcove Vinson froze. For a few seconds he stared at the bathtub, his body rigid. He tried to shout to Colonel Harriman, but instead he made a low gagging noise and stumbled backward. He vomited, staggered, and fell to his knees on the submerged tile floor.

He had found the Roberts family. They were all in the bathtub together; the shower head was spraying a jet of water on them and the tub was overflowing. Their dead, naked bodies lay pressed together in the fetal position, curled like snails, swollen and blistered almost beyond recognition. The mass of cooked flesh was a mottled reddish gray, and as Vinson regurgitated onto the floor, he thought—and the thought made him retch again—that their glazed, protruding eyes looked like poached eggs.

At first glance the kitchen appeared neat and tidy, except for the ruptured Budweiser can on the counter. Doheny picked it up. The can was empty and there was a dried stain beneath it.

Two framed samplers hung on the wall near some cabinets. One said "Some people sell themselves to the Devil; others rent themselves out by the day." The other said "Makin' love don't last, cookin' do."

Then Doheny heard muffled, frantic shouts coming from the back of the house. He hurriedly left the kitchen, ran through the living room, and raced down the narrow hallway.

Vinson was still on his knees when he reached him. He had stopped vomiting, but his head still hung, mouth open, the gauze mask askew.

When Doheny glanced inside the bathtub and saw the Roberts family, he felt the bile rise in his own throat. Reflexively, he stepped back and swallowed. Then he helped Vinson to his feet.

Harriman joined them, his eyes wide, face pale. A moment later the other members of the search-and-rescue party entered. They stared in horror, unable to avert their eyes.

The burly airman with the halligan tool became ill, feeling no shame as he doubled over and loudly spilled his guts into the toilet. He flushed it and staggered out.

Doheny watched the senior medic examine the bodies. He fought to control his stomach.

"They're all here," announced the medic in an impersonal nasal tone. He was trying to hold his breath. "We found a recent photo album in the master bedroom. Parents and their three young sons."

Harriman shook his head sorrowfully. "They tried to survive the heat by submersing in the tub. Instead they were boiled alive."

The entire party became silent, each man mentally painting his own picture of what it must have been like in those last few seconds. The very air inside the bathtub alcove had screams smeared on it.

The guilt that Doheny felt was worse than the assault on his physical senses. He had given the order to activate the solar satellite. And the Roberts family had died an excruciating death because of it.

Doheny knew he had lost his struggle. He pushed past one of the medics, hung his head over the toilet, and vomited into the bowl, wishing he could clear his conscience as easily as his stomach.

Chapter 7 *

THREE MILES AWAY, at the solar power plant, Everett Judson Nore was deep in thought as he briskly walked down the corridor toward the VIP lounge. He was preoccupied with the White House phone call he had received a few minutes before. The call had been routed through the special Pentagon trunk line linked to the scrambler phone in his office. Jack Conley, the assistant for national security affairs, had personally phoned Nore to advise him of the emergency presidential directives concerning the first-order event. When the conversation had ended Nore was deeply troubled. He had grave doubts about the President's decisions.

He nervously fingered the folded sheet of paper in his breast pocket. Printed on it in bold black letters was the carefully prepared press statement regarding the satellite malfunction. Nore knew it was a damned lie couched in engineering jargon and half-truths. The statement had been the result of a forced collaboration between Conley and himself. The newspapers won't swallow it, he thought, but the television networks and video services might.

He paused outside the entrance to the VIP lounge just long enough to glance at his watch. It was 9:15 P.M. According to Jack Conley, the soldiers from Fort Union would be arriving at any minute to seal up the plant. It will take all of his persuasive abilities to smooth over the ruffled feathers, he thought wryly. The reporters and plant personnel aren't going to like being confined to the premises for God knows how long. But he was more concerned about Mike Doheny. Conley had ordered him to brief Doheny on every aspect of the Sunstroke Project. Nore instinctively knew that Doheny would take it hard. Well, we've all got our burdens to bear. He swallowed hard and opened the door.

The VIP lounge was the size of a small theater, with simulated mahogany-paneled walls and dozens of plush leather couches arranged in a semicircle around a lectern. The TV reporters, their assistants, and cameramen were sitting close together, exchanging notes and sipping hot coffee from foam cups.

Deputy Energy Secretary Howard Averson sat alone in a corner of the room, appearing sullen and pensive. His brief period of limelight in front of the TV cameras had passed; the reporters had quickly learned that Averson didn't know any more than they did.

The group had been waiting in the lounge for nearly two hours. They were irritated and impatient, tired of each other's company, and feeling imposed upon.

When Nore entered the room and took his place at the lectern, TV lights flared on, cameras whirred, and a forest of microphones appeared.

He raised his hands to ward off the volley of attempted questions, then let his eyes rove over the somewhat hostile two dozen people before him. He immediately spotted the tall slender blond in the severely tailored suit, standing in the front row, notebook in hand. Diane Bradford, the reporter from Cable News Service, wore an expression of suspicious apprehension. Nore was not eager to answer her pointed questions.

The clamor subsided and Nore cleared his throat. "Ladies and gentlemen," he said in a deep resonant voice, "I apologize for my delay in meeting with you here and sincerely hope that you haven't been too seriously inconvenienced. As promised, the project director's office has released a statement concerning the technical difficulty which occurred earlier this evening."

He took the sheet of paper from his breast pocket and unfolded it. The prepared statement was brief; Nore read it aloud slowly, attempting to hide the contempt he felt toward the charade.

"A malfunction of the attitudinal-control system aboard the solar satellite occurred tonight at seven-oh-one P.M. Mountain Standard Time. A high-resolution radar scan determined that the satellite had drifted a fraction of an arc degree from its geosynchronous orbital position directly above the U.S. Department of Energy's solar power plant. However, the on-board phase-control devices immediately shut off the microwave transmission beam. As a result, the plant operation was terminated, causing a temporary power outage in Albuquerque. Ground controllers are attempting to resolve the problem."

His last two sentences were drowned out by an angry outburst from the reporters.

"That's bullshit!" shouted Video News.

"What kind of hype is this?" demanded ABC.

Diane Bradford raised her voice in an effort to be heard over the tumult. "It didn't happen that way, Mr. Nore," she protested. "We were inside the control room during the malfunction, remember? Those fail-safe devices of yours didn't work."

Nore waved aside the questions. "Just a minute now," he said heavily. "Let me finish this statement first, then I'll answer your questions."

He resumed reading in a stronger voice. "An investigative team of specialists, led by project director Michael Doheny, strongly suspect that the malfunction was caused by intentional sabotage. Apparently the on-board guidance computer was fed—"

Suddenly there was the sound of many footsteps in the corridor outside and Nore turned toward the lounge entrance.

The door was thrown open and a half dozen uniformed MPs with submachine guns filed into the room and took up parade-rest positions around the astonished reporters and political aides. The murmur of conversation stopped and everyone stared at the MPs and the grim-faced officer who followed them in. His badge identified him as a provost marshal, a supervisory military police officer. He was carrying a blueprint of the plant.

The old order changeth, Nore thought cynically, giving way to the new. He eyed the intruders uneasily. They were in their early thirties, he guessed. Hard and well-trained professionals brandishing their ugly weapons with flourish.

The army provost marshal walked directly to the lectern and speared Nore with his small steely eyes. Nore studied the man's features for a moment before stepping aside. The provost marshal was above average in height, with a massive torso and thick arms and legs. His eyebrows merged in a dark line above the bridge of his nose, a barely discernible scar crossed his left cheek, the backs of his hands were covered with coarse black hair. He had the patiently relaxed posture of a toughened combat veteran.

The provost marshal laid the blueprint on the lectern, then faced the startled audience with one hand resting lightly on his holstered side arm.

"I'm Marshal Earl Clayton of the Fort Union Military Police Corps." His voice was boulder firm and his words had the slow emphasis of a drumbeat. "We have reason to believe that a covert act of sabotage has taken place at this facility. To prevent any further incidents, the entire plant is now operating under martial law according to Article Three, Section Seventeen of the National Espionage Act."

Clayton's eyes swept the room in a direct challenge.

"Anything you may have seen or heard since entering this facility tonight will not be discussed either with plant employees or among yourselves. For the next forty-eight hours, none of you will be permitted to leave these premises, nor will you be allowed to communicate with the outside. Living quarters and provisions will be provided for you here. We will notify the wives of those of you who are married and inform them of the situation." He paused, obviously expecting protests.

The room was completely silent. Nore scanned the captive audience and saw shocked expressions on their faces.

Clayton continued. "Your cameras and other equipment will be temporarily impounded until the detention period is over. I am not prepared to discuss further the reasons for these orders. Your cooperation will be appreciated."

Nore could feel the tension in the air building to a fever pitch. Then angry shouts filled the room.

"This is some kind of cover-up, isn't it?" accused the young, soft-faced reporter from Video News.

"What the hell is going on?" demanded CBS.

"You can't keep us here against our will," protested NBC.

"You're gonna be up to your armpits in lawsuits," threatened ABC.

Within moments the uproar tapered down to an incessant murmur, like the drone from a beehive.

Diane Bradford stepped forward, walked past the provost marshal at the lectern, and stood facing Everett Nore. She felt Clayton's eyes on her. "Mr. Nore, would you please tell us what this is all about?" she demanded in a voice with a wire edge to it.

Nore decided to be partly truthful. "Ms. Bradford, as I'm sure you're aware, this plant is under the jurisdiction of the U.S. Department of Energy. Apparently the DOE officials in Washington have decided to take matters into their own hands and"—he gestured to the MPs—"this is the result." He shrugged his shoulders. "I'm afraid we're stuck with it, at least for a while."

Deputy Energy Secretary Howard Averson moved toward the front of the room. "Everett, I wasn't informed of any decision affecting plant security. I think there's been a misunderstanding of some sort." He turned to Marshal Clayton. "Marshal, which government office contacted your fort?"

Clayton glared at Averson. "Sir, I've already told you that I won't discuss my orders," he said coldly. "But I can assure you there's been no mistake."

Averson glanced at his watch. "Well, if you'll excuse me, I have a plane to catch. I'm due back in Washington in the morning."

"I'm sorry, sir," Clayton said firmly, "but no one here is to leave this plant."

Averson was incredulous. His long face seemed to stretch further. He stiffened. "Your orders can't possibly apply to me. I'm the Deputy Secretary of Energy."

Clayton was not impressed. "No one here is to leave this plant," he repeated emphatically.

The correspondent from Video News flailed his arms. His face was red, contorted with rage. He pulled on his plaid sports coat and strode briskly toward the door. The others stirred, but were reluctant to follow.

Nore was suddenly alert, knowing instinctively what was going to happen next.

Provost Marshal Clayton nodded to a couple of MPs standing in a corner of the room. The two guards slung their weapons over their shoulders, then moved with a relentless stalking skill. They flowed by each couch and table and person as if this were a daily routine. Before the Video News reporter had reached the door, they came up behind him quietly and with an enormous confidence.

The reporter turned and saw the two big MPs flanking him. They gently took him by both arms and attempted to quietly escort him back to his seat. But the young man panicked and pulled free. "Keep your fucking hands off me!" he yelled.

When the MPs tried to restrain him, tears of anger flooded down his cheeks. He shoved and slapped without landing a telling blow. He had never learned how to fight.

They had him then. One of the MPs clamped the reporter's arms behind his back while the other grabbed his feet. The young man became desperate and started kicking furiously at them.

Nore shouted at the top of his voice, "Leave him alone, goddamn it! Don't hurt him."

But his warning came too late. An audible snap echoed through the room and the reporter suddenly grimaced and sagged. The audience watched in stunned silence.

"My arm!" screamed the Video News reporter. He sucked in his breath. "You broke my arm!"

Nore ran to the injured reporter, shoved the MPs aside, and examined the fractured limb. The lower part of the man's right arm hung at an unnatural angle. The blood was drained from his contorted face. He was breathing shallowly and sweating. Nore was certain the man was going into shock.

The provost marshal approached warily. His eyes widened when he saw the obviously broken limb. "I'm sorry, sir," he said lamely to Nore. "They had no intention of injuring him. It was an accident."

Nore looked up. His face grew tight. "This man needs immediate medical attention," he said harshly. "I want him taken to the infirmary *right now*."

Clayton gestured to the MPs. They quickly half carried the faint, listless reporter out of the lounge.

Nore felt a rising tide of anger building within him as he watched them leave. He gripped his right wrist with the palm of his left hand and squeezed hard. He spun on his heels to face Clayton. "Your men didn't have to break his arm, damn it. It was completely uncalled for."

Clayton studied Nore for a moment. "Sir, it was an accident. My men were just trying to restrain the man, to keep him from leaving. They were trained to follow their orders to the letter."

Nore's face flushed. His eyes seemed to flash sparks of anger. He stared at Clayton with a fierce intensity. "Marshal," he said in a low voice, "if your men perpetrate any more violence on these premises, I'll personally see to it that charges are brought against you by the adjutant general of the U.S. Army."

Clayton's small eyes narrowed. He opened his mouth to reply, but then shut it. There was something in Nore's eyes that told him the man wasn't bluffing. He decided to change the subject. "Sir, I have orders to see that the governor is escorted to his mansion. Exactly where is he?"

"In the control room," Nore snapped. "I'm on my way there now. You can follow me."

As he left the VIP lounge Nore wondered what Doheny's reaction would be to the military takeover of the plant. Doheny was all engineer and no politician. It would be difficult for him to accept the military's presence. And infinitely harder for him to accept the true nature of the solar satellite. Nore was not anxious to confront him on either subject. But he had no choice.

Diane Bradford stood motionless a few feet away from the lectern, nervously glancing at the hard faces of the heavily armed MPs stationed around the large room. She hadn't moved since the MPs had dragged the Video News correspondent out of the lounge. In all her twenty-eight years she had never before felt so vulnerable and scared. Her mind whirled with unanswered questions and a nagging uncertainty. A degree in journalism from the University of New Mexico and six years' experience in the local broadcasting industry hadn't equipped her for tonight's ordeal.

In one corner of the lounge several MPs were sorting through the TV lights, microphones, and cameras that had been hastily surrendered by the cameramen and their assistants. The other reporters stood nearby, numbly watching the MPs efficiently labeling each piece of equipment before putting it on a tan-colored dolly.

We're being treated like common criminals, Diane thought bitterly. Imprisoned inside a high-tech power plant gone wild. She shook her head and squeezed her eyes shut in an effort to expel the entire nightmarish scene from her mind. But when she opened her eyes the MPs were still there; they had become part of the harsh reality surrounding her.

The initial shock and confusion slowly began to metamorphose into analytical thought. Her professional journalist's instincts were suddenly aroused and her mind started racing back over what she had seen and heard inside the control room. She was now more certain than ever that Everett Nore was desperately trying to cover up the magnitude of the solar satellite malfunction. Even if it meant illegally confining her and the others. She didn't believe Nore's claim about sabotage because to her it sounded too contrived, too convenient. Possibly Nore may have learned his company was at fault, perhaps because of improper design or poor workmanship. But even the head of NSI doesn't have the authority to call up a contingent of military police to protect his corporate interests. No, she thought, other more important factors were involved, probably political.

Diane shuddered as she realized the implications. She and the other reporters were caught in a strange web of conspiracy enveloping the Solar Satellite Project. And from her perspective there was no easy escape.

She immediately wondered if all the plant personnel were involved. It was difficult for her to believe that the project director was willingly participating in the cover-up. She had interviewed Mike Doheny earlier that day in his private office at the plant. He had briefly outlined the technical aspects of the project to her with the aid of artists' renderings and a videotape presentation. The interview had been followed by an extensive tour of the plant. At one point during the tour she had questioned him regarding the safety of the entire operation. She had been impressed by the apparent candor and straightforwardness of his replies. He had seemed to genuinely believe in the integrity of the so-called fail-safe devices.

Afterward Diane had made a professional assessment of Doheny. She had found him to be an honest, hardworking, and dedicated engineer-administrator. She had been pleasantly surprised by his appearance. Definitely not a stereotype engineer. His imposing height, strong build, good looks, and no-nonsense demeanor made him a standout in any profession. He had revealing blue eyes and the perpetual inquiring frown of a scholar. She had half smiled to herself. Quite a combination. As part of her job as a TV journalist she had researched Doheny's personal life and discovered he had divorced his wife four years ago. Since then he had completely immersed himself in his work.

Presently, she recalled how decisive and commanding he had been during the control room crisis, when everything went wrong. She could not bring herself to believe such a man could condone Nore's blatant lies and the brutal strong-arm tactics of the MPs. She had an intuitive hunch that Doheny wasn't involved.

Driven by her irresistible reporter's curiosity and by the outrage she felt at being imprisoned against her will, Diane resolved to unravel the conspiracy and bring it to the public's attention. Every nerve ending in her body told her this could turn out to be the story of the century. The once-in-a-lifetime opportunity that could place her in a position to demand anything she wanted in the industry—such as her own prime-time network news show with an ironclad ten-year contract. She had long since realized that her present position as a correspondent for the local Cable News Service affiliate was a dead end.

Although she had no idea how she was going to conduct her investigation under the harsh circumstances, Diane felt it represented the greatest challenge of her career that could only be met by using whatever means were available to her. Men were attracted to her. This was a simple fact of Diane's life. In some cases her mere proximity constituted a kind of subtle seduction. She disliked taking advantage of this biological accident, but she was determined that if it became necessary to seduce Doheny or anyone else to get her story, she would do it.

But where, she thought, where *is* Mike Doheny?

Chapter 8 *

WITH ITS ANTICOLLISION strobes making tiny, brilliant flashes, the Skyguard FH-2 helicopter descended toward the plant's front parking lot. Doheny was startled to see several armored personnel carriers and jeeps parked near the main gate. When he asked Harriman about them the colonel merely shook his head. It was the same response Doheny had gotten earlier when he had asked Harriman where the bodies of the Roberts family were being flown to.

As the helicopter gingerly settled on its landing gear, the two CBR medics who had examined and treated the rectenna substation crew sprinted toward the aircraft. According to their report the substation crew were suffering from severe dehydration and were recuperating in the infirmary.

Doheny thanked the two medics and Colonel Harriman for their services, then climbed out and dropped to the ground. He watched the air force helicopter as it vaulted into the night sky with its grisly cargo.

Doheny raced up the steps to the control center building, a starkly lit, windowless monolithic structure. Sentries were stationed at the entrance, in the lobby, and at the elevator bank. Lean, hardened men with bleak eyes and a professional air, Doheny thought. They gave him the impression of being hired killers. He took an elevator down to the first sublevel, got out, and went to the control room.

Inside, the air was filled with the acrid smell of ozone and warm electrical insulation. Several electronic consoles were lifeless, their lights extinguished, their guts spread out in front of them. A handful of technicians led by propulsion systems engineer Jenkins were searching through the jungle of wires and silicon wafers like diviners seeking oracles in the entrails of chickens.

"We've just finished the post-mortems on the guidance and

microwave consoles, Mike,'' Jenkins reported. ''There's nothing wrong with the circuitry.''

Doheny nodded, then walked over to Everett Nore, who stood to one side of the exposed consoles. ''What the *hell* is going on around here, Everett?'' he asked sharply.

As if on cue the control room doors snapped open and Provost Marshal Earl Clayton entered. Nore made the introductions smoothly, then instructed Clayton to briefly outline the new security procedures in effect at the plant.

Clayton recited the rules and regulations in a droning, monotonous voice.

Doheny was incredulous. ''I don't believe it, Everett. You can't just lock up everyone inside the plant. This is a civilian facility. At any rate, our people are going to be bone weary soon and anxious to get back to their families. Why—''

He was interrupted by Clayton. ''Sir, overnight accommodations have been provided for all personnel, including the television reporters and yourself.''

Doheny fought to stem the swell of anger and resentment rapidly building within him. He didn't want a confrontation. ''Marshal,'' Doheny said in a reasonable tone, ''you can't confine the reporters to the plant. They're not company employees.''

''I'm just following orders, sir,'' Clayton said smoothly. ''They are presently being held in the VIP lounge.'' He studied Doheny with small steely eyes. ''It's my duty to inform you that one of the reporters willfully violated the National Espionage Act by attempting to leave the premises. He forcibly resisted arrest and assaulted two of my men. Unfortunately, during the struggle he sustained a minor injury. Purely accidental, I assure you.''

''How badly was he hurt?'' Doheny demanded.

Clayton was visibly irritated at being questioned by a civilian. He stiffened slightly. ''His right arm was fractured,'' he murmured.

Nore decided to interrupt. ''I've already spoken to the marshal about this,'' he said in a conciliatory tone. ''It *was* an accident.''

Doheny's face felt hot, flushed. His first impression of the MPs had been correct. They were nothing but thugs. He stared fiercely at the provost marshal. ''I want you and your soldiers to leave here within the hour,'' he said quietly in a voice that dripped with hostility.

Clayton assumed an air of mock ease, a recklessness attributed to physically powerful men, a vanity as if their strength had no limits. "Sir," he said coolly, "you don't have the authority to countermand my orders." It was a direct challenge.

Doheny's throat felt tight, and he clenched his teeth, popping the muscles on both sides of his jaw. All of the pressure and strain he had been under that night came to a head. He glared at Clayton. "As director of this facility," he said slowly, spitting out each word with the emphasis of a jabbing forefinger, "I'm ordering you to leave these premises."

Clayton was not intimidated. "Only my commanding officer at Fort Union can issue that directive, sir."

The tense silence that filled the room was broken by a couple of jittery coughs from the technicians gathered around the exposed consoles.

Nore moved closer to Doheny. "Mike," he pleaded, "there's nothing we can do. Washington wants—"

"To hell with Washington," yelled Doheny. He stormed to the main control console and picked up the phone. "Operator, put me through to Fort Union. The C. O.'s residence."

A harsh voice came on the line. "This is a security intercept. We cannot allow outside calls without authorization from Marshal Clayton."

Doheny stared at the phone blankly for a moment, then slammed the receiver down in disgust. He suddenly felt a hand on his shoulder.

It was Nore. The head of NSI looked tired and older than his years. "Mike, I'd like to speak with you in my office." There was a desperate urgency to his voice.

Doheny pulled one of the overstuffed black leather armchairs closer to the massive walnut desk in front of him, sat down, and silently watched Nore pour three fingers of Scotch into two tumblers. When Nore held out the glass, he accepted it with a murmur of thanks and took a sip. The fiery liquid burned his sensitive stomach but soothed his jangled nerves. Then he saw the red scrambler phone perched on the desktop. He had never seen it before. The curious lack of buttons or dial told him it was a special trunk-line phone.

Nore caught his glance. "They installed that thing a few days ago," he said in a forced offhand manner.

"Who's on the other end?"

Nore downed his drink, leaned back in his chair, and folded his hands. His knuckles became mottled with red. "The Pentagon."

Doheny shut his eyes and massaged his temples. "All right, Everett," he said in a tired voice. "You'd better start from the beginning."

Nore stood up and crossed the bristly carpet to the bookshelf lining the rear wall. It was filled with stacks of aerospace periodicals and textbooks. He pushed the books to one side to reveal a wall safe. The combination consisted of his wife's birthday in reverse prefixed by the first two numbers of his home zip code. After punching in the eight digits he turned the handle and opened the door. A bulb lit the interior, like a refrigerator. Inside was a red-banded file, a heavy thick wad of paper bound in gray.

Nore took out the file, rapidly leafed through it, then closed the safe. "Skim through it, Mike," he said slowly and distinctly, as if anticipating a stoppage in his throat. "I'll tell you the whole rotten story."

Doheny looked at the thick folder and frowned. Stenciled on the gray cover was PROJECT SUNSTROKE, and underneath, the words TOP SECRET. The seal of the Advanced Weapons Research Group, a Pentagon organization, appeared on the bottom.

Although he felt sapped by fatigue from the numbing events of the past few hours, Doheny opened the file and began reading. He became instantly alert upon scanning the first page.

FOREWORD

Harnessing solar energy for use as a military weapon is not a modern concept. The first solar weapon was designed and constructed over two thousand years ago by the Greek mathematician Archimedes. The device consisted of an immense magnifying glass capable of concentrating the sun's rays to set fire to enemy ships. It was used to defend the city of Syracuse against the invading Roman forces. Unfortunately the concept has been largely ignored throughout most of history because of its ineffectiveness at night and on overcast days.

However, the advent of spaceflight capability has enabled the solar weapon concept to overcome the limitations imposed upon it by both the diurnal cycle and atmospheric conditions. Once deployed in a high earth orbit a solar device could continuously tap the sun's energy and transmit it to earth. Indeed, this was the basis for Project Headlight.

In 1967, during the height of the Vietnam War, a Pentagon study group proposed the deployment of an orbiting solar mirror to illuminate the Southeast Asia jungles at night. This would have prevented the elusive Viet Cong guerrillas from seeking shelter under the dense foliage canopy to evade American ground and air forces. During daylight hours, the orbital mirror could have been used to blind enemy troops by intensifying sunlight. But Project Headlight was abandoned when certain government officials incorrectly predicted the Vietnam War would be over before the orbital mirror could be built and launched.

Presently we have the opportunity to erect a space-based solar weapons system capable of neutralizing enemy population centers in addition to shielding this nation against a nuclear attack. This is Project Sunstroke, an advanced weapons concept based on the Solar Satellite Project proposal recently submitted to the Energy Department by Nore Space Industries, Inc. As originally proposed by NSI, a solar satellite would be placed in geosynchronous orbit to collect solar radiation for conversion to high-intensity microwaves for transmission to a receiving antenna on earth to produce base-load electricity. With relatively minor modifications, the NSI satellite can effectively test the feasibility of the Sunstroke weapons system.

This report summarizes the test phase of the Sunstroke program. The design modifications of the NSI proposal are presented here as well as the framework in which the test satellite should be publicly exhibited.

The compilation of this report was greatly aided by the advice of a distinguished advisory panel and by the participants in three specialized study groups: one on satellite conversion, one on the biological effects of high-intensity microwaves, and another on foreign government reactions. The important analyses and recommendations provided by the prime contractor and by numerous individuals within the armed forces who gave generously of their time are gratefully acknowledged.

Dean M. Stratton

Dean M. Stratton, Lt. General, USAF
Chairman
Sunstroke Project Commission

Doheny turned liquid inside. He rubbed his hand over his face, pressing heavily against it. He did not want to believe what he had just read was true. It was some kind of morbid joke, he thought, an elaborate prank. Then he remembered that armed soldiers were stationed throughout the plant, making sure that no one leaves or enters.

When Doheny turned the page he was confronted by a computer schematic illustrating the effects of high-level microwaves on the human body. He glanced with revulsion at the diagram.

Doheny found that the bulk of the file consisted of the required modifications listed in detail and carefully cross-referenced with the original NSI proposal. He had finished leafing through them when he came to a section pertaining to him personally.

PAGE 598

PROJECT CODE: SUNSTROKE
PRESENTATION AS CIVILIAN SOLAR POWER GEN-
ERATING STATION
SUMMARY:
To reduce the risk of an enemy military attack on the Sunstroke demonstration satellite the entire weapons system will be contained within the present framework of the NSI proposal with a civilian project director temporarily in charge. All military affiliations must be kept distant and tenuous. Sixty days after start-up, satellite control will shift to the SDS Division of the U.S. Space Defense Command Headquarters in Colorado Springs.
By executive order, the designated project director will <u>not</u> be briefed on Sunstroke unless circum-

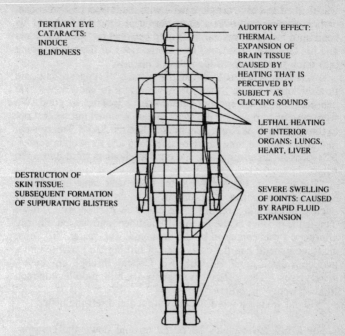

TERTIARY EYE
CATARACTS:
INDUCE
BLINDNESS

AUDITORY EFFECT:
THERMAL
EXPANSION OF
BRAIN TISSUE
CAUSED BY
HEATING THAT IS
PERCEIVED BY
SUBJECT AS
CLICKING SOUNDS

LETHAL HEATING
OF INTERIOR
ORGANS: LUNGS,
HEART, LIVER

DESTRUCTION OF
SKIN TISSUE:
SUBSEQUENT FORMATION
OF SUPPURATING BLISTERS

SEVERE SWELLING
OF JOINTS: CAUSED
BY RAPID FLUID
EXPANSION

stances require it. An on-site civilian observer will be appointed to relate vital developments to the appropriate authorities through a secure trunk-line during the sixty-day conditioning period.

Doheny closed the file and gazed vacantly into space while his mind fought to reject, to somehow escape, the indisputable knowledge that the Solar Satellite Project had been turned into a monstrous weapon. Feelings of disbelief followed by white-hot anger washed over him. It was all there and he could not deny it. An advanced alternative energy source had been perverted and twisted into an obscene killing machine.

Enraged, Doheny suddenly got up and slammed the file onto Nore's desk. He stood there, flexing his hands uncertainly, glaring first at Nore, and then at the partially empty whiskey bottle. He said nothing.

Nore sat slumped in his chair, looking up at Doheny. His face was flushed and his eyes were wide with the impact of a great deal of liquor consumed over a short period of time. He lowered his head until his neck was almost buried between his wide shoulders and his face was broadened by parallel rows of flesh that sprang into thick furrows down the sides of his jaw.

It was Nore who finally broke the silence. "I suppose," he said in a thickened voice, "that you have a right to know why." He paused. "Six years ago our future wasn't looking so good. We were counting on getting the space station contract but we lost out to those bastards at North American. Then the SALT Treaty went into effect and our long-range missile contracts went up in smoke. NSI stock hit an all-time low and our shareholders were starting to panic.

"But then you bright boys in the think tank came up with the Solar Satellite Project. You told me it would beat the piss out of nuclear power and Arab oil." He chuckled mirthlessly. "So we dangled it in front of the Energy Department and waited. Shortly afterward I was contacted by the Pentagon. Top-secret shit. Some air force general had the crazy idea of turning our satellite into a goddamn death ray." He looked at Doheny through unfocused, watery eyes. "They offered us a twenty-six-billion-dollar contract, Mike. Twenty-six *billion*."

Without saying a word, Doheny turned and left the office.

For a full ten minutes he paced up and down the corridor, struggling to comprehend the ugly ramifications of Project Sunstroke. Finally he gave it up and went to the Central Computer Room. He wanted the CCR team's analysis of the satellite telemetry that was transmitted during the malfunction so he could include it in his final report. He planned on typing it up that night and submitting it in the morning along with his resignation.

The CCR was only forty by fifty feet in size, yet it contained more computer intelligence than the entire country had possessed a decade earlier. The cold, windowless main data facility of the plant was packed with ultra–high speed, superconducting Cray 9 computers. The electronic powerhouses required a constant temperature of sixty degrees, stabilized electrical lines, and special color-corrected lights that did not interfere with their sensitive circuitry. Programming crews in white lab coats and sweaters sat crouched in front of humming terminals, their eyes riveted to the glowing screens before them.

Doheny shivered when he went inside. As he walked between

the rows of consoles he saw his own face reflected in the polished aluminum and chromium surfaces. His eyes stared back at him hauntingly, accusingly.

Dr. Theodore Matsuko Kitami, head of the CCR, glanced up from his console. His dark, smooth, bespectacled face wore a pleasant expression of bland dispassion. His self-possession was an oasis of calm in the presence of his tense subordinates. Kitami held a doctorate in computer science from M.I.T. and had personally designed the on-board artificial brain for the solar satellite, the crowning achievement of a distinguished career.

"We've been expecting you, Mike," Kitami said cheerfully. "I have something to show you." He got up and led Doheny to a nearby console. His long, slender fingers played the keyboard like a pianist. A series of tiny green characters flitted across the display screen.

Doheny looked expectantly at Kitami, who smiled benignly, revealing a set of small, perfect white teeth.

Kitami cleared his throat. "These numbers are readings we received from the impedance sensors aboard the satellite. As you know, they register vibrations due to course corrections, friction with the solar wind, variations in the earth's gravitational field, and so on. Now watch the numbers very closely."

On-screen the numbers winked, then leaped significantly in value.

Kitami pointed to the flickering digits. "These readings conclusively show that the impedance sensors registered a massive impact just before the satellite's microwave power beam left the rectenna." He stood back, looking triumphantly at the screen. "A collision," he said softly. "A silent collision in space."

A vein bulged down the center of Doheny's forehead. "Do you mean something hit the satellite?"

"Undoubtedly."

"That would explain a great deal," Doheny murmured. "No wonder we couldn't defocus the beam. The collision must have jarred the phase-control circuitry inside the microwave transmitter. This also explains why the satellite is drifting along a new orbit: it was literally knocked out of its geosynchronous position by the impact."

He turned to Kitami. "Have you determined what caused the microwave transmitter to shut down by itself?"

"Yes indeed." Kitami held up a sheaf of printouts containing satellite temperature data. "The heat sensors within the transmitter's housing registered a temperature surge at the exact moment of impact.'' He touched a finger to the side of his nose. ''The computer ascertained that the heat continued to build until the klystron tubes inside the transmitter simply burned out.''

Doheny slowly nodded. ''The klystrons turn off when the temperature exceeds one hundred degrees Centigrade. Higher temperatures will cause the oscillator circuits within them to fuse.'' He frowned. ''But if we're wrong and the klystrons haven't burned out, could the transmitter turn on again when it cools down?''

Dr. Kitami raised his eyebrows, then lowered his head slightly and peered gravely at Doheny over the rim of his glasses. ''According to the computer it is physically impossible. The microwave transmitter is completely dead.''

''All right, thank you, Ted,'' Doheny said quietly, letting his breath out slowly. He felt a sense of relief. But it was offset by a nagging doubt in the back of his mind.

September 11
The Second Day *

Chapter 9 *

AT AN ALTITUDE of over twenty thousand miles above the earth, the command computer aboard SOLSAT X-1 made a startling discovery as the satellite drifted through the silent vacuum of space. The spacecraft was being slowly pulled by invisible fingers of gravity toward the planet below. The computer quickly determined that the satellite could no longer counterbalance the earth's gravitional field because its own orbital momentum had been considerably reduced by the collision with the intruder. Now SOLSAT X-1 was being drawn closer and closer to the great globe slowly rotating beneath it.

Fierce, unfiltered sunlight was steadily beating down upon its two huge solar-paneled wings, generating a constant flow of electricity. This powerful current surged through the satellite's cylindrical hull directly to the hundreds of klystron tubes embedded within its microwave transmitter. But the rows of klystrons were dark and lifeless, unable to produce the microwave radiation according to the instructions in the subroutine currently in control of the satellite. The man-sized tubes were kept in an overheated state by the raw solar energy streaming through the crack in the microwave transmitter housing. The internal argon gas pressure within each tube had increased to the danger level. In addition, the heat expanded the sensitive oscillator circuit connections at the base of the klystrons, shutting off the current flow.

For the past several hours, as it swept over the night side of the earth, SOLSAT X-1's computer had repeatedly tried to bring the dead klystrons to life. Each of its efforts had been in vain and the tubes had refused to light. If the heuristic logic circuits in the incredibly complex artificial brain had been programmed for emotional responses, SOLSAT X-1 would have felt infinitely deep sorrow and regret at its failure to complete its assigned mission.

But there was hope.

Its infrared sensors detected an immense cone of darkness directly ahead. For the first time in its short existence SOLSAT X-1 was about to lose the sun. Unbearably bright and searing, it had been the satellite's constant companion since launch, two weeks ago. Now the satellite's orbit was diving into the earth's shadow, where the temperature approached absolute zero.

Minutes passed and the cone of darkness drew nearer. Soon the light was fading. The last flaming rays of the sun spread out along the curvature of the earth, then contracted and died in a brief blaze of chromatic glory as the solar disk plunged behind the world. A purple twilight hue—the glow of many sunsets—was falling across the satellite's outstretched solar wings as they entered the earth's gigantic shadow. In another moment the purple glow disappeared and it became very dark; the stars were shining in a sky blacker than a winter midnight.

With all of its solar-powered systems now temporarily shut down during the short night, SOLSAT X-1 was suddenly deprived of all inputs. The satellite was never intended to be eclipsed by the earth for more than a few minutes in any given six-month period. Now it would be in darkness for several hours. The only on-board system functioning was a small battery-driven tape recorder that dutifully stored the ground-based radio commands on magnetic tape for future use.

As SOLSAT X-1 dived deeper and deeper into the earth's frigid shadow, the temperature dropped sharply. The brutally intense cold was penetrating its microwave transmitter housing. The slow minutes dragged by and the quartz crystal klystron tubes inside were beginning to cool down. The internal argon gas pressure within was rapidly decreasing as the tubes gave up their excess heat to the unbelievably cold vacuum. Within ten minutes the pressure had returned to normal. During that time the oscillator circuit connections at the base of the tubes had cooled and contracted in size; the electrical pathways to the klystron tubes that had been previously blocked were now open. The damage from the solar heat had been undone.

SOLSAT X-1's sloping orbit carried it southeast over the continental United States. And yet the great landmass below was not wholly obscured by the night. The blackness was broken here and there by necklaces and garlands of twinkling lights—the gleam of sleeping cities showing through gaps in the clouds. The satellite silently swept over San Antonio, Houston, and New Orleans. Then the smooth, coal black waters of the Gulf of Mexico appeared, alive with the green and red lanterns of slowly moving ships.

At last, far ahead, there was a sudden burst of light along the earth's curvature. This flare signaled the end of the short night. The satellite's orbit was now swinging out of the vast shadow. Dawn flashed like an explosion along the planet's rim when SOLSAT X-1 emerged from the cone of darkness and headed out into the sun. Its solar-paneled wings glowed a brief crimson, then gold, then blazed with the pure white light of day.

A tremendous surge of power coursed through the satellite's hull as its solar panels instantly converted the sunlight into electricity. A microsecond later SOLSAT X-1's on-board systems snapped on. Its infrared sensors became operative again and started imaging the fast-approaching Florida coast, brilliantly outlined by an endless string of cities shimmering in the early-morning light.

SOLSAT X-1 registered the current surging into the klystron converter assembly within its microwave transmitter housing. One by one the klystron tubes became suffused with a pale orange luminescence. Then tenuous shapes moved across their surfaces and in their depths. The shapes coalesced into shifting bars of light and shadow, then formed spokes that began to rotate. The wheels of light spun faster and faster. . . .

The subroutine controlling the satellite contained the instructions for supplying the ground below with the microwave transmission beam. Once again SOLSAT X-1 would fulfill these commands: in the next few minutes the satellite would discharge another invisible burst of high-intensity microwave radiation.

Far below, the warm waters of the Gulf of Mexico gently lapped the shore along Westport Beach, Florida. The broad expanse of sand was a glittering gold in the first rays of the rising sun. The sky was cloudless and a light onshore breeze stirred the moist tropical air. It was the beginning of another beautiful day.

There was a lone figure jogging along the beach near the water's edge. Fifteen-year-old Chris Hollister trotted across the hard, damp sand, his long, sun-bleached blond hair flying in the wind. He was tall and muscular for his age, and he moved with the careless grace of youth. A book bag was slung over his right shoulder and an old blanket was bunched up in the crook of his left arm. The bag held his school books and a Radio Shack boom box he had gotten for his birthday. Occasionally he splashed through the lacy fringe of the gentle surf, his sneakers sinking in the softer sand and splattering his stone-washed jeans with seawater.

A casual observer would have thought that Chris was out running to get in shape for track or basketball. In reality the teenager was on his way to a secret, early-morning rendezvous with his girl.

He had met her two weeks ago, on the first day of class after summer vacation, during the break following second period. Her name was Jeanne and she was a real looker. They had sort of run into each other in the hall, and at the time Chris had known for sure that she was going to be the main woman in his life. A mutual infatuation for each other quickly developed. They met between classes, spent lunchtime together, and walked home hand in hand every day after school. Chris began to really care for her.

On Friday and Saturday nights they sat at a dark corner table at Tommy's, the downtown teen nightclub, and kissed and necked amid the swirling lights and pounding rock music. Soon they started making plans. First, Jeanne was going to have their baby, then Chris would find a good job so they could get married and leave home.

Three nights ago the teen lovers decided they had to find a place where they could be alone. No parental supervision, no eavesdroppers. Just themselves. They gave the problem much thought over cherry Cokes and Marlboro cigarettes. It was Chris who came up with the solution. He knew the perfect place. The Billingses' shorefront estate on Fairmount Road.

Old Mr. Billings had recently died of a heart attack and his grieving widow was staying with relatives in the time of her sorrow. She had put the estate in the hands of a local realtor, but it was overpriced and there had been no takers. Chris had gone to the deserted house numerous times during the summer to smoke weed. While exploring the huge yard one night, he had discovered a gazebo that Mrs. Billings had erected in her ornamental garden.

For the past couple of days he and his girl had been meeting clandestinely at the little summer house in the morning before school and at night after dinner. They smoked weed, listened to music, and made out. Both of them thought it was really trippy.

Presently, as Chris raced down the beach toward the Billingses' house, he saw passing gulls dive into the placid sea for their breakfast. The fluid beauty of their movements did not affect him; he perceived the birds only as moving targets for the pellet gun in his bedroom closet. He fondly recalled the rush he had gotten when he shot one in midair.

Now and then he looked down at the little shells and tangles of seaweed littering the crisp, cool sand. Dozens of bugs—small black beetles—skittered out of his path before he could stomp them, and when the wave wash receded, he saw the tiny bubbles pop over the holes made by sandworms. The whole shoreline was alive.

Inland, to the east, he spotted the glistening white steeple of the First Fundamental Church of Christ, jutting above the rooftops. He felt a twinge of guilt when he glanced at the majestic spire. It belonged to his folks' church. In the past he had attended the Sunday services with his parents and listened wide-eyed to Reverend Parmenter's rambling, sulfurous sermons. However, as he grew older, Chris felt hemmed in by the strict moral laws and guidelines. So he had drifted away from the flock and started enjoying a happier, freer life-style. But the years of religious indoctrination had planted a seed deep within him that had sprouted into a meandering vine. Lately it had been giving his insides a little squeeze.

He continued trotting until he came to the red brick walkway leading up to the Billingses' estate. He stopped suddenly. Something out at sea had caught his eye. He swept his gaze seaward and saw wisps of white cloud billowing upward from an area of frothy, churning water about two miles offshore. He stared in awe as the wisps became a swirling shroud of fog, thick and seamless, hovering over the patch of rolling sea. He frowned. It was coming closer with each passing second. Must be a squall, he thought, puzzled. But it didn't look like one. Too small and low. And the sea had been so calm and clear just a minute ago. Well, it had to be *some* kind of storm. He shrugged. What the hell, a little rain can't hurt. He turned and ran up the walk.

The shorefront entrance was guarded by two big gates of wrought iron, but they were never locked. Chris slipped through, leaving the gate ajar for Jeanne. He crept past a small grove of fruit-laden Valencia orange trees as he made his way onto the grounds. He headed straight for the spidery wood-latticed gazebo standing on a well-tended lawn near a tropical planting of philodendrons, birds of paradise, King palms, and pink frangipani. The gazebo was octagonal, topped with a black steel weather vane. Inside the air smelled of mildew and spent passions. There were two chairs and a love seat of iron cast in a Victorian grapevine pattern, painted white. They might have been decorative but without cushions they were hell to sit on.

Chris Hollister squatted on the hard-packed sand floor and spread out the old blanket he had brought. Then he took out the radio from his book bag and tuned in a popular Miami rock station. They were playing "Wet and Wild" by the Medusans, his favorite group. He had bought their latest video last month but his mother had thrown it out because all the guys in the band wore makeup and high heels and looked like cute chicks. She didn't understand heavy metal glam.

He faced the seashore, peering through the gaps in the latticed wall to see if Jeanne was coming. No sign of her yet. But he could see the dense, throbbing mass of fog creeping closer. The sight made him feel uneasy, but he wasn't going to let it spoil his fun. He shot a glance at the Billingses' house to see if Jeanne had entered through the front gate. Nothing. The house of course was empty. Like most of the others in Westport Beach it was made of stuccoed cinder block built on a concrete slab, anchored to pilings driven deep into the sand. The roof had red Spanish tile set in a fish-scale pattern.

Satisfied that he was alone for the moment, Chris began to dance to the music. He was too self-conscious to dance in front of others, even Jeanne. His body moved in time to the beat, heels kicking, arms flailing, torso gyrating wildly.

"Hey, don't you look cute," said a youthful feminine voice.

Red-faced with embarrassment, Chris planted both feet firmly on the floor and looked up at the giggling girl in the doorway. "Hi," he said meekly.

Jeanne Pierson took him by the hand and kissed him first on the lips, then on the tip of his nose. She was slender, had dark eyes, fair skin, and long brown hair streaming down to the middle of her delicate back. Her untethered breasts jutted slightly beneath the thinnest of cotton jerseys. She was fourteen and a half. Rubbing up against him, she said in a serious tone, "You dance pretty good. I want you to do it at Tommy's like that, okay?"

"No way," protested Chris. "Everyone will laugh." Anxious to change the subject, he pulled out a joint from his hip pocket. It was tightly wrapped in a dollar bill to protect against breakage. He held it up, grinning. "How 'bout some killer breakfast?"

They lighted up, sat down on the blanket and passed the joint back and forth, smiling vacuously, talking about one subject after another. School, mutual friends, parties and stuff. Jeanne mentioned the weird cloud she had seen off the coast on her way over. Chris said it was just a little freak storm that had come up; he was certain it would pass quickly. Soon they were down to a tiny roach that couldn't be held without burning their fingertips.

Then Chris lay sprawled on his back, his arms stretched out. He giggled and drummed his heels on the packed sand in rhythm to the music. The whole world softened, hard edges blurring. The morning seemed blander, almost fluffy. He felt himself beginning to dissolve.

Suddenly the music from the radio was drowned out by shrieking static. Chris jumped up and twisted the dial frantically but the earsplitting screeching sound continued unabated. He angrily switched the radio off and muttered, "Fuck."

"What happened to it?" asked Jeanne.

"Hell if I know," said Chris, disgusted. He sat cross-legged on the blanket and sulked.

Jeanne didn't care about the radio; her mind was on something else. One moment she was sitting there quietly, knees drawn up, head bowed, and then suddenly she uncoiled and pounced. She dived on him, throwing her body against his, knocking out his breath, her frantic mouth seeking his. Her hot, wet tongue was darting wildly, forcing his lips.

Then she began rubbing, clutching, stroking him through the soft cloth of his jeans, her hungry eyes watching his face. Chris felt his body responding.

"It's mine," she said. "It's all mine, isn't it, Chris?"

"Yeah," he said throatily. "All yours."

They fumbled with each other's clothing, wrenching them off and flinging them aside. Her cool fingers guided him. He was crude, ferocious, hard. Exactly what she wanted.

Her knees rose, bare ankles and feet locked behind his back.

By that time Chris was bucking and plunging like a demented mustang. He slipped out, he slipped back in. He chewed on her pink nipples. She tugged his hair, bit his lips, sucked his neck, raked his bare torso with her fingernails. His hands were pulling on her ass, and her hands were pulling on his, and nothing short of the apocalypse could have made them stop. They thrashed together again and again with the urgent ardor of extreme youth.

He pumped, going, "Hah! Hah!" as if he had slain some mighty beast. His body went rigid and shook violently. She felt his warm gush and moaned with pleasure. Not wanting it to end, she wouldn't let him roll away, but clutched him so tightly that his ribs ached. He could feel her throb, deep, a pulse that gradually diminished. She was so hot. And wet.

Finally she let him withdraw and roll free. He lay on his back, panting, trying to breathe. The sky was whirling through the latticed gazebo roof. A flock of sea gulls flying overhead seemed to be caught in the vortex. He wondered where he was, had to think a moment to recall his name, the place, the date—he was that disoriented. After a minute or two he glanced at Jeanne. She lay on her side, dozing. She always went to sleep right after her climax.

This was the period of time he dreaded the most, when the guilt set in. He knew that he had willfully sinned against the Lord. And he had done it repeatedly. He recalled one of Reverend Parmenter's sermons. The minister had said sex outside marriage was an abomination in the eyes of God. This type of sin made your soul so rotten and ugly even the Lord couldn't bear the sight of it; He would cast it straight down into the eternal fires of hell.

Chris was quietly pondering the corruption of his soul when a hissing sound rose immediately, drowning out his thoughts. It was something like the sound of air escaping from a million inner tubes. The hissing swelled and grew. Soon it became a muted roar like the noise from a nearby waterfall.

He sat up and peered through the latticed wall at the beach. A moment elapsed before his brain understood what his eyes saw.

The water along the shore was boiling, sending plumes of white steam into the air. Huge bubbles were forming and breaking on the surface of the sea. The roaring sound went on and on. Then white fog drifted across the stretch of sand, and the bright autumn sun cast crazy arcs of rainbow in the cottony moisture.

Chris stared at the horrifying sight with a kind of euphoric fascination. His eyes were wide and his lips parted as he watched the clouds of steam billowing majestically into the sky above the angry bubbling roar. The smell of a thousand laundries reached his nostrils.

So it's not a storm, after all, he thought suddenly. No, the sea is . . . boiling. . . . But it can't be!

He saw fingers of white mist snaking toward the Billingses' estate. They swirled around the little orange grove and crept across the lawn, enveloping the tropical plants near the gazebo.

It's the weed, Chris thought desperately, it's gotta be the fucking weed. I'm really freaking out. He couldn't remember ever having had such vivid hallucinations from just a few tokes of marijuana. He screwed his eyes shut, hoping the nightmarish images would go away.

Within moments the roar from the sea began to fade and he opened his eyes. The fog had lifted and the plumes of steam above the water had dissipated. He sighed with relief. The bad trip was over. He glanced at Jeanne; she was still sleeping peacefully.

He was about to bend down and kiss her, when he suddenly heard strange popping noises coming from outside. Startled, he looked around the yard for the source. Something weird was happening to the orange trees near the gate. All of their leaves were turning brown, shriveling, and dropping off. Then he saw what was making the noise. The ripe oranges hanging on the trees were swelling and bursting open, shooting fragments of peel and flesh in all directions like shrapnel from exploding grenades. The pungent, sweet smell of freshly cooked orange marmalade permeated the air. After a few seconds there wasn't a single orange left intact.

One by one the tree trunks bulged for an instant, then split apart with a loud wrenching, cracking sound. Streams of hot glistening sap shot out. Then each tree collapsed into a heap of skeletal branches and broken wood. In another moment the whole grove looked as if it had been destroyed by a bulldozer.

"Hey," cried Jeanne, now fully awake. "What's making all that noise?" She made a mad scramble for her clothes.

Chris mumbled something incoherent in a low, piteous voice. His attention was riveted to the columns of steam rising from the expanse of green lawn. The grass was turning to slime.

He knew for certain he was hallucinating again. But this time he felt his scalp tingle and the hair standing erect all over his naked body. Tics pulled at the corner of each eye. He began to feel hot. Rivulets of sweat were running down his face, tickling his nose. He was now scared to death.

The long, wide philodendron leaves and palm fronds right outside the gazebo rapidly curled and shriveled. The sight looked like a time-lapse film of the growing process—leaves unfolding and expanding—only in reverse. The birds of paradise turned into a sticky, fibrous mess.

"Chris, let's get out of here!" shrieked Jeanne. "It's so hot." She pulled on her pants, but the heat was too intense for clothing and she started kicking them off in a panic. The furious effort threw her off balance and she tumbled, falling backward on the hard-packed sand.

"Help me, Chris," she begged.

Chris reached over to her. He felt dizzy, lightheaded. He seemed to be moving in slow motion.

Suddenly they heard a loud *whack* on the roof above them. Both teens looked up, their eyes wide. Jeanne screamed and Chris started gagging.

A sea gull's smooth, rounded head was poking through a gap in the latticed roof. Its glazed eyes had been popped out of their sockets and were dangling from white threads of tissue. The beak was twitching, opening and closing.

Chris looked away from the hideous sight and tried helping Jeanne up, but he was too weak from the heat. He fell on top of her. She stiffened beneath him and shrieked in pain. He thought he had never heard such an awful sound in his whole life; it was as if all the plants and trees and creatures of the sea had screamed. Summoning all of his strength, he managed to roll off her, but the screaming seemed to go on and on. Finally it ended in a series of agonized gasps.

He lay beside her, breathing harshly, unable to get up. A cry of pain strangled in his throat. He felt an incredibly intense burning sensation spread over his body, seizing his soft genitals and then his arms and legs. Flames seemed to be licking him everywhere, but there was no fire. His skin was blistering, his eyeballs and lips swelling. Mucus streamed down his nose. Every time he inhaled, something inside him hurt viciously. He heard a strange clicking sound reverberating in his head.

It came to him with a sudden numbing reality that he was going to die. For an instant he experienced a mindless, animallike panic. He thrashed about, clawing at his hair, pulling it out in handfuls. Then he lay still.

He saw brilliant spirals of light expanding before him, widening outward to infinity. A moment later he was completely blind. His skin swelled until it became one enormous blister. His body curled, limbs jerking and contracting.

Then Reverend Parmenter appeared out of nowhere, huge and forbidding, his angry face glowing in the darkness. Chris heard the booming voice of the minister damning him to the fires of hell for all eternity.

Chapter 10 *

MINUTES BEFORE THE deaths occurred Mike Doheny had been in his office typing his final report. Without warning, the klaxon horns throughout the plant had begun screaming. Then he heard Jenkins shouting over the intercom, telling him to report to the control room, that they had another emergency. The satellite's microwave transmitter had mysteriously turned on by itself. Doheny had jumped up and raced to the control room, where he had found a tight cluster of engineers and technicians huddled near the IR screen, their faces drawn, the consoles around them alive with flashing red lights.

Presently Doheny turned to Phillips, the young technician manning the microwave systems console. "Status report," he snapped.

Phillips's hands swept over the panel, pushing buttons, twisting knobs. His face was lit from beneath by flickering dials.

Doheny glanced at his watch. It was 5:30 A.M. He had been up a full twenty-four hours. He ignored the dull throbbing at his temples, the quivering ache in the muscles of his neck and back. He tried to blink away the milky membrane that seemed to cover his eyes.

Phillips looked up from his panel, his eyes red. "I don't know how"—he spread his hands—"but the satellite is transmitting at full power again."

Doheny stared in angry disbelief at the infrared screen. The satellite was now transmitting a thermal image of the Florida peninsula. Hovering above the Gulf coastline was a glowing bright spot—the focal point of the microwave beam.

The nightmare was starting all over again.

Two floors above the control room Diane Bradford sat motionless on the edge of her narrow cot in the VIP lounge, listening with growing apprehension to the eerie wailing of the klaxon horns. They had been blaring steadily for the past few minutes. The first time she had heard the piercing alarms was the night before, when the satellite had malfunctioned and endangered the plant. She wondered what was happening now. Dressed only in a white satin chemise and panty hose, she pushed her blond hair from her forehead, rubbed the sleep from her eyes, and looked around the room.

The interior of the theater-sized guest lounge resembled a wartime refugee camp. It was filled with army cots to accommodate the television reporters and their assistants and Deputy Energy Secretary Howard Averson—a total of two dozen people. The women lay separate from the men according to U.S. Army regulations. All had been rudely awakened and frightened by the alarms. Some were loudly voicing their concern and pulling on their clothes while the rest lay under heavy tan blankets, reluctant to leave the warmth and security of their makeshift beds. Several people got up and went to the chemical toilet cubicles propped up against the back wall.

Across the room, near the entrance, stood four grim-faced MPs armed with machine pistols. Their hard, intent eyes were continually flicking back and forth as they scanned the prisoners. One of them calmly spoke into his radio transceiver, seemingly oblivious to the screaming klaxons.

Diane reached under her cot, took out a notebook from her purse, and wrote down the approximate time the alarms had begun sounding off this morning. Afterward she put the notebook back and began to dress. As she buttoned her blouse she lapsed into a review of the previous night's events. . . .

When Everett Nore and Provost Marshal Clayton had left the lounge, she and the other reporters had stood by and watched as their TV cameras, lights, and microphones were loaded aboard a dolly and wheeled away. Then the MPs set up cots, mess tables, and toilet facilities. By 10:30 P.M. everything was ready and a late dinner was served. The food consisted of bland but nourishing army rations—canned beef, rehydrated potatoes with gravy, mixed vegetables, white sugary bread, and coffee. During the meal, Diane joined in subdued conversation with her colleagues. They spoke in hushed tones about the injured Video News correspondent who was still in the infirmary. A half hour later the lights were dimmed and everyone was ordered to bed down for the night.

Diane lay on her cot, unable to sleep, her mind racing. The fear she had experienced when the MPs had broken the Video News reporter's arm had returned. A faint hint of panic came over her. The determination she had felt earlier had vanished and was replaced by a gnawing frustration that made it increasingly difficult to concentrate. She found it hard to pursue a line of thought through to its finish. Instead her mind jumped from one subject to another. What would she do if she ever got out of this room? Should she try to leave the plant? They had probably impounded her car. Would it be possible for her to make it to a pay phone on foot and report to her boss at Cable News Service? But she really didn't have the whole story yet. Should she try to find Mike Doheny, the one man who could possibly give it to her? She still didn't know where he was.

She spent an hour or so in this frenzied state of mind. Finally her random thoughts became more ordered, started to follow a cohesive pattern, and then crystallized into a coherent design. She now had a plan. As a consequence she was filled with a warm feeling of resolve and a sense of purpose. However, she realized that to be able to implement her scheme she was going to have to accomplish a great deal the next day. It would be necessary to memorize the schedule of all activities within the lounge, such as the precise time when meals were served, when the guards changed shifts, and so on. She would have to eavesdrop on conversations between the MPs whenever possible to try to ascertain the approximate positions of the soldiers stationed throughout the plant. Earlier that night she had overheard them discussing the showers set up outside the rest rooms on the ground floor. Did that mean she and the other captives would be escorted there once a day for personal hygiene? She would probably find out in the morning.

Lastly she would have to determine the exact location of Mike Doheny. He must be somewhere inside the plant. Most likely in the control room, trying to find out what went wrong with the satellite. Undoubtedly he would also be spending a lot of time in his office on the first sublevel, writing an endless series of reports.

Satisfied that she at last had a workable plan, she dropped off to sleep. She slept lightly, fitfully, plagued by disturbing dreams. She woke repeatedly during the night, feeling confused, disoriented. But each time she managed to doze off. . . .

Diane awoke startled and unnaturally alert that morning when the klaxons went off. Her defenses were working and her mind quickly recoiled from the unpleasant dream images of the night. But she found it unbelievably difficult to emerge from the warmth and slight comfort of the army cot. She wanted to wrap the heavy blanket around her like a cocoon to shut out the reality pressing in on her. Instead she forced herself to get up and investigate what was going on.

Diane had just finished dressing when she suddenly heard angry shouts coming from across the room. The CBS correspondent, a slender dark-haired man in his late thirties wearing a rumpled white shirt, was arguing with an MP at the entrance, the one with the radio transceiver.

"Why the hell can't you tell me what's going on?" yelled CBS, his face flushed, arms akimbo. The dark circles under his eyes indicated he had slept poorly. He was unshaven, his hair disheveled. "How come they turned on the alarms? Is there a fire or what? We have a right to know."

The MP looked at him from under thick, heavy brows. It was not a friendly look. "Sir, you'll have to return to your place," he said coolly.

CBS refused to budge. "I want to talk to Marshal Clayton," he demanded, his voice cracking.

"That's not possible."

"Fuck you," snarled CBS. His eyes swept over the soldier in a direct challenge.

Diane hurriedly pulled on her shoes and stood up, her heart beating rapidly. The last thing they needed, she thought, was another confrontation with those goons. If her plan was to succeed she would somehow have to keep the friction between the soldiers and the reporters down to a minimum. She had confidence in herself. She approached the lounge entrance warily, trying to ignore the flutter of anxiety in her stomach.

The others in the room remained seated in their cots, unable to move, as if the tenseness had sapped the strength in their limbs.

Diane stepped quickly between CBS and the MP with the transceiver. "Please," she said frantically, "we don't want any trouble. We're scared and upset by the alarms." She felt a chill as the silent MP regarded her with stony eyes. He was tall, lean, hard. There were calluses on his hands. She noticed the retaining strap on his machine pistol was unfastened.

Diane swallowed. "We're concerned for our safety," she pleaded. "Last night, before you arrived, there was some kind of accident here at the plant and those alarms were activated. Could you possibly tell us if we're in some kind of danger?''

The MP continued to stare at her. After a moment he said, "I'm sorry, ma'am, but we don't know any more about it than you." There was a midwestern twang to his voice. The hard look in his eyes softened slightly. "That's all I can tell you."

"Thank you," Diane murmured. "Thank you very much."

The CBS correspondent looked disgusted. He opened his mouth to protest, then shut it and walked away.

Diane returned to her cot, sat down heavily, and let out a long, deep sigh. That was close, she thought. But her strategy had worked; she had kept the peace. At least for the time being.

She lay back on her cot, trying to think despite the commotion around her and the ominous sound of the alarms. She recalled what Everett Nore had said about the satellite during the previous night's press conference in the lounge, just before the MPs showed up. He had said something about it being adrift. Diane wondered just how far it had drifted by now.

At that moment, high above the earth where the sun shone with indescribable fury in a perpetually black sky, SOLSAT X-1 swept along its new orbit, beaming its lethal flood of radiation to the planet below. Through multifaceted infrared sensors it monitored the beam's progress along the Gulf coast of Florida.

The infrared scan detected frenzied thermal heat patterns swirling upward in all directions as the microwaves brought the surf to a boil. To the satellite's command computer this infrared signature was positive proof that it was fulfilling the subroutine's instructions to provide the world below with an unbroken microwave link.

But once again solar radiation was streaming into the jagged fracture in the microwave transmitter housing that had been caused by the collision with the intruder. The temperature inside was becoming unbearably hot. In a reflex as automatic as it was useless, the computer immediately sent an electrified command to the turbopumps connected to the coolant storage tanks deep inside the satellite's hull. The effort was fruitless: the tank values were still stuck as a result of the collision.

As the minutes elapsed, one by one the klystron tubes started to overheat and shut down. SOLSAT X-1's computer began monitoring the steady drop in the microwave power output.

*   *   *

Provost Marshal Earl Clayton walked into the control room. He looked fully rested and clean-shaven. His uniform was fresh and crisp, his close-cropped hair neatly combed. A sidearm and a radio transceiver were strapped to his waist. He walked slowly toward Doheny with the easy economical movement and balance of a predator.

"Why did you people sound the alarm?" Clayton asked forcefully, his face impassive. "The noise woke up everyone in the lounge. The reporters are all agitated." His eyes were drawn to the ghostly image on the infrared screen.

Doheny ignored him, riveting his attention to the bright splotch on the screen. There was no doubt the area surrounding the beam's focal point was inhabited. Prime seaside real estate. He knew there wasn't enough time to warn the residents. It was all happening too fast. There was nothing he could do to stop it. He was in a terrible agony. With his rigid stance, his ravaged face, and his burning eyes, he looked like a statue of anxiety.

Suddenly the bright splotch shimmered, faded to a blur, then disappeared. The console in front of him began emitting an odd humming sound. Red lights flickered across the indicator panel. Before he could react the console went silent and the indicators winked out.

He glanced at his watch. The satellite had transmitted its deadly beam for twenty-nine minutes. Exactly like last night, he thought. It had killed five people then, he recalled grimly. He wondered how many had died this time.

He desperately wanted to know what had caused the satellite to become operative again and why it had turned off. His mind raced for the answers but none were forthcoming. His capacity for deduction had been sapped by fatigue. He needed some rest.

Jenkins, the guidance engineer, tapped the console with his fingertips. He was edgy, upset. When he spoke there was a mean crackle in his voice; it was not due to lack of sleep, but to painful frustration and fear. "Do you think that thing will turn on again?"

"After what just happened," Doheny said slowly, "I'd say it's a definite possibility, one we've got to be prepared for." He kneaded the bridge of his nose and tried to think. "Our first priority is to find out why the satellite became functional again. There must be some type of mechanism or set of conditions affecting it that we don't know about. Something even Ted Kitami's computers couldn't predict. The collision up there obviously altered the micro-transmitter in some way."

"What collision?" Jenkins asked sharply.

"Ted analyzed the telemetry we received during last night's malfunction," Doheny explained. "The data indicates the satellite had collided with an object moments before we lost control."

Jenkins blew out a spastic sigh and stroked his beard. His massive forehead was puckered with consternation. The others gazed at Doheny in speechless amazement.

"At this point it's only a theory," Doheny said, "an extrapolation of available data. But it does fit the facts."

"Sir," shouted Phillips, "we're losing the IR image. The satellite must be moving out of range." He consulted some readouts, then said, "We're past all lateral correction limits."

Doheny glanced at the infrared screen and saw patches of electronic snow partially obscuring the image. He realized the signal strength was decreasing as the satellite drifted farther away. He knew it was absolutely essential to maintain a constant vigilance over all systems aboard the rogue spacecraft. As he watched the image dissolve he tried to determine a solution to the telemetry blackout problem.

His years of experience in the aerospace industry provided the answer. He would have to contact NASA and have them begin tracking the satellite with their Deep Space Network. The DSN consisted of three radio tracking stations distributed evenly in longitude around the world. These installations were normally used to receive telemetry from interplanetary space probes. He would request a direct feed to the plant via military and civilian communications satellites. In addition, he would alert the Pentagon to initiate a continuous infrared and radar surveillance of the Sunstroke satellite.

Doheny thought about the hot line in Nore's office. He believed it could be used to effectively bypass the endless maze of bureaucracy. He made his way to the control room exit doors where he was confronted by the provost marshal.

"Just a minute, Mr. Doheny," said Clayton. His neck was thrust pugnaciously forward, his compact shoulders hunched. A prizefighter's stance. He fixed Doheny with a threatening stare. "As military commander of this installation I demand to know what's going on with this satellite of yours."

Doheny drew himself to his full height and returned Clayton's glare. He was considerably taller than the provost marshal. "I'm sorry," he said coldly, "but we have a crisis situation here and I can't spare the time."

Clayton's eyes became hooded, his expression masked.

Doheny turned on his heels and left the room, the doors whisking shut behind him. Out in the corridor he realized Clayton had not been briefed on Project Sunstroke. The provost marshal and his men had been brought in for the sole reason of holding everyone at the plant incommunicado.

Doheny felt tired and yet vaguely restless. He stopped at a refrigerated water fountain and splashed the icy liquid on his face and on the back of his neck. The sensation was unpleasant but invigorating. It sent a shock wave through the dulling mixture of exhaustion and nervous tension that was blunting his mental acuity. He could think more clearly now.

It occurred to him that outside experts should be consulted regarding the satellite. His mind became filled with names and organizations. First on his mental roster was a brilliant but outspoken engineering professor from Caltech, a man who had just recently publicly criticized the Solar Satellite Project. Then there was the lead scientist for the Bioelectromagnetic Research Laboratory, a renowned physicist currently investigating the environmental effects of high-energy microwaves. The others included a space-propulsion specialist from NASA, and the air force general who had masterminded Sunstroke. Doheny believed these individuals should be contacted without delay.

Seconds later he entered Everett Nore's private office. There had been no response to his rapping on the door. Inside he found the head of Nore Space Industries slumped over his desk. The nearby bottle of Scotch was empty. Nore had obviously been here throughout the emergency. Doheny felt Nore's pulse; it was rapid but steady, his breathing shallow and raspy. Doheny was stunned that Nore had been so devastated by alcohol. He knew Nore drank heavily at times, but in the past he had controlled it, grown expansive with it. Apparently the crisis had become too pressing, and Nore had tried to escape. Doheny was dismayed, ashamed. With great care he gently shook the sleeping man.

Nore awoke with a start. His flesh was loose, papery, and his eyes were sunken and dark circled, his hair disheveled. He rubbed his head. How come, Doheny thought, people find a hangover so comical, like a black eye or somebody slipping on a banana peel and cracking his pelvis?

Doheny said in a soft but firm voice, "The satellite discharged again. The thing irradiated a portion of south Florida before it shut down. It was a repeat performance of last night."

Nore's bloodshot eyes seemed to recede farther into their sockets. He pointed to the squat red scrambler phone on his desk. His voice was a hoarse whisper. "You've got to make the report, Mike. I can't do it. Too goddamn sick."

Both men's eyes met, and for an instant Doheny experienced a fleeting tremor of uncertainty. Nore was staring at him with a strange, pleading expression. A request, he thought. The pained look on Nore's face indicated this was undoubtedly one of the rare instances in his life that he had ever asked anyone for a favor.

"Make the call," wheezed Nore. "Just pick up the phone and you're patched through. Code Sunstroke. Tell them everything that happened." Keeping his head level, he slowly got to his feet, staggered to the lavatory, and closed the door.

Doheny sat for a time at the littered desk, staring at the red phone. He was a little sickened by the thought of cooperating with the people who had turned the solar satellite into a space-based weapons system, a monstrosity. But he had to make the call now if they were to find some way of stopping the satellite before it became operative again.

He picked up the receiver and waited.

Chapter 11 *

IN THE LIVING quarters on the top floor of the White House the President of the United States was awakened by the unrelenting buzz of the special telephone beside his bed. Even in his bleary, semiconscious state James William Kendall recognized the unique sound of the instrument connecting his suite with the teletype room downstairs. He had heard it only twice during his presidency. The first time had been a test of the phone system; the second occurred when an emergency session of Congress had reached an eleventh-hour agreement with the railroad unions to call off a strike that had been crippling the nation's economy.

Kendall opened his eyes, cleared his throat, and reached for the handset. The phone felt cold to the touch. "Yes."

A youthful voice said, "Mr. President, this is Lieutenant Fallon, Comm Room duty officer. Sir, we just received another coded EMCON message from the NMCC at the Pentagon."

The President sat up. The words had torn through the soft gray veil of grogginess enveloping his brain. "Send a courier up to my study immediately," he snapped.

Kendall hung up the phone and glanced at his wife, Caroline, lying next to him in the spacious bed. When the phone had sounded she had stirred and nuzzled down beside him, pressing her soft warm body against his. She was a tall, beautiful woman with finely etched cheekbones, long black hair, and electric eyes.

"Why don't you call them back and tell them to leave you alone?" she murmured sleepily. "You were up half the night."

"I'm all right," replied Kendall, brushing his lips against her silky hair.

"Is it getting better or worse?" she asked with sudden worry in her voice.

"Too early to tell," said Kendall with a forced smile, trying not to reveal the inner dread he felt. "They're sending a messenger boy up here with the latest news. I'd better get ready."

Last night, when Caroline had returned from presiding over a dedication ceremony at the new Grosvenor Hall of Modern Art, she had found her husband deep in conference with his closest advisers. Later, in bed, he had confided to her about the Sunstroke crisis and the catastrophic damage it could do to his career.

As she watched her husband climb out of bed and put on the colorful brocaded robe she had given him for his birthday last month, her thoughts drifted to the day she had met young James Kendall, the newly elected senator from Maine. At the time she was a striking twenty-two-year-old New York fashion model making the Washington circuit. Her boyfriend, a state representative who had attended Harvard Law School with Kendall, had taken her to one of those interminable dinner parties at the nation's capital.

Slightly drunk on champagne, Caroline's boyfriend said: "You see that guy over there? Someday he's going to be president."

"Sounds interesting," said Caroline. "Why do you think so?"

"Because he wants to."

At Caroline's insistence, her escort introduced her to Kendall and they became friends instantly. Then lovers. She traveled with him, slept with him, cooked for him, and loved him. Several months later they were married. She had no regrets at giving up a successful modeling career. During the sixteen years of their marriage she had never wanted another man. She found his jaunty, optimistic outlook on life and his effortless charisma quite irresistible.

President Kendall quietly bent down and kissed his wife on her full lips, jarring her thoughts back to the present. Then, dressed in his pajamas and robe, he left the bedroom.

He walked into the big oval study where he met the Army Signal Corps sergeant, a thin swarthy man in his early twenties who stood stiffly at attention. After taking the sealed EMCON printout from the courier, Kendall dismissed him and promptly tore open the message and read it.

For the first time in many years he was shocked.

He stared at the flimsy printout. A fist squeezed shut behind his navel. Then tension and anger sent a wave of nausea through his stomach. He was angry because no one had told him the satellite could become operational again. No one had predicted that it would attack south Florida this morning. Christ, he thought, more casualties. The damn thing struck a portion of the Gulf Coast. Now, how the hell are we going to explain this to the public?

Kendall read the message again quickly. It was in three parts. The first section was a brief report of this morning's attack on south Florida. The second part summarized Dr. Kitami's collision theory. This was followed by several urgent recommendations by Doheny that impressed Kendall. First, NASA should immediately begin tracking the Sunstroke satellite with their Deep Space Network and transmit all telemetry to the solar power plant for analysis. Second, Doheny requested continuous infrared and radar surveillance of the satellite to enable them to accurately predict the exact path of the microwave beam in the event of another discharge. This "doomwatch" would act as a distant early-warning system for the evacuation of inhabitants in the target zone.

For security reasons Kendall was unsure of Doheny's last recommendation in which he strongly urged the Sunstroke officials to assemble a team of specialists to determine how to safely disable the rogue spacecraft. Doheny included a list of four names and their respective organizations:

ROSEN, AARON D, CALIFORNIA INSTITUTE OF TECHNOLOGY
GAITHER, FREDERICK J, BIOELECTROMAGNETIC RESEARCH LABORATORY
COURTLAND, MALCOLM I, NASA
STRATTON, DEAN M, USAF, SPACE DEFENSE COMMAND

Kendall frowned at the first name. He knew Dr. Rosen was an outspoken critic of the Solar Satellite Project. A few months ago *Scientific American* had published an incisive article written by Rosen that stated the inherent dangers of the project should it be implemented. The President was unfamiliar with the other names except, of course, for General Stratton.

Damn it, he thought, last night they had this thing under control. He had authorized the detention of everyone at that plant and the removal of those farmhouse casualties. With a little coercion and some luck, the first satellite attack would have been completely contained. And now this. He stared angrily at the EMCON printout, balled it in his fist, then shoved it into the pocket of his robe.

He started pacing the room in an effort to regain his composure. It was a trick he had learned years ago while in the Senate. After a few minutes he glanced at the ship's clock on the mantelpiece below the Matthew Jouett portrait of Thomas Jefferson. It was 8:20 A.M. Washington time. He picked up the phone on his desk and called Jack Conley, his assistant for national security affairs, and told him to come up to the study right away.

A moment later there was a knock on the door and Kendall opened it wide to admit a waiter wheeling a service cart with coffee, croissants, and the morning paper. It was brought in every day at this time. Behind the waiter stood the tall, angular figure of Jack Conley, his eyes red from a sleepless night.

"You'd better sit down, Jack," said Kendall after the waiter had left. "I'm afraid that we're going to have to earn our salaries this week," he added with a tired, faint smile. Then he briefed his adviser on the contents of the second EMCON message.

Conley's face became a mosaic of worry lines. He was astonished the satellite came to life without prior warning. The implications were staggering. Both men were in agreement an emergency conference in the Crisis Room should be held as soon as possible. Conley left to set up the meeting.

The President poured himself a cup of coffee from the service cart and pondered this latest development in the Sunstroke crisis. It was all so incredible, he thought. Thousands of miles above his head was a multibillion-dollar satellite, a gigantic miracle of science and technology that had twice turned the vast energy of the sun into a death ray and fired it at the earth. Who knew how many persons were roasted to death in the second attack? The irony was not lost on Kendall. They had set about designing, building, and lofting into orbit the ultimate offensive/defensive weapon, which would shield the United States from enemy attack. Now the thing was out of control, killing the very people it was supposed to protect.

Kendall was also cognizant of the historical significance of the present situation. He realized this was the first true space crisis the nation had ever faced. Never before had an orbital device attacked American citizens. What made matters worse was the possibility put forth by Doheny that the satellite could discharge again, perhaps at another country. The international ramifications sent a cold shudder through the President's body. Suddenly he felt the pressures closing in on him from all sides.

For an instant, terror, pure and simple, clawed at his guts. His hands were trembling slightly.

What he needed now was to touch base with the everyday world, to reconnect with some object that represented substance in his life. He picked up the morning paper from the stainless steel tray beside the coffee urn and glanced at the headline screaming at him in bold black print: "Solar Satellite Mishap Blacks Out Albuquerque."

He quickly scanned the article and was grateful there was no mention of any casualties. The FBI had done a thorough job last night in "sanitizing" the isolated farmhouse struck by the satellite. Apparently the attack on south Florida had not made the news—yet. Maybe fate would be kind to him, Kendall thought, maybe they could keep this whole thing under wraps. He was shot through with doubt.

He put the newspaper down and went to get dressed for the meeting.

It was a few minutes past nine A.M. when President Kendall strode into the National Security Council conference room at the West Wing of the White House. He was wearing his old corduroy, Jack Conley saw; it was what the President called his good-luck suit. He had worn it on election night six long years ago. Maybe, Conley thought, the corduroy just might bring him some luck. Privately, Conley was grateful that the President, not he, carried the burden of decision this morning.

Kendall nodded his greetings to each of the men sitting around the oval table. The advisers who were physically present included Conley, chairman of the Joint Chiefs General Willis Thompson, Defense Secretary Hugh Fitzpatrick, FBI Director Harold Sorensen, and Energy Secretary Donald Addeo. One of the large television screens on the wall above them displayed the image of General Dean Stratton, head of the Space Defense Command, broadcast live from Cheyenne Mountain, Colorado.

"Well, gentlemen," said the President as he slowly paced about the room. "We have another problem." His voice was soft, his eyes hard. "It seems our satellite up there isn't through with us yet. As you know, it fired at Florida shortly after dawn this morning. And according to the project director at the solar-power plant there is a good possibility of more casualties." He shot an angry glance at General Stratton's bespectacled image. "Dean, why the hell wasn't I told it could start transmitting again by itself?''

On-screen, General Stratton cleared his throat, his face grim. ''Sir, apparently the Sunstroke satellite is in a highly unstable condition, making it impossible to predict its activity.'' He had a dry, precise way of speaking, which irritated Kendall.

''The EMCON message mentioned something about a collision in space,'' said the President, his voice sharp. ''Do you concur with this assumption, Dean?''

''Yes, sir,'' Stratton replied unhesitantly. ''Just before your office called, I finished reading a report from NORAD that offers some substantiation. As you know, NORAD maintains a constant radar watch over the space above the North American continent. Last night, as instructed, their scanners were focused on the region of space surrounding the satellite during its start-up period. One of their technicians reported a radar ghost—a barely discernible echo—in the vicinity of the satellite during that time. It was visible for only milliseconds on their radar scopes. Although the NORAD technicians believed it was a reflection from the satellite itself, they conducted a thorough investigation consisting of detailed computer analyses of videotapes of the echo, a complete instrument check, and so on. Their final report, finished this morning, speculates the radar ghost may have actually been a stealth kinetic-kill antisatellite vehicle. I was about to inform you by scrambler when Jack Conley phoned me. As I'm sure Hugh Fitzpatrick can tell you, the Russians have been experimenting with such a device recently.''

A shocked silence filled the room. Defense Secretary Fitzpatrick slumped in his chair, hand on his brow, deep in thought. Thompson bowed his head, chin on chest, like a man at prayer. FBI Director Sorensen took out his silver cigarette case and stared at it with large mournful eyes. Energy Secretary Addeo ran a hand over his bald pate. The President stood with his back to the table, gazing at the bank of communications consoles on the far wall. National Security Adviser Conley nervously glanced from one to the other.

President Kendall turned to face the table again. ''Fitz,'' he said, ''do you have any specifics on this?''

The defense secretary sat erect, his face pinched and bleak. His clear gray eyes were nested in fine lines and seemed tired, his white hair slightly disheveled. ''The CIA has determined they have been trying to develop an antisatellite device specially shaped and sheathed with certain composite materials to enable it to escape radar detection. But the Agency thinks they're years away from deployment.''

''I find it hard to believe,'' the President said, frowning, ''that the Russians would pull something like this. Not after all the billions of dollars worth of aid we've given them. But we can't rule it out entirely. Is there any way we can know for certain whether or not they were responsible for the attack?''

Fitzpatrick nodded thoughtfully. ''Our recon satellites routinely monitor every launch from the Russian Republic's Plesetsk Space Center. If the CIA conducts a comprehensive review of all photoreconnaissance records for the past few months, they might find a suspect rocket payload, one fitting the approximate size and weight of the Russians' new ASAT weapon.''

''Then I think we should have Russell Tanner investigate this further,'' said President Kendall. Tanner was the director of Central Intelligence.

Kendall went to his place at the table and pulled open a drawer containing a secure telephone. He picked up the phone. ''Julie, get me Russell Tanner at Langley.'' A moment later the DCI came on the line. ''Hi, Russ,'' greeted the President. ''How are you? Fine, thanks. And Karen and the kids? Glad to hear it. Ah, listen, Russ, I need to know something about the Russians' ASAT program. Can your people verify if they've launched one of their new stealth models within the past two months or so? Yes, I'm aware you believe it's still in the design stage. However, some information has come across my desk which indicates otherwise. No, I can't at this time. That's right. Make this top priority. If you can find out anything, report to me directly on a secure line. Thanks, Russ.''

Kendall replaced the phone, then glanced at his advisers. ''Although I'm not convinced the Russians are responsible for damaging our satellite, it'll be interesting to know if they possess the capability of evading normal radar.'' He shot a questioning look at the defense secretary. ''If I remember correctly, Fitz, our own stealth ASAT program is still on the boards?''

''Presently,'' rasped Fitzpatrick. ''But we're expecting a test shot early sometime next year.''

''Mr. President,'' said Energy Secretary Donald Addeo, ''the fact that our Sunstroke satellite malfunctioned immediately after it became operational is in itself highly suspect.'' The black arcs of his eyebrows shot upward, causing the mole in the middle of his forehead to dance on a ridge of flesh. ''Taking into account

NORAD's radar ghost, it's obvious someone tried to knock it out of action. And who but the Russians would have both the motive and resources to carry out such an act?" He had seized upon this idea in the hope of avoiding any personal blame for the crisis.

The President frowned. "Hold on a minute, Donald. We can't blame anyone until all the evidence is in. Until we know for certain the Russians have orbited a stealth ASAT we'll have to restrain our accusations."

General Willis Thompson, chairman of the Joint Chiefs of Staff, leaned over the table, his right hand flat on its surface. The four stars on each shoulder and the rows of medals decorating his tunic glistened as he moved. The effect resembled a highly tinseled Christmas tree being jostled. "Sir, if we discover the Russians are responsible for crippling the satellite, we may have a dangerous situation on our hands, to say the least." His prominent jaw was thrust forward, his lips a thin tight line. "At best, their attack could be considered an aggressive, provocative act. At worst, it could be interpreted as a prelude to invasion."

President Kendall could feel the sweat starting in his armpits. "Now let's not get ahead of ourselves, Will," he said cautiously. "At this time we don't know for sure whether they're responsible or not. Remember, we bent over backward to set this thing up as an alternative energy source under purely civilian control."

"That's true, of course," conceded General Thompson. "But we have to keep in mind the possibility of leaks. The Russians may have found out the truth about the solar satellite through their intelligence network and decided to try to take it out."

"Gentlemen," said President Kendall with some exasperation, "until we get some hard facts in we're just indulging in pure conjecture." He swept a challenging gaze around the table and at the TV screen. "Now, let's try to define the areas which require our immediate attention."

He reached into his breast pocket, took out the EMCON message, and unfolded it on the tabletop. He jabbed a finger at the printout. "First in south Florida: what are we going to do about it?" He twisted in his chair to face Harold Sorensen. "What are your recommendations, Harold?"

Before replying, the head of the FBI lit a cigarette with a lighter bearing the presidential seal. He looked at the President with sad, protuberant eyes. "According to the national security adviser we have a repeat of last night's first-order event. In my opinion we should treat any Florida casualties in the same manner."

"That reminds me, Harold," said Kendall. "What exactly did your agents do at that New Mexico farmhouse?"

Sorensen inhaled deeply on his cigarette and blew out a cloud of thick smoke. "Shortly after the bodies were recovered the house was burned to the ground." When he saw the shocked expressions on the faces around him he quickly added, "It was the most expedient way to remove all evidence of their bizarre deaths."

A cold shiver went up the President's spine. He closed his eyes and rubbed his temples. When, he wondered, will this nightmare end?

"Once again our main concern is to keep this out of the media," continued FBI Director Sorensen. "Undoubtedly we should contact the authorities in south Florida right away and have them announce that a fire broke out in the area. This ploy worked for us in New Mexico."

Jack Conley, the national security adviser, frowned. He leaned forward. "But can we afford to use this same strategy again?" he asked pointedly. "If we contact those people then there will be that many more outsiders involved. We'll just be begging for a leak."

Sorensen shook his head. "Not if it's handled properly," he said coolly. "If we exert pressure on their top brass they'll really try hard to keep the whole thing under wraps." He tapped cigarette ash into an ornate crystal ashtray and glanced at Kendall. "In my opinion, Mr. President, this is the only course of action open to us."

There was a long silence as each man contemplated the merits and drawbacks of Sorensen's proposal.

The look on Defense Secretary Fitzpatrick's face was one of tortured indecision. For the past few minutes he had listened quietly to the exchange between the FBI director, the national security adviser, and the President. During that time he had been wrestling with his conscience. He viewed the whole affair as being monstrous, out of control. They were not upholding the Constitution of the United States as they had sworn to do; instead the highest office in the country was shredding it in the name of political and personal gain like some banana republic. He decided it was his duty to make his stand clear to everyone present.

"Mr. President," rasped Fitzpatrick, "I wouldn't carry this thing any further than we already have. I've been in government thirty-five years." He was speaking with an aloof dignity. "I've held elective office and am aware of the horrible responsibility of power. It can tear you apart. You go on making decision after decision, hoping each one will be better than your last. But there comes a time when you begin justifying your actions according to the end result.'' He paused. ''This is when you have to draw the line. Nixon didn't know when to draw it and he ended up making history.''

The President stared at the thin, deeply lined face of the defense secretary. ''What are you saying, Fitz?'' he demanded skeptically. ''That we should just lay back and do nothing?''

''Of course not,'' snapped Fitzpatrick. ''All I'm trying to say is that we've stripped American citizens of their constitutional rights. Or have you forgotten the reporters and others who are imprisoned at that plant?''

''I haven't forgotten, Fitz,'' said the President heavily.

''We're fast approaching the point where we're going to have cover-ups on top of cover-ups,'' warned Fitzpatrick. ''Then it won't take much to bring the whole thing down on top of our heads. Do we want to do that or''—he searched for the right words—''should we reconsider our position?''

''In what respect?'' asked President Kendall sharply.

Hugh Fitzpatrick hesitated, his eyes hooded, his expression masked and composed. ''Maybe we should go public on this and tell our side of the story before someone leaks it to the press.''

Kendall was incredulous. His voice rose. ''You mean I should appear on television tonight and calmly tell the nation all about Sunstroke and how it was secretly financed. Tell the hardworking taxpayers how the thing went crazy and roasted a young family and God knows who else to death? Is this your advice?''

The defense secretary spoke carefully, but with emphasis. ''If you don't inform the public now on your own accord I'm certain you'll be facing impeachment charges by the end of the week.''

The President took a deep breath, stood up, looked at Fitzpatrick, and said slowly, ''But surely you realize that if I divulged Sunstroke the result would be the same?''

''Mr. President,'' said Jack Conley, ''we're all a little out of sorts on this. I'm sure the secretary has only the best intentions in mind and didn't mean that literally.'' His tone was placatory.

''No, he meant it,'' said Kendall softly, his handsome face expressionless. He started pacing. Finally he said firmly, ''I don't think we have a choice here.'' He looked through the defense secretary rather than at him, his eyes burning as if with fever. ''I can appreciate your stand on this, Fitz, but if the Russians are responsible for disabling the satellite, then we could be on the brink of war.'' He let the one word, *war,* hang heavy in the air. ''The country would surely cave in if I were impeached now. No, it's my duty to remain in office during this crisis to see us through it.''

The President's suddenly restored confidence was contagious. An electric current seemed to flow through the room, affecting everyone except Defense Secretary Hugh Fitzpatrick, who sat slumped in his chair, eyes screwed shut.

''We're going ahead with Harold's suggestion,'' announced President Kendall with impersonal calmness. He glanced at General Stratton's televised image on the wall above him. ''Dean, I want you to have the air force dispatch a CBR unit to south Florida. Order them to comb the microwave track for casualties. Any bodies are to be taken to that lab in Richmond.''

Kendall turned to face the head of the FBI. ''Harold, do whatever is necessary to keep this out of the press.'' Then he scanned the EMCON printout. ''Next, we have to decide what to do about our ailing satellite. The project director of the solar-power plant believes it could discharge again. Only next time we might not be so fortunate. I'm certain all of you can figure out the repercussions if the thing fired on Russia, China, or even on one of our allies.''

There was a low murmur of voices around the table.

The President's fingertips stroked the printout. ''The project director over there has recommended we assemble a group of specialists to determine why the satellite is continuing to malfunction and how to stop it. He included a list consisting of three outside experts, the best in their fields, and Dean Stratton.'' His eyes swept the room. ''All right, let's toss this around,'' he said quietly.

They tossed it around, but not quietly.

General Thompson wanted a joint service committee comprised solely of military experts from the army, navy, and air force. He emphasized the army but didn't name any individuals.

Jack Conley, a former army brigadier general, supported General Thompson's views.

FBI Chief Sorensen agreed with an all-military team for security reasons. However, he wanted the FBI to provide background checks on everyone involved.

Defense Secretary Fitzpatrick argued the team should be

composed of scientists and engineers from NASA and aerospace defense contractors.

General Stratton was adamant that only air force personnel should be considered for the job. He read off a list of qualified specialists from air force installations around the country.

Energy Secretary Addeo strongly believed a representative from the Energy Department should be on the team.

The President recognized the law of bureaucracy in action: when dealing with a difficult issue most committee members will inevitably argue over turf. Therefore their respective recommendations were debatable. "Gentlemen," he said tersely, "since we're working against time I think it would be best to go along with the project director's original selection. I've got a gut feeling we need fresh ideas, a new outlook. The men on his list might be able to provide them."

"Very well, sir," said JCS Chairman General Thompson. "If I may point out, they'll require a secure command post with immediate access to all Sunstroke satellite data as well as high-speed computers." He proceeded to name several army installations possessing the required electronic equipment.

President Kendall shot a glance at the large TV screen above them. "Dean, what are your thoughts on this?"

On-screen, General Stratton clasped his hands before him and leaned forward. "The facilities at the solar power plant are more than adequate. We've installed the most powerful computers in the country there to handle all satellite functions and telemetry. Once the plant is tied into NASA's Deep Space Network the on-site control room will be in constant contact with the satellite. Also the entire plant is under tight military security. It's perfect for a command post."

"I agree," replied Kendall. "Dean, I want you to be there to coordinate the team, to take charge of the operation."

He turned to FBI Chief Sorensen. "Harold, have the bureau run a thorough check on these people." He indicated the first three names on Doheny's list. "Once they're cleared, your agents are to track them down and provide immediate transportation to the solar power plant." He thought for a moment. "If the specialists refuse to cooperate, have them arrested or put in protective custody. Just make sure they get to the plant."

Hugh Fitzpatrick stirred uneasily. His face wrinkled into a reflection of inner conflict. "We can't arrest private citizens without—'' the defense secretary started to protest, but the President cut him off.

''Stopping the satellite is our number one priority, Fitz,'' declared the President. ''If certain individuals have to waive some of their rights in the service of their country, then so be it.''

Fitzpatrick shook his head almost imperceptibly. He was genuinely saddened by the decisions being made this morning.

The final point for discussion was the continuous infrared and radar ''doomwatch'' over the satellite suggested by Doheny. JCS Chairman Thompson and General Stratton were charged with its implementation.

When the meeting broke up several minutes later, Kendall eyed his defense secretary with concern. He wondered if the strain was becoming too much for Fitzpatrick.

As he watched the others leave the room, the President hoped they would all be able to bear up under the steadily mounting pressure.

He sat there alone, his lower lip curling downward with smoldering rage and frustration. He was thinking about General Stratton's revelation that a stealth ASAT may have attacked the satellite. He found it almost beyond belief that the Russians were responsible. But if they didn't do it, he thought, then who the hell did?

Chapter 12 ✳

THE ANSWER TO an anguished President's question lay deep in a remote rain forest in French Guiana, a territory of France situated on the northeast coast of South America. The land is bounded on the north by the Atlantic Ocean, on the east and south by Brazil, and on the west by Suriname, formerly known as Dutch Guiana. The infamous Devil's Island penal colony had been located on one of the isles off the Atlantic shore.

Rising above the dense forest and piranha-infested waters was the launchpad for the unmanned European *Ariane* rocket that had challenged U.S. supremacy in space for nearly two decades. Over the years the *Ariane* had successfully deployed dozens of communications and weather satellites belonging to Italy, Spain, Canada, Mexico, Japan, Germany and China. The current manifest called for twelve launches, which included an Arab satellite named *Arabsat 1A,* an Italian one called *Italsat 1,* France's *Inmarsat 2 F3,* and Spain's *Hispasat 1B. Ariane* was subsidized by the European Community, and its sales executives sweetened deals with discounts, deferred payments, and other inducements to recruit customers. The program was overseen by the European Space Agency, NASA's foremost competitor in the multibillion-dollar space-transportation business.

The sleek 155-foot-tall, three-stage *Ariane* rocket was capable of inserting a payload of 3,850 pounds into geosynchronous transfer orbit 22,300 miles above the earth. Its first and second stages were fueled by a hypergolic combination of terebenthine and nitrogen tetroxide. The third stage was powered by the cryogenic propellants liquid hydrogen and liquid oxygen. The rocket was jointly manufactured by France's Société Européenne de Propulsion and Germany's Messerschmitt-Boelkow-Blohm.

Today the huge launchpad was seemingly deserted; the only people present were the maintenance teams that clean up after a launch. The giant *Ariane* booster that had sat on the pad for the past two weeks had lifted off late yesterday afternoon bearing a special payload. The crew who had sent it aloft had long since departed. Because the launch had gone off without a glitch and had been precisely on time the crew had been given generous bonuses. Most of them had spent the extra money on endless rounds of drinks at the Salut, a fly-blown bar in nearby Kourou, a town that had sprung up over the years near the Guiana Space Center. The crew had descended on the bar last night after confirming the deployment of the rocket's payload in geosynchronous orbit. Some of them were still there, celebrating with the extra francs that management had given them.

The Salut was dark, had wooden floors covered with sawdust, a long well-scrubbed bar with stools, and a few tables. The walls were decorated with cheap colorful murals depicting the *Ariane* booster blasting off. The atmosphere was syrupy and thick with smoke. A jukebox in the corner played lilting calypso music. There were a few dozen men inside, all in a partial stupor, with puffy red-rimmed eyes and glazed expressions. Most were native Indians, descended from the aboriginal Carib tribes, who had been educated at French technical schools and hired and trained by the European Space Agency as launch crew technicians. They were tall and dark skinned, and sat together at the bar, speaking to each other in their native language.

Their launch crew chief was a Frenchman named Jacques Bourges, who sat alone at a table separate from his men. He was a swarthy, preoccupied man of about thirty-three, with tight disagreeable lips, a smooth sallow face, and an irritating way of sticking his tongue hard in his cheek when trying to assert himself. He had been a technician at the Aerospatiale company in Paris for seven years before being recruited by ESA to head the launch crew at the Guiana Space Center.

Bourges sat at the table, sullen and listless. His 2,000-franc bonus should have made him happy, but it did not. It had been in an envelope given to him by the clerk at the disbursement office. Along with the check was a note warning him to regard this particular launch with utmost confidentiality, for purposes of security. Bourges was disturbed by the payload that he had helped insert into geosynchronous orbit. He didn't know what the devil it was.

He was wondering if he should have another drink or go home when suddenly he noticed a man standing by his table.

"Mind if I join you, monsieur?" asked the man in thick, glutinous French.

Bourges squinted through alcohol-hazed eyes. He did not recognize the man. The stranger was plump, exuberant, with large projecting ears, a full head of tightly curled light hair, and an irrepressible smile. Bourges guessed he was Dutch. He shrugged and gestured for the man to be seated.

The man sat down heavily at the table. He glanced at Bourges's glass and said, "Can I buy you another brandy?" Without waiting for a reply he waved to the bartender. "A brandy for my friend and a beer for me," he shouted. A moment later the burly bartender, who was wearing a dirty white apron, brought the drinks over. Bourges murmured his thanks and took a gulp.

"Monsieur Bourges," said the man softly, "I need to talk with you."

Bourges was taken aback. "How do you know my name?"

The man identified himself as Gerard van Eeden, a security operative for ESA. He said he was investigating last night's launch and wanted to know if Bourges had noticed anything unusual about the *Ariane*'s payload.

Bourges nodded to himself. He had been right. Something suspicious had been going on. He leaned toward van Eeden and said in a low, conspiratorial tone, his voice slurring, "The launch manifest called for an *Arabsat 1A* meteorological satellite to be boosted into stationary orbit. Yesterday the transport plane brought the payload to the launchpad." He shook his head vigorously. "But when we opened the packing crate there was no meteorological satellite inside."

"What did you find?" van Eeden prompted, his eyes eager.

Bourges snorted in disgust. "A weird spherical black thing."

That same morning, inside the kitchen of a modest home in Pasadena, California, Mrs. Ann Rosen was preparing breakfast for her husband, who was upstairs taking a shower. She was a small, slight woman of sixty-three wearing a bright yellow house dress. Her gray hair was pulled back in a bun. She had just put two slices of whole wheat in the toaster when she heard the sound of a car pulling up in their driveway. She moved quickly to the window above the sink, stood on her tiptoes, and saw two men get out of a white sedan.

The men were strangers. They glanced at the house, then came up the brick path toward the door. One was hefty, completely filling out his charcoal suit. He was ruggedly handsome with thick brown hair and light eyes. His skin was tanned, as if he worked outdoors. The other man was taller and leaner and wore a navy blue suit. He had jet black hair with fierce eyes deep set in a long, sad face.

The fierceness of those eyes frightened Ann Rosen. She backed away from the window and called to her husband in a shrill voice.

In the bathroom upstairs Professor Aaron Rosen turned the shower tap to cold with a small pawlike hand and gasped as the icy stream hammered his skull and shoulders. He was a diminutive fireplug of a man, barely five feet, six inches tall. He was nearly bald and in two weeks he would be sixty-four. Yet vitality still sparked from him as static electricity snaps from light switches in cold, dry weather.

Rosen was the chairman of the aerospace engineering department at the nearby California Institute of Technology. He was a rebellious, often abrasive scientist-engineer who had played a major role in designing spacecraft for the immensely successful *Viking, Voyager,* and *Magellan* unmanned missions to the planets. For his efforts he was awarded the NASA medals for Distinguished Public Service and for Exceptional Scientific Achievement. He also had served as president of the physics section of the American Association for the Advancement of Science. He had been teaching space propulsion physics at Caltech for the last twelve years.

During the past few months Rosen had become infamous in certain government circles because of a paper he had submitted to *Scientific American.* It was entitled "An Analysis of the Biological Hazards Accompanying the Deployment of a Solar Satellite in Geosynchronous Orbit." The following excerpt was published in major newspapers around the country:

> The proponents of the Solar Satellite Project have repeatedly stated that the microwave beam generated by the satellite will supply sufficient baseload electricity to power a city the size of Albuquerque at a fraction of the cost of conventional nuclear plants. What they have not publicized is the inherent susceptibility of the orbiting energy station to a random impact with space debris which could alter the beam's precise alignment and direct it at populated areas. The Department of Energy maintains the on-board "fail-safe" devices would automatically

defocus the beam to a relatively harmless level in
such a situation. This paper investigates the hypo-
thetical scenario of a collision which renders these
safety devices inoperable while simultaneously altering the microwave beam's critical alignment.

After describing the devastating results of a space collision,
Rosen concluded his paper with the statement that many more
years of research and testing were needed before solar satellite
technology could be made reasonably safe.

As he showered Professor Rosen had no idea his prediction had
come true. Also he had never heard of Project Sunstroke. Nor was
he aware his daily routine was about to be radically disrupted.

When Rosen shut off the water he heard his wife calling him in
an urgent voice. Puzzled, he stepped out shivering, clawed his
towel off the rack, hurriedly dried himself, then threw on his
bathrobe. "I'm coming," he shouted. "I'm coming." As he raced
down the stairs he heard the doorbell ring. Now, he thought, who
the hell would be stopping by for a visit this early in the morning?
He saw his wife's anxious face as she met him at the front door.

"Two big men in suits," she said breathlessly. "I don't know
who they are. They parked in our driveway like they own the
place."

The doorbell rang again.

Rosen grunted and looked out the security peephole which he
dubbed "the Judas hole." He could tell at a glance the two men
were not from Caltech. They had a grim, determined look about
them that he found unsettling. He frowned. A strange fear touched
him like a premonition, but he quelled it, slipped the chain on, and
opened the door a crack.

The ruggedly handsome one was in front of it. He had his I.D.
out, ready to show him. The gold shield glinted in the California
morning sun. The big man was an FBI agent named Samuel Strain.
His partner was Frank Merrill.

"I'm sorry to disturb you, Professor Rosen," began Strain, "but
there's an emergency requiring your professional assistance."

Rosen scrutinized their credentials through the gap in the door,
then looked from one agent to the other. His eyebrows twitched
into peaks of incomprehension. "What kind of emergency?" he
asked, incredulous.

"May we come in?"

"Of course, of course," mumbled Rosen. He released the chain from the door and invited the two men inside. After gesturing impatiently for them to sit down on the living room sofa, he asked his wife to serve coffee. He sat in the overstuffed easy chair opposite the FBI agents and asked, "Now, would you please tell me what this is all about?"

By way of reply Special Agent Strain reached into his coat pocket and withdrew a sealed envelope. "Sir, this is a letter from the U.S. secretary of energy explaining the situation. I've been authorized to turn it over to you."

Rosen took the envelope, opened it, and read the letter twice. It was carefully worded, saying that because the nature of the solar satellite malfunction was more serious than had first been believed, Project Director Michael Doheny urgently requested Rosen's immediate assistance to help resolve the problem. Transportation to the solar power plant site would be provided by the government and generous compensation would be made for services rendered.

Rosen shook his head. "You know," he said sharply, "I was against the deployment of this thing from the very beginning. I told them how susceptible the system would be to disruptive elements in the space environment. Heat. Cold. Meteoroids. Space junk." His words succeeded each other in little barks, like a string of Chinese firecrackers. "But no one listened. Now that it screwed up, they're begging me to help bail them out." He spread his hands. "Don't get me wrong. When I heard about the satellite malfunction last night on the news I sure as hell didn't gloat. That thing is dangerous. Thank God no one was hurt."

The other agent, Frank Merrill, spoke for the first time. "Then you'll offer your services and accompany us to the solar power plant?" His eyes glared at Rosen with a fierce intensity.

"Impossible," growled Rosen. "I can't take a leave of absence from the institute at a moment's notice. This has to be planned out months in advance. Why, I haven't even had a vacation in ten years. Too damn busy."

The presence of the FBI men sitting in front of him suddenly disturbed Rosen. "By the way," he said slowly, "why did the Energy Department send a couple federal agents over here to deliver this letter? It doesn't make any sense."

The two agents exchanged glances.

"Professor," said Strain in a quiet, sincere voice, "I'm going to be honest with you, sir." He paused and studied the puzzled expression on Rosen's face. "I want you to understand that my partner and I have absolutely no choice in this matter. We've received special instructions from our superiors to escort you directly to the solar power plant in Albuquerque without delay." He held up one hand to forestall Rosen's protests. "Please understand this is very difficult for us. I'm not supposed to divulge this information to you at this time, but from what little we've been told, the situation at that plant is critical. Lives are in danger. Will you please reconsider?"

Rosen's face flushed red with anger. He jumped out of his chair and seemed to bounce across the room to confront the men on the sofa as though he were being propelled by springs hidden in the soles of his shoes. "You're telling me that I have no choice!" He punctuated his words with a jabbing forefinger. "What are you going to do? Knock me over the head and handcuff me?"

In the kitchen, Ann Rosen had been listening intently to every word. She slammed the coffeepot down and hurried into the living room. Shaking with both fear and rage, she shouted, "This is an outrage! We're living in America, not Nazi Germany. You have no right to do this. My husband is a respected scientist with friends in high places. You'll be sorry, believe me."

Rosen held his wife. "Ann, Ann," he pleaded. "It's all right. I've decided to go with them. They need my help. There are lives at stake." His voice was resigned, his face slack, expressionless. It seemed to her like a bad dream. She was afraid and worried.

Rosen turned to the FBI men. "Listen, do I have time to phone my office, tell them I won't be in?"

"No, sir," said Strain. "I'm afraid not. You'll have to pack quickly. There's a military jet waiting to fly you to Albuquerque." He smiled slightly. "You'll be taking an extended sick leave. Everything's been arranged."

"I see," grunted Rosen. "For how long?"

"An indefinite period. Pack what you can in the next few minutes, and then we'll go. Breakfast will be served on the plane."

Rosen hugged his wife, left the room, and went upstairs to the bedroom. As he threw several changes of shirts, slacks and underwear into a suitcase, he wondered exactly what was wrong with the satellite and why the project director wanted his assistance.

He remembered that Doheny had been an outstanding engineering student at Caltech. Serious, determined, brilliant. They had kept in contact over the years up until the beginning of the Solar Satellite Project. Since Rosen had been vigorously opposed to the scheme, he wanted nothing to do with its implementation and broke off all ties with his former student.

How ironic, thought Rosen, grimly, that despite his public and private condemnation of the solar satellite, he was now being forced to help put it back together.

That same morning, Dr. Frederick Gaither entered his office at the Bioelectromagnetic Research Laboratory, a long, low concrete building in the middle of the University of Washington campus in Seattle. Gaither was an obese man in his mid-fifties with thinning hair and a ruddy complexion. His main pleasures in life consisted of eating to excess, drinking fine wines, and chain-smoking slim, expensive cigars.

Each day on his way to the BRL he stopped at a gourmet bakery and purchased Danish pastry, powdered doughnuts, an assortment of cookies, and a pint of half-and-half for his coffee. Today he shoved a two-foot stack of documents to one corner of his desk and carefully unwrapped his pastry goods and spread them out before himself. As was his custom, he spent several moments surveying each item with eager anticipation, leaning over and inhaling the sweet, fresh-baked aroma.

Gaither was the head of the technological assessment department at BRL whose primary function was to determine the environmental impact and potential health risks of various government and private-sector projects involving the use of both ionizing and non-ionizing radiations. He possessed doctorates in medicine and physics. Eighteen years ago, while doing biochemical research at the University of Washington, he had conducted experiments with rats suggesting that close proximity to high-voltage electric power lines, sleeping on electrically heated waterbeds, or using electric blankets could cause higher cancer rates and longer gestation periods and an increase in miscarriages among pregnant women. Because he knew precious government grants went hand in hand with sensationalism he published his findings. As predicted, the public outcry was sufficient to force the government to fund a complete investigation into the subject. Gaither found himself at the hub of the controversy, with an $875,000 grant and a position as assistant research director of the technological assessment department of BRL. Since then he had been promoted to director, overseeing the work of seventeen full-time researchers.

Three years ago, while ascertaining the impact of radio broadcast towers on a remote tract in North Dakota for the U.S.

Environmental Protection Agency, Gaither became interested in the long-term effects of radio waves on the population at large. His interest soon became an obsession. Anxious to uncover another controversial subject garnering more public acclaim and funds, he saw great potential in the study. Being very cost-effective, he went on line with his time-sharing computer terminal at night and on weekends, when the time was far cheaper. His determination paid off: within a year he had found that exposure to electromagnetic radiation caused definite behavioral and physical changes in laboratory animals. He correlated this data with health statistics for the entire U.S. population who had been exposed for decades to leakage from microwave ovens, to television and radio broadcasts, microwave transmissions from satellites, air traffic control systems, police and military radar, cellular telephones, and other communications systems employing high-energy radio waves that continuously bombarded the atmosphere. The results were shocking. His study indicated constant exposure to the electromagnetic radiation and elevated magnetic fields produced by modern technology generated an abnormal increase in heart problems, cancer rates, and, far less severe, headaches and loss of memory within the general population. BRL was deluged by grants for further research into the matter.

Presently, the two-foot stack of documents, which Gaither slid to one corner of his desk, represented $33 million worth of research spent by NASA and the U.S. Air Force to develop a plane capable of flying continuously for months at a time at the edge of space without fuel. The unmanned craft would draw power from a beam of microwaves sent up from the ground. It could be used to study the tenuous reaches of the stratosphere or be utilized as a cheap alternative to a spy satellite. BRL was hired to evaluate the health risks accompanying the project.

Gaither had just stirred half-and-half into his coffee and took his first bite of Danish when the intercom buzzed. His secretary told him two FBI agents wanted to see him right away.

The office door opened and two men in their early thirties dressed in three-piece suits entered with credentials in hand.

In accordance with his reputation of possessing a quick wit, Gaither said, "The last I heard, I didn't owe any back taxes. What can I do for you gentlemen?"

"We're FBI," replied one agent dryly, "not Treasury." He handed Gaither a letter from the Energy Department similar in content to the one given to Professor Aaron Rosen.

Gaither scanned the letter quickly, trying to read between the

lines. He was fascinated by the implied ramifications. His department at the Bioelectromagnetic Research Lab had assessed the
environmental impact of the Solar Satellite Project several years
ago and had found it to be quite severe. If the Energy Department
needed his help in determining the extent of last night's malfunction, then either something catastrophic had already taken place or
was about to. The idea intrigued him.

"When am I expected at the solar power plant?" he asked
woodenly.

"A plane is waiting to take you there now, sir."

Gaither frowned. "Do you mind if I finish my breakfast first?"
he asked with some irritation. "I don't like flying on an empty
stomach." He helped himself to the doughnuts and cookies. "Care
to join me?"

The agents declined. "I'm afraid you'll have to hurry, sir."

The third and final civilian member of Doheny's team was
contacted by the FBI that morning at NASA's Launch Control
Center in Cape Canaveral, Florida.

Malcolm I. Courtland was a tall, thin aerospace engineer in his
late thirties. His cocoa brown skin shone, and his face mirrored a
curious mixture of culture and restrained violence. He moved with
a slow, deliberate calm. He was NASA's foremost rocket trouble-
shooter, a man with a talent for quickly determining the nature of
a spacecraft malfunction whether on the launchpad or in space.
Today he had been brought in to find out why *Satcom XXII* had
failed to lift off on schedule.

For the past two hours Courtland had paced about the cavernous
control room, inspecting readouts and interrogating hapless technicians. From time to time he shot an angry glance at the huge
projection TV screen on the far wall, which displayed the
gleaming but lifeless spacecraft sitting on its concrete-and-steel
launchpad two miles away. He was no closer now to finding the
answer than when he had first started. Consequently he was in a
foul mood when the two federal agents entered the room and
approached him.

A few moments later Courtland pounded the top of a console
with his open hand, startling the nearby technician. "No way," he
shouted. "I'm not leaving until"—he jerked a thumb at the TV
screen—"that bird out there is in orbit."

"In that case, sir," said one of the stern-faced agents, "you're
under arrest."

*   *   *

That morning General Dean Stratton put on his cap, adjusted his spectacles, and left his private cubicle within the U.S. Space Defense Command operations center, a self-contained two-story steel blockhouse suspended by giant springs and shock absorbers located a half mile inside Cheyenne Mountain in Colorado. Stratton was a short man with a soft face, long arms, and stooped, rounded shoulders. His silver-white hair was crew cut. Behind the thick lenses of his glasses, his eyes were a clear, cold green. He strode purposefully through the vast theaterlike room on the second story, where twenty-three officers controlled and monitored all phases of the strategic defense Space Shield.

Cheyenne Mountain had originally been hollowed out to accommodate the NORAD missile warning center to ensure the facility's survival in the event of nuclear war. For several decades NORAD had kept track of every spacecraft, missile, and aircraft over North America. Later, military planners including Stratton had decided it would be an ideal location to house the Space Shield control center. Consequently the site had been expanded to include both operations. Stratton had been placed in command of the entire installation, a position he had maintained for the past nine years.

As Stratton made his way to the exit leading to the main tunnel, two air police sentries gave him a smart salute. Outside in the dark tunnel another air policeman sat in a jeep waiting for the general. The engine was idling and the headlights were on. Stratton climbed in and told the sentry to take him directly to the airfield outside the mountain. They rode in silence along the curving half mile of primary tunnel, wide as an avenue, that led to the outside portal.

The air inside the tunnel was musty despite the constant air conditioning. Even though it was morning it might as well have been midnight. There was no sunlight. The only illumination came from widely spaced mercury vapor lamps. As they made their way through the winding artificial cave an occasional bat was caught in the jeep's blazing headlights.

The men who spent their tour of duty here found it a strange experience. They lived a buried, nightmarish existence. Subterranean life was hard, demanding. The crew who manned the operations center were not ordinary men. They had been carefully screened by hard-eyed navy psychologists and thoroughly trained for their tasks. Living inside the center was not unlike serving aboard a nuclear submarine, where space was severely restricted and claustrophobia could send a man into a deadly panic. The crew referred to Cheyenne Mountain as "the Mausoleum."

Stratton was able to deal with the pressures of this cavernous life because he was basically a nerveless man. Before his failing eyesight grounded him, he had been a superb jet-fighter pilot with intentions of becoming an astronaut. When his vision dimmed he had found solace in the world of science, vigorously studying chemistry and physics at M.I.T., where he earned his doctorate. He became interested in developing advanced weapons technology. This led him to coordinate research and development of the strategic defense Space Shield and, later, Project Sunstroke.

When Stratton had first proposed converting the Energy Department's solar satellite into the Sunstroke demonstrator he had envisioned total military control over every stage of the project. However, budgetary constraints and the pressing need to deemphasize the military nature of the satellite forced him to turn it over to the civilians. At best Stratton considered the private sector to be a necessary evil in American society. Although the taxpayers financially supported the military, he believed they were untrustworthy, unreliable, out of control. He thought private industry was no better. Almost every firm he had dealt with cheated the air force through massive cost overruns, kickbacks, and monstrous overcharging of inexpensive items. He never forgot the $2,500 toilet seats that the contractor had charged during the Cheyenne Mountain renovation. It had been personally humiliating when the fact was disclosed at a Senate hearing on Pentagon overspending.

For these reasons he distrusted all civilians, including the project director of the solar power plant.

His jeep came to a sudden stop at the outside portal, a massive steel blast door fourteen feet tall and three feet thick. Stratton gave the two heavily armed sentries who were stationed there the egress code for the day. One of the sentries touched a panel embedded in the granite wall and the huge door slowly slid open with a hydraulic sigh.

As he drove through the open portal into the cool, crisp Colorado morning Stratton pondered his orders. Under a presidential directive he was to assume command of the SOLSAT X-1 control site—the solar power plant—and take whatever steps were necessary to render the Sunstroke satellite inoperative. Privately, General Stratton interpreted these orders to mean that he was to regain control of the satellite, for he could not conceive of destroying such an elegant weapons system.

Chapter 13 *

AFTER CONTACTING THE Pentagon on Nore's hot-line phone, Mike Doheny had made use of the showers set up by the MPs just outside the rest rooms on the ground floor of the solar power plant. A half-dozen plastic stalls with heavy twill curtains had been fitted together in the corridor. Thick hoses snaked from the stalls to the lavatory faucets. The water, to Doheny's irritation, had been lukewarm.

On his way back to his office he had stopped at the Central Computer Room to obtain a set of compact discs containing all of the satellite schematics. He wanted to reacquaint himself with every on-board system, subsystem, and component.

Now, inside his office, Doheny shaved and changed his clothes. The night and early morning had taken a heavy toll on his energy; he could feel a dead weight of fatigue pressing down on his brow and eyes. But there was no question of sleeping. He informed the control room he would be in his office for an hour or so. He told the weary personnel to work in rotating shifts so they each could get some rest. Then he put a fresh packet into his coffee maker and returned to his desk.

As he waited for the coffee to brew he inserted one of the compact discs into his personal computer. He leaned forward to study the intricate diagram of flowing green lines on the screen, a schematic of the satellite's microwave transmitter housing. More images and data flickered onto the screen in a steady hypnotic pattern. Doheny tried to keep his eyes open but it was useless. In a minute fatigue overcame him and he slowly slumped back into his chair.

His sleep was soon invaded by the Dream.

He was standing beside a control panel outside the propulsion systems test chamber, a steel-walled blockhouse, at Nore Space Industries' complex in Salton City, California. They had been

testing one of the satellite's attitudinal-control thrusters in the
chamber when it developed a minor glitch. The test was postponed
and two technicians were sent inside to replace a burned-out
circuitry module on the thruster. A safe, simple operation. Doheny
remained outside the chamber to monitor the instruments.

As always, just as it had actually happened two years ago, there
was an explosion. Doheny looked up to see a blinding white-hot
flame licking at the plexiglass window in the hatch to the test
chamber. A voice from inside shouted, "Get us out of here!" and
there was a cry of pain. Other technicians wearing face masks and
asbestos gloves tried to open the hatch but were driven back by the
intense heat. Doheny grabbed a crowbar, pried the hatch open, and
went in. The flames had subsided but superheated air seared his
lungs. The entire chamber was filled with black greasy smoke. He
nearly suffocated. Coughing deeply, he made his way to the
crumpled figures on the floor. As he crouched down to help them,
he was shocked.

Somehow the Dream had changed.

Instead of two charred bodies there were now five. He looked
closer. Staring up at him through unseeing, poached eyes were the
members of the Roberts family, the Sunstroke satellite's first
victims. He stood up and jumped back in horror.

Peering out through the plexiglass window, he saw familiar
faces watching him. They were the men and women he saw every
day at the plant. He shouted to them for help. One of them reached
over and pressed a red button. The chamber was suddenly filled
with the sound of an alarm.

Doheny bolted awake, rubbed his eyes, then stared at his watch.
It was a little past 8:30 A.M. He had dozed off for nearly two and
a half hours despite himself. His own dream shouts and the sound
of the emergency alarm were still ringing in his ears as if they had
gotten nested in the corners of the room.

He blinked his eyes. His desk intercom was flashing and
emitting a shrill whine. A firm male voice told him that General
Stratton had arrived and was waiting in the conference room.

Stratton wasted little time on social amenities and uttered only
a few short words of greeting as he shook hands with Doheny. The
polished buttons on his uniform shirt and the silver decorations on
his cap visor glistened under the bright conference room lights.
Although Stratton stood as erect as possible, he was still a full
head shorter than Doheny. This did not stop him from trying to
take command of his first meeting with the civilian project

director. He sat down at the head of the table and motioned for Doheny to be seated.

The conference came down immediately to the rapid exchange of facts and figures, a hard-driving effort by both men to familiarize each other with every aspect of the crisis at hand. Stratton quickly outlined the status of the Pentagon's attempt to set up a "doomwatch" according to Doheny's recommendations. The operation had been code-named Earthnet. By that afternoon every available military, meteorological, and earth resources satellite with infrared capability would be scanning for any telltale signature from the microwave beam. Also fourteen long-range reconnaissance aircraft similarly equipped would go aloft, filling in the gaps between the orbital scans.

In addition, ten oceangoing satellite-tracking vessels and fifty-four radar ground stations around the world would begin continuous radar surveillance of the Sunstroke spacecraft. Stratton went on to report that NASA had been ordered to start tracking with their Deep Space Network. Lastly he said a detachment of air force technicians would arrive at the plant later that morning to install the necessary receivers and other equipment.

"What about the three outside specialists I requested?" Doheny inquired.

"I understand the men are on their way here right now." Stratton eyed him steadily. "I assume you've been briefed on Project Sunstroke?"

"Yes."

There was an oppressive blankness to Stratton's expression. "I must ask you not to divulge any information concerning Project Sunstroke to any of the civilian specialists."

Doheny felt a flush of anger. "I'm sorry, General, but we don't have the time for that kind of bullshit." His voice was firm, adamant. "Our job is to stop the satellite before it kills more innocent people. We're going to have to make use of every scrap of data we can get our hands on. And this means briefing each member of the team on Project Sunstroke and anything else of value."

Stratton sat back in his chair and stared coldly at Doheny. His lips tightened back over his teeth. He did not tolerate blatant disrespect from anyone. But unfortunately he needed this man's assistance to regain control of his satellite. "Very well," he said quietly. "All vital information will be disseminated to everyone on the team."

It was a major concession, Doheny thought. If he keeps his word.

Twenty minutes later Doheny entered the plant lobby to greet his former instructor from Caltech. He thought it was a strange place for a reunion.

Professor Aaron Rosen glanced angrily at the MPs flanking him at the lobby entrance. "What do you mean I have to show some identification?" he shouted. "For crying out loud, the FBI brought me here! Isn't that good enough for you soldiers?"

Doheny studied the short, animated figure for a moment. He was engrossed by the man's personality. Some people never change, he thought wryly.

"Welcome to the club, Professor," he called out.

Rosen turned around slowly, as if he heard a note of enchanting music. A crooked grin came over his round face. "Mike, what the hell is going on around here? I thought this was supposed to be a civilian operation."

"So did I, Professor," said Doheny heavily. He briefly explained the emergency to Rosen.

As they talked, the detachment of air force technicians from Kirtland wearing khaki overalls and carrying cases of electronic equipment came into the lobby. Doheny escorted the entire group to the control room, where he and General Stratton spent the next few hours supervising the installation of the Earthnet relay and the DSN telemetry link.

The next member of the team, Dr. Frederick Gaither from BRL, arrived at noon and was taken directly to the control room. When he stepped inside he immediately sat down in an unoccupied swivel chair, which barely contained his bulk, and started patting his perspiring face with a handkerchief. After recovering from the exertion of his walk through the plant he lit a slender cigar, glanced around the crowded room filled with military and civilian technicians, and remarked to Rosen, "I see we've got a full house here. At least I won't be lonely."

Later that day a gray sedan pulled up at the plant and NASA engineer Malcolm Courtland and his FBI escort got out. Courtland was understandably upset at being arrested and had been demanding to see his attorney ever since they had left Cape Canaveral. The agents placed Courtland in the custody of Provost Marshal Earl Clayton, who signed the necessary release forms.

Courtland became nervous and apprehensive when he caught

sight of the MPs brandishing their ugly machine pistols. "Jesus, Mary, and Joseph," he muttered.

During that same day a coded message from the Pentagon was dispatched to satellite operations centers around the world. The controllers of all infrared-equipped spacecraft not engaged in priority surveillance missions were ordered to begin global scanning. The men who received the instructions were told this was just another routine exercise to test their capability of detecting thermal heat patterns from nuclear detonations in the event of war. The code name for the test was Earthnet.

Three hundred and fifty miles above the earth a U.S. spy satellite hummed and chattered as its battery of Schmidt wide-scan infrared television cameras was aligned at the planet below. The satellite was passing over the Red Sea, the Sinai Peninsula, and the eastern Mediterranean. A protective metal shield over the IR cameras opened like an iris and they began scanning.

Within minutes after the Earthnet message was transmitted, a total of eleven satellites in orbit over the major oceans and landmasses had their heat-sensitive instruments trained on designated areas. These spacecraft bore exotic names such as *Hermes, NOAA, Landsat, SAMOS, IRAS, Daystar, SATMET, Orion.* All were U.S. owned and operated.

Also participating in the Earthnet operation were those air bases possessing Nighthawk surveillance aircraft. Always on constant alert status, these ungainly long-range jets were normally used in high-altitude reconnaissance missions over enemy territory. They were equipped with wing and fuselage pods housing sophisticated ground-search radar, image-enhancing cameras, and Bausch and Lomb infrared sensors. The multimillion-dollar aircraft were stationed at top-security bases in California, Utah, Hawaii, South America, and Western Europe. Fourteen Nighthawks went aloft that day to provide infrared coverage of those areas missed by the satellite scans.

A different set of orders was dispatched to the control room at the DSN-2 radio telescope near Madrid, Spain. This sprawling facility was part of NASA's Deep Space Network of ground stations used to receive and relay telemetry from space probes. Presently the huge dish was listening to the electronic uproar from 50,000 light-years away at the center of the galaxy. Then a new program was fed into the radio telescope's control computer. Accompanied by the groaning and creaking of protesting steel, the massive dish slowly pivoted in its moorings until it was locked on the Sunstroke satellite.

Similar scenes would be repeated in the hours to come at the radio observatories situated in the vast, dusty scrub land outside Canberra, Australia, and in the Mojave Desert in California.

Another message code-named SATSCAN was sent by the Pentagon to ten special U.S. Navy vessels plying the waters of the Pacific, Atlantic, and Indian oceans. These ships, which bristled with radar dishes and antenna masts of unearthly configuration, were satellite-tracking vessels assigned to coordinate points around the world; their purpose was to maintain constant surveillance of specific orbital spacecraft. Today they were ordered to begin tracking the largest manmade object orbiting the earth, something far more interesting than just another Russian Cosmos spy satellite.

Thousands of miles above the earth, the object of the most extensive tracking scan ever conducted swept through the intensely hot airless sunlight on a southeast trajectory.

As it drifted through space, SOLSAT X-1's radiation sensors registered the gentle touch of a radar probe on the metal surface of its hull. This electromagnetic contact stimulated the satellite's command computer to immediately trace the radar probe to its source by using the on-board radio wavelength directional finder, the same device it utilized to direct the microwave beam at the solar power plant rectenna. The computer scanned the area on the planet below with the infrared sensors and compared the signature to a set of thermal patterns stored in its memory. In microseconds the computer identified the source of the radar probe as an oceangoing vessel.

Directly ahead of the satellite lay the zone of darkness. The cool night side of the world was approaching. Minutes later SOLSAT X-1 glinted in the last golden rays of the sun just before plunging into the brief night.

At sunset a group of longshoremen were unloading a cargo ship anchored off the African coast at Benguela when they spotted a brilliant light shining high in the western sky. The dockworkers pointed upward, talking furiously among themselves.

Suddenly the light dimmed and winked out. The men shook their heads and became silent. They believed the apparition in the sky was an evil omen. Each of them offered a quiet prayer to their deity, begging to be spared from the tribulations to come.

Chapter 14 *

A WAVE OF relief came over Doheny now that they were finally ready to make use of the Earthnet/SATSCAN distant early-warning system. He surveyed the gleaming equipment that had been newly installed in the control room.

Covering the back wall was a huge glowing blue screen showing a simple Mercator map of the world. The familiar continents and oceans were crisscrossed with lines of latitude and longitude. Beneath it sat two Cyber 3440 high-speed computers that had been airlifted from Kirtland AFB. The one on the left would show the rogue satellite's orbital position over the earth by projecting a corresponding red blip on the big screen. The other computer would pinpoint the exact location of a telltale infrared signature from a microwave discharge by flashing a white light onto the Mercator map.

Doheny eyed the red phone squatting beside the new computer consoles. It was an extension of the hot-line phone in Nore's office. This special phone was to be used for reporting the specific geographic location of the microwave beam's infrared signature the moment it occurred. Once this information was relayed to the Pentagon, the designated military officials would take appropriate action to evacuate anyone directly in the path.

Doheny watched a couple of air force engineers take their places at the two computer consoles and begin thumbing through programming manuals. At a cue from Stratton the two men pressed buttons and flicked switches. Indicator lights came on as the machines hummed and whirred. A bright red blip—the present location of the Sunstroke satellite—appeared on the big screen over the Indian Ocean midway between South Africa and the islands of Indonesia. Doheny could make out its position to be 30 degrees 8 minutes south latitude, 74 degrees 22 minutes east longitude.

The control room danced with the rhythmically oscillating colored computer lights and the pulsating glow from the screen. Apparently the entire system was working. Data on the Sunstroke satellite was being successfully relayed from the radio telescope in Australia to the down-link antenna atop the plant's roof via a Telstar comsat in geostationary orbit.

Across the room civilian technician George Phillips was perplexed when he saw that the readouts on his microwave systems console were still blank. Now that they had the telemetry relay from Australia hooked up he was certain they should be receiving something from the satellite itself besides its orbital position. But they weren't. He reported this to Doheny.

Puzzled, Doheny glanced at the red blip on the big screen. It was edging closer toward Indonesia. Then the answer came to him.

"The satellite has entered the earth's shadow," he announced. "Since the solar panels aren't receiving any sunlight they're not producing electricity to power the on-board radio transmitters. All systems are inactive—for the time being." He turned to Phillips. "You'll get some readings when the satellite moves into the daylight side a few hours from now."

Doheny wondered about the earth's diurnal cycle. In space the temperature difference between the sunlit and dark sides of the world was extreme. Was this one of the mechanisms affecting the satellite's microwave transmitter? He asked Stratton. The general was too preoccupied with matters at hand, but said they would discuss the subject at the conference that night. Doheny joined him, and the two men spent the next hour evaluating, checking, and rechecking the Earthnet/SATSCAN setup. From time to time they glanced at the menacing red blip slowly moving across the big screen.

Upstairs on the ground floor Cable News Service correspondent Diane Bradford stepped into the shower stall. With a screech of plastic hooks along metal, she whipped the heavy shower curtain closed, then unbuttoned and removed her blouse. Her bra followed. After slipping out of her slacks she flung the clothes over the curtain rod and turned on the water full force. She let it crash down on her head while she slowly rotated, cupping her hands over her high, firm breasts to protect them from the needlelike jets of tepid water. The liquid massage effect was soothing and enabled her to think clearly.

She and eleven other prisoners had been escorted by the MPs to the half dozen showers set up in the corridor outside the ground-floor lavatory. Each person was allocated five minutes for personal hygiene. Diane was grateful for the privacy the stall provided. Being imprisoned in the guest lounge all night and day had been a humiliating and degrading experience. She didn't mind her colleagues—they were basically decent, respectable people—but she had never imagined they would all be living together in such close proximity. And she especially didn't like the leering glances from the MPs the night before, when she and the other women had partially undressed before going to bed. It was a relief to get out of that place, at least for a little while.

She felt depressed, beaten. She had all but given up on getting her exclusive interview with Mike Doheny, the one man who could tell her exactly what happened after the satellite had malfunctioned. Her earlier plan to slip away undetected was impossible to implement; the goons watched her and everybody else like hawks. Even Deputy Energy Secretary Howard Averson. There didn't seem to be any possibility of meeting secretly with Doheny. She had heard him being paged earlier in the day, so at least he was still inside the plant. But he was so damned inaccessible. She began to wonder if he was as much a prisoner in this place as she. It seemed that she wasn't going to get her story of a lifetime, the one big break she so desperately needed to further her career. She would have to be content with working for the Cable News Service affiliate at Alburquerque until something better came along, if it ever did.

She hungered for some good rigorous exercise to help release the tension. The muscles of her long, lithe body ached for physical activity. For the last year she had religiously played tennis five nights a week with her number one cameraman, Andy, at a high school tennis court near the TV studio. She had natural balance and good rhythm. She hadn't played since being assigned to cover the dedication of the solar power plant three whole days ago.

After lathering and rinsing she decided to do a simple stretching exercise. Naked, standing on her tiptoes, she raised her arms above her head as far as she could, palms open. Diane was tall and her fingertips nearly touched the low ceiling. She took a deep breath and, straining her muscles, put more effort into her stretching. It felt good. Then she saw the loose vinyl ceiling tile above her head. The tile was large, about two feet by three. There was a quarter-inch gap on one side between it and a metal support. The tile must have been jostled when the soldiers installed the portable showers, she thought.

An idea came to her. Clenching her teeth, she tried with all her might to touch it with her fingertips but couldn't quite reach it. The molded step above the shower floor was the answer. She stood on it and carefully probed the loose tile. With a little push she lifted it off the metal supports to reveal a ceiling space, an uninviting dark world inhabited by pipes, wires, and ducts. It was big enough to accommodate a person crawling on hands and knees. She wondered if the ceiling spaces throughout the plant were all interconnected. She studied the gaping hole, her mind racing. She decided this find was too valuable to waste in a hastily devised operation.

She suddenly grew concerned that the two MPs outside might spot the dislodged tile through the two-inch gap between the top of the stall and the ceiling. She cautiously lowered the tile back in place and stepped down to the shower floor shortly before a harsh voice shouted, "Time's up. Everybody out."

On the way back to the lounge Diane found it difficult to suppress a smile. She felt certain she was going to get her story after all.

At the Salut bar in Kourou, French Guiana, *Ariane* crew chief Jacques Bourges felt that dangerous glow when he might say something he would later regret. He sat at the table in the corner talking to Gerard van Eeden, the man who had identified himself as a European Space Agency security operative. Bourges had drunk too much brandy and knew he was saying too much.

Van Eeden seemed to be an ebullient, cheerful man who loved conversation, good food, and drink. After listening intently to Bourges's description of the strange payload that had been shot into space by yesterday's *Ariane* launch, he had asked if anyone else had been disturbed by the mysterious object. Bourges had said none of the members of his launch crew had cared much about anything except doing their job so they could get their bonuses. Then van Eeden had wanted to know if Bourges had told anyone else about the payload. Bourges had said no.

Presently van Eeden was drawing Bourges into a conversation about his marital status. "I'm not married," Bourges murmured.

Van Eeden gave him a knowing smile and winked. "The native girls around here are quite a temptation, no?"

Bourges's face blushed but he did not reply. When van Eeden

asked if he had any family in Guiana he shook his head. He was beginning to suspect that van Eeden was investigating him, and the thought terrified him.

Van Eeden stood up and put a wad of francs on the table. "Come, my friend. It's time for you to go home and get some sleep." He gave Bourges a friendly pat on the shoulder. "You had better let me drive you," he said sincerely. "You've had a little too much to drink." Bourges protested, but van Eeden squeezed his arm. "I insist."

Outside the Salut the sun burned away the morning chill and the clinging damp mist. In the distance the fringe of the rain forest could be seen, a solid wall of trees rearing into the sky.

The brandy had hit Bourges hard, and his legs were wobbly. Van Eeden gripped him with surprisingly strong arms and escorted him to a mud-splattered four-wheel-drive Range Rover. He opened the door and helped Bourges inside. He started the car and pulled onto Saint-Elie Boulevard. "Where do you live, my friend?"

"The Saut-Tigre district," Bourges said thickly. That area was a wedge of French colonial homes located on the east side.

The car bumped over the cobbles in the street, and Bourges braced himself for the sharp right turn that would take them to Saut-Tigre. The next moment he lurched sideways in his seat as the Range Rover swerved to the left. "We were supposed to turn right," he complained. "This will take us into the jungle."

Van Eeden's pale eyes did not flicker as he pulled out a Glock nine-millimeter pistol and leveled it at Bourges. "Keep quiet," he said in a low growl.

Bourges's skin broke out into a cold sweat.

Chapter 15 *

AFTER INSTRUCTING CARL Jenkins to provide him with a satellite tracking report at twenty-minute intervals, Doheny went up to the conference room. Professor Rosen, Dr. Gaither, and Malcolm Courtland were already seated at the table. So was Everett Nore. The toll of the previous night still showed in Nore's pale skin and the dark pouches under his eyes, but he was sober and appeared to be in control. He shifted his bloodshot eyes away from Doheny and looked down at his coffee cup.

Doheny turned to the others and officially welcomed them. He apologized for the unpleasant circumstances in which they had been contacted and for the severe inconvenience of having their normal routine disrupted at such short notice.

As he spoke, two women from the plant's commissary wheeled a food cart into the room and served steaming trays containing rehydrated steak with mushrooms, baked potatoes, vegetables, rolls, and a slice of hot apple pie. They left after refilling everyone's cup with fresh coffee.

Doheny was so hungry that even the rehydrated vegetables tasted good.

Dr. Frederick Gaither, the obese medical researcher from the Bioelectromagnetic Research Laboratory, scrutinized the contents of the tray in front of him. He frowned and asked, "Are these army rations?"

"I'm afraid so," Doheny said apologetically. "We don't have much choice around here."

Gaither prodded the baked potato with his fork as if it were a laboratory specimen. "I wouldn't eat these tubers if I were you," he warned.

"Why not?" asked Professor Rosen with concern. "They look perfectly good to me."

Gaither cut into his steak and propelled a piece into his mouth before answering. "The army irradiates all of its fresh produce for the sake of preservation. Irradiated produce can keep for months without refrigeration. Marvelous, isn't it?" He beamed and winked. "Trouble is that the radiation also causes some potentially unhealthy chemical reactions in the treated food." He paused to butter a roll. "Years ago at BRL we fed white mice a steady diet of irradiated fruit and vegetables for six months."

"And?" asked Doheny.

"Their digestive tracts hemorrhaged."

NASA engineer Malcolm Courtland, who sat across from Rosen, suddenly lost his appetite and abruptly pushed his chair back from the table.

The conversation in the room was interrupted by a loud buzz from the intercom.

"Tracking report," said Jenkins's small, tinny voice. "Satellite is over open sea above the Java Trench. Position: ten degrees twenty-six minutes south latitude, one hundred sixteen degrees fifteen minutes east longitude."

When the trays had been cleared away, General Stratton and Provost Marshal Earl Clayton entered the room. Following a brief introduction by the general, a grim-faced Clayton took the floor and outlined the security restrictions in effect at the plant. At the end of his speech he asked if there were any questions. There weren't any. He swept his eyes around the table for a moment, then strode toward the door.

"Brusque bastard, isn't he?" Courtland observed—judiciously waiting until the provost marshal had left before offering his appraisal.

"He's just doing his job," Stratton said sternly.

Courtland ran his hand through his short-cropped black hair and said in an exasperated voice, "This morning at the Cape I was literally arrested by two FBI agents, put on a military transport jet, and whisked to this godforsaken place. Now a military policeman tells me I'm a prisoner here and can't even use the phone to tell my wife I won't be home for dinner. Now tell me what this is all about?"

Rosen glanced accusingly at Stratton and Doheny. "Soldiers with guns, no outside communication, no fraternizing with the other people locked up here," he barked. "You've turned this place into a goddamned concentration camp. Why?"

Doheny got up and stared levelly at the new arrivals. "You were brought here because we need your help very badly." He related the events of the past twenty-four hours, explaining how a collision in space had caused the satellite's microwave beam to veer away from the rectenna and create a five-mile-long swath of devastation through the New Mexico desert before shutting down. The trio of specialists listened in tense silence as he recounted his overflight of the irradiated area. Keeping his emotions in check, Doheny went on to describe the discovery of the Roberts family and the condition of their bodies.

"My God," muttered Rosen.

Doheny told them about the early-morning discharge on south Florida, then turned to Stratton and asked if there had been any casualties.

Stratton looked up sharply with a glint of spectacles. He rose from his seat and stepped to the front of the room. "Tonight I learned that the bodies of a young couple were found near a beach house. Specimen samples matched those taken from the Roberts."

The general's voice cut through Doheny like a knife. The satellite had killed seven people so far. How many, he wondered, would die before this was all over?

Before Stratton could return to his seat Doheny asked, "Would you like to brief our colleagues on Project Sunstroke, General, or shall I?"

Stratton's mouth tightened into a thin line. It went against his grain to divulge military secrets to civilians. But he needed their help to repair the satellite. He briefly outlined Project Sunstroke, explaining the solar satellite's potential military use as an offensive/defensive space-based weapons system. When he finished he was met with a stunned silence.

Then Gaither uttered a low whistle. "With all due respect, General, when this hits the fan the mob will want the Pentagon's collective head in a basket."

Rosen's face was reddened and distorted with outrage. He shot question after question at Stratton in an attempt to learn more of the military's scheme.

"I'm not at liberty to give you any more details," said the general, giving the remark a distinctly sharp edge. "This information is all highly classified. I assure you that the decisions regarding Project Sunstroke were made with this nation's best interests in mind."

"Are you serious?" shouted Rosen, contemptuously. "This satellite of yours burned seven innocent people to death. How can *that* possibly serve this country's best interests?"

"Gentlemen," Doheny interrupted, "right now our job is to determine how to safely deactivate the satellite."

Rosen turned sharply to Doheny. "Mike," he said incredulously, "I can't believe you've thrown in with this bunch of warmongers!"

Everett Nore put his hands on the edge of the table and spoke up for the first time that evening. "Professor, Mike Doheny didn't know anything about Sunstroke until late last night," he said in a reasonable tone. "Mike was intentionally kept in the dark so he could effectively promote the civilian nature of the project to the press." He glanced at the others. "Undoubtedly the general and I will have to face some future board of inquiry, and frankly"—he shook his head sadly—"I'm not sure we'll be able to answer some of the questions that will be put to us. . . ." His voice trailed away. "But this is beside the point," he said quickly, firmly. "Presently we should concentrate on the reason why you've been brought here. Let's get on with the conference."

"I think we should reacquaint ourselves with what we're up against," said Doheny. He pulled open a drawer, took out a videocassette, and inserted it into a VCR slot recessed into the middle of the table. A projection TV screen on the far wall sprang to life and a diagram of the solar satellite appeared.

Doheny let the tape run for a few minutes, allowing the group to familiarize themselves with the basic technical aspects of the satellite from launch to geosynchronous orbital insertion. Afterward Doheny switched the VCR off and the screen died. "Well," he said, "this is what we're dealing with. A ten-thousand-ton spacecraft. The most massive man-made object ever put into space. Any comments?"

"If that sucker's solar cell array was set down in New York," observed Courtland, "it would stretch from Thirty-sixth Street to Forty-sixth Street—ten city blocks—or in London from Charing Cross station to well past the Savoy." He grinned. "She's a beautiful bird," he added admiringly.

The intercom buzzed and everyone listened to the tracking report. The satellite was over open sea, twenty-five miles west of Ceram Island. Its position was 3 degrees 6 minutes south latitude, 128 degrees 29 minutes east longitude.

Dr. Frederick Gaither shifted his immense bulk in an effort to get into a more comfortable position. There was a mischievous glint in his eyes. "Mike, I know you're anxious to get down to business, but before we do, I'd like to get something straight. I'm talking about nomenclature here. Just what are we going to call this orbiting enemy? Do we refer to it as 'him' or 'her'?"

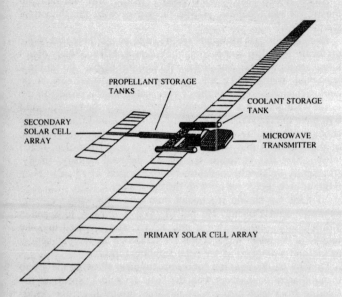

PROPELLANT STORAGE TANKS

COOLANT STORAGE TANK

SECONDARY SOLAR CELL ARRAY

MICROWAVE TRANSMITTER

PRIMARY SOLAR CELL ARRAY

Doheny smiled. He welcomed a little levity to smooth over the rough edges, to help boost the morale. "I'll settle for 'it,' Fred."

"Seriously now," said Gaither in a professional tone, "I believe its sheer size will be our biggest obstacle to overcome. The satellite is so large that specular sunlight reflections from it have hampered optical astronomers at the Hale Observatories in California and at Kitt Peak in Arizona. They've raised hell about it since those solar wings were unfurled."

Stratton nodded solemnly. "Understandable. Before last night's collision sent it into an elliptical orbit the thing had a visual brightness amounting to about one-fifth of the full moon. In subsequent orbits it will become even brighter as it moves closer to the earth." He thought for a moment. "The sight of it could possibly cause panic among the world's populace," he said gravely.

Rosen had scribbled a few calculations on a pad. He looked up. "I don't think so. To a ground observer directly beneath its path the satellite is only visible for a few minutes before sunrise and just after sunset, as it crosses the terminator. Remember, when it's passing low over the night side there's no sunlight to reflect, and on the daylight side the sun outshines it. The thing will be visible during the day, but just barely.''

"Professor," said Doheny, "you've just brought up an important point. The sunlight factor. Judging by that last tracking report, the satellite will be emerging from the earth's shadow and into the sun very soon now. It'll be like stepping out of the deep-freeze and into a blast furnace. There will be a buildup of internal stresses and strains throughout the entire structure, of course, but I'm mainly concerned about the effect on the microwave transmitter. Bear in mind the satellite was never intended to leave sun-synchronous orbit and enter into the earth's shadow for prolonged periods.''

Rosen glanced up from his notes. "Are you talking about cumulative effects?''

Doheny frowned. "Possibly. This afternoon it went from full sun into the shadow, just the reverse of what's happening now.''

"And don't forget this morning," said Rosen. When he saw the puzzled look on Doheny's face, he added, "During the videotape show I made some quick calculations on the satellite's orbital trajectory. They indicate it also crossed the terminator at dawn today, over the Gulf of Mexico or thereabouts.''

Although the conference room was kept at a comfortable temperature of seventy-two degrees Fahrenheit Doheny felt a chill run up his spine. He should have realized earlier that the satellite had crossed the terminator this morning, but at the time he had been too preoccupied with responding to the crisis instead of attempting to analyze it. Also he had been simply too tired to think clearly. Then later on he had spent most of the day concentrating on setting up the Earthnet/SATSCAN operation.

He turned to Stratton. "Do you think the alternating cold and heat activated the klystrons when the satellite was over south Florida?''

The general shook his head. "No," he said adamantly. "They're encased inside the transmitter housing, a thick-walled, heavily insulated structure. You know as well as I that neither solar radiation nor intense cold could penetrate it.''

Doheny kneaded the bridge of his nose. "That's true," he conceded, "but only under normal circumstances." He recalled the sharp vibrations registered by the satellite's impedance sensors just prior to last night's malfunction. "What if the force of the collision ruptured the housing's integrity, exposing the klystrons to the space environment?''

Stratton blinked; he was less sure of himself now. "But the housing was shielded against impact," he stated flatly.

"Against impact with random orbital debris," corrected Doheny. "Not against a deliberate assault by an antisatellite device."

The three specialists were shocked. "Do you mean it was attacked?" asked Courtland skeptically.

"We're investigating the possibility," replied Stratton noncommittally.

When it became apparent the general wouldn't answer any further questions on the subject, the group spent the next few minutes discussing how the satellite's klystron tubes would react if exposed to extreme temperature differences, the solar wind, and micrometeoroids.

Downstairs in the control room Phillips stared anxiously at the microwave systems console before him. It was still blank. He slipped the plastic wrapper off a fresh pack of cigarettes and crumpled it. He played with the wrapper, crumpling it, smoothing it out, crumpling it again. He was agitated, tense, jumpy. He wheeled his chair to face Jenkins, the bearded guidance engineer manning the Earthnet station. "Carl," he said with obvious irritation, "do you really think it'll start up again?"

Jenkins's face was illuminated by the eerie moonglow from the big screen. "Mike thinks so," he said.

"He's been shitting bricks since last night. Running around, double-checking every single component till he's blue in the face. Christ, he's driving me crazy."

"Come off it," Jenkins said with a wry smile. "You're just pissed off because you can't go to that dolly bar again tonight," he teased. "Hey, if they don't wear panties, where do you tuck the dollar bills?"

Phillips waved his arm at Jenkins as if swatting a flying insect, then spun back to his console. He nearly jumped out of his seat when he saw the red lights flashing on his readout board. "Shit!" he yelled. "It's turned on again. Power levels are rising fast." The indicator lights painted his face a deep crimson. He could feel perspiration forming on his face and beneath his shirt.

Jenkins hit the intercom button and informed Doheny in a low, unnatural voice.

Seconds later the control room doors snapped open and Doheny lunged inside. He was followed by Nore, Stratton, Rosen, Courtland, and a panting Gaither.

Doheny studied the active readouts, then looked at the big screen. A strange white shape slowly blossomed under the satellite blip approximately 100 miles north of New Guinea in the Pacific Ocean. The moment the infrared signature appeared the Earthnet computer tripped the klaxon horns and they began braying throughout the plant.

"There it is," Doheny said quietly. "The thing is discharging again. Thank God it's over open ocean. It'll miss New Guinea completely." He turned and shouted to Jenkins, "Kill those klaxons."

A tense, breathless silence filled the room.

In an urgent voice Doheny told Stratton, "General, you'd better get on the hot line and report the position of the beam's signature."

Stratton moved quickly to the Earthnet station, picked up the red scrambler phone, squinted at the big screen, and read off the infrared signature's latitude and longitude.

Doheny told Phillips to activate the satellite infrared screen. "Go to fifty microns. I want a good overview of the vicinity." The others swarmed around the console and watched the focal point of the microwave beam as seen from the satellite.

Suddenly they saw a rapidly moving reddish streak appear at the lower right corner of the screen. It was headed directly for the blinding-white focal point.

"Aircraft," said Jenkins. "I'm certain of it."

"Their on-board electrical systems will go haywire if they get anywhere near that beam," cried Phillips, his voice taut.

Gaither quickly stepped up to the console. "If that plane flies through the microwave beam," he warned, "everyone aboard will be flash-cooked like roasts in an oven. This was one of the worst-case scenarios we hypothesized at BRL when evaluating the satellite's environmental impact."

Doheny turned sharply to Stratton. "General," he yelled, "there's an aircraft heading right for the beam. Warn them *off*!"

Stratton spoke clearly and succinctly into the phone. "Emergency. Emergency. Broadcast an immediate warning to approaching aircraft on target heading."

Doheny returned his gaze to the satellite infrared screen and saw the reddish streak closing in on the fiery spot. He felt nauseated, sick with nervous apprehension. His face seemed set in concrete, the worried grimace hardened there. He stared for a long while at the screen, praying that the plane would change course in time.

Chapter 16 *

QANTAS AIRLINES, FLIGHT 26, a Boeing 787 carrying 258 passengers, sped toward Manila faster than a bullet leaves the muzzle of a .45-caliber pistol. For the past three hours since its departure from Sydney, Australia, the aircraft had been cruising in smooth air at 33,000 feet. The predawn sky above was lit by a sprinkling of stars burning like gemstones. But as the flight passed over the lush islands of Indonesia far below, the sky brightened and took on a tarnished silver hue, the first hint of daylight. Soon the sun would appear in the east, and another long, hot day would begin in the tropics. None of the passengers or crew aboard Flight 26 had any idea of just how hot it was going to get.

In the first-class section stewardess Blair Mitchell, a slim, dark-haired young woman in her early twenties, served a light breakfast of hot tea and croissants with marmalade to those who were awake. The exclusive china cups, saucers, and plates all bore the insignia of Australia's number one airline. As she wheeled the breakfast cart down the aisle Blair observed that some of the passengers continued dozing quietly in the comfortable seats while others were checking their itineraries or reading newspapers.

When she came to the large man in the ill-fitting suit sitting in a third-row window seat, she put on her best smile and took special care in arranging the food on his tray. She had been told by the head stewardess that he was Dr. John Fraser, some kind of nuclear scientist working for the government who was on his way to an important meeting in Japan. For most of the flight he had been studying thick sheaves of paper he had taken from his briefcase. The papers were covered from top to bottom with all kinds of crazy equations. His rumpled suit, his ruddy face with slicked-back hair, and his battered briefcase made him look more like an encyclopedia salesman than a scientist, she thought amusingly. He wasn't much for small talk but at least he was polite. His only attempt at conversation had occurred shortly after takeoff, when he had asked the duration of their stopover at Manila. Deep creases in his forehead had appeared when she told him it would be for about an hour. He obviously was in a hurry to get to that meeting in Tokyo.

Another passenger who rated special service was a girl her own age wearing a bulging, brightly colored maternity dress, sitting in a fifth-row aisle seat. Her name was Sue Waring and she was headed for Manila to join her husband, a computer engineer, who had been recently transferred to the Philippines. Blair asked if she was comfortable, rearranged her back cushion, then served her.

The young stewardess's smile turned cold when she came to the two women who sat four rows behind Sue Waring. She was certain they were lesbians. Several times during the flight she had seen them holding hands. And they sat close to each other, knees touching. One was bleached blond, the other brunette. Both were in their late thirties. Except for their obvious intimacy, the two women appeared perfectly normal. Definitely not stereotypes. Both were very feminine and attractive, even pretty. Blair hurriedly served them and moved on.

Her heart started beating rapidly as she approached the ex-Rugby player sprawled in a left-hand window seat in the last row. She was captivated by Bruce Gibson's rugged good looks, his enormously wide shoulders, and casual demeanor. From a previous chat she had learned he was twenty-seven, single, and had been a forward with Queensland University's Rugby team, the Outbackers, during his college years. Presently he was employed by a mammoth international realty firm. He was en route to the Philippines to assess a tract of undeveloped land along Subic Bay, about forty kilometers northwest of Manila.

The only thing she didn't like about Bruce Gibson was that he tended to drink too much. Since takeoff he had consumed two Wallabys and four beers, and now he wanted his favorite early-morning eye-opener, a Bloody Mary. But the strong uneven features of his tanned, youthful face and the way his suit clung to his powerful athlete's body were just too irresistible. She had been fantasizing about him since he first stepped aboard.

"Good morning," greeted Blair, nervously.

"Well, hello," said Gibson with a wolfish grin. "How're you doing?"

She served him with exaggerated care, doing her best to engage in meaningful conversation.

Dr. John Fraser, the VIP in the ill-fitting tweed suit sitting in the third row, sipped his tea, then ate the croissant slowly, dabbing bits of marmalade on the pieces as he broke them with his hands. Fraser had been appointed by ATECH, a multinational scientific consortium, to head the new accelerator project on the outskirts of Canberra in the Australian Capital Territory. When completed, the accelerator would probe the structure of matter and shed light on how the universe was born. Although the ATECH machine was designed to be a smaller version of America's Superconducting Super Collider, it would utilize an improved magnetic system to push the protons to a higher energy level of 12,000 giga-electron volts.

Fraser was fifty-seven years old. He knew that construction of the new machine would be a five- to eight-year job, which meant that it would probably be the last big project he would ever tackle. As it turned out, this was the way he wanted it. Upon graduating from the Australian National University with a doctorate in nuclear physics, he became a junior member of the team that built the CERN 500 GeV machine in Geneva, Switzerland. He'd progressed in thirty years from 500 GeV to 12,000 GeV. He believed it was a fair enough achievement for a lifetime's work. After the project's completion he'd be content to leave nuclear physics to younger men, primarily because the majority of the problems these days were political and financial in nature rather than scientific.

He was flying to Japan to negotiate a contract for the vast amount of steel work needed to build the tunnel that would house the accelerator. The tunnel was to be built in the shape of a circular racetrack, forty-eight kilometers around. This called for a lot of steel, and Fraser had the unenviable task of bargaining with Japan, Inc. He dreaded going to Tokyo because he knew they would work him to death. They'd meet him at the airport, straight off the plane, and go right to the office for a business conference. There wouldn't be any time to wind down. They were such keen fellows.

He had hoped for a longer stopover in Manila to rest up for the ordeal to come. But the stewardess had told him it would be only for an hour or so. If he was lucky he'd be able to nap sometime between now and his arrival in Japan. He could sleep like a log in his home in the countryside outside Canberra, but sleep never came easily in big cities. He wondered how he'd fare tonight in Tokyo. He glanced enviously at the passenger in the seat next to him, a portly, middle-aged businessman who was snoring softly.

In the mood for more tea, Fraser looked around for the stewardess. He spotted her chatting with the handsome young chap in the back row. He smiled to himself, slipped on his reading glasses, and took out the early-morning edition of the *Australian Telegraph* from his briefcase. His eyes fell on the headline: "Is America's Giant Satellite Lost in Space?" Scanning the article, he read that some Africans had sighted the thing last night, shortly after sunset.

How typical of the Yanks to build something so huge and powerful, he thought wryly, only to lose control of it in such a short period of time. He remembered when NASA's 100-ton *Skylab* space station was allowed to reenter the earth's atmosphere in 1979 because the necessary funds to boost it into a higher orbit were lacking. Portions of it survived reentry and rained down on southwestern Australia. Fortunately no one was killed. He recalled how NASA had tried to make light of the situation by offering a $10,000 reward to anyone who salvaged a piece of the spacecraft.

As a physicist Fraser was aware of the hazardous microwave intensities generated by the solar satellite. He thought it was very fortunate indeed that no one had been injured during the satellite's malfunction.

Sue Waring arched her back as a new pain shot through her swollen abdomen. Her hand gripped the armrest and she breathed sharply through clenched teeth. In a few moments the pain lessened and she sighed with relief.

"Are you all right?" asked the short, balding young salesman seated beside her.

"Yes, I think so," Sue said, getting back her breath. "Little junior just decided to exercise a bit." She opened her compact and applied powder and lipstick to her face.

When Sue had first boarded the plane she had been squeezed into the window seat. The young man in the aisle seat next to her had observed her difficulty and offered to change places to give her more room to stretch out. She had gratefully accepted. But throughout the flight he had seemed overly concerned and too solicitous regarding her condition. Every few minutes he would ask how she was, if she needed anything. He was becoming a damn nuisance. She wished he would just mind his own business.

She rummaged around for a magazine, any magazine, found one, opened it up, and pretended to read. She hoped the annoying passenger would get off at Manila.

Four rows behind Sue Waring sat Madeleine Brown and Shelley Hunter. They were traveling to Japan together for a holiday, something they had wanted to do for a long time. They had skimped and saved for months to be able to afford the trip. Madeleine, the blond, was a dental hygienist while Shelley worked as a secretary for a large construction outfit in Sydney. They had met nearly a year ago, when Shelley had gone to a new dentist for a checkup.

Both women were married at the time but neither of them had any children. Their relationship, as they referred to it, had begun almost immediately after Shelley sat down in the hygienist's chair. It had been something automatic, a strong mutual attraction that both women felt. There was nothing masculine about either of them. Quite the contrary, it was each other's complete femininity that they found so desirable.

When they began their tender experimenting, neither considered it infidelity. To them it was just plain fun. With their fingertips, as lightly as possible, the tips of their nails barely touching, they took turns slowly tracing an outline from shoulders all the way to the crotch.

"Do you like this?"

"Mmmm."

"How does this feel?"

"I'm not sure."

"How about right here?"

"Ummm. Definitely."

They explored, feeling, touching, with slight feathery contacts. Sometimes they spent a whole hour not moving, just holding, gently pressing their bodies together. They soon discovered one another's preferences, mentally filing them away for future selfish and unselfish use.

Two months later, after intimate encounters in a dozen different motels throughout Sydney, they kissed, openmouthed, for the first time. For some reason this act was the stimulus that made them decide to divorce their husbands and live together. It meant the end of the deceptive double standard they had been living. Shortly afterward they moved into a pleasant apartment on Strathfarrar Lane and began a loving, lasting relationship.

During the flight the two women talked quietly, read, held hands, and snoozed. This morning both were ravenous and ate their breakfasts quickly. Shelley glanced out the window and saw the hazy dark outline of the northwestern tip of New Guinea approaching far below. She excitedly pointed it out to Madeleine. The sky above was rapidly brightening, and both women anxiously awaited the sunrise.

Bruce Gibson, the ex–Rugby player from Queensland, was scared to death of flying. He tried not to think of how high they were nor did he look out the window. Also the tight quarters inside the plane made him uneasy. Earlier, when he had walked through the tourist section on his way to the first-class compartment, he had been dismayed by the sight of all those people packed together, three abreast. He had been dreading this flight for the past few weeks.

He was grateful for the pleasant distraction that Blair Mitchell provided. As she bent over to place his Bloody Mary and a plate of croissants on his tray, he surreptitiously laid his hand on her thigh. Her short, tight-fitting uniform accentuated her ample breasts and long legs. He wondered if the two of them could slip away to someplace private during their stopover in Manila.

Gibson worked for CIE Hoshita, a Japanese firm that had plunged into the Australian real estate marked over a decade ago. Through the years they had quietly bought up much of Queensland's beautiful shoreline. On the face of it, Japan's solid investments should have been welcome. Yet over the years Queenslanders had protested that they had become a service class of waiters and cabdrivers for the wealthy Asians. The final blow to Australian pride came when Japan's Ministry of Trade and Industry encouraged CIE Hoshita to build a city for retired Japanese expatriates on the eastern Gold Coast. Angry Australians organized an anti-Japanese protest march to stop the project. The realty firm was forced to abandon its plans for the retirement city. Since then they'd maintained a low profile, yet still continued to acquire much of the Gold Coast without attracting undue attention by hiring young, acceptable native Australians to act as their brokers.

Gibson was one of their most successful agents. Australian landowners who were reluctant to deal with Japanese brokers were happy to bargain with one of their fellow countrymen, especially a sports celebrity like Gibson. Recently CIE Hoshita wanted to buy up desirable land in the Philippines, another location where anti-Japanese sentiment ran high because of World War II. They decided to send the ex–Rugby player there to handle the transaction. He was offered a handsome commission, an amount large enough to get him to fly on a plane.

Gibson gulped his drink, then leaned close to Blair and whispered his proposition to her. Not surprisingly, she consented.

On the flight deck Captain Peter Daniels silently monitored the confusing array of pointers, dials, and blinking indicator lights surrounding him. He was a tall man with a seamed, weatherworn face and sharp blue eyes. His stomach rumbled and he thought half-consciously of breakfast. On an early flight like 26 he never bothered to eat at home. The extra time was better spent in bed with his wife. Instead he usually had one of the stewardesses bring him snacks. He wondered where Blair Mitchell was.

He glanced at the temperature indicator and saw it was *minus* forty degrees Centigrade outside the aircraft, a paralyzing, deathly cold. "Tom," he said, "give me the FOD."

Behind him, Flight Engineer Thomas Breen, a nervous thickset man, reported their fuel over destination was precisely 22,512 kilograms.

Captain Daniels grunted his acknowledgment. He had just entered the figure in the flight log when First Officer Geoffrey Taylor, the pale, thin young crewman sitting beside him, said in a mildly excited voice, "Captain, we've got a bogey at two o'clock."

Daniels peered out the curving flight deck window and saw a huge, strange light shimmering in the predawn sky above. For an instant he wondered what it was, then he remembered the TV news reports. "That's the runaway Yank satellite they were talking about on the telly."

"God, it's bright," murmured Flight Engineer Breen.

First Officer Taylor turned to the captain. "Think we should explain what it is to the passengers? They'll have spotted it, too, you know."

Daniels shook his head. "Most of them are probably still asleep. Won't do any good to wake 'em up."

As they talked, the sun slowly rose above the ocean horizon, a globule of orange fire flattened by refraction. The satellite was still visible, although somewhat fainter because of competition from the rising sun. Below them, the northwest tip of New Guinea slid past, and then they were over open sea.

Suddenly an alarm sounded on the flight deck. Simultaneously, on a radio panel in front of the throttles, an amber light winked on. The alarm and light signaled a special call on the Emcal radio system through which an airliner could be contacted individually, as if by private telephone. Each aircraft had its own code.

Daniels thumbed his microphone button and acknowledged, "This is Qantas Twenty-six. Over."

"Flight Twenty-six, this is Qantas dispatcher, Manila." Sudden crackling static erupted from the speaker and the message started to fade in and out. ". . . urgent . . . make an immediate course . . . danger . . ." Then the words were completely lost in a burst of shrieking static.

Daniels felt beads of perspiration forming on his face. He thumbed the microphone button again. "Manila Operations, this is Qantas Twenty-six. Repeat message. Over."

Nothing but high-pitched static came over the speaker.

Without warning the pointers and dials before them went wild. Indicator lights flashed on and off across the readout board, then dimmed out.

As a stunned Captain Daniels helplessly watched the dying instrument panel in front of him, a part of his mind was aware of how warm it was becoming on the flight deck.

He depressed the microphone button, his thumb reddening from the pressure, and said in a calm voice, "Mayday, mayday. This is Qantas Twenty-six. We have a failure of all on-board electrical systems. Over."

His distress call was answered with another crash of static.

Throughout the aircraft ceiling lights flickered, startling the passengers, most of whom were awake by now. Some remarked about the lights while others complained about the heat.

In the first-class section Sue Waring felt uncomfortably warm. She hoped she wasn't coming down with some kind of virus. Since becoming pregnant she worried about catching the flu. She was relieved when she heard the other passengers talking about the heat.

Dr. John Fraser had been watching the strange light in the dawn sky. He also realized it was the American satellite. Now he took off his coat and loosened his tie. He wiped his sweating face with a handkerchief and wondered what was wrong with the plane's air-conditioning unit.

Several rows behind, Madeleine Brown and Shelley Hunter used magazines to fan themselves, but it didn't seem to help. It just kept getting hotter and hotter.

In the back of the compartment, former Rugby player Bruce Gibson gulped his Bloody Mary, then turned to Blair Mitchell, the young stewardess, and said, "Hey, tell those guys in the cockpit to turn up the air conditioning. It's stifling in here." He took off his tie and partially unbuttoned his shirt. He was becoming panicky.

Blair fanned herself with one of the plastic trays from her breakfast cart and looked up at the flickering lights. "Odd," she said. "We've never had any trouble like this before."

In a few moments the heat was seething, coming in waves. Passengers were standing in the aisles, pulling off their clothes, shouting for help.

Breathing rapidly, sweating profusely, Dr. Fraser heard an odd clicking sound coming from nearby. He glanced out the window at the satellite glinting in the early-morning sun. He recalled that its purpose was to convert sunlight into microwaves. No, it can't be! he thought wildly. Suddenly he knew what was happening to them.

Madeleine Brown and Shelley Hunter frantically peeled off each other's sweat-soaked clothing. They felt faint, but above all, frightened. Both looked up in horror as the overhead lights dimmed and went out, plunging the aircraft interior into semi-darkness; the early-morning sun was too low on the horizon to provide sufficient illumination. Despite the incredibly intense heat, they embraced, holding one another tightly.

Drenched in perspiration, Sue Waring desperately clawed at her blouse. She tore it off and flung it on the floor. But she was still too hot. Then she leaned forward as a new, not-to-be-ignored spasm of pain pulsed through her abdomen. My God, she thought, not now. She gritted her teeth and grabbed the armrest. The pain was so agonizing that she screamed.

For one second there was a silence in which no one moved or said anything, the only sound being the steady background whine of the jet engines.

Then it began. There was no sense, no pattern, only frenzied madness and confusion. Sue Waring's scream produced a mass exodus from seats. People pushed, shouted at, and kicked each other. Someone punched the half-naked, balding young salesman who had annoyed Sue earlier. He had been standing in the aisle, pulling off his clothes. Now he lay prostrate on the floor, bleeding.

With great effort, Dr. Fraser slowly rose from his seat. He was determined to reach the flight deck to warn the pilot to steer the plane away from the satellite's microwave beam. Just as he got to his feet, an elbow bashed his cheek. Then someone slammed into his side, knocking him back down.

In the rear of the compartment Bruce Gibson couldn't stand the heat any longer. He was obsessed with the idea of getting outside, breathing the cool air. He grabbed Blair's breakfast cart and, straining mightily, hurled it again and again at the plexiglass window next to his seat.

"Stop it!" screeched Blair. "Stop it!" She tried to reach Gibson's arms but the narrowness of the aisle and the intervening seat prevented her.

At that moment, a mosaic of fractures appeared in the window. Gibson battered the glass several more times with the heavy cart before it blew out with the din of a thunderclap. Explosive decompression had occurred. Shocked, Gibson dropped the cart and fell back onto the seat, clutching the armrests with all his strength, gasping for breath. With a roar of tornado force, the air inside the plane—until now maintained at normal pressure— swept through the open window into the high-altitude near-vacuum outside, creating a horrific suction. Gibson managed to keep himself from being pulled out the opening.

Blair Mitchell was not so fortunate. She flew through the air and was sucked out the window, her flesh ripping against the razor-sharp pieces of plexiglass. She was pulled out with such force that her body was dismembered in a cloud of rich arterial blood. Every loose object—magazines, discarded clothing, luggage, teapots— swept after her.

Throughout the plane, emergency compartments above each seat automatically snapped open and blue oxygen masks sprang out, each one connected by a short hose to a central oxygen supply.

Although the aircraft's interior filled with the savagely biting, thin icy air, the heat inside continued to build. All of the passengers now lay gasping on the floor or in their seats, dying, the skin blistering all over their bodies.

As he lay motionless on his seat, Dr. John Fraser could feel the microwaves thickening his blood, burdening his heart, slowing his brain. His hand made a feeble move toward the oxygen mask dangling before him, then fell lifeless. As the fluids within him became heated to the boiling point his oozing body slowly curled into the fetal position.

Sue Waring had become one great blister, thrashing about on her seat. Then she went limp and contracted into a ball as both she and the unborn child inside her died.

Four rows behind her, Madeleine Brown and Shelley Hunter lay writhing in agony, their limbs entwined. A moment passed and both women's hearts mercifully stopped beating.

In the back, Bruce Gibson let out a deep sigh and finally released his grip on the armrest. His lifeless body slowly, spasmodically moved toward the broken, jagged window, the external near-vacuum drawing him out to follow Blair Mitchell.

On the flight deck Captain Peter Daniels made a gurgling sound and pitched forward, arms stiffly outstretched, his teeth clenched in a rictus grin. Just before he died, his clutching, insensate hands struck the control column with surprising force, sending the aircraft into a steep, screaming dive.

Minutes later, Flight 26, a metal coffin containing the burned corpses of its passengers and crew, slammed into the calm waters of the Pacific Ocean 150 miles north of New Guinea. At the moment of impact the fuselage disintegrated aft of the flight deck, both wings broke away, and the tail assembly tore free and tumbled in the air before crashing into the sea. The flight deck section and the tail assembly, both somewhat intact, rapidly filled with seawater and sank. Large fragments from the fuselage and wings, light and buoyant due to their honeycomb structure, floated on the surface.

In a few days severed body parts and other debris from the wreckage would wash up on the picturesque beaches along the northern shore of New Guinea.

Chapter 17 *

DOHENY FELT AS though he had been kicked in the stomach. He fought an impulse to pound the top of the microwave systems console with his fists to vent the anguish twisting his guts. Despite the multimillion-dollar Earthnet "doomwatch" system, they had been powerless to save the plane. Once again he had to stand by and watch people die. He looked away from the infrared screen and lowered his eyes.

Professor Rosen frowned and spread his hands. "The general's warning should have gotten through in time," he growled. "Why didn't they change course?"

"They were too close to the beam," snapped Doheny. "The message was probably drowned in static. The microwaves are of sufficient strength to interfere with radio communications."

Nore approached Doheny. "You were right about the satellite, Mike," he said. "The microwave transmitter discharged the moment it came out into the sun."

Doheny nodded, grateful for the opportunity to turn his thoughts to the purely technical aspects of the crisis. "There's a pattern here, Everett, I'm certain of it. Remember, last night the transmitter shut down by itself after functioning for about thirty minutes. The same thing happened this morning. If the transmitter housing had been fractured by the collision, then solar radiation poured into it, causing the klystron tubes to overheat and turn off. They're probably heating up right now."

"And when the satellite enters the earth's shadow," said NASA engineer Malcolm Courtland, "the klystrons cool down. Then as it crosses the terminator into full sunlight, they begin transmitting again until they overheat." He shrugged. "Makes sense."

"I think we've just identified the mechanism at work behind these microwave discharges," stated Doheny. "We'll know if our theory is correct''—he looked at his watch—''in about twenty minutes from now.''

Phillips swiveled around in his seat. ''But what about the on-board coolant system? Liquid nitrogen should be pumping through the klystron tubes and cooling them down.''

''Thank God it's *not* working,'' Doheny said with emphasis. ''Otherwise the satellite wouldn't shut off until it reached the night side.''

Dr. Frederick Gaither turned to Doheny. ''Now that we know the sequence, we should be able to predict the location of the next discharge.''

''Exactly,'' said Doheny as he studied the big Mercator map on the far wall.

Across the room General Dean Stratton put down the hot-line phone. ''I've just been informed,'' he announced solemnly, ''that the downed aircraft was a Qantas airliner out of Sydney bound for Tokyo.'' He paused, then said gravely, ''There were two hundred fifty-eight passengers plus the flight crew aboard. The Manila controllers confirmed that the aircraft ditched in the Pacific.'' His left hand plucked blindly and persistently at one of the shiny buttons on his tunic. ''They died quickly, humanely,'' he added.

Doheny's mind blurred out of focus. He slumped down into the nearest chair. He felt hollow and sick inside. He rubbed his face, pressing heavily against it.

Everett Nore jabbed a finger at Stratton's tunic. ''Can you imagine what it must have been like inside that plane?'' he asked in an intense half whisper, staring savagely. ''Everything was normal for a while. Then it started getting hot. Unbearably hot. No way to cool off, no place to run. The heat kept building and building inside their bodies, roasting them. They must have gone crazy up there, General.'' He shook his head. ''No, sir, they didn't die 'humanely.'''

Startled more by the fierce look in Nore's eyes than by his words, Stratton stepped back and blinked. His hand unconsciously moved to the end of his tie. He clamped the end between his fore and middle finger, and began working the point of the cloth in under his thumbnail. His hand froze when he saw Nore watching the movement.

''You want to save that killer satellite, don't you?'' accused Nore. ''You intend to repair it and test it, as if nothing had happened.''

Stratton's eyes narrowed behind the thick lenses of his glasses. "It's the logical course of action, Mr. Nore, for both of us."

"Perhaps," Nore said angrily. "But the *humane* thing to do is to destroy it." He strode toward the exit and left the room.

Doheny got up from his chair and stood there, leaning against the console. "Two hundred fifty-eight passengers," he murmured. "If only—"

"Mike!" barked Professor Rosen. "Stop it. It's not your fault that it discharged. No one's blaming you." Doheny smiled weakly, and Rosen burst out, "Self-incrimination is a luxury you can't afford. We've got a lot of work to do." Rosen clenched his little fist and squeezed his fingers together emptily. "We've got to put that thing out of action, Mike."

At that very instant the satellite's infrared signature on the screen faded and disappeared. As predicted, the satellite stopped transmitting.

Doheny stared at the screen above him for a long moment. It was obvious in retrospect that the klystron tubes would overheat and shut down due to solar radiation. Was there anything else, Doheny wondered, that would prove obvious in retrospect?

Upstairs in the guest lounge everyone sat at the mess tables discussing the latest outburst from the klaxon alarms as they ate their evening meal.

Diane Bradford put down her fork and lightly touched the hand of Andy Johnson, her TV cameraman, a lean but muscular blond-haired man in his middle twenties who sat beside her. Needing an ally, she told him of her plan to privately interview Mike Doheny.

"I need your help on this, Andy," she whispered.

Johnson glanced at her nervously. "It sounds too dangerous, Diane." He indicated the Video News correspondent sitting across from them who was trying to eat with his left hand because his right arm was in a cast. "If you ask me, I think those grunts broke his arm last night on purpose just to show us they mean business," he whispered.

Diane closed her eyes and sighed softly. Her recruitment of Andy was proving to be more difficult than she had thought.

She brushed her leg against his and said quietly, "We've been through all this. No one's going to get hurt. All I need is a little, simple diversion tomorrow when they take us to the showers. You won't get into any trouble." She squeezed his hand. "I promise."

He hesitated for a moment, then nodded. "Okay, you can count me in."

Diane smiled sweetly, drew him to her, and kissed him lightly on the cheek.

Alone in his office, Everett Nore unlocked the top left drawer of his desk, pulled it open, and took out a fresh bottle of Scotch and a tumbler. He sloshed two fingers into the glass and gulped it with a snap of his wrist. He poured another and sat back to ponder the latest first-order event in the Sunstroke crisis.

Nore was certain that the President and his cabinet had somehow managed to keep the earlier deaths under wraps and out of the news. But tonight's Australian airliner disaster will be impossible to cover up, he thought. The best anyone could do was to try to pass it off as an accident, or the result of a terrorist attack. He wondered what Stratton and his Pentagon friends had told Manila Qantas Operations to get them to put out a warning to all air traffic. A wind shear alert? Hurricane warning?

He recalled his conversation with Stratton in the control room. He had shaken up the man and the memory of it made him grin. And he had found out something he had suspected all along: the general was intent on salvaging the blessed satellite instead of disabling it. In addition, Stratton had hinted he wanted his support. That bit about it being "the logical course of action for both of us" also contained the carrot. Nore sighed deeply. If the President and his men somehow kept the lid on the whole sordid mess, and it was a big "if," and presuming the satellite was brought under control, then the Sunstroke project could go ahead as planned. Nore Space Industries would be awarded the biggest contract in the history of aerospace to build several larger, heavily shielded versions of the satellite.

However, at this time, backing Stratton was risky, dangerous. Nore wasn't at all sure they could repair the satellite, or even if they should try. But the prospect of a history-making contract nagged at him.

The head of NSI swallowed his drink and stared at the beautiful amber liquid inside the squat, square-faced bottle in front of him. He wondered how many successful decisions he had made throughout his career while under its influence.

Inside the control room General Stratton finished copying the last of the instrument readings into his logbook, then looked apprehensively at his watch. The President should be receiving the EMCON message on the Qantas plane crash any time now, he thought.

The general told Doheny he'd be in his office for the next couple of hours and left the room. He walked down the corridor and took an elevator up to the first floor. As he approached the door to his office an MP stationed there saluted. Stratton returned the salute, went in, and, not wanting to be disturbed, locked the door behind him and sat down at his desk.

He glanced speculatively at the projection TV screen and miniature television camera mounted on the wall in front of him. It was a two-way video link with the White House and the U.S. Space Defense Command within Cheyenne Mountain, having been installed by the same air force technicians from Kirtland who had set up the Earthnet/SATSCAN system at the plant. The TV communications equipment utilized a military satellite to relay the signals to and from Washington, D.C., and Colorado. After checking to see that it was operating properly, Stratton tried to relax and collect his thoughts.

He wished they had been able to avert the Qantas airliner mishap. It would have made it easier for him to present his case to the President for continuing with Project Sunstroke. Presently the best he could hope for was to dissuade his commander in chief from taking any rash action against the satellite. He had been counting on Nore's full support in the matter. Therefore he had been both surprised and disappointed by Nore's emotional outburst in the control room. He found it difficult to understand why a major U.S. defense contractor should be so overwrought by the deaths of some foreigners. After all, NSI had been manufacturing ballistic missile systems for nearly two decades. Did Nore actually believe these weapons of war would never be used, that they were just meant to be stockpiled over the years?

As a general of the United States Air Force, Stratton had devoted his entire life to the conduct and strategy of war. He had lived each day with the possibility that he would have to send men to die in some remote corner of the world. Long ago he had learned to view death as a numerical abstraction to be programmed into a computer for evaluation as either a tactical loss or gain. It was the only way to preserve his sanity. He would have liked the civilians here at the plant to be equally disciplined. He thought of Doheny and the way he had been torturing himself over these first-order events. It made Stratton sad. Doheny was an excellent engineer, and he possessed a fine, intuitive mind. It was a pity, he thought, that Doheny and the others were being taken to the edge of the abyss and forced to look over the edge without being prepared for it in advance. Only careful military training could have provided them with the strength and ability to see beyond the present crisis to the magnificent opportunity for America that lay ahead.

After jotting down some notes General Stratton waited expectantly for the White House teleconference to begin.

Chapter 18 *

WHEN THE PHONE rang in President Kendall's private
study on the second floor of the White House, there were five men
sitting amid the litter of a late dinner. Kendall, National Security
Adviser Jack Conley, chairman of the Joint Chiefs General Willis
Thompson, Secretary of Defense Hugh Fitzpatrick and FBI
Director Harold Sorensen had dined at the long teakwood coffee
table. The President had barely touched his food, only drinking
coffee and nibbling a slice of bread while the others ate a full
meal. They had been discussing a long-term strategy for maintaining a tight lid of secrecy on Project Sunstroke once the crisis
was over.

Kendall had the phone off its cradle before it could ring twice.
"Maybe the team in New Mexico has found a way to stop the
satellite," he said, explaining the reason for his haste.

His face dropped slightly in disappointment when he heard the
voice at the other end. Then he stiffened and listened intently. The
call was from Russell Tanner, the head of Langley, in response to
the President's earlier inquiry regarding the status of the Russians'
antisatellite program. The DCI informed Kendall that he had just
received a report from one of his operatives, a mole planted at the
Plesetsk Space Center, their counterpart to Vandenberg Air Force
Base. According to the report, they launched a rocket three days
ago bearing a classified payload, which the agent suspected as
being a stealth kinetic-kill vehicle. Shortly after launch, control of
the spacecraft was turned over to the Flight Control Center at
Kaliningrad, a suburb fifteen miles northeast of Moscow. This
installation oversaw Russia's military space missions.

Kendall's face was drawn. His grip tightened on the receiver.
"You told me their stealth ASAT program was still in the
development stage," he said angrily. "Now you're informing me

that they put one in orbit several days ago? Why didn't we know about this earlier?''

The voice in the receiver explained that security at the Plesetsk facility had become unusually heavy, preventing his operative from reporting sooner. ''It was pretty rough for her to transmit this data tonight,'' said Tanner, his voice taut. ''Because of the urgency of your request, I pushed a little too hard. Her cover has been jeopardized. We're trying to get her out.''

President Kendall expressed his concern for the agent's safe escape and thanked Tanner for the information. After he hung up, he relayed the DCI's report to his advisers.

''If I may say so, Mr. President,'' said FBI Director Harold Sorensen, ''it seems our intelligence operation needs to be overhauled.''

Kendall ignored the remark. ''Does anyone have something more useful to say?'' he asked sharply, with a hint of sarcasm.

Jack Conley, the national security adviser, pressed the palms of his large hands onto the polished surface of the coffee table. ''Sir, it appears the Russians stepped up development of their stealth ASAT program with the intention of deploying it against our satellite. The time frame we're talking about here is too coincidental to support any other hypothesis. They launched their ASAT only two days before the scheduled activation of our satellite. And last night our NORAD scanners at Cheyenne Mountain detected a suspicious echo just prior to the satellite's malfunction. We've already heard expert testimony from General Stratton concerning the nature of the 'radar ghost.' He believed it was a stealth ASAT.'' He lifted his hands from the table and spread them, palms upward. ''And we now know that Russia put one in orbit.''

General Willis Thompson, the chairman of the Joint Chiefs of Staff, spoke next. He thrust his rugged jaw forward and said in a voice that boomed through the room, ''Mr. President, there's only one conclusion we can draw from the CIA report.''

''Which is?'' asked Kendall, still frowning by the phone.

''Obviously the Russians tried to destroy our satellite with their new ASAT,'' declared Thompson. ''Clearly this is a vicious, provocative act of aggression against the United States. Even worse, it could be a prelude to war.''

FBI Director Sorensen locked his hands behind his head, leaned back on the sofa, and closed his protuberant frog eyes. ''Did our Kremlin friends want to take out the satellite,'' he said thoughtfully, ''or was it their intention to make the thing go haywire and fire its beam at random so the rest of the world would turn against us?''

General Thompson shook his head. ''No, I don't think this was the case.'' He shifted his position to face the president. ''Their stealth kinetic-kill vehicle was probably the most destructive long-range antisatellite weapon in their arsenal. There is no doubt they intended to completely disable our satellite to prevent us from using it against them when they launch their first strike.''

Defense Secretary Hugh Fitzpatrick ran the long, bony fingers of this hands through his disheveled white hair and said, ''Or the Russians may have acted out of sheer desperation to protect their own national security.'' His voice was almost as harsh on the ears as the sound of gravel spilling down a metal chute. ''If they know about Project Sunstroke,'' he added, ''then our satellite up there probably intimidated the hell out of them.''

The President paled noticeably. All of these thoughts had crossed his mind during his phone conversation with the DCI. Each analysis had one common denominator, which he now voiced. ''I take it, then,'' he said with a note of finality, ''all of you are in agreement that the Russians were the ones who attacked our satellite last night? That NORAD's 'radar ghost' was actually their stealth ASAT?''

The four men sitting around the coffee table nodded.

Kendall held his hands behind his back and started pacing the study. He looked tired. The crushing pressure of the crisis and his attempt to throw off the press by keeping his White House appointments schedule as usual were grinding him down. President Kendall had once confided to Jack Conley, his national security adviser, that he wished there were two presidents, like in the old story about every ocean liner having two captains—one to socialize with the passengers and one to run the ship.

He stopped pacing and turned to the advisers. Cupping his chin with his right hand, he said in a strangely calm voice, ''What I'd like to know is, how did they find out about Sunstroke? We were so damn careful to keep everyone off the track. It was all set up to look like an innocent solar energy project. We were even going to supply a whole city with electricity. How the hell did they find out? *How?*''

''Sir, if we were able to penetrate their space center at Plesetsk,'' said Jack Conley gravely, ''then it stands to reason they may have infiltrated Cape Canaveral and examined our satellite before it was launched. One of their trained experts could have spotted certain modifications that were not part of the original publicized design.''

"Or they could have infiltrated the Pentagon,'' interjected Hugh Fitzpatrick.

General Thompson gave Fitzpatrick a look of ill-concealed anger tinged with outrage. "Impossible,'' he bellowed. "Our security is too tight to allow such a thing. I can assure you there are no Russian agents in the Pentagon.'' His eyes darkened into narrow slits as he regarded the defense secretary. "I believe it is far more likely that someone in the Defense Department leaked the information,'' he said in an accusatory tone.

"Only a handful of key defense personnel had access to the knowledge, General,'' Fitzpatrick shot back. "While on the other hand, dozens of Pentagon employees have been briefed on Sunstroke.''

"Will, Fitz,'' said the President, exasperated. "This argument is pointless. There'll be plenty of time to pass the buck later. Let's return to the main issue here, namely the Russian assault on our satellite.'' Thompson and Fitzpatrick became silent, pensive, and Kendall continued. "At this time I have to agree with Will: beyond a doubt their attack was an act of aggression.'' He carefully pondered his next words. "Their action demands an appropriate response from us. Let's give this some thought.''

General Thompson sat bolt upright on the sofa, his face stern. "Mr. President, we must be prepared for a possible first strike. I strongly urge that Trident Groups Alpha and Beta and other nuclear SSBN submarines be ordered to Condition Yellow via the ELF transmitter. In addition, all other air, land, and sea forces should go to alert-level-four status—one step above routine. Of course the Russians may detect the change of status of our strategic forces, but this could work to our advantage. It would tell them in no uncertain terms that we're on our guard.''

The President listened carefully to the chairman of the Joint Chiefs' recommendations. Outwardly, Kendall appeared slim, handsome, at ease. But inwardly he was anything but cool or calm at the prospect of pushing the world to the brink of nuclear war over the Sunstroke crisis. His eyes were screwed tight as if to shut out the vision of a world in radioactive ruins.

The anguished President was about to ask Jack Conley for an opinion when suddenly someone rapped sharply on the door to the study.

"Come in,'' shouted Kendall.

The door opened and an Army Signal Corps officer entered. He walked briskly to Kendall and handed him a sealed EMCON printout. When the courier left, Kendall muttered, "This had better be some good news," and tore open the message.

He glanced quickly at the first few sentences, then lowered his hands and looked up. Holding the flimsy printout as if it were a small dead thing, he said softly, "I don't believe it." Stunned, he grasped the arms of a nearby chair for support. "The satellite discharged again. This time it shot down an Australian airliner with two hundred fifty-eight people aboard." He passed the EMCON message around.

Kendall closed his eyes, and with a visible effort got himself in hand. "I think we should go to the Crisis Room," he said quietly.

Within a few minutes a gray veil of cigarette smoke hung above the large oval table inside the National Security Council conference room at the West Wing of the White House. It was just past nine P.M. Washington time.

FBI Director Harold Sorensen tapped the glowing end of his cigarette over a heavy crystal ashtray. "Mr. President," he said confidently with a crooked grin, "we've just had a lucky break."

Kendall stared at him, then slowly shook his head. He indicated the EMCON printout laying on the middle of the table. "You call this . . . this catastrophe lucky?"

"Not exactly, sir," said Sorensen quickly, his smile gone. "What I mean is that we anticipated the satellite would discharge again, possibly on foreign soil. We were right. But unlike the other first-order events, we're in the clear on this one. The plane went down at sea. There were no witnesses. As far as the world is concerned this is just another unfortunate aircraft accident. These mishaps occur every month of the year. We don't have to worry about smoothing it over."

Kendall sank back into his chair. He had to admit the man's cold analysis was correct. But the thought brought on a conflict of conscience, which quickly turned to anger. He desperately needed to blame someone, anyone. "This accident shouldn't have happened." There was cold fury in his voice. His hard eyes swept over the men at the table. "I thought our people in New Mexico had some type of distant early-warning system in effect. Why didn't it work?" he demanded.

"That's what I want to know," said General Thompson brusquely.

President Kendall turned to his national security adviser. "Jack, if I remember correctly the plant now has a direct video link to this room. Contact them right now. I want to sound out Dean Stratton on this.''

Jack Conley went to the console beneath the bank of TV screens and opened the circuit to the solar power plant. A light showed on his control console and Stratton's image appeared on the huge color screen. ''General Stratton is standing by, sir,'' Conley announced to the President.

Kendall shifted his seat to face the television screen. He got right to the point. ''How did this tragedy off the coast of New Guinea happen, Dean? I thought your 'doomwatch' equipment was supposed to prevent something like this. For Christ's sake, that system is costing us over a million dollars a day to operate.''

Without a moment's hesitation Stratton replied, ''Sir, we did our best to warn the airliner away from the danger zone, but interference from the microwave beam disrupted communications.'' He went on to explain that they were successful in keeping other aircraft and seafaring traffic away from the beam.

Kendall leaned forward. ''Exactly what did you tell the Qantas people in Manila?''

''We informed them our meteorological satellites registered an area of severe wind shear and asked them to issue a SIGMET.''

The President frowned. ''What's a SIGMET?'' he asked dryly. He didn't like to admit his ignorance in the presence of his cabinet members.

''A weather advisory concerning meteorological conditions significant to the safety of all aircraft in the vicinity,'' said Stratton smoothly. ''In this case it was issued due to extreme turbulence.''

As the President paused to reflect on this information, Stratton took the initiative. ''Sir, I'd like to inform you at this time that we have determined the precise reason why the satellite periodically transmits its microwave beam.''

Kendall listened carefully as the figure on the screen explained how the klystron tubes inside the satellite's microwave transmitter were activated when the spacecraft traveled from the earth's shadow into sunlight.

After Stratton finished his explanation, Kendall pressed a finger to his lips and thought hard. Finally, he asked, ''Then we can expect the satellite to fire its beam every time it swings out into the sun?''

On-screen, Stratton nodded. ''That's correct, sir.''

"Can you predict where it will strike next?" asked the President sharply.

"Yes, sir," said Stratton. "We're presently engaged in the process of determining the precise time and location of the next discharge."

While General Stratton was in his office on the first floor of the plant briefing the President, Mike Doheny stared in disbelief at the readout on the SATSCAN computer in front of him.

Minutes earlier he had fed the satellite's velocity, altitude, orbital parameters, attitude, and present ground path along with the earth's rate of rotation into the computer and instructed it to predict the geographic location of the next microwave transmission. For several moments the machine had chattered and whirred as relentless streams of numbers flickered across the display. Within seconds the torrent of data had converged into the angular degrees representing the requested latitude and longitude. At the same time a corresponding green blip had materialized on the immense Mercator map projected on the wall.

Now Doheny shifted his gaze to the huge blue screen above his head and studied the green blip, the exact spot where the microwave beam would touch down shortly after dawn the following morning. It was located approximately thirty miles inland from the all-too-familiar coast. He estimated the time of tomorrow's sunrise over the area, glanced at his watch, and felt his pulse quicken.

His face set in tense rigid lines, he punched out General Stratton's office number. The phone rang several times in his ear before the general answered.

"Yes," said Stratton with half-suppressed irritation.

"General, this is Doheny in Control—"

"I can't talk now," interrupted Stratton. "I'm in conference with Washington," he said impatiently.

"I don't give a damn who you're talking to," snapped Doheny, struggling to keep his temper in check. "We've got to hold an emergency meeting at once. The satellite will be transmitting in less than twelve hours from now." He paused to catch his breath. "I've just found out the location of the next target," he said urgently.

"Where?"

"Los Angeles."

Chapter 19 *

THE PRESIDENT OF the United States stared with growing irritation at the television monitor on the wall of the Crisis Room. On-screen, General Stratton was still on the phone, his face expressionless. President Kendall couldn't make out the words, and this added to his annoyance. What, he wondered, was so important that it took precedence over a presidential conference?

Kendall glanced at the other men sitting around the oval table. Jack Conley sat stiffly in his chair, legs crossed. JCS Chairman Willis Thompson took a deep breath and exhaled a loud sigh. Hugh Fitzpatrick sat motionless, but the twitching of his bushy white eyebrows betrayed his impatience. FBI Director Harold Sorensen looked bored as he doodled a sketch of the earth on his pad.

As Kendall waited he thought about General Thompson's recommendation to elevate the status of America's strategic forces to Condition Yellow—just two steps removed from a full-blown nuclear attack alert. Such a status change would indicate to the Kremlin that the United States was fully prepared to meet any further acts of aggression. However, it could also force the Russians to raise their own alert status to meet the U.S. threat. Then the United States would go to the next stage, daring them to do the same in a very dangerous game of nuclear chess. The process of escalation would continue until one side backed down; or it would result in a war in which there could be no victor.

Kendall was uncertain at this time whether the attack on the Sunstroke satellite was truly intended to provoke a war between the superpowers. Their assault could have been an isolated act with no premeditated follow-up. The Russians may have felt justified in attempting to disable the satellite because they believed it was a violation of the Anti-Ballistic Missile Treaty. Kendall knew that the conversion of a solar satellite into a military space-based weapons system did in fact constitute a violation. If the issue was debated in an international court of law, he had no illusions about the outcome: the U.N. would find America guilty as hell. Legal matters aside, his problem at the moment was to decide upon an appropriate response to the Russian attack, and the answer eluded him.

The President was pondering these thoughts when, on-screen, General Stratton put down the phone and turned to the camera. His face had the pinched look of ulceration.

"Mr. President," said Stratton tensely, "please accept my sincere apology for the interruption. We have just ascertained the approximate time and location of the satellite's next microwave discharge. Be advised, sir, that we are currently rechecking all available data to fully substantiate this prediction." He hesitated, as if choosing his words before continuing.

The President waited, anxious and silent, for Stratton to go on. He was aware of a growing tension in the Crisis Room.

General Stratton took a deep breath and said, "We have determined the satellite will discharge over Los Angeles at approximately oh six four five hours Pacific Standard Time, tomorrow morning."

Kendall suddenly felt very ill, shaken with a chilling nausea that was half fear and half anger. His hands trembled and he clasped them together to hold them steady. "Did I hear you right?" he asked, incredulous. "Are you telling me that thing up there is going to fire on Los Angeles?"

Stratton cleared his throat nervously. "Yes, sir. In about eleven hours from now. We estimate it will irradiate a zone approximately three square miles in area before the microwave transmitter overheats and shuts down."

The President pursed his lips and looked at his advisers. Across their faces flowed a rapidly shifting montage of shock, bewilderment, and fear.

Kendall turned his gaze back to the television screen and stared hard at Stratton. "No, Dean," he said in a flat, controlled voice, "you're wrong. The satellite is not going to strike Los Angeles."

Stratton frowned. "I beg your pardon, sir," he said, puzzled. "Our preliminary analysis clearly indicates—"

"The satellite is *not* going to discharge again," interrupted Kendall, his tone final. "You and the other experts over there are going to neutralize the thing before it reaches California."

Stratton lowered his head and his voice accompanied the

movement. "Sir, you can be assured we will make every effort to prevent it from transmitting. In a few minutes from now I will hold a conference to consider the options available to us."

"You'll do more than that," said Kendall with vehemence. He had dropped all pretense of formal protocol or even simple courtesy. "Listen closely. I'm ordering you to destroy that satellite before tomorrow morning. Is this clear?" He leaned back in his chair and waited for a reply from the bespectacled man on the screen.

Stratton, seated in his office at the solar power plant fifteen hundred miles away, looked searchingly at his commander in chief. Kendall could almost feel the pressure of his scrutiny through the Syncom communications link that connected them. Stratton was thinking furiously of some way to convince the President to reconsider. "Sir," he said hesitantly, "I believe we can prevent the satellite from discharging at Los Angeles without actually destroying it. Would this comply with your orders?" he asked imploringly.

"Then you've found a way to stop it?" asked Kendall in a skeptical tone.

"Yes, sir," replied Stratton easily. "At this point there are several alternate courses of action open to us."

The expression on the President's face softened slightly, encouraging Stratton to continue. "The civilian specialists and myself are about to choose the most expedient method of rendering it inoperative," said the general, emphasizing each word. "Whichever procedure we decide upon will be selected on the basis of its effectiveness *and* the safety of its implementation."

"What does that mean?" asked Kendall.

"Sir," said Stratton confidently, "we must remember the satellite is still in a highly unstable state. We have to be careful not to aggravate its condition by acting rashly. Our primary objective is to safely neutralize it in the given time frame."

"All right, Dean," said Kendall impatiently. "We're wasting time here." He raised his hands above the table and gestured. "Do whatever is necessary to put that satellite out of action before it gets anywhere near Los Angeles. Keep me posted on your progress."

"Of course, sir," replied Stratton solemnly.

The President kneaded the bridge of his nose. "Just one more thing, Dean."

"Sir?"

There was a cold hardness in Kendall's eyes. His voice was dispassionate and impersonal. "If for some reason you fail," he said slowly, "then I want your resignation on my desk before noon tomorrow."

Stratton's eyebrows lifted slightly. He opened his mouth to speak, then thought better of it. He had gotten what he wanted from the President: a precious reprieve for his satellite. He didn't want to push his luck.

With a sharp wave of his hand, Kendall signaled Jack Conley to break the connection. The image on the screen shrank to a dot and disappeared.

Kendall rubbed his eyes wearily. "Well, gentlemen, you've all heard the latest glad tidings from New Mexico," he said acidly. "It seems our satellite up there is intent on providing us with more victims. The Australian airliner wasn't enough. Christ, now it wants to decimate L.A."

"Dean Stratton seems confident in his team's ability to deal with the satellite," rasped Defense Secretary Fitzpatrick, his face bleak.

Kendall's fingertips stroked the tabletop. "Yes, he was cock-sure of himself." He glanced at each of his advisers, his eyes dark. "But let me tell you this," he said sharply. "If that thing does strike L.A., then we've had it. There'll be the biggest congressional investigation you ever saw." There was a raw edge to his voice. "Some young, shit-kicking senator will wave the flag and dig as deep as he can until he hits pay dirt. And Sunstroke will be there for all to see. He'll scream bloody murder about our creative accounting to divert funds, our kickbacks and bribes to people in the military and industry, and maybe he'll even find out how we covered up the first casualties. It'll be a Roman circus. He'll toss piece after piece to a starving media and we'll have a feeding frenzy on our hands like you've never seen before. Watergate will look like a ladies' tea party by comparison. For certain it will mean the end of this administration." He speared the four men with a steely glare. "And, gentlemen, we could all end up in prison. Yes, *prison*."

He jabbed an accusing forefinger at Fitzpatrick. "This morning you mentioned about impeachment. Well, let me assure you if that satellite discharges tomorrow everyone in this room will be brought up on charges of criminal conspiracy."

FBI Director Harold Sorensen drew a skull and crossbones in orbit around his sketch of the earth.

JCS Chairman Willis Thompson turned to the President, his chest ablaze with decorations, shoulders glittering with silver stars. His graying hair was cut so close that his pink scalp showed through. "Sir, I'm certain Dean will accomplish his job," he boomed. "The Space Defense Command at Cheyenne Mountain was in disarray before he took over. He integrated the Space Shield and NORAD into a viable strategic-defense and radar-monitoring system that is unparalleled anywhere in the world."

Kendall considered Thompson's overwhelming endorsement of Stratton for what it was worth. When under duress or close scrutiny the military could always be counted on to band together. He stroked his right cheek and said pensively, "Maybe. But I want a contingency plan in case he fails."

"Mr. President, there is something else we can do," rasped Defense Secretary Fitzpatrick, his voice grave. "Evacuate Los Angeles," he said with sullen reluctance.

Kendall let out a short deprecatory laugh. "Oh sure, I can just pick up the phone and tell the mayor of L.A. that he has less than twelve hours to evacuate over three million people." His voice hardened. "For Christ's sake, think, man! The panic alone might kill more than that satellite. Besides that, we'd be tipping our hand. Our opponents would start digging the moment they heard anything about an evacuation." He shook his head. "No way, Fitz."

"I quite agree, sir," remarked Sorensen. "Evacuation is out of the question."

The President thought hard for a moment. "Could we blow it up with one of our orbiting explosive devices?"

National Security Adviser Jack Conley answered the question. "We don't have anything powerful enough in geosynchronous orbit. All of our antisatellite vehicles were designed for infinitely smaller targets."

Kendall squinted reflectively at a communications panel on the wall linking the Crisis Room to SAC Headquarters and the M-X Peacekeeper silos. Finally he said, "Why can't we hit it with a nuclear warhead? Vaporize it out of existence?"

Conley was the first to answer. "Theoretically, yes. The problem is the distance involved. The satellite is over twenty *thousand* miles above the earth. Now the maximum attainable altitude of our ICBMs—including the M-X missile—is only seven *hundred* miles."

General Thompson clasped his hands before him. "Sir, we need something far more powerful than a missile booster. We need a geosynchronous launch vehicle like a Taurus 44E or a Pegasus. They could do it. Either rocket could easily be fitted with a nuclear device and launched on an intercept course.''

Harold Sorensen twirled his ballpoint pen in his hand. ''What concerns me is the time factor. How long does it take to prepare one of those rockets for launch?''

Kendall frowned. ''A good question, Hal.'' He felt his skin prickle with nervous apprehension. ''Check with Canaveral and Vandenberg,'' he told Jack Conley. ''See what they've got on the launchpad.''

Conley rose from his seat and moved quickly to the bank of television screens lining the wall. He tapped instructions on a keyboard beneath the NSSLS screen. The National Security Space Launch Status screen showed all pending military and intelligence agency launches. The display lit up:

VANDENBERG AFB—TAURUS 44E BEARING KH-31 PHOTORECONNAISSANCE SAT PAYLOAD SCHEDULED FOR LIFT-OFF AT 1520 HOURS 9–12. STATUS: FUELING OF LAUNCH VEHICLE AND CHARGING OF ON-BOARD BATTERY SYSTEM COMMENCING. COUNTDOWN IN PROGRESS.

''We're in luck, sir,'' announced Conley. ''There's a Taurus scheduled for launch tomorrow night from Vandenberg. A KH-31 recon satellite.''

''Who's the base commander over there?'' asked Kendall.

''Barry Wisneski,'' answered Conley. ''He's been briefed on Project Sunstroke,'' he added.

''Contact him right now,'' ordered the President. ''Find out how long it will take them to replace the spy satellite with a nuclear warhead.''

Conley nodded briskly and went to the phone.

Hugh Fitzpatrick, who had been silent throughout the exchange, spoke up. ''Sir, if we go ahead with this, we'll be violating the 1967 Space Treaty, which expressly forbids the detonation of nuclear weapons in space.''

Kendall smiled grimly. ''I know, Fitz, but this is an emergency.'' How ironic, he thought, that we had to break one treaty to put the Sunstroke satellite into orbit, and now we may very well be forced to break another in order to stop it.

Fitzpatrick wasn't through. "If we put a nuclear missile into orbit the Russians may think we're about to launch a first strike against them," he warned. "Have you considered that?"

The President had been trying hard to suppress the inner rage and frustration he felt all evening. Now he exploded. "*The Russians?*" he shouted, his face crimson with anger. "If those people in the Kremlin hadn't fired at our satellite we wouldn't be in this insane predicament now. They started this whole mess. They're the ones who are really responsible for the nearly three hundred people who have died so far. My God, don't push me, Fitz."

"I'm sorry, sir," wheezed Fitzpatrick, "but it's my duty to analyze any action we may take which could possibly jeopardize the security of this country."

Kendall's cold eyes focused on Fitzpatrick's thin, haggard face. "I am prepared to do everything possible to protect Los Angeles." He doled out the words with the slow, measured cadence of a funeral drum. "If it means violating an outdated treaty we made decades ago, then I'll do it. We're at the mercy of what Hal has pointed out as being the crucial factor in this crisis"—he glanced up at the clocks mounted on the wall—"time. We have less than twelve hours."

Fitzpatrick leaned back in his chair, his head lowered. He felt like a tired old man.

"As for the Russians," said Kendall, "I think it's time we checked up on their recent activities." He nodded to General Thompson. "Will, I need a report on their present military status."

Thompson immediately opened a drawer and pulled out a secure phone. Within seconds he was consulting with the Joint Chiefs in the War Room at the Pentagon. Moments later, when he replaced the phone, his face was grim. "Mr. President," he said in an official tone, "the Russians are engaged in several unannounced ancillary maneuvers. They have seventy Hammer long-range bombers aloft on airborne alert. Their ICBM force of SS-9/SL11s is on the line." He paused. "These are strong indications of a preparation for launching a first strike, sir."

"Now wait a minute, General," Fitzpatrick said hurriedly. "They've conducted readiness exercises with their bombers and missiles in the past, just as we have. I can't see how you can jump to the conclusion that they're preparing to attack."

Thompson glared at Fitzpatrick. "This is the official evaluation of the Joint Chiefs of Staff, Mr. Secretary," he said icily, "not my personal opinion."

The President lapsed into silence, trapped now in that lonely, uncomfortable place referred to in Harry Truman's plaque on his desk, the end of the line where the buck comes to a halt. It was a place where only one man can make the decisions affecting an entire nation, and the world. Kendall closed his eyes and retreated to the solitude of his mind, to the depths of his soul.

A minute later he turned his head with exquisite slowness toward General Thompson. "We can't risk underestimating their intentions," he said in a quiet, reflective voice. A pause, then, "Order our Trident and SSBN missile-carrying submarines to go to Condition Yellow, Will. This action should be sufficient to get our message across. Now it's President Gorodin's turn to start sweating."

Once again Thompson reached for the secure phone. This time he began issuing orders to the commander of the navy's ELF transmitter located near the Wisconsin and Michigan state border.

Fitzpatrick was stunned by the decision. He sat staring at Kendall, unable to move, as if the tenseness of the situation had sapped all his strength. He couldn't believe that the President had just moved the nation a giant notch closer to World War III.

At that moment Jack Conley replaced the phone at the communications console at the far wall of the room and returned to the oval table. For the past few minutes he had been in contact with the base commander at Vandenberg AFB discussing the feasibility of converting the huge Taurus launch vehicle into an extreme-range nuclear missile. His long, angular face was sullen. "They need a full twenty-four hours to refit the Taurus, sir," he informed Kendall. "It's a physical impossibility to do it in less than twelve."

The President drew a deep breath through his gritted teeth but said nothing. His eyes were shut, his body motionless. A moment passed and he said wearily, "It looks like we'll have to depend on Dean Stratton and his team. We don't have any choice," he said, sighing. Then a thought occurred to him. "Jack, tell Wisneski at Vandenberg to go ahead and refit the Taurus. Even if Dean finds a way to stop the satellite from firing on L.A., I want the thing blown out of the sky"—he eyed Fitzpatrick—"no matter what."

He glanced at General Thompson and Jack Conley, who were now both on the phone, executing their separate instructions. The chairman of the Joint Chiefs of Staff was speaking with the precision of a drill sergeant, ordering the navy commander at the ELF transmitter site to broadcast a state of Condition Yellow to America's undersea fleet. Conley, the national security adviser, spoke in low, measured tones with the base commander at Vandenberg, directing him to replace the Taurus's spy satellite payload with a nuclear device to be removed from the nose cone of an M-X Peacekeeper missile.

Now it can go either way, the President thought. Either the crisis is defused, or it escalates beyond control.

Within minutes after General Thompson contacted the commanding officer at the control center for the navy's ELF transmitter situated near the Wisconsin/Michigan state border, a low, deep rumble shook the earth.

The extremely low frequency transmitter was a forty-mile-long antenna buried under the farms and forests of northern Wisconsin and the upper peninsula of Michigan. It was the most reliable communications system ever conceived, being impervious to electronic jamming and disruption by nuclear detonations. Its powerful, slowly pulsed radio waves built up resonating vibrations in a vast subterranean granite formation called the Laurentian Shield, which sprawled across much of America's heartland. This pulsating signal could penetrate the murky depths of every ocean on earth.

Now, for the first time in its operational history, the massive antenna broadcast a series of three deep pulses, the code for Condition Yellow—"nuclear attack possible."

This grim message was received and decoded by the huge Trident submarines that lurked three hundred meters down in every ocean of the Northern Hemisphere. Each Trident carried twenty-eight launch tubes housing thermonuclear missiles locked on specific targets throughout the world. In addition, this signal was also received by forty-seven SSBN nuclear submarines equipped with sixteen launch tubes apiece. On board each of the undersea craft, preparations were made in an efficient, predetermined manner. Nuclear weapons with a combined explosive force equivalent to billions of tons of TNT were readied.

Vandenberg AFB, north of Santa Barbara on the California coast, was a miniature city with its own schools, shops, and housing projects, costing $3 billion to set up and close to $1 billion a year to operate. It possessed highly classified research facilities, ten launch platforms, and several dozen M-X and Minuteman III silos.

Inside a heavily reinforced concrete bunker that served as the control center for Pad 9B, the launch director, a short balding man wearing a blue air force uniform shirt with the sleeves rolled up, slammed down the phone. Red faced with anger, he swore loudly, then thumbed the switch on the loudspeaker at his console. "This is Launch Control. We have an abort on Taurus. The mission is scrubbed. Repeat. We have an abort."

A weary technician nearby turned to him. "Sir, there's no reason to abort," he said, incredulous. "The countdown is going smoothly. No anomalies. We're still go for lift-off."

The launch director shook his head. "I know, but the old man just ordered me to scrub. We're to stand down and wait for further instructions." His eyes narrowed. "I think our Polack commander has been talking to Charley Horse," he said conspiratorially. Charley Horse was military parlance for the Pentagon or the White House.

The irate launch director then ordered his team to shut down the electrical umbilical to the KH-31 satellite payload. Afterward, he sat there, fuming, waiting for additional orders from his base commander.

Outside on the concrete launchpad stood the twenty-three-story-tall Taurus 44E satellite carrier, brilliantly illuminated against the night sky. The immense rocket was partially obscured by weird clouds of vapor from the liquid oxygen in its fuel tanks. At the very top of the spacecraft, an electrical cable clamp attached to the nose cone was disengaged and swung away, dangling back and forth through the thick mist like a great pendulum.

Chapter 20 *

SAINT-ELIE BOULEVARD BECAME a narrow gravel road as it entered the French Guiana rain forest on the outskirts of Kourou. The Range Rover bumped up and down as its tires hit good-sized rocks and deep ruts. Gigantic trees with trunks fifty feet in diameter soared two hundred feet overhead, blotting out the sunlight with their dense foliage. Vines and creepers hung down from the branches, and giant ferns grew in profusion around the moss-covered roots. Everything was wet with dew.

The two men inside the Ranger Rover rode in silence. During the past hour Jacques Bourges had sobered up quickly and had repeatedly demanded, then begged, to know what was going on. The driver, Gerard van Eeden, had gripped the steering wheel with one hand and held his Glock semi-automatic pistol with the other, keeping it trained on the ESA crew chief. He said nothing.

The car turned onto what appeared more like a footpath than a road. The going was rough. The car penetrated deeper and deeper into the jungle. Bourges was horribly frightened and confused. The perspiration on his face felt cold. The blood was thundering in his head, and his breathing was quick and shallow. Finally they came to a stop. Van Eeden grabbed a satchel from the backseat, then ordered Bourges out. They marched several hundred yards into the forest.

The air was thick with moisture, and overhead wide-spreading branches shut out the daylight. There were occasional bird calls, but otherwise a profound stillness settled over them. Van Eeden paused to inspect the trunks of two sturdy young trees that grew about three feet apart. He pulled out a hunting knife and sliced off the thin branches so that the trunks were smooth up to a height of about six feet. He eyed Bourges the whole time. When he was through, he took four pairs of chrome-plated handcuffs from his satchel. He gripped Bourges, shoved him between the two trees, and handcuffed his wrists and ankles to the trunks so that he was bent over with legs spread wide apart. A horrified Bourges pleaded to be let go, then struggled against the restraints. The steel only bit deeper into his flesh.

With his knife, van Eeden carefully cut away Bourges's trousers and let them fall to the ground. Next he gingerly sliced the terrified man's briefs so that his genitals were exposed.

Van Eeden grabbed a nightstick from his satchel, the same type of billy club used by policemen the world over. His eyes became curiously glazed. He gently prodded Bourges's buttocks with the club, then with an underhanded swing he struck his exposed genitals once, sending the man into a screaming paroxysm of pain. Bourges's shriek turned into a gurgling retch.

Smiling, van Eeden drew close to Bourges, leaning intimately toward the pain-wracked man as though to kiss him. "And now, my good friend," he said gently, "who else did you discuss the *Ariane* payload with?"

Bourges shook his head violently. "No one else," he wheezed.

"Liar," accused van Eeden. He hit Bourges again.

Half a continent away, in the conference room at the solar power plant in New Mexico, NASA engineer Malcolm Courtland turned to Doheny and asked, "How large of an area will be irradiated?"

"Approximately three square miles," Doheny replied, his eyes hard but with a new fatigued look in them.

"Whew!" This was from Dr. Fred Gaither, the head of the Bioelectromagnetic Research Lab in Seattle, who ejected the whistle with the automatic reflex of a man unable to stifle a cough. The fleshy pouch that sagged from his chin to his collar shook as he spoke. "Then over twenty thousand people will be killed," he cried. "My God, that's how many would die if an atomic bomb went off."

"Or if an earthquake of seven point five on the Richter scale struck," said Professor Aaron Rosen, sick with worry.

Courtland gnawed his lip. "Just what *are* the microwave intensities involved here?"

"We're talking about more than one hundred kilowatts per square meter," Doheny answered. "This intensity is powerful enough"—he glanced at the steam rising from his coffee cup—"to bring one acre-foot of cold water to a boil in seconds."

Fred Gaither took a long, slender cigar from his breast pocket and lit it. "There's going to be immunological and hematological bioeffects that will occur far beyond those three square miles." He drew on the cigar and released a curling ball of blue smoke. "Not to mention the thermal overloading extending for miles outside the irradiated zone that could build to the death temperature. This is why the plant here is located in such an isolated area, and"—he waved his flabby pink hand around him—"why these walls are lined with lead."

Doheny breathed in and out slowly, his mind whirling with ideas, schematics, plans. A chain reaction of thought like a lightning bolt shot through his brain. He got up, went to the blackboard at the front of the room, and began writing furiously, the chalk screeching. Then he stepped back and examined what he had written:

PHASE ONE: U.S. STRATEGIC DEFENSE SYSTEM (SPACE SHIELD)
PHASE TWO: REPROGRAMMING OF ON-BOARD COMPUTER

"What's proposed here," said Doheny, "is a two-prong attack on the satellite. An assault on its structural integrity and a psychological subversion of its brain."

Stratton smiled thinly. "Your proposal corresponds quite closely with modern warfare," he observed.

"That's right, General," Doheny said. "We're at war with this thing, and I intend to win."

Gesturing with his cigar, Gaither asked, "Mike, why can't we just shoot down the satellite with a nuclear-tipped missile?"

"None of our ICBMs can reach it," replied Doheny. "Remember, the satellite is orbiting at more than twenty thousand miles above the earth. Even the most powerful long-range missile—the M-X—can only reach a maximum altitude of slightly more than seven hundred miles. The reason it's capable of striking targets thousands of miles away on other continents is because of its artillery shell–type trajectory, a low, wide arc close to the earth. The only way a nuclear warhead could be directed at the satellite would be to put one atop a multi-stage satellite launch vehicle capable of attaining geosynchronous orbit."

"And it would take at least twenty-four hours to refit a satellite carrier with a nuclear device," interjected General Stratton. "I know. The air force has investigated the possibility of using one against clusters of enemy space surveillance platforms in the event of war.'' He glanced at his watch. "We have barely eleven hours left before the satellite discharges. Not enough time for a refit."

"Now returning to our proposal here," said Doheny, tapping the blackboard. "General, you're the expert on phase one, the Space Shield. Can you give us a rundown on the arsenal under your command at Cheyenne Mountain?"

Stratton opened his briefcase, extracted a red-banded folder, and sorted through its contents. He took out copies of a particular document and handed one to each member of the team.

Doheny shot a glance at Nore. The head of NSI was studying his copy with obvious fascination. Many of the elements comprising the Strategic Defense System had been built by rival firms.

Doheny scrutinized the sheets before him with a fierce intensity in the hope of finding the means of disabling the satellite. Having occupied a high-level position in the aerospace industry for many years, he was used to reading classified documents. But this particular one overshadowed all others. It represented over a hundred billion dollars' worth of research and development stretching nearly two decades.

U.S. DEPARTMENT OF DEFENSE

CLASSIFICATION: TOP SECRET
CODE: ALPHA COBRA 1189-A-A-29
SUBJECT: STRATEGIC DEFENSE SPACE SHIELD
COMPONENTS

CATEGORY A: SPACE-BASED DIRECTED ENERGY
WEAPONS
1. PALADIN Free-electron Laser Platform—
   Deployed in geosynchronous orbit (GEO). Orbital
   weapon generates a coherent beam of one megawatt intensity at a wavelength of one microme-
   ter. Range: 1,000 miles. Power source: nuclear
   reactor. Four units deployed in GEO. Status: operational.
2. ALAMO Charged Particle Beam (CPB) Platform—
   Deployed in Low Earth Orbit (LEO). Accelerates
   electron beam to 5 million electron volts (5MeV)
   to be directed against orbiting targets and/or
   missiles during boost phase. Range: 400 miles.

Power source: nuclear reactor. Twelve units deployed in LEO. Status: operational.

CATEGORY B: CONTACT ASSAULT WEAPONS

1. STARBURST Air-to-Space Antimissile/Antisatellite Missile. Launched from F-117B interceptor at 40,000 feet. Range: 600 miles. Propellant: solid, powdered aluminum/polybutadien matrix. Stationed at select USAF bases (listed page 243). Status: operational.

2. ICARUS Maneuverable Destabilizer Antisatellite Vehicle (MDAV)—Highly maneuverable vehicle with multiple restart capability. Orbital device destabilizes target by attachment with magnetic coupling. After attachment is accomplished vehicle activates reaction engines in spin mode to cause change of attitude. Propellants: long-storage UDMH as fuel, N_2O_4 as oxidizer. Four units deployed in GEO. Status: operational.

3. MACE Kinetic-kill Antisatellite (ASAT) Vehicle—orbital device for intercepting and disabling target utilizing stored kinetic energy from orbital velocity. Range: LEO to GEO. Propellants: UDMH as fuel, N_2O_4 as oxidizer. Fifty-seven units deployed in LEO. Status: operational.

Doheny had the vague feeling that the list was incomplete, that something was missing. He was trying to remember when Nore suddenly interrupted his thoughts.

"What about the Paladin laser?" Nore asked. He sat back in his chair and folded his arms. "Could it knock out the satellite's microwave transmitter?"

"It's not powerful enough to penetrate the shielding," answered Stratton.

Doheny looked thoughtful. "But could the laser be aimed through the cracks in the shielding?" he asked hopefully. "If so, it might be able to raise the interior temperature to keep the klystrons overheated."

"The Paladin laser generates only a single megawatt of power," said Stratton, his voice quiet and unemotional. "I'm afraid it's far too weak."

Doheny scanned his copy of the document. "The other

directed-energy weapons don't have either the range or sufficient power to do the job," he announced sullenly.

"That takes us to the contact assault ASATs," stated Malcolm Courtland. "How much of a punch do these Mace kinetic-kill vehicles pack, General?"

As though stating a fact that was self-evident and hardly needed mentioning, Stratton said, "Not enough. They're far too small to generate enough energy to affect the satellite."

Doheny frowned. "General, what type of ASAT do you believe was used against the satellite last night, the one that caused the malfunction?"

Professor Rosen curled his right hand into a fist. "Who attacked the satellite?"

"We don't know at this time," Stratton said noncommittally. "Our radar picked up a faint echo indicating a kinetic-kill ASAT far greater in size and mass than our Maces. Computer scans of the echo indicate a mass slightly less than two tons. Ours weigh in at only five hundred pounds."

"Then they wouldn't have a ghost of a chance," said Doheny. "The satellite is traveling too fast now."

"Are you referring to its increased momentum, Mike?" asked Professor Rosen.

Doheny nodded. "The satellite is nearing its closest approach to earth and in doing so, it's gaining in both speed and momentum. This means it'll be traveling faster than at any other point in its orbit. Its increased momentum will deflect the ASATs because of the kinetic-kill vehicles' infinitely smaller mass and lower velocity."

"Of course," stated Rosen flatly.

Peering myopically at Doheny through his spectacles, Stratton said with emphasis, "I believe the Icarus destabilizing devices could alter the satellite's present attitude in space sufficiently enough to divert the microwave beam away from earth. They attach magnetically to the target and use their own rocket motors to change its attitude."

"How much thrust does each device produce?" asked Doheny hopefully.

"Eighty thousand pounds."

A muscle rippled in Doheny's cheek. "The satellite has a mass of ten thousand *tons*. I doubt whether even all four devices could budge it more than a few hundredths of a degree. That wouldn't be enough to divert the beam away from earth."

Stratton nodded. "Under normal circumstances, I would unhesitatingly agree. However, according to the telemetry you received last night after the collision, your people were unable to activate the satellite's thrusters."

"That's right."

"There is a good possibility," Stratton said in a dry, clipped voice, "that the thruster propellant lines were ruptured in the collision, and the fuel and oxidizer were dumped in space."

Doheny performed some quick mental calculations, then looked sharply at Stratton. "Yes, the satellite would be light enough for your devices to move *if* it lost its fuel load. The problem is we have no way of knowing down here for certain. The collision wrecked the propellant sensors."

"We'll know for certain at twenty-one hundred hours," Stratton said cryptically.

Doheny glanced at his watch. "That's only fifteen minutes from now," he said, puzzled. "What do you mean?"

"I ordered my command center to maneuver a surveillance spacecraft into the same orbit as the solar satellite," the general announced. "It should be close to the rendezvous point now. The craft possesses a battery of high-resolution television cameras. The TV images will be transmitted to the Earthnet/SATSCAN screen in your control room. We'll know soon enough if the propellant lines were ruptured."

Five minutes later Doheny, Stratton, Nore, and the three civilian specialists were inside the control room, gathered around the big screen watching the satellite's slow progression across the Mercator map. Stratton entered a code into the computer and the map flickered into static. When the image cleared they saw a sprinkling of stars against a velvet background.

Doheny could make out the constellation Cygnus the Swan quite clearly. He searched the screen but could not as yet see any sign of the Sunstroke satellite in the darkness of space above the other side of the world. Mentally he divided the huge screen into grids, then carefully examined each of the small units. After a few moments he found it, a small light patch obscuring the constellation Cepheus.

"There it is," he announced, pointing to the upper left-hand corner of the screen.

Everyone drew closer to the big screen, anxious to see their first glimpse of the enemy.

Chapter 21 *

THE LIGHT PATCH became steadily larger, growing in both size and detail until the image filled the screen. The satellite's huge central cylinder, portions of the outstretched solar panels, and the underside of the vast octagon-shaped microwave transmitter were clearly visible.

They all saw the breaks in the fuel lines at once.

Pointing to them, Doheny said, "That's why we couldn't maneuver the thing. Every ounce of fuel must have shot out into space. You were right, General."

Stratton nodded. "Now that we've confirmed the satellite lost its propellant load, I think we should discuss the exact placement of the Icarus destabilizing devices."

Doheny disagreed. "Let's finish the visual reconnaissance first. I want to see the full extent of the damage from the collision."

They could make out great jagged fractures in the microwave transmitter's titanium-alloy shielding. Through these cracks they could see the crystalline klystron tubes inside, glistening like gigantic jewels. The sight filled them with awe.

"It's incredible," exclaimed Professor Rosen. "We're looking at the things that have killed almost three hundred people. And for the life of me, I've got to admit they're beautiful."

"You're very right," said Dr. Fred Gaither. "Beautiful but deadly."

As he surveyed the damage, a frightening thought occurred to Doheny. "The only reason the microtransmitter overheats when exposed to the sun is because its liquid nitrogen coolant system malfunctioned. This could be due to any number of factors. The collision may have broken their lines, too, or caused them to become obstructed, or the tank valves are simply jammed." He eyed Stratton sharply. "Now, if we use your destabilizing devices, the vibrations from their attachment could possibly loosen the obstruction in the lines or unstick the valves.'' He paused. ''Think about it, General. If the coolant system becomes operative, then the klystrons will be prevented from overheating and the micro-wave beam will continue to discharge until it reenters the earth's shadow. In the meantime the beam will burn a swath halfway across the world.'' He shook his head slowly. ''I don't think we should risk it.''

Stratton's mouth tightened and his eyes narrowed. ''We don't have much time, Mr. Doheny. Do you have an alternate method?''

''Yes,'' Doheny replied. ''Like I said in the conference room, we can try reprogramming the satellite's computer to force it to disengage the microtransmitter.''

He turned to Malcolm Courtland. ''You've troubleshot more ailing spacecraft than anyone. Some of your more esoteric radio signal procedures are in the textbooks. What I have in mind is using the plant's directional antenna to transmit a pulsed carrier signal to the satellite when it comes into range.'' He paused to consider the signal design. ''We'll need a carrier at something like one hundred eighty megacyles. Then it'll have to be pulsed at one kilocycle, length six microseconds.''

Courtland leaned forward, his long brown hand gripping the edge of a console. ''Trouble is,'' he said worriedly, ''I'll have to know the layout of the on-board logic circuits. Also, I'll need help developing the new programs.''

''We have the man who designed the satellite's brain right here at the plant,'' Doheny said encouragingly. ''Ted Kitami, the head of our Central Computer Room. He wrote the original program.'' He depressed a button on the intercom and asked Dr. Kitami to come down to the control room.

Kitami entered the room cradling a cup of hot cocoa with both hands. He listened quietly as Doheny recounted the grim events that had transpired since their last meeting the night before. Kitami's smooth bespectacled face remained expressionless when Doheny told him the satellite would strike Los Angeles shortly after dawn the next day.

''Now,'' said Doheny, ''we need your help to reprogram the satellite's computer.'' He waved a hand at Malcolm Courtland. ''Malcolm here will design the pulsed carrier signal. I want you to come up with a new superseding program to command the computer to disengage the microtransmitter. Once you've devel-oped it Malcolm will translate the instructions into a binary-coded signal and transmit it to the satellite when it comes within range.''

He glanced at his watch. "We've got about ten hours left. Can you do it, Ted?"

Kitami sipped his cocoa, sat in a chair, and touched a finger to the side of his nose. He was silent for a few moments, deep in thought. Finally he shook his head sadly. "It took me a full year to write the original program, Mike. What you're proposing now is equally complex, involving a multitude of intricate subroutines. It would take months, I'm afraid."

Doheny felt his shoulders sag. He hadn't realized the full complexity of the task. But he wasn't through yet. "All right, Ted," he said briskly. "So completely rewriting the program is out of the question. Can we somehow alter the original one, maybe erase portions of it and fill in the blanks with new commands?"

"Yes," said Kitami hesitantly, "this is feasible. However, I must point out that a defense subroutine is currently operating in the present program to circumvent unauthorized tampering."

"But you know the entry codes," protested Courtland. "The computer will *have* to accept the new instructions."

"Not necessarily," replied Kitami quietly. He glanced sideways at General Stratton, who nodded almost imperceptibly.

This surreptitious communication did not escape Doheny's notice. He tried to suppress the anger he felt toward the pointless charade of secrecy. He assumed Kitami was a member of the Project Sunstroke staff since he was the one who had designed the satellite's artificial brain and had programmed it to enable the spacecraft to function as a weapons system.

"Ted," said Doheny, irritated, "our group here has been briefed on Sunstroke. There's no need to conceal anything." He sighed heavily. "Now, I think you'd better explain why the on-board computer won't accept an altered program."

Dr. Kitami stared into space, his high fine cheekbones catching the light. His dark eyes sparkled angrily for a moment, as if he'd suddenly realized he'd been backed into a corner. "I suppose you blame me for being a part of this military project, Mike. But please bear in mind I had no choice in the matter."

"Nobody is accusing you of anything, Ted," said Doheny. "We're only concerned with stopping the satellite. Tell us why you think the computer won't accept the new instructions."

Kitami held up one finger as if testing the direction of the wind. "Last night the satellite was no doubt attacked by an enemy vehicle." He shot a glance at Stratton, who once again nodded. "It is my belief that its on-board computer is now in a defense mode as a result. This means all of its defensive capabilities have been activated in anticipation of another attack, whether physical or electronic in nature. Therefore it may refuse to accept a new set of commands, even if we use the appropriate codes.''

"Why?" asked Doheny.

"Because it is in an agitated state due to the collision.''

"Are you saying that it's upset?'' asked Fred Gaither, tapping his cigar over an aluminum ashtray.

"Perhaps,'' replied Kitami solemnly.

"But it's only a machine,'' said Professor Rosen, incredulous. "Aren't you being too anthropomorphic in your analysis?''

Kitami speared him with his cold, dark eyes. "The computer is heuristic, self-learning, a breakthrough in artificial intelligence. It has an incredibly flexible capability of dealing with problems that is remarkably similar to human thought processes.''

Courtland straightened up and smiled wanly. "How is this possible?''

Before answering, Kitami took another sip of cocoa. "The great speed with which the computer operates and its vast memory storage capacity are due to its superconducting silicon microchip circuitry. Unlike ordinary chips, these are coated with a thin deposit of high-temperature superconducting material, yttrium barium copper oxide, which offers absolutely no resistance to the flow of electricity. The computer's self-learning capability is a direct function of the algorithmic program that I formulated.'' An expression of unmistakable pride flowed across his face. "Very briefly, this program contains a set of rules for resolving all predicted problems and events. But it doesn't stop there. It allows the computer to draw on its accumulated knowledge to deal with unpredicted events. Each time it faces a new situation it evaluates all pertinent data from its memory in order to cope. If the data is insufficient it will make the best possible decision and proceed from there. The results of its decision, whether positive or negative, are stored in memory in case a similar situation is encountered in the future. In this manner the computer is able to learn from its mistakes.''

"For this reason,'' said Doheny thoughtfully, "you believe the satellite will do everything possible to ward off another attack, including our attempt to alter its program?''

Kitami nodded slowly.

Everett Nore came forward. "Ted, there's no doubt in my mind that your computer and the program you developed for the satellite represent a revolution in artificial intelligence,'' he said matter-of-factly. His forehead crinkled. ''What I don't understand is why it failed to detect the kinetic-kill vehicle last night.''

Before Kitami could reply, General Stratton placed the palms of his hands on the computer console and said, ''Dr. Kitami, will you permit me to answer that?'' He swiveled in his chair to face Nore. ''The satellite's intruder-detection system was unable to pick up the stealth ASAT for two reasons. First, because it was only partly activated during the initial start-up of the satellite's microwave transmitter. At that critical period the on-board electrical power systems hadn't stabilized yet. Secondly, the stealth ASAT vehicle's configuration and special anechoic coating enabled it to avoid detection. We believe the ASAT was spherical because this shape disperses rather than reflects radar waves. Also it was undoubtedly almost completely black, close to being a perfect absorber of light and other electromagnetic radiation. Technically speaking, its albedo was probably somewhere in the ninety-nine point nine percent region—infinitely blacker than coal. Nor was there any sheen on it. The exceedingly small amount of light that it reflected was scattered more or less equally in all directions.'' He stood back and rubbed his face absently. ''Frankly I wish we had that ASAT in our arsenal.''

Although fascinated by the preceding discussion, Doheny was also acutely aware of the time factor. He wanted to crystallize a plan of action. ''Ted,'' he began, ''from what you've told us the satellite's computer is prepared for another assault. I think we should put its mind at ease, so to speak, convince it there's no possibility of a future attack. Then, when it's off guard, we can erase some of its program and feed it the new instructions.''

''A subterfuge,'' said Kitami meditatively. ''Your idea has some merit. It may work.'' He pressed two fingers to his lips. ''We can alter the original program with a surgical tapeworm. That is, we can introduce a limited subroutine containing the commands that will precisely erase only those parts directly related to the microwave transmitter functions. I can assemble a simple tapeworm very quickly.''

Doheny turned to Courtland. ''What about the carrier signal, Malcolm?''

Courtland looked up from his notepad. ''I've already outlined the signal design. All I have to do is plug in the binary code as soon as it's written out.''

''Good,'' said Doheny. ''We've got a technician here, Glen

Larsen, who knows our multiplex console like the back of his hand. We'll let him handle the actual transmission." He looked at his watch, then glanced at Kitami and Courtland. "Better get started, gentlemen," he urged. "There isn't much time left."

As if to underscore Doheny's last statement, from across the room Jenkins read off the satellite tracking report. Its position was over open sea, 32 degrees 13 minutes north latitude, 170 degrees 21 minutes east longitude. The satellite would discharge in ten hours.

"Thunder is approaching on the right?" asked Kitami cryptically.

Over the months Doheny had become used to Kitami's occasional poetic license. "Pardon me, Ted?"

"Just a little ancient Roman phrase. The Romans were aware that thunderstorms usually moved from west to east, like our satellite, due to the earth's rotation. The Roman senate building faced south. If they heard thunder on the left, this meant a storm was moving away from them. A clap of thunder on the right meant a storm was approaching. Figuratively speaking, thunder is rapidly approaching Los Angeles from the right."

Doheny smiled grimly. "This is one storm we're going to break up."

"With Mr. Courtland's assistance," said Kitami, "our subterfuge message, the tapeworm, and the new instructions should be ready within the hour." He smoothed his lank, glossy black hair, turned to Courtland, and asked if he was ready to go to work. The two men got up and went to the Central Computer Room.

Doheny's spirits were buoyed up. At last, he thought, we're taking the offensive. He was pleased with the team effort. They were working together now in a common cause to put the satellite out of action.

He felt light-headed, euphoric, almost as if his body were charged up like a generator running at peak capacity. He knew that when it was all over he'd probably collapse in a heap from fatigue.

Stratton gave Doheny an approving nod. "I'm impressed enough with your scheme," the general told him, "to hold off on the Icarus attachments. I'm anxious to see the reaction to your signal transmission."

Chapter 22 *

FORTY MINUTES LATER Dr. Kitami and Malcolm Courtland burst into the control room, talking excitedly as they
converged on the communications console. Kitami held a sheaf of
computer printouts containing the codes.

Across the room Doheny was using the SATSCAN computer to
determine how much time they had before the satellite entered the
earth's shadow. He knew that once it crossed into the darkness
there wouldn't be any sunlight to power its on-board computer;
the thing would become dormant and unreceptive until it emerged
into the sun at dawn the next day. The calculation took only an
instant.

Doheny strode to the communications console and told Kitami,
"We've got eighteen minutes left before the satellite is eclipsed by
the earth. We'll have to move fast."

Glen Larsen, the communications technician, sat at his station
thumbing through a manual. He was a compact, sandy-haired man
in his late twenties, wearing russet cowboy boots and a western
shirt under his white lab smock. He listened intently as Doheny
briefly explained what they were going to do.

"We'll have to modulate a high-frequency carrier containing
coded, multiplexed data," Doheny informed him. "You'll be
using frequency-division-multiplexing to modulate the sinusoidal
subcarriers to handle the load and speed up the transmission.
Malcolm Courtland here will give you the precise technical
description of the signal, and Ted Kitami will provide the actual
code."

"What system?" drawled Larsen.

"Binary," replied Doheny. "Let's get started." He studied the
blip on the big screen for a moment and estimated the satellite's
position in the sky relative to the power plant's location. "Bring

the uplink antenna to fourteen hours nine minutes right ascension, twenty degrees thirty minutes south declination.''

''Understood,'' said Larsen. He pushed a series of levers and turned several dials to align the huge rooftop antenna with the Sunstroke satellite, now coming into range low in the western sky. A green indicator at the top of his console winked on. ''On center,'' he reported.

Doheny stepped back and nodded to Courtland and Kitami. ''It's your show, gentlemen.'' He felt a burst of elation. This was it. They were going to put the satellite out of action and save Los Angeles.

Beside him stood General Stratton, Everett Nore, Professor Rosen, and Dr. Fred Gaither. All watched the proceedings intently.

When Courtland approached the console Larsen looked up and said laconically, ''When this is all over, I've got a couple textbooks you wrote that I'd like you to autograph.''

''Be glad to,'' Courtland said, grinning. Then he glanced at his notes. ''First, I want a carrier at one hundred eighty-three megacycles. Then pulse it at one kilocycle, length six microseconds.''

''Carrier at one hundred eighty-three m.c.,'' repeated Larsen, moving a small dial on his multiplex panel. ''Pulse one k.c., length six microseconds.'' He changed over to another circuit. A small display screen at eye level lit up. A bright green pulse danced across it and settled down, allowing him to set the length at six microseconds.

''Second,'' said Courtland, ''we need a separate multiplex transmission at forty-one point seven two megacycles, frequency modulated, amplitude six decibels below the first. We'll key in the final numerical combination on the frequency modulation.''

''Ready,'' said Larsen after making the required adjustments.

''Check subcarrier frequency,'' ordered Courtland.

''All okay,'' replied Larsen, scanning his panel.

''Multiplex key plugged in?''

''Set.''

Courtland turned to Ted Kitami. ''We're ready to encode, Doctor.''

Kitami sorted through his printout sheets and stepped up to the console. The renowned scientist possessed a superhuman fluency in the language of computers. He swam in binary mathematics like a fish in the sea. To Doheny, he said, ''Our first transmission will contain the subterfuge message we discussed earlier. It should convince the satellite that it is not under attack, that last night's assault was a mistake." He adjusted his glasses and read the first series of binary digits to Larsen.

"One zero one one, zero one one one, zero one, one one zero."

Larsen's fingers flitted over his touch-pad keyboard as he encoded the numbers.

As Kitami read off another binary series, Fred Gaither eased his immense body into a swivel chair beside Doheny. Whispering, he asked, "Are they transmitting now, Mike?"

"No," said Doheny. "Larsen is recording the message on a reel of magnetic tape inside here." He pointed to a shiny metal cabinet beneath the multiplex console. "When the first message has been completely encoded, it'll be transmitted in two high-speed bursts."

"How will we know if the satellite accepts it or not?" asked Gaither.

"It'll tell us on that small receiver display just above Larsen's head," replied Doheny. "In plain English."

When Larsen finished recording the last numerical series, he flung a frequency switch open, checked his dials, then turned to Doheny and announced, "Ready to transmit, sir."

Doheny felt a cold lump in his throat. If the satellite responded positively to this first message then it should accept the follow-up commands. He swallowed and said, "Transmit *now*." His voice was dry, harsh.

Larsen snapped the transmit button down. It glowed amber, and a high-pitched whine emitted from the console.

Doheny counted the passage of time with the beats of his heart, and after several moments of absolute and unearthly silence, he saw the satellite receiver display above Larsen light up. Then it buzzed like a bee trapped in a jelly jar. An instant later the entire screen was filled with numbers.

"What is the significance of those numbers, Dr. Kitami?" asked General Stratton, puzzled. His voice was less firm than usual, almost shaky.

"I think," replied Kitami, "that we will find out very shortly."

The screen went blank, and printed out the words:

MESSAGE ACKNOWLEDGED

"Look!" shouted Professor Rosen. "It worked. The thing believed the story."

"I sincerely hope so," said Kitami solemnly. Something about his calm, measured voice ran like a cold shadow across the room.

Doheny pressed his hand against the back of his neck and pulled it around the taut muscle that corded down his shoulder. "Let's get on with the rest of the transmission," he ordered.

Several minutes later Dr. Kitami backed away from the console and lowered his head.

Larsen spun around, propelled by his Texan boots, and informed Doheny they were ready to transmit the "surgical tapeworm."

Doheny was aware that all eyes were on him now. "Transmit," he said hoarsely.

Larsen pressed the transmit button, hard. The console whined as it broadcast the urgent message at the speed of light.

A second passed. Two seconds.

The receiver display on Larsen's console came to life. The satellite's reply to the second transmission was simple, clear, succinct. A single word appeared on the screen.

NO

Ten feet above the control room Diane Bradford lay on her thin narrow cot in the guest lounge, sleeping fitfully, tossing and turning. Suddenly she was startled awake by muffled voices. After blinking her eyes open she pushed the coarse army blanket aside, propped herself up on one elbow, and looked around the room. It was dimly lit by a night-light and she could just make out the rows of cots.

Except for a few snoring noises and one or two others who moved restlessly in their sleep, the lounge was quiet. From a cot farther up the aisle, a man broke wind softly, moaned, then went silent again. The other occupants of the long room were quiet except for their measured breathing. Even Andy, her Cable News Service cameraman, was asleep.

For a moment Diane thought the voices had been part of a dream. Then she heard them again. They were coming from directly beneath her. The voices began alternating with a high-pitched whine and an odd buzzing sound. Seconds later there was an incessant beeping. Electronics. She realized the noises were coming from the control room in the basement sublevel below. She wondered what was going on down there.

She drew the blanket around her and lay there, listening intently to the muted voices. Although she couldn't make out the words she could perceive the underlying tenseness behind them. She heard someone shout. A few minutes passed and the sounds subsided. At least, she thought, they didn't turn those damn klaxon alarms on. Those wailing sirens would have awakened the whole room, putting everyone in a foul, ugly mood, including the MPs. She didn't want anything to jeopardize the plan she would put into effect the next day.

After failing to go back to sleep, she started mentally rehearsing the elements of her scheme to privately interview Mike Doheny. Earlier that night she had worked them out in detail with Andy, her cameraman. She had even drawn up a floor plan of the power plant based on memories and impressions from their guided tour of the place the day before. It had not been easy to persuade Andy to participate in her plan. Shortly before the lights were turned out, they had gone over it again in hushed tones. He had brought up every excuse he could think of for abandoning the scheme. He was worried because he was the one who had to create the diversion.

"Look," Diane had said, exasperated. "It all gets down to one thing: timing. All you have to do tomorrow morning is to wait for the men's rest room to clear so nobody will see you. Then do what we've talked about and leave. It's that simple." She had lightly stroked his arm. "Don't worry, nothing can go wrong," she had assured him. "So we're all set?"

He had nodded reluctantly, eyes closed.

As Diane reviewed her plan in the quiet, dark room she began to have second thoughts. Earlier, making all the preparations had been exciting, even fun. Something to do to keep her mind occupied and her spirits up. But now, as she lay in the gloom, she could no longer ignore the risks. Even if she managed to locate Doheny by scrambling through the crawl spaces above the ceiling, she couldn't evade the MPs forever. They would eventually find her. Then what?

Diane almost decided to call the whole thing off. She realized that she and the other reporters would probably be released within a few days. After a stern warning not to divulge anything they had seen or heard at the plant, they would be free to go. Then she would go back to her dead-end job at the Cable News Service affiliate in Albuquerque without ever knowing what really happened at the world's first solar microwave power plant.

"Fuck it," she said aloud. She was going to go through with it. If anything, she had to get to the bottom of what was going on around here just to satisfy her curiosity. With her mind firmly made up she closed her eyes and felt the muscles of her body slowly relax. In minutes she was asleep.

Doheny stared at the receiver screen. He felt the breath of panic when he realized the satellite's computer had exceeded its parameters.

Professor Rosen made a guttural sound, the meaning of which Doheny instantly understood.

They had failed.

Everett Nore slowly unfolded his arms, uncrossed his ankles and stepped up to the communications console. Jabbing his finger at the screen, he said angrily, "Is this some kind of joke, Larsen? Did you deliberately goose the satellite to print this?"

"No sir, Mr. Nore," protested Larsen vehemently. "I only transmitted what Dr. Kitami encoded."

General Stratton turned sharply to Kitami. "How do you explain this reply, Doctor?"

Kitami's expression was clouded. "Apparently," he said calmly, "the defense subroutine I mentioned earlier is in full operational control of the central logic elements. Very simply, it will not allow the computer to accept our reprogramming instructions."

Stratton's mouth twisted. "Why not?"

"Because it is now in a complete defense mode. While in this state it will reject all commands to circumvent its operation. The collision with the ASAT has led our satellite to believe it is under attack."

"Your defense subroutine was designed for the express purpose of preventing an enemy nation from gaining control of the satellite," Stratton said loudly. "But we transmitted the special entry codes that should have given us access to its program. Why didn't it accept them?"

Kitami lightly touched his finger to his chin. "Perhaps our satellite no longer trusts us."

"The goddamned thing has become paranoid," cried Malcolm Courtland.

Dr. Fred Gaither swiveled in his chair. "Once bitten . . ."

Doheny glanced at his watch. "We're not through yet," he said firmly. "There are four and a half minutes left before it's eclipsed by the earth." Turning to Dr. Kitami, he said, "I want to communicate with the thing, Ted. Can you ask it why it won't accept our commands?"

Kitami looked down at the sheaf of printouts he was holding. "I think we can formulate your question from these codes." His voice sank to a whisper as he scanned the sea of binary numbers before him. He read off a short numerical series to Larsen, who recorded them on tape.

On Doheny's order, the query was transmitted to the satellite. In seconds they had the answer.

YOU ARE THE ENEMY

Kitami uttered a short, harsh laugh. His cackle attracted irritated glances from some of the others in the room. "Forgive me," he apologized, "but the irony here is too much to bear. I was ordered to develop this special defense subroutine to provide our satellite with the capability of defending itself against enemy attacks. And now it believes *we* are the enemy."

Doheny was about to reply when the screen buzzed and printed out a second message in bright green letters:

THIS COMMUNICATION IS TERMINATED

The glowing words on the display turned the marrow in Doheny's bones to water. Now there was no possibility of reprogramming the thing. Their only hope of safely deactivating the satellite was lost.

Suddenly the screen dissolved into shifting lines of static. The satellite had just crossed the terminator and plunged into the night side of the world.

Doheny realized that Ted Kitami had indeed achieved a breakthrough in artificial intelligence when he designed the on-board computer. The built-in heuristic, self-learning capability allowed it to effectively deal with any situation. Doheny resolved never to underestimate the thing again.

At the guidance console Jenkins nervously combed his fingers through his beard and announced, "Nine hours to microwave discharge."

General Stratton pursed his lips and adjusted his glasses. "We have no choice now but to use the Icarus destabilizing devices," he said gravely.

"Remember what I said about the satellite's coolant system," Doheny warned. "If the devices jar—"

Stratton cut him off. "It's a calculated risk we'll have to take. There are over twenty thousand lives at stake in Los Angeles. I'm going to Cheyenne Mountain at once to implement the operation." He indicated Jenkins's radar scope. "You'll be able to observe the attachment on radar." Then he turned and quickly left the room.

Inside his office at the plant, Stratton contacted the White House and informed the President of his intention to use the Space Shield to prevent the satellite from discharging at Los Angeles. Kendall gave him the go-ahead to activate the Icarus destabilizing devices, then ordered the general to keep him posted.

After hurriedly packing his belongings, Stratton summoned Provost Marshal Clayton, officially handed over command of the plant to him, then drove to the nearby airstrip and boarded a military jet.

In Washington, the President sat at the oval conference table in the White House Crisis Room, deep in thought. "It seems," he told Jack Conley, "that Dean has things under control."

Conley nodded. "Do you want to call off the Vandenberg missile shot?"

Kendall shook his head. "No, I want them to proceed with it. Just in case." He cupped his chin. "I'm thinking about Doheny and those specialists at the power plant. They know too much."

Conley shrugged. "We've got them incarcerated over there under military guard, with no outside calls allowed. There shouldn't be any trouble."

"They still have access to that trunk line in Nore's office. I'd feel better if it was disconnected."

"It wouldn't hurt," said Conley.

"Do it."

At that moment, 2,500 miles to the south, a murder was about to take place deep in the rain forest of French Guiana. Night had fallen and the forest hooted, buzzed, and rustled with living things. Gerard van Eeden played his flashlight beam at the pitiful figure jackknifed between the two trees before him. *Ariane* crew chief Jacques Bourges had passed out from the inhuman torture van Eeden had inflicted on him throughout the long day.

Van Eeden had determined that Bourges had not told anyone else about his suspicions regarding the *Ariane* payload. Now it was time to put the poor man out of his misery. Van Eeden placed the muzzle of his gun to Bourges's temple and fired once. He was not concerned about anyone hearing the shot; hunting was prevalent in the area. He quickly dug a grave in the moist, loose soil with a collapsible shovel he had brought with him. Then he laid Bourges's battered body to rest. He knew that within minutes the large black beetles living in the soil would begin consuming the flesh right to the bone. Nothing was wasted in the rain forest.

An hour later he was in his hotel room at Kourou, taking a shower. Afterward he ate a leisurely dinner in a café down the street. When he finished his meal he used the pay phone near the men's room. He placed a transatlantic call to a number he had been given. It was for an extension line belonging to a low-level diplomat at the Netherlands' embassy in Moscow. The man doubled as van Eeden's contact with the Russian military.

There was a series of clicks, then a voice answered in Dutch. "Yes?"

After giving his I.D. number van Eeden said, "I have an urgent message to be transmitted immediately."

"Go ahead," said the voice.

Van Eeden gave him a coded message to send, then hung up.

On the other side of the world, inside the basement of the Dutch embassy in Moscow located in Dzerzhinsky Square, a middle-aged man with a heavy brow, light hair, and a tense expression on his face carefully checked to make sure no one was watching as he entered the radio room. Satisfied no one was about, he sat down at the radio transmitter in the corner and began translating van Eeden's coded message into Russian. Five minutes later he started sending it over a special military wavelength.

Van Eeden's message traveled 1,600 miles southeast of Moscow to the Tyuratam Antisatellite Facility in the Dzezkazgan Province.

Lieutenant Colonel Leonid Brusavitch, the duty officer in charge of communications, eyed the winking light on his console with an arched eyebrow. At first he thought it might be a message from the Flight Control Center in response to America's Condition Yellow alert. But when he glanced at the frequency-tracer readout below the flashing indicator light he saw that the incoming radio signal had originated from a nonmilitary source in Moscow. He activated the laser-driven radiotelegraph printer, which rapidly typed out the incoming message.

Brusavitch tore off the sheet and stood up from the console. He was thirty-five, about average height, with a determined-looking face, dark, lank hair, expressive eyes, and laugh lines at the corners of his mouth. He read the message over twice, shook his head slightly, and sighed. The radiotelegram was intended for his commanding officer, General-Lieutenant Rybinsk, the head of Tyuratam. There had been a dozen such messages, similarly cipher-coded, sent to Rybinsk over the past year. Rybinsk had explained to him that he was playing the European Community's stock market, that the messages were sent from his broker. The general-lieutenant also dispatched his own coded radiotelegrams to that same source. Consumed by curiosity one night three months ago, Brusavitch had used his console to trace the transmission. He found out it originated from the Dutch embassy.

There were other things that also didn't seem quite right. Last May one of Brusavitch's friends, an officer working in the computer operations center at Tyuratam, had confided during lunch that someone had illegally accessed classified data from their computers. An investigation had been launched at once, but when the final report was turned over to the general-lieutenant he apparently shelved it. Since then Brusavitch had kept copies of the radio dispatches between Rybinsk and the Dutch embassy. He was deeply concerned that the general-lieutenant may be in the business of selling classified material.

He made a copy of the current dispatch, then hand-carried the original printout down the long corridor to his commander's office.

From behind his huge desk General-Lieutenant Erik Rybinsk grinned and shrugged as he took the dispatch. He was fairly tall, with lean, muscular cheeks and a light tan that contrasted well with a head of short-cropped graying hair. A long nose and thin lips gave him a somewhat predatory air.

"Another tip from my broker, no doubt," he said a little too casually. He eyed Brusavitch for an instant, looking for any telltale signs of suspicion. His subordinate's face was expressionless.

After dismissing Brusavitch he scanned the message. A smile creased his face and he nodded to himself. So we're in the clear, he thought.

At fifty-eight years of age, Rybinsk had found a way in which to accumulate a vast amount of funds in a short period of time. Last year, when he learned all military retirement pensions would be slashed by 60 percent in a desperate effort by the government to save the faltering economy, Rybinsk had become greatly embittered. He had devoted his entire life to serving his country and believed he was entitled to something better. He let it be known to specific individuals that he had something valuable to sell. He had hired van Eeden, a paid assassin, to eliminate any potential leaks.

Presently he went to his office safe, removed a notebook, and flipped to a page listing the itinerary for the *Arcturus*, a luxury liner currently being chartered by his overseas business associates. Rybinsk calculated that the ship would be within radio range of Tyuratam in a few hours. He sat down and composed the message he would send them.

Chapter 23 *

GENERAL STRATTON'S JEEP came to a halt at the outside portal to the U.S. Space Defense Command Headquarters within Cheyenne Mountain, Colorado. The massive three-foot-thick, fourteen-foot-high steel blast door slid open with an oily purr, and the jeep drove inside the dark meandering tunnel.

Moments later he arrived at the operations center, a 3,000-square-foot, two-story bunker with four-foot-thick walls of steel welded by minute nuclear explosions in industrial reactors. The structure was cushioned from atomic bombs by huge shock absorbers. Forty-six men lived and worked here in reasonable comfort for months at a time.

General Stratton took an elevator to the Space Shield command room on the second floor. The room was huge, theaterlike, and manned by twenty-three officers, each one an experienced specialist in space-based strategic defense systems. Stratton went to the master control board and unlocked the clear plastic cover encasing the switches and buttons. He would personally activate the powerful Icarus antisatellite devices presently in geosynchronous orbit over Colorado and use them to tilt the Sunstroke satellite forty-five degrees on its axis. That angle would direct the microwave beam away from earth and shoot it into space, preventing it from discharging on Los Angeles.

On his plane flight to Colorado Springs Stratton had been in constant communication with the Space Shield controllers, ordering them to reprogram the Icarus navigational computers for an interception of the satellite. They were to begin deorbiting the Icarus spacecraft upon his arrival at the facility. There were four of these ASATs in parking orbit high above Cheyenne Mountain. Stratton had calculated all four were needed for the operation.

The Icarus devices were officially classed as MDAVs, Maneuverable Destabilizing Antisatellite Vehicles. They were designed to physically attach themselves to a target satellite using articulated magnetic clamps. Then the vehicles would activate their large rocket motors for either deorbiting the target or making it spin like a top to prevent it from transmitting data to ground controllers. Each ASAT possessed an RL-95 rocket motor capable of producing 80,000 pounds of thrust with a multiple restart capability.

The general studied the activation switches for the spacecraft on the panel before him. There were three switches for each ASAT. The first one activated an electromechanical interlock that committed a deorbit-and-attack interception of the target fed into the tracking computer. Even if the entire U.S. Space Defense Command complex was disabled by a power failure, the ASATs' internal circuitry could still process an attack on the target. The second switch initiated a fully automatic attack preparation, with final guidance corrections, target processing, opening of the ASATs' muzzle shutters, and preparation for mixing of thousands of gallons of hypergolic fuel. Switch number three was labeled Attack Commit. It activated the huge centrifugal pumps that would bring the fuel and oxidizer together in the rocket motor thrust chamber, where they would ignite spontaneously. This switch would not be thrown until the ASATs were attached.

For the next few minutes Stratton listened to the calm, steady litany of voices around him as an exhaustive check was made on all critical systems of the Icarus vehicles. During this period he moved from station to station, personally inspecting the flashing alphanumerical readouts. He peered at the target radar screen and saw the green blip representing the present position of the Sunstroke satellite. It was now passing over the Northeast Pacific Basin on its west-to-east orbit. He estimated the tail chase interception of SOLSAT X-1 would take about six hours.

When the systems check was finished General Stratton sat down at the master control console. Slowly, almost reverently, he brought his hands down on the first set of switches for the Icarus antisatellite vehicles. Then he sat back and laced his fingers.

In space, 22,300 miles above Cheyenne Mountain, four large cigar-shaped spacecraft designated MDAVs 1, 2, 3, and 4 responded to a series of radio commands. Each vehicle was 120 feet in length and 18 feet in diameter. They had been the second stage of the USAF Titan 4D rockets, which had lofted them into their parking orbits. The ASATs looked like flying fuel tanks, which was precisely what they were considering the vast amount of fuel each one carried.

The dark forms of the four vehicles were suddenly lit by tiny maneuvering jets, which flashed on and off like spotlights. The spacecraft seemed to slowly fall through space as they descended to the Sunstroke satellite's orbital altitude. The tail chase to intercept SOLSAT X-1 had begun.

In the solar power plant control room Mike Doheny peered at Jenkins's radar scope. With each revolution of the radar sweep hand he saw four green blips move closer to the Sunstroke satellite.

"He's activated them, all right," he told the members of his troubleshooting team. "They'll probably make contact in a few hours." When he looked away from the scope there was a worried expression on his face.

Professor Rosen flashed a deep-eyed look at Doheny. "What's wrong, Mike? Don't you think they'll work?"

"I'm concerned about the extent of damage from the collision," Doheny replied. "You saw the fractured housing, the broken fuel lines, the tangled circuits. The thing is in a highly unstable state, to say the least. When those devices attach themselves there's going to be a hell of a jolt. From what we've seen so far, anything could happen." Frowning, he said, "There's one method of preventing the discharge on L.A. that we haven't discussed yet."

"Such as?" asked Everett Nore.

"Physically obstructing the beam," answered Doheny.

Fred Gaither heaved his bulk out of a console chair with an audible grunt and stood up to stretch his legs. "Dr. Kitami's remark a while ago about thunderstorms reminds me of something that may or may not be of value," he said laconically. "A number of years ago the National Oceanic and Atmospheric Administration asked me to evaluate the environmental impact of a meteorological project called Stormbreak." He closed his eyes in concentration for a moment. "It was a methodical program for fragmenting severe thunderstorms before they reached inhabited regions. The first stage involved the seeding of rain cells by bombing the clouds with alectoes, cartridges filled with fine silver iodide crystals. An old trick."

Gaither waved his cigar through the air. "Now, the most interesting feature about Stormbreak was the second stage. Lightning suppression. They made use of metal chaff, six-inch-long strips of aluminum foil used by pilots to confuse radar. Planes were filled with negatively charged chaff, and tons of the stuff were dropped into a storm. It effectively grounded the storm's electrical charges, diminishing the lightning by eighty-seven percent, if I remember correctly.''

He took a deep breath and turned to Doheny. ''Microwaves and lightning are both manifestations of electromagnetic radiation. Maybe there's some way we can neutralize the satellite's microwave beam, like they did to the lightning.'' He tucked his pudgy hands into the pockets of his voluminous trousers. ''What do you think, Mike, is this of any use?''

For a moment Doheny was reflective, incommunicative, desperately trying to dig deep into his memory. He recalled the nagging feeling he had experienced earlier when reading General Stratton's list of Strategic Defense System components. He had felt that it was incomplete, that some element was missing. Now he remembered.

''Dipoles,'' he said abruptly. ''Instead of aluminum strips we could use copper dipoles to disperse the microwaves. Gentlemen, do you remember the Needles satellite program?''

Professor Rosen grimaced. ''How could I forget,'' he growled. ''We thought it would put astronomy out of business for good.''

Doheny saw that Ted Kitami was at once alert, nodding and thinking intensely.

Nore looked up with a sour expression on his face. ''We lost that contract to Rockwell,'' he muttered. His eyebrows arched. ''You were with them then, weren't you, Mike?''

''Right, Everett. I was assistant project manager on Needles eleven years ago.''

''Needles,'' murmured Malcolm Courtland. ''That was a primitive Star Wars ASAT, wasn't it?''

''I feel left out,'' lamented Gaither, his round face set in a pugnacious expression, as if the man in the moon were scowling. ''Will someone please tell me what this 'Needles' thing is all about?''

Doheny explained that Project Needles was an early Space Shield experiment conducted by the U.S. Air Force involving two antisatellite spacecraft placed in geosynchronous orbit. Each satellite contained millions of copper-wire dipoles, each about a half inch in length. The purpose of the experiment was to determine the feasibility of preventing an enemy spacecraft from either transmitting or receiving radio signals by screening it with a cloud of dipoles.

One of the Needles spacecraft was maneuvered alongside a target, an aging Tiros meteorological satellite scheduled for replacement. The dipoles were released and the test was successful. However, optical and radio astronomers protested vehemently, arguing that the dipoles would quickly disperse and spread throughout the satellite's orbit, interfering with astronomical work for years to come. As it turned out the interference was minimal. The air force decided to abandon Project Needles because the dipole cloud broke up too quickly, allowing signals to reach the target spacecraft after only a few hours.

"Our rectenna outside the plant," Doheny said, "is composed of billions of dipoles that reflect the microwaves into a receiver for DC conversion. Beyond a doubt dipoles scatter microwaves." Doheny shot a glance at the big Mercator map on the far wall. "As far as I know, the second, unused Needles spacecraft is still in orbit, probably in the air force's graveyard slot above Hawaii. Theoretically, we should be able to reactivate it."

"After eleven years?" asked Rosen skeptically.

"I think so," Doheny said encouragingly. "Its engines use long-storage hypergolic fuels. And the dipole launching mechanism is spring-actuated. There's nothing to wear out."

He strode across the room to the SATSCAN computer and immediately began calculating an interception course from Needles' position over Hawaii to the solar satellite's present location seven hundred miles off the California coast.

Without warning Provost Marshal Earl Clayton walked into the control room. He was conducting an inspection of the plant, making sure that everything was secure. No one paid any attention to him. He glanced first at the Mercator map, then at the blips on Jenkins's radar scope. With his thumb hooked in his holster, he approached Doheny.

"Scuttlebutt around here says your satellite is going to fry L.A.," Clayton said in a low voice. "Do you really think you can stop it?"

"We're going to try," Doheny muttered without looking up from the computer console.

"Maybe you can, maybe you can't," said Clayton. He swept his hand through the air. "Not much discipline here."

Doheny glanced up at Clayton in amazement. Why, he thought, is this man trying to bait me? Then he recalled that he had challenged Clayton's authority when they had first met. Since then the friction between them had grown steadily. He decided to ignore the provost marshal and concentrate on the task at hand.

Clayton leaned closer to Doheny. "Discipline. Self-control. That's what's missing in this place. For instance, did you know that your boss is an alcoholic? He's halfway through his second bottle of whiskey."

Doheny felt the pressure building behind his eyes. "Get out."

"You don't have the authority to order me to leave," whispered Clayton, grinning. "Or the balls to make me."

Doheny sat there, firmly gripping the edge of the console, staring at the digits on the screen.

Clayton waved his hand at Rosen, Gaither, Courtland, Nore, and Kitami. "You've got some fine people here," he said with heavy sarcasm. "The best. An old Jew, a fat man, a nigger, a drunk, and a gook. Yessir, fine people."

The numbers on the screen before Doheny exploded into a white-hot brilliance as his mind seethed with an intense and consuming anger. He sprang up from his seat, put the palm of his hand flat against the provost marshal's chest, and pushed hard. "I said *get out!*" he shouted.

Clayton staggered backward from the force of the shove.

For a moment they stood there, eyes locked. To the others in the room it seemed as if the two men might come to blows. If it came to that, Doheny's height would give him some advantage. He was six foot three, limber, and had an athlete's huskiness. Clayton was several inches shorter, but had a thicker, compact body of beef with heavy arms and legs and the training to use them in combat.

Everett Nore swung toward them, his face twisted with irritation and his forefinger in motion. He looked at Clayton with eyes that were as friendly as a cracking glacier.

"Marshal," snapped Nore, pointing his finger, "you're interfering with control room operations. Leave here at once," he warned, "or I'll report you to your commanding officer at Fort Union. Have I made myself clear?"

Clayton nodded, but his expression remained rigid. He knew Nore's Pentagon connections could cause him big trouble.

"I don't want you setting foot here again," ordered Nore. "Now get out."

Somebody laughed.

Without a word or a backward glance, Clayton left the room.

The heat was gone now from Mike Doheny's mind. Slowly his

body began to relax and he returned to his calculations. Within minutes he had the interception orbit plotted. He turned to Nore and said, "It'll take the Needles spacecraft about five hours or so to make the rendezvous from its parking orbit. I think we can pull it off here." He swept his hand around the room. "We've got the equipment and personnel necessary to reactivate Needles. All we require are the exact coordinates of its present position and the activation codes."

Nore nodded thoughtfully. "General Stratton can supply us with that information." He eyed the hot-line extension near the computer console. "I'll call him now and explain the situation."

Nore went to the red scrambler phone and picked up the receiver. There was no dial tone, no high-pitched hooting sound, no voice on the other end. He slammed the receiver down. "They've disconnected it," he shouted. He was angry and unnerved by this strange turn of events. "*What the hell is going on?*"

"It seems," Doheny said heavily, "your friends in Washington have written us off."

General Stratton's eyes were riveted to the large display screen, which showed the 24,000-mile scan of the immense high-resolution radar dish atop Cheyenne Mountain. He had electronically squelched out all objects detected by the radar that were less than five tons in mass, as well as all ground returns. This left six blips on the screen, each one possessing a code assigned to it by the command center computer. The most prominent blip was the Sunstroke satellite. The four blips in a V formation closing in on it were the Icarus ASATs, while the fainter blip at the upper right-hand corner represented a Westpac military communications satellite in geosynchronous orbit. Data on the Icarus devices' flight paths were displayed on the margins of the rectangular screen.

Stratton glanced at the big digital clock on the wall. It was two minutes to midnight. Less than seven hours to the microwave discharge.

September 12
The Last Day *

Chapter 24 *

FOUR HOURS LATER the Space Shield officer seated at the radar console pointed to the ICARUS blip nearest the Sunstroke satellite. "MDAV One will reach attachment point in five minutes, sir."

Stratton nodded, then flicked open the second set of switches for each Icarus antisatellite vehicle. These switches activated the automatic attack sequence, began final corrections and target processing, and opened the muzzle shutters at the front end of each vehicle to expose the magnetic attachment clamps.

An officer across the room reported that all four ASATs had properly responded to the remote slaving commands and had begun their attack sequences. He read off a series of alphanumeric codes from his displays.

A voice near Stratton said, "Four minutes to attachment."

The other men in the room worked quickly and efficiently at their stations. They had practiced hard for this moment, one of the rare instances when a Space Shield component was to be actually deployed against a live orbital target.

"Three minutes to attachment."

Stratton recalled the grim warning that Mike Doheny had given him regarding the use of these ASATs against the satellite. Doheny feared that the Icarus devices would activate the satellite's coolant system, enabling the microwave transmitter to operate continuously. However, Stratton believed the coolant lines had been severed by the collision, rendering the entire system inoperative.

"One minute to attachment."

The general felt his pulse quicken. He stepped closer to the radar screen, peering intently as the first of the small blips started to merge with the largest one.

*   *   *

High in space, the first intruder, a cigar-shaped object 120 feet in length, closed in on the tail section of SOLSAT X-1. A dozen thick tentacles dangled from the intruder's front end, which earlier had opened like an iris.

The intruder drew closer and closer. Soon it was only five hundred feet away. Then three hundred . . . one hundred and closing.

Had SOLSAT X-1 been operative its sensors would have registered a gentle thump at its aft section. Moments later there were two more thumps. Now three devices were attached to the tail section: one at twelve o'clock, one at three o'clock, and another at six o'clock.

The fourth Icarus had to perform a more difficult maneuver than the others to reach its nine o'clock attachment point. Numerous course corrections were required, and the device had to fire its thrusters repeatedly. This complicated maneuver taxed the abilities of the ground controllers far below and cost them nearly an hour and a half of precious time. It also caused the vehicle to build up considerably more momentum and velocity than its sister spacecraft. It struck SOLSAT X-1 hard.

The satellite shuddered violently from the force of impact, but all four Icarus devices clung stubbornly to their host.

The sudden jarring set up strong vibrations deep within the satellite's hull, causing a twelve-inch-diameter aluminum coolant line to break free of its fasteners. Swinging wildly, the heavy coil struck the frozen turbopump valves. The effect was like tapping ice from an outdoor water faucet with a hammer. The coating of ice on the valves was shattered by the blow. They were now unstuck and functional. Only a single electrical impulse from SOLSAT X-1's command computer was needed to open them.

However, this singular event went completely unnoticed by the inoperative computer.

General Stratton nervously glanced at the big digital clock. Barely six minutes remained before the scheduled microwave discharge on Los Angeles. His eyes flickered across the propellant readouts on the Icarus guidance console. For an instant there was a flash of red and Stratton felt his heart lurch. Then all indicators turned green.

The general swiveled in his chair to face the master control panel. With quick, precise movements of his fingers he flicked each of the activation switches for the ICARUS propulsion systems, then stared with a fierce intensity at the readouts on the guidance console.

At the solar power plant Doheny and the others huddled around the satellite infrared screen saw the thermal image of Los Angeles begin to slowly rotate in a lazy wide arc, then disappear off screen.

Doheny turned to Jenkins. "Give me the satellite's attitude, including coning/nutation motions," he ordered.

Jenkins ran a computer analysis of the radar scan, then reported, "Positive clockwise rotation to forty-five degrees. Coning/nutation motions amount to minus one-nineteen degrees right ascension, minus seventeen degrees declination. Right on target," he added, grinning.

"He did it," said Nore, relieved. "Goddamn it, he really did it."

"Thank God," sighed Rosen.

Gaither stroked his pendulous cheeks. "That satellite is going to have quite a surprise when it wakes up this morning."

"Yes," Doheny said quietly. He couldn't shake the feeling that the operation had been too easy.

In the vast black silence of space twenty thousand miles above Los Angeles, SOLSAT X-1 rushed toward the sunlit portion of the planet below. Although the huge satellite was still enveloped in darkness, it would soon cross into the daylight and become operational.

Seconds passed. Then, directly ahead, a gray stain seeped along the edge of the world. Dawn was about to break. Steadily, inevitably, came a brilliant thin line of blazing incandescence. A moment later the sun itself leaped above the horizon with sudden swiftness, and its first rays struck the satellite's solar-paneled wings. Its on-board systems suddenly came to life.

There was a new subroutine controlling SOLSAT X-1. It had switched on during the night and had ordered the command computer into a defense mode. The Pentagon had intended to activate this subroutine at a later date to test the satellite's defensive capabilities. Instead, this new set of instructions had been activated out of sequence due to the memory shifts caused by the collision with the ASAT device two days ago.

By analyzing data from the pressure sensors studding the satellite's hull, the command computer calculated that four intrud-

ers were clinging to the aft section. At that instant the microwave
transmitter housing began throbbing and pulsating with electricity.
However, the computer determined the satellite's position had
been altered and that the microwave beam was not being directed
at earth.

A gently warming sun shone down on Washington that morning, bathing the lawn and garden outside the White House with its
bright, cheerful rays. Sunlight streamed through the French
windows on the second floor of the stately mansion, pleasantly
illuminating the private study of the Western world's most
powerful leader. This room was his personal sanctum, the one
room where he could concentrate on doing the job for which he
had been elected. But today he was having a difficult time carrying
out the routine duties of his office.

President James Kendall sat at his desk, glowering at the pile of
papers stacked before him—the clerical chores of the chief
executive of the United States, untouched since the Sunstroke
crisis had begun. There were policy papers from the State
Department to be read, two dozen commissions and executive
orders waiting for his signature, and eight recommendations from
the attorney general for judicial appointments.

He was making an attempt this morning to conduct business as
usual because of the urging of Jack Conley, his national security
adviser. Conley had wanted to quell any suspicions among the
White House press corps, and the best way to do it was to have the
chief executive carrying out his normal duties.

Kendall sat alone in his study, angry, tired, his nerves frayed.
He was anxiously waiting to hear from Dean Stratton. Damn it, he
thought, why hasn't he called? What's happening up there in
space?

He scrawled his signature on one of the judicial appointment
recommendations and was reaching for another when the light on
his secure phone started blinking. It was General Stratton calling
from Cheyenne Mountain. The call was being relayed to the White
House via a multi-channel military communications satellite
code-named Westpac. This comsat was in a fixed orbit directly
above the Sunstroke satellite. Stratton informed him that the Icarus
devices had successfully reoriented the satellite so that its microwave power beam was directed away from the earth during its
thirty-minute discharge.

Kendall let out a long sigh of relief. "Congratulations, Dean. You did an excellent job. Excellent."

"Thank you, sir," replied Stratton.

Kendall crossed his legs and closed his eyes. His brow drew into a rigid knot above the bridge of his nose. "Now," he said slowly, "the way I understand it, the satellite fires its beam every time it swings out into the sun."

"That's right, sir."

"And the only reason the beam missed L.A. was because your ASATs pointed the working end of the satellite away from earth."

"Yes, sir."

"Will the thing be kept in this position permanently, or do you have to nudge it from time to time?"

"Sir," said Stratton, "our ground controllers must periodically adjust the satellite's attitude to maintain it at the correct angle."

"I see." The President sat back in his chair, massaging his chin. He proceeded to inform Stratton about the nuclear supermissile being assembled at Vandenberg Air Force Base. He told the general the missile would be launched later that day to destroy the satellite.

Both the President and General Stratton would have been shocked to learn their conversation was being overheard as it bounced off the Westpac military communications satellite. The two men had no way of knowing that another entity was monitoring their call.

A portion of the self-defense subroutine currently directing SOLSAT X-1's functions had originally been designed to instruct the on-board command computer to receive and analyze all radio transmissions between enemy ground stations and their spacecraft. Now, due to its jumbled circuits, the computer was unable to differentiate between the Westpac military comsat and an enemy spacecraft.

SOLSAT X-1's parabolic communications antenna had tuned in to the frequency wavelength linking the White House and Cheyenne Mountain the instant Stratton made the connection. The computer monitored the transmission, silently interpreting and analyzing. Finally it collated this information with the data stored in memory.

In microseconds the computer made the connections between the unsuccessful attempt by the enemy ground station to reprogram it, the fact that four enemy spacecraft were attached to its hull, and the recently acquired knowledge that a nuclear-tipped missile would soon be launched to destroy the satellite. This correlation was automatically processed and stored.

Suddenly SOLSAT X-1's parabolic antenna began receiving a series of slaving commands being transmitted to the four intruders attached to the hull. The computer instantly recorded the radio commands on magnetic tape. Then the satellite's gyroscopes detected a change in attitude. Its position was being adjusted for orbital drift.

The SOLSAT X-1 computer began deciphering the remote slaving codes that had been transmitted to the Icarus devices.

That morning Major General Barry Wisneski, the base commander of Vandenberg AFB, stood at the edge of a huge yawning pit set in the tarmac. With his feet wide apart and his arms akimbo, the commander's short, stocky body was held in a posture that was almost arrogant as he peered down into the hardened M-X missile silo. The cylindrical concrete-lined pit before him was 30 feet in diameter and 115 feet deep.

Fifty feet below the rim, illuminated in the harsh glare of the California sun, six figures wearing hoods and heavy radiation suits moved like priests along the scaffolding surrounding the nose cone of the buried missile. They were cautiously disengaging the 425-kiloton Mark 5 atomic weapons used as multiple independently targeted reentry vehicles in the M-X Peacekeeper. Each of the nuclear devices were separately encased in a black cone-shaped ablative shield made of laminated carbon fibers for protection during the fiery reentry phase of their trajectory.

Although the missile carried ten of these powerful bombs, only three would be needed to completely destroy the immense Sunstroke satellite. After being removed from the missile the devices would be fitted into a titanium-alloy collar, custom built overnight, which would then be fastened to the Taurus 44E satellite carrier waiting on Launch Pad 9B two miles away.

General Wisneski and the others with him stepped back several yards from the mouth of the silo to allow an overhead crane to lower its hoist into the pit to lift the nuclear devices to the surface. Soon all three atomic bombs were gently deposited onto the back of a shock-mounted, pneumatically cushioned transport vehicle. Each of the weapons were approximately four feet in height, one and a half feet in diameter, and weighed four hundred pounds.

Wisneski consulted briefly with Lieutenant Colonel Milton W.

Jackson, chief of the M-X Division of the 7595th Missile Group, and was told the good news that they were ahead of schedule. They watched the atomic bombs begin their slow two-mile journey to the Taurus rocket, jutting against the bright morning sky like a great needle.

Chapter 25 *

THAT MORNING DIANE Bradford's heart was beating like a rabbit's when one of the MPs, a man of medium height with a deep suntan and heavy muscles bulging under his uniform, jerked a thumb at her and eleven other prisoners.

"You people are first. Come on, let's move it."

Diane took a deep breath and exhaled slowly in an effort to calm her nerves. The moment she had been anxiously waiting for—as well as dreading—had finally arrived. It was time to execute her plan. She had noted the day before that the MPs had selected a dozen people closest to the lounge entrance and escorted them to the showers first. Ten minutes were allowed for the actual shower, and another ten for toweling off and using the rest rooms.

She hoped desperately that Mike Doheny would show up in his office today, the one room in the plant she thought the MPs would never search. She believed it was the safest place for her to conduct the interview.

As she got up from her cot she exchanged glances with Andy. There was a ghost of a smile on his lips but his eyes betrayed the fear and apprehension building inside him. The rest of the group included Deputy Energy Secretary Howard Averson and two television reporters plus their assistants. Three MPs quickly herded them out of the room and down the corridor.

The ground-floor hall was well lit but deserted. Diane ticked off the signs as they passed along the hall. Accounting, Personnel Services, Badge Control. Then they rounded a corner and came upon the half dozen shower stalls set up outside the rest rooms. She surveyed the area. The heavy twill shower curtains were still damp from yesterday and puddles of water coated the plastic mats on the floor in front of each stall. She eyed the thick black water hoses that ran from the stalls to the faucets inside the lavatory. So did Andy.

Diane immediately went to the second stall from the right, the one with the loose ceiling tile above it. She kicked off her high heels and climbed in, then took off her outer clothes and draped them over the curtain rod. The other women in the group also entered the stalls and undressed.

From the pockets of her pantsuit Diane took out her notebook and penlight and stuffed them both into the top of her panty hose. She stood on her tiptoes and inspected the vinyl ceiling tile above her head to make sure it was still loose. It was. After pointing the shower head away from her, she turned on the water and waited for Andy to create the diversion.

It had been arranged beforehand that while the women showered the men went to the lavatory for a shave. An MP at the rest-room door passed out army shaving kits—a can of lather and a disposable razor—to each man. Andy Johnson and the others took their kits inside and headed for the washbasins.

Andy was a likable young man in his mid-twenties, thin but wiry, with curly blond hair. He had come to love and admire Diane during the past two years he had held camera for her. Now was his chance to show her how much he really cared.

Knowing he had only a few minutes in which to act, he quickly surveyed the scene around him. There was one MP inside, positioned near the open door. The soldier was leaning against the wall, looking bored. For a moment Andy studied the half dozen water hoses snaking across the floor from the door to the washbasins. The black hoses bulged with water pressure. He stood there, fumbling with his shaving kit as he tried to determine which hose went to which shower stall.

He noticed that all of the basins except for one had hoses connected to the faucets. Four men were fighting for space around the one free basin, each man trying to get at the stream of water from the single faucet as he shaved. Former titles of authority meant nothing here, for even Deputy Energy Secretary Howard Averson had to wait his turn.

Andy walked across the room to the toilet stalls and entered one. He was aware that two were already occupied. After securing the door he took handfuls of tissue paper and threw them into the toilet, enough to plug it. He flushed it, then left the stall and joined the group at the washbasins. The large mirror on the wall before him enabled Andy to observe the MP at the door.

At that moment there was a loud gurgling followed by the sound

of water sloshing. When the MP's gaze turned toward the dark
stain rapidly spreading across the tile floor, Andy's hand shot out
to the nearest faucet with a hose connected to it. Guiltily, he shut
off the hot-water valve, instantly turning the warm water in one of
the shower stalls to icy cold.

Outside in the corridor, Diane and everyone else heard an
earsplitting screech, then the sound of a shower curtain being
whipped open. Diane peered out and saw a small dark-haired
woman leap from the stall, screaming. The woman clawed
frantically at a towel, but it slipped from her fingers and fell to the
floor. She stooped awkwardly to retrieve it, exposing her naked
breasts and buttocks. Two smiling MPs raced over to investigate.
Both soldiers' backs were turned to the other stalls.

Diane moved fast. She jumped on the molded plastic step above
the shower floor, reached up to the loose ceiling tile, and pushed
it off the metal supports. Then she slid the tile sideways to allow
access to the ceiling space. She placed her hands firmly on the top
of the shower stall, got a good grip, then put one foot flat against
the wall. Using her arms for support, she planted her other foot on
the wall. By applying pressure with her legs and supporting herself
with her hands she managed to elevate her right foot a little higher,
then her left one. The strain on her arms was brutally painful and,
at one point, she almost gave up. But she kept at it, using every
ounce of strength in the process, and slowly inched herself up like
a mountaineer climbing a sheer cliff.

When her head rose above the top of the stall she could see
down into the corridor. The two MPs were talking to the woman,
who was still shivering. One of them offered her another towel.

Diane's legs entered the dark cramped ceiling space first,
followed by her upper torso. She had made it. A feeling of elation
rushed through her, masking the exhaustion and aching muscles.
She began sliding the heavy vinyl tile back in place. But she
shoved too hard and it fell against the metal supports with a dull
thud that jarred the whole suspended ceiling.

She did not see the startled lead MP turn around sharply, did not
see his expression change as he instinctively realized his attention
had been diverted away from the other prisoners, did not see him
head for the shower stalls fast, his partner at his heels.

Heedless of the screams of outrage from the other women in the
showers, the two MPs tore open the curtains to each stall. They

froze when they found the empty one. Both men exchanged worried glances.

Directly above their heads Diane switched on her penlight and its thin pencil of illumination cut through the gloom. She saw a maze of electrical conduits, pipes, and air-conditioning ducts wrapped in fuzzy fiberglass insulation. Assuming that she had only a few minutes at most before her absence was noticed, she took out her notebook containing the floor plans she had drawn. She examined them for a moment, then started moving.

The ceiling space was not more than three feet high and she had to crawl on hands and knees. She had the irrational fear that rats might appear at any time, chirping and squealing. She continued on, the dust from the insulation swirling as her back brushed the ducts. It smelled musty and irritated her nasal passages. She sneezed. More than once she had the sensation of being buried alive, and that the concrete floor above her was pressing down, about to crush her. Ahead in the thin light beam she could see a mass of twisted pipes and wiring, some of them in her path. She swallowed her claustrophobic fear and moved on.

The concrete floor pressed more heavily on her back as she was forced to crawl over the tangled assembly of pipes and wires. She felt them poking her stomach as she maneuvered over them. A burr on one of the pipes tore the crotch area of her sheer pantyhose.

She had to move partly by feel, advancing forward slowly, cautiously. Her confidence in her ability to successfully traverse through this strange world between floors grew steadily. Then she accidently touched a steam pipe with her elbow and it burned her. She stifled the urge to cry out.

Diane wondered what other dangerous obstacles lay ahead in the darkness.

In the commissary on the floor above Diane, Provost Marshal Earl Clayton was interrupted by an incessant beeping from his belt. He took another bite from the buttered roll in his hand, put it down on the plate of food before him, unclipped his radio transceiver, and responded to the call.

"Sir, this is Owens at security detainment post three, first floor," the lead MP told Clayton. A pause, then, "We have an escape, a white female reporter, blond, late twenties, about five eight. Name is Diane Bradford, she's with Cable News Service.

Last seen entering the showers here. Left her clothes and shoes behind. Request instructions."

"Give me the whole situation," ordered Clayton. After the lead MP briefed him, he said, "Take the prisoners back to the lounge. I'll be down there in a few minutes. And, Owens?"

"Yessir?"

"You're on report," Clayton said, switching off. He sat there for a moment, angry, absently scratching the thick hair on the back of his neck. He had been half expecting an escape attempt by one of the cocky young employees at the plant. But he never thought a woman reporter would try it. "Bradford," he muttered. The name was familiar, but he couldn't quite place it. Then he remembered and smiled. Well, he thought, there's no way she can get out of the plant.

He pressed the button on his transceiver and ordered the corridor security details to freeze all elevators until further notice. He gave them Diane's description, her last known location, and her alleged intent of leaving the premises. He clipped the transceiver back on his belt and got up from the table. When he was through interrogating the prisoners he intended to personally lead the search for Diane.

Three floors below the commissary Mike Doheny was hunched over Jenkins's radar scope, completely unaware of Diane's escape and the hunt for her. He was peering closely at the green satellite blip, watching for any severe change in its orientation. Aside from some minor attitudinal corrections implemented by General Stratton there had been no activity since the satellite's microwave discharge above Los Angeles. Its overheated microwave transmitter was still aimed away from earth.

Suddenly communications technician Glen Larsen tore off his headset. "I'm picking up a high-frequency radio transmission," he told Doheny in an excited voice. "It's coming over the L-band, the frequency reserved for the satellite."

"Put it on the speakers," Doheny ordered.

A hissing crackle came over the control room speakers. Larsen turned a knob and the sound became something like what Tennyson had called the "murmuring of innumerable bees." He turned the knob once more, and the sound was a babble of distant electronic voices, some shouting, some conversing normally, some screaming, some whispering—all of them trying beyond desperation to communicate an unintelligible message.

Startled by the noise, the others in the room grouped around the console.

Doheny screwed his eyes shut and listened closely. Finally he said, "It sounds like a code of some kind. Try decoding the signal with the multiplex computer."

Larsen donned his headset, studied the dials and gauges before him, then punched a keyboard to feed the signal into the computer, which instantly began chattering. A moment later it printed out the contents of the message.

Doheny tore off the printout and scanned it. It contained a numerical sequence for activating a hypergolic propulsion system. He immediately recalled that the Icarus destabilizing devices had that type of rocket motor. He showed the sheet to the others.

Jenkins examined it and cocked his head toward the speaker. "Do you think the military is broadcasting that signal, bouncing it off the satellite, and we're picking up the reflections?"

"No," said Doheny, pointing to a dial. "Look at the power level. The signal strength is way too high for an echo."

A sudden, frightening thought occurred to Doheny. He turned to Larsen and said sharply, "I want you to pinpoint the source. Use your dampeners to filter out all radio noise from that portion of the sky, and from the ground. Then boost your EME phase modulation. That should enable you to get a good fix."

Larsen spun dials and turned knobs. Three minutes later he looked up from his console, his face taut, his eyes bulging whitely. "The satellite," he yelled. "It's coming from the solar satellite."

Beads of perspiration formed on Doheny's forehead. A new horror had now been corroborated by Larsen's simple pronouncement. The implications were staggering.

"I think," Doheny said gravely, "it's trying to activate the propulsion systems for the Icarus devices. General Stratton may have inadvertently supplied the thing with maneuverability."

In the deep haunting blackness of space high above Southern California SOLSAT X-1 was broadcasting the original activation signals that General Stratton had transmitted to the four Icarus ASATs. Moments earlier its command computer had broken the codes. Then, on the basis of the correlation it had made between the recent attempts by ground controllers to commandeer the satellite and the fact that a nuclear missile was being readied against it, the self-defensive subroutine driving the computer ordered it to calculate a new orbit, one that would take it out of missile range.

A vast number of non-synchronous orbits had been stored in memory for military testing purposes on varied terrain. The computer accessed a polar orbit for two reasons. First, this trajectory would carry the satellite furthest away from the missile's point of origin. Secondly, the computer had been programmed with extensive instructions for carrying out a polar orbital insertion without the need for ground guidance. This program involved a limited test of the microwave power beam on the Arctic environment.

An instant later the subroutine instructed the computer to transmit the coded Icarus ASAT activation signals that had been stored on magnetic tape. These signals also contained the thrust vector control codes for swiveling the Icarus rocket nozzles to the proper position for effecting an orbital change.

This procedure had been programmed into the SOLSAT X-1 computer to provide it with the capability of commandeering hostile spacecraft in close proximity. Defense Department strategists had never thought it would be used against their own craft.

Geysers of bright red flame erupted from the main rocket engines at the rear of each Icarus device. Slowly, ponderously, the immense satellite navigated a ninety-degree turn as it broke loose from its west-to-east trajectory. Then the command computer fired all four Icarus engines in a simultaneous burn to propel SOLSAT X-1 into a polar orbit.

Chapter 26 *

A BABBLE OF voices broke out among the Space Shield controllers inside Cheyenne Mountain. The guidance officer, his face strained, turned to General Stratton.

"Sir," he said tautly, "the Icarus MDAVs have fired their main engines. They're not under our control. The satellite is changing course."

An intricate pattern of furrows appeared on Stratton's forehead. He shot a glance at the radar screen above the master control console and saw the large satellite blip slowly moving toward the top of the display on a northern trajectory. Somehow the satellite had broken free from its west-to-east orbit.

He flicked each of the Icarus activation switches off, but there was no response. Something was preventing the ASATs from responding to the cut-off command. Their engines continued to fire.

Frustrated, Stratton threw the switches again and again, with no result. He spent the next five minutes doing a circuit of the room, peering closely at all the dials, gauges, and readouts in a desperate attempt to find some clue as to what went wrong. Then he questioned each of his senior officers, demanding an explanation for the malfunction. No one could offer one.

In a last desperate move to shut down the rocket engines he ordered the guidance officer to boost the cut-off signal, then he snapped the switches closed again, hard. When he saw that the engines continued to burn, his hands went limp and his shoulders sagged. He suddenly felt immensely weary and older than his fifty-five years. He would have to immediately inform the President that they had lost control of the satellite.

He picked up the secure phone beside his console and, in a tight voice, informed his commander in chief of this latest inexplicable development.

The President's familiar New England–accented voice was high pitched and urgent and barely under control. He demanded an explanation, but Stratton was unable to provide one. Recovering his breath, Kendall ordered him to find out what happened, and to determine the satellite's new course. This information was to be relayed without delay to Vandenberg AFB's base commander.

In the Crisis Room at the White House President Kendall angrily hung up the phone. He was furious at Dean Stratton for losing control of the satellite. Thank God, he thought, that I had the foresight to set up the Vandenberg missile shot. He took solace in the knowledge that the thing would be destroyed before the day was over.

He sat at the oval conference table, glaring at the handful of advisers surrounding him. "Dean lost the satellite," he told them. "His ASATs are taking the thing along some northern orbit, and he can't do a damn thing about it."

"Does Vandenberg know about this?" asked chairman of the Joint Chiefs of Staff General Willis Thompson.

Kendall nodded. "Dean is informing them right now. Nothing," he said emphatically, "is going to stop their missile from blowing it up. You can bank on it."

He turned his thoughts to the more pressing matter at hand, the Russians' reply to his order to elevate the status of America's missile-carrying submarine fleet to Condition Yellow. He had ordered the warning during the night, after learning that they had put their own long-range bombers and ICBM forces on alert. However, instead of stepping down, their response had been to send more bombers aloft, to put additional ICBMs on line, and to place their own submarine fleet on alert status. The game of nuclear chess, which no one could win, was well under way.

The President asked General Thompson, "Will, could you give us a precise picture of what the Russians are doing at this very minute?"

General Thompson rose from his seat at the conference table holding a remote control device in his hand and stepped up to one of the large projection TV screens. The wall-size display was tied in to the network of KH-14 surveillance satellites girdling the globe. Thompson flashed a Mercator map on the screen showing the precise positions of all Russian nuclear missile-carrying submarines, each one pinpointed by a blinking red light.

The general took out a collapsible aluminum pointer from his

pocket and indicated several of the lights in the Atlantic and
Pacific oceans. "These are the present positions of their
Dobrinyin-class submarines, each of which carries ten SS-N-34
nuclear missiles. In a few hours they will have maneuvered within
target range of virtually every American city." He paused and
eyed the President. "Sir, as you know, this maneuver is in
response to your ordering our own sub fleet to Condition Yellow."

Kendall swallowed hard and nodded. As he watched the
blinking lights slowly moving toward the American shores he
began to regret issuing that order.

General Thompson flashed a series of live television pictures
taken from low earth orbit of Russian SS-9/SL-11 nuclear missile
sites. The resolution was so fine that the men in the conference
room could see technicians engaged in a flurry of activity around
the silos. It was obvious the missile sites at Stangusta and those
along the Oder and Amur rivers were being readied for launch.

The high-resolution images of air bases at Baku, Tashkent, and
a dozen others under Kremlin control appeared with almost
bewildering speed. But even the untrained eyes of the President
and his advisers could make out scores of heavy bombers racing
down the runways and streaking into the skies. According to
General Thompson, these were long-range Bear bombers being
sent aloft to join the other bomber squadrons that were already
airborne. The men at the oval table watched the television images
in silence.

General Thompson plunged the screen into darkness with a
touch of a button. "Mr. President," he said gravely, "clearly the
Russian armed forces are moving for a first strike. I'm afraid we
have no choice but to meet this threat with a State Orange strategic
alert."

Hugh Fitzpatrick, the white-maned defense secretary, suddenly
spoke up, his face pale and perspiring. "But that's only one notch
away from a nuclear war alert," he croaked. "If we go to State
Orange it'll provoke them even further." He shook his head and
turned to Kendall. "We can't afford to do it, Mr. President," he
pleaded. "We can't go to war just because the Russians tried to
shoot down one of our satellites."

"With all due respect, Mr. Secretary," interrupted General
Thompson, "Sunstroke isn't just an ordinary satellite. It's an
advanced space-based weapons platform. A logical military target
which they took out as a prelude to a first strike."

Fitzpatrick swiveled around sharply, the color returning to his cheeks. "Damn it, General, we don't know that for certain. I still think they attacked the satellite because they felt intimidated by the thing. I don't believe they had any intention of going to war."

"Fitz, Will," said President Kendall, rapping the table, "we've got to discuss this without letting our emotions get carried away."

"A difficult thing to do," rasped Fitzpatrick, "when we're discussing an action that could bring about hundreds of millions of radioactive corpses and the world bombed back to the Stone Age." He paused for breath, his chest rising and falling rapidly like that of a man who had just run a marathon. He continued in a more reasonable tone. "Escalating our forces now will push them too far, too soon. Look what happened when we went to Condition Yellow last night. The Russian reply was to engage their own submarine fleet, launch more aircraft, and bring their big ICBMs on line. They sure as hell didn't back down like we hoped. If we go to State Orange they'll be forced to go to their own equivalent alert status and only a hairsbreadth will separate us from an all-out nuclear exchange. We can't risk pushing Gorodin to the edge like this."

National Security Adviser Jack Conley leaned forward. "Sir," he said to Kendall, "from what we know of President Gorodin, his outward demeanor of being a self-assured, single-minded head of state is illusory. The State Department believes he's under constant pressure from Clausenko, the vice president, who has strong ties to their military regime. State thinks Clausenko is trying to depose Gorodin at this time. As you're well aware, President Gorodin is pro-democracy and has developed an economic rapport with the West. An escalation of our forces could play right into Clausenko's hands and help him to topple Gorodin. Of course at this moment we can't be absolutely certain if Gorodin is still calling the shots over there."

The President sat back in his seat, chin in hand. "I remember a briefing I got once—maybe two years ago. The man quoted a think-tank treatise from the late eighties. It was a convincing treatise about avoiding nuclear war. Beautiful arguments. Perfect logic. For example, it argued against civil defense as an unnecessary and ineffective countermeasure. And it was probably right. But at the end of the treatise the writers said there was no defense against a desperate Russian leadership." He smiled thinly. "I agree with that analysis."

General Thompson, who was still standing beside the television monitors, looked at the President and said, "If we fail to order a State Orange alert now, this afternoon, it could be a clear case of dereliction of duty."

Kendall nodded. "I'd say that's putting it right on the line, General," he said dryly.

"I'm sorry, sir. I never meant you *wouldn't* act."

Kendall held up his hand. "Will, we're not going to decide to plunge ahead with another alert until we've got this entire situation put into proper perspective. We need a strong overview." He glanced at Thompson, who averted his eyes, then glanced at Fitzpatrick, whose craggy face now wore a faint smile. "Let's reiterate what caused this mess. One step at a time," he added.

Jack Conley folded his large bony hands on the tabletop. "I'm certain we're all in agreement the Russian ASAT attack on the Sunstroke satellite initiated these events. For reasons of their own they tried to take it out."

"Exactly," said General Thompson. "The warning shot of a preemptive first strike."

"That's *your* assessment, General," snapped Fitzpatrick.

"Are you disputing the fact the satellite attack was followed by a provocative series of unannounced ancillary maneuvers involving an airborne alert?" asked Thompson in a contemptuous tone.

The President stepped in. "He's right, Fitz. That's the way it was. Whether or not the Russians' ASAT assault was the beginning of an all-out first strike cannot be conclusively proven, however. But we couldn't take the chance. We had to go to Condition Yellow."

"But it started a nonstop escalation," warned Fitzpatrick. "Less than twelve hours later we're ready to call up State Orange." There was a tired, frightened look in his eyes. "Do you really want this administration to be the one that starts World War Three?" he asked accusingly.

Kendall felt a jab of pain in his intestinal region, a certain constriction in his chest. The defense secretary's point-blank question got to him, as intended. "We're not going to war, Fitz," he said quietly.

"Then you've got to defuse this crisis," rasped Fitzpatrick, "while you still can. Talk to Gorodin on the hot line, explain our intentions to him. Admit Sunstroke was a mistake, tell him you're preparing to dismantle it, then ask for a simultaneous mutual stand-down of both nuclear forces."

Kendall sat there, stroking his temples. The inner tension

showed. He talked at a tremendous pace, in machine-gun bursts. "When the time is right I'll speak with Gorodin. As for Sunstroke, it'll be blown up sometime late this afternoon. I will tell Gorodin about the Vandenberg missile shortly before launch. That will give us something to bargain with."

He turned to General Thompson. "Will, let's briefly review State Orange"—he shot a glance at an exasperated Hugh Fitzpatrick—"to refresh our memories."

"First of all, sir," said the general, "State Orange means that a nuclear war is *likely,* but not imminent. It is designed to move our strategic forces into position in anticipation of an attack launched by the enemy, in this case the Republic of Russia. I can give you a report on the current status of our armed forces right now if you wish, sir."

At a nod from the President the general stepped up to another projection screen. Using his hand-held remote he punched in the code for MEECN, the Minimum Essential Emergency Communications Network—a two-way secure teletype link between the White House and every Minuteman and M-X Peacekeeper silo situated from Vandenberg AFB on the West Coast to Ellsworth AFB, South Dakota; to every USAF nuclear bomber squadron stationed around the globe; and to America's Trident and SSBN submarine fleets cruising the world's oceans. He read off each line of data as it scrolled across the screen.

As he listened to the readiness status of America's immense nuclear arsenal the peace-minded civilian side of Kendall was sickened by the destructive capability possessed by this nation, a force which he may have to mobilize. A single thought came to mind. Cockroaches. He remembered Secretary of State Hank Jacobsen had once told him, "Cockroaches will inherit the earth." According to Jacobsen they were the only life-form capable of surviving the deadly radiation effects from nuclear detonations. Kendall lamented that Jacobsen was in Central America on a six-day goodwill tour instead of being here in the Crisis Room. The secretary of state's calm logic and sense of humor would have been appreciated. Kendall had thought of recalling Jacobsen but abandoned the idea because of the risk of alerting the press to the crisis.

When Thompson finished his report on the status of the U.S. strategic weapons systems Kendall called for a vote. Should they go to State Orange? The vote was deadlocked. Thompson and Conley were for it, with Fitzpatrick and Kendall against.

The President leaned back in his chair. "We will wait awhile longer."

At that moment, high above the world, SOLSAT X-1 soared through the heavens. After being locked in a useless orbit for three days it was now pursuing an independent course away from the Vandenberg missile's launch point.

The on-board command computer had not detected that the coolant valves to the liquid nitrogen tanks had been unstuck during the Icarus attachments. The valve sensors had been snapped off and could not relay this information. If the subroutine controlling the computer had been informed the valves were functional it would not have had to order the course change to evade the nuclear supermissile.

As the satellite continued on its polar heading, the earth below slowly turned like a globe beneath the hand of a schoolteacher.

SOLSAT X-1's progress was also being monitored by the Russian radar controllers at the Tyuratam Antisatellite Facility. The lead radar technician immediately phoned General-Lieutenant Erik Rybinsk, the commander of the installation, who was in his office on the second floor of the administration wing.

Rybinsk angrily acknowledged the report and hung up. He sat at his desk, absently drumming his fingers, lost in thought. Somehow the Americans regained control of their satellite, he surmised. Undoubtedly due to those devices that docked with it a short time ago. But why would they send it on a polar heading? It did not make sense. This development came as a surprise to him. He had thought that the stealth ASAT launched by the *Ariane* had completely disabled the satellite, that the Americans would abandon it. What were they up to?

He glanced at his watch and saw it was time to send his radio message to his business associates on the *Arcturus* luxury liner, which should now be cruising the Mediterranean. He knew they would be upset if they learned the American satellite had not been fully incapacitated. Only a fool would tell them, he thought. Rybinsk reasoned that such a disclosure would cause him to forfeit the second installment of his payment. The first one had been for selling them the design for the Elektron Stealth Antisatellite Device. This second installment was contingent on its success. He needed the extra money to pay off his hired killer, van Eeden.

Rybinsk took out the sheet bearing his message to the *Arcturus* and sandwiched it between a stack of radio dispatches that were to be sent to the Flight Control Center at Kaliningrad near Moscow, and to the Ministry of Defense. Then he summoned Lieutenant Colonel Leonid Brusavitch, his communications officer. When Brusavitch showed up, Rybinsk handed him the dispatches and told him to transmit them without delay. The colonel took them, saluted, and left.

As he walked down the corridor Brusavitch scanned the sheaf of dispatches. When he came to the cipher-coded personal message he noted with a wary eye that it was to be transmitted at a commercial maritime radio frequency to a specific set of coordinates. More funny business, he thought.

Inside the communications room, he sent the other dispatches, then plotted out the coordinates Rybinsk had given him on a wall map. He determined they were in the Mediterranean Sea between Spain and Algeria. Next, he made a quick call to the Maritime Department of the Russian Naval Operations Center in Moscow and found out that the call letters for Rybinsk's message were for the Saudi-owned ocean liner, *Arcturus*, scheduled to be plying those waters right now.

This was serious. His commanding officer intended to communicate with a foreign vessel in international waters during a military alert. Brusavitch was faced with the most difficult decision of his life, something which he had been putting off for some time. Should he report his commander's activities to the Ministry of Defense? He struggled with himself for several moments before making his decision. Brusavitch knew that if he refused to send this message, the general-lieutenant could have him court-martialed on some fabricated charge and he would rot in prison while Rybinsk covered his own tracks. No, Brusavitch thought, I must send it now. When his shift was up he would fly to Moscow and report the entire matter to the ministry. He would show them copies of the Dutch embassy dispatches and this latest one. He would also bring up the matter of the computer tampering that Rybinsk had all but sanctioned. He would let the Ministry decide if his commander was guilty of treason.

The S.S. *Arcturus* was steaming through the warm blue waters of the Mediterranean. To her portside lay the picturesque Spanish shoreline at Aguilas, and far to starboard the lush coastal farms of Beni-Saf in Algeria. The enormous luxury liner had been chartered by COEC, the Consortium of Oil Exporting Countries.

Representatives from several Middle Eastern nations had gathered aboard to fix the current price per barrel of crude.

The messenger boy from the radio room, a swarthy young Arab about nineteen, raced down the narrow halls toward the dining–saloon. He strode past the many tables to the one on a raised platform and went to the heavyset man with the glistening bald pate who was smoking a cheroot stuck between thick, pendulous lips. The messenger stood behind the man's chair and handed him an envelope. The man was Abu Siwa, the chairman of COEC. When the messenger left, Siwa slit open the envelope very precisely with a knife and began reading:

WHEN THE BLACKBIRD'S EGG HATCHED THE BABY BIRD DEVOURED THE GREAT GLOWWORM. A WEASEL TRIED TO GET AT THE NEST BUT IT WAS CAUGHT BY THE HUNGRY TRAPPER.

Abu Siwa smiled, then touched the flame from his jewel-encrusted cigarette lighter to the radiogram, dropped it in an ashtray, and crushed the burning embers with his cheroot.

Chapter 27 *

AT THE SOLAR power plant the search for Diane Bradford was intensifying. The MPs positioned at the plant's entrances and exits and those stationed throughout the labyrinth of corridors were maintaining a watchful vigilance. A party of five soldiers led by Provost Marshal Earl Clayton was combing the first floor for any sign of her. The men were walking slowly, looking around like bird dogs, inspecting every room, closet, and cabinet.

Earlier Clayton had interrogated each of the prisoners in the guest lounge, but was unable to uncover any clues to Diane's whereabouts. Although he suspected some kind of conspiracy he failed to obtain a confession from any of the captives. Nor did he learn exactly how she escaped. He had examined her shower stall but didn't find anything suspicious. The ceiling tile that Diane had dislodged had fallen back into place when she dropped it. Clayton assumed she had simply run from her stall while the guards' attention was distracted. He was determined to search every square inch of the plant until he found her.

The provost marshal had no idea his quarry was just a few feet above him, silently crouching on hands and knees in the dark stuffy ceiling space.

Diane Bradford was peering at her floor plan of the solar power plant, conscious that she was draining her precious penlight battery in the process. According to her hand-drawn map and her memory Mike Doheny's office was on the basement sublevel, three floors below. That meant she would have to use the main utility core to travel between floors. The utility core was a concrete chimneylike vertical shaft that housed electrical conduits, pipes, and ducts. Andy Johnson, her cameraman, had suggested using it to descend to the basement sublevel. He had told her every multi-story office and industrial building had one.

In the pencil beam from her tiny flashlight Diane could see the ducts, wires, and pipes converging ahead of her. She surmised the utility core lay in that direction. To conserve the penlight battery she switched it off and followed a pipe with her hands. When her eyes had adjusted to the gloom she saw a faint glow coming from a large, dark rectangular shape about thirty feet from her position. She was certain it was the core.

She was moving by feel now, being careful to put most of her weight on the metal supports for the ceiling tiles rather than on the tiles themselves. Once or twice she heard voices filtering up from the floor below. She thought they were either coming from the power plant employees imprisoned at the facility, or from the MPs out searching for her.

The going was not easy. Moving only a few feet at a time, she tried, not always successfully, to avoid the blistering hot steam pipes. The air was musty and the dust from the fiberglass insulation covering the air-conditioning ducts coated her mouth and made her eyes water. Her progress got more difficult as she drew closer to the utility core because the wires, ducts, and pipes came together to form a tangled mass. More than once she thought about turning back. But realizing her desire to be the only reporter to uncover the true story behind the solar satellite mishap made the ordeal worth it.

Then, halfway to the core, Diane's right forearm brushed against a steam pipe. The pain shot through her like an electric shock. She lost her footing on the metal tile supports and fell onto the suspended ceiling.

Directly below, MP John Owens was inspecting the chemical supply room on the first floor when suddenly he was startled by a loud thump above his head. He looked up and noticed one of the ceiling tiles was protruding from the rest. A few seconds later he heard a scrabbling sound and saw the tile being pulled back into place. At that moment he realized someone was up there. So, he thought, that's where the bitch is.

Owens had been the lead MP in charge when Diane had made her escape. After having been reprimanded by the provost marshal he had been hoping he'd be the one to collar her. Now was his chance. He leaped up at the low ceiling and hit the vinyl tile with his fist.

The tile flew upward from the force of the blow and struck Diane in the forehead. Her head snapped backward, and she was almost knocked unconscious. Although stunned and hurt, she pitched forward and struggled with all her might to push the tile back into place, but it wouldn't budge. Through the opening she caught a glimpse of John Owens, his blocky face contorted, holding the tile up with one hand while frantically groping inside the ceiling space with his other. Diane threw her entire weight against the tile and pushed with every ounce she could muster, but his greater strength prevailed despite her best efforts.

Then Owens's free hand caught her left wrist in a viselike grip. He had her now and began pulling her closer to the opening. When she tried to free her wrist from his grip he started twisting it, making her grimace. She was helpless and he knew it. When Diane felt herself being pulled downward she panicked, and pure animal instinct took over.

She bit his hand, sinking her teeth into the fleshy part just below the thumb. Grunting with anger and pain, he quickly released his grip. Just before Diane slammed the tile down she heard him yelling into his radio transceiver, calling for backup.

Expecting pursuit at any moment, Diane moved fast and covered the remaining distance to the utility core with amazing speed. When she reached the core's vertical concrete walls she began probing for an entrance. She rounded a corner, following a cold water pipe with her hands and felt it enter the core through a large access port, then turn down at a ninety-degree angle. The other pipes did the same. Leaning over them, she stuck her head into the port and looked down into the darkness. There was a faint glow filtering up from far below.

Diane took out her penlight and played the small beam first over the dense cluster of pipes and wires, then on the four interior walls of the shaft. She determined they were about four feet wide, giving the core an inside area of sixteen square feet. The bundle of pipes went down the center of the shaft, leaving just enough room for a maintenance person to climb between it and the walls. She was wondering if they used a rope and tackle to make the vertical ascent when suddenly she spotted metal rungs protruding from the far wall. Being careful not to touch the steam pipes, she entered the access port and lowered herself into the core. She got a firm grip on the rungs and started climbing down.

Peering into the darkness, she could see the pipes and wires angling out horizontally from another access port, and she realized she had reached the ceiling space for the first basement sublevel. She felt a momentary elation at the good progress she was making. But it evaporated when the thought entered her mind that if she could use the core to travel down, an MP could be using it to go up. The possibility sent a chill up her spine.

She continued climbing down. Below her there was more light filtering upward. Then, in the dim glow, she could make out the access port for the second basement sublevel. When she heard the progressively louder sound of electronic equipment, Diane knew she was above the control room. The hardest part was over. There wasn't far to go now.

Mike Doheny anxiously studied the Mercator map on the big blue screen mounted above the Earthnet/SATSCAN computers. The satellite blip on the screen was slowly creeping northward, toward the top of the screen. Doheny knew that no human controlled the thing; General Stratton's Icarus ASATs had been commandeered. The satellite and the Space Shield devices were now functioning as one spacecraft. But why was it heading north?

He rushed to the SATSCAN computer and instructed it to predict the satellite's new orbit. Within seconds a bright green line arced from top to bottom across the huge screen.

"That's a classical polar orbit," cried Jenkins, who had joined Doheny at the console. His brow was furrowed in consternation. "Why would it want to fly over the poles?"

"Think about it for a minute, Jenkins," said Doheny. "As the satellite shuttles from north to south, the earth steadily rotates at a uniform speed inside the thing's orbit. This gives the satellite virtually complete access to any point on the globe." A chilling thought occurred to him. "A polar orbit will also allow it to cross the terminator more frequently than before. Probably six or seven times a day."

"And it'll discharge its microwave beam every time it comes out into the sunlight," interposed Jenkins.

Doheny nodded gravely. "In one week," he said with calm, slow emphasis, "it could fry every major city in the world."

He thumbed the intercom switch and told the members of his troubleshooting team to report to the control room for an emergency conference. Minutes later the specialists were sitting in the swivel chairs beside the consoles. The only member of the team absent was Everett Nore; he had not responded to Doheny's urgent call. The others listened in stunned silence as Doheny briefly described the commandeering of the Icarus devices and the ramifications of the polar orbit. Throughout the explanation he stood beneath the big screen, occasionally gesturing to the orbital track woven across it. His voice was strangely calm.

Afterward he nervously eyed the screen. Just in the short amount of time it had taken him to explain the situation the satellite had crossed the border from New Mexico to Colorado.

Dr. Fred Gaither was the first to speak. "I don't understand how the satellite was able to take over those Icarus devices." He shrugged his shoulders, making his huge soft body ripple like a pond.

Ted Kitami adjusted his black-rimmed glasses and said, "The answer is very simple. Our satellite's communications system is equipped with a battery-driven tape recorder for the purpose of recording ground-based radio commands made during the brief eclipse periods. Remember, it was calculated that even in geosynchronous orbit the satellite would enter the earth's shadow for up to seventy-five minutes during the spring and fall equinoxes, and would be unable to generate enough electricity to power its own systems. It seems that early this morning the satellite recorded General Stratton's slaving commands to the Icarus devices and played it back later."

"The satellite had to have been programmed to do something like this, Ted," Doheny mused. "Do you know anything about it?"

Kitami took a sip of pineapple juice from a cup. He explained that part of the satellite's original computer program included instructions for radio manipulation of enemy spacecraft. "Now, on its own initiative, it tried out this technique on the general's antisatellite devices. How remarkable!"

Malcolm Courtland frowned thoughtfully and leaned forward. He shifted his gaze from the green orbital track on the big screen to Doheny. "Could there possibly be another reason why the satellite is assuming a polar orbit? Something we've maybe overlooked?"

Doheny spread his hands and said, "I can't think of anything else." He glanced questioningly at the others.

Kitami said quietly, "There is one other possibility." After a reflective pause he continued. "When the satellite's guidance computer system was first programmed we inserted instructions for a specific test of the microwave power beam's thermal effects on different regions of the earth's surface. One of these future tests included a sustained discharge on the Arctic ice cap to determine if a sufficient quantity of the polar ice could be melted within a reasonable period of time to cause coastal flooding. The test would be performed on a small scale, of course.''

Doheny's jaw dropped. He couldn't believe that he had heard correctly. ''Do you mean the satellite has been programmed to melt a portion of the Arctic ice cap?''

Kitami nodded solemnly. ''As I said, the test was to be very limited in scope. If my memory serves me right, approximately one square kilometer of surface ice was to be irradiated to a depth of one meter.''

Doheny sat down heavily in a swivel chair. The blood seemed to drain away suddenly from his head, leaving it hollow and light. His chest felt as if a steel band were tightening around it.

Fred Gaither's hand twitched and a neat cylinder of gray ash from the cigar he had lit up fell onto the top of a console and disintegrated into a powdery explosion.

Professor Aaron Rosen gestured helplessly, and the little sound he emitted, a cross between a groan and a sigh, expressed how he felt.

Malcolm Courtland shut his eyes and ran a hand over his hair.

Doheny took a gulp of coffee from his cup and swallowed hard. His face pale, he said, ''This throws a new light on the reason for the satellite's course change. It may have entered a new orbit in order to reach the ice cap, not just to target the world's major cities. Once it gets there it could change its orbit again to cross the terminator near the Arctic Circle, cool down its klystron array, then discharge at the ice when it comes out of the shadow.'' He realized for the first time that the Sunstroke satellite could threaten the survival of the human race.

The moment Diane climbed out of the core onto the suspended ceiling she lay on her back for a few seconds, breathing hard and letting the tense, aching muscles of her arms and legs relax. She knew she couldn't rest for long. Lying on her back, she once again consulted her map. All she had to do now was to crawl past the control room, check her bearings by looking through the ceiling cracks, then continue past the next two rooms. At that point she should be directly over Mike Doheny's private office.

Diane kept to the fixed ceiling above the sublevel corridor. It took her eight minutes to crawl the length of the control room, and another three to pass over the next two rooms, which were, respectively, a small electronics lab and an instrument supply room. Then she stopped and listened. There was no sound coming from below.

Slowly, carefully, she lifted the corner of a ceiling tile. When she looked down through the crevice she realized she had made a mistake in her floor plan. The figure slumped over the desk below wasn't Mike Doheny. It was Everett Nore. He was asleep, snoring loudly, his legs propped on his desk, head thrown back. She replaced the tile and moved on.

Fred Gaither waved his cigar like a baton. "At one hundred kilowatts per square meter," he warned, "the power beam is quite capable of melting the entire polar ice pack. How long the process would take depends on the duration of each discharge."

Doheny once again thought of the satellite's on-board liquid nitrogen coolant. "Fred, if the thing could discharge continuously, how long would it take?"

Gaither engulfed himself in an alarming quantity of cigar smoke, then waved it clear. "Two, three weeks. Something like that. Of course that much water released into the oceans over such a short period of time would raise their level by a couple dozen feet. That doesn't sound like much, but the results would be catastrophic. There'll be tidal waves you wouldn't believe, three hundred to four hundred feet high. All the coastal cities will be immediately inundated. Then, as the tidal waves wash inland, they'll flood the world's continents." He broke off. Into a silence as deep as a well his next words dropped like heavy stones. "The face of the earth would be changed forever."

"We need to brainstorm a method of disabling the satellite before it reaches the Arctic," announced Doheny.

"What about that Needles spacecraft you mentioned?" Courtland asked.

Doheny shook his head. "The satellite can easily outmaneuver it now. Besides that, the copper dipoles would be dispersed in a few hours by the solar wind."

Rosen sat up abruptly. "Now we calculated that Needles' dipoles would attenuate the microwave beam, decrease its intensity to below the lethal level by scattering the microwaves. That gives me an idea. What if we were able to somehow reflect the beam back at its source?"

Doheny took a deep breath and exhaled. "It would burn out the klystrons in the microwave transmitter." Nodding, he said, "I think you're on to something here, Professor."

Rosen snatched up a notepad from a console and set to work calculating the minimum percentage of the beam's total output that would be required to overload the klystron array. After several minutes he looked up. "Twenty percent. That's all we need. But the problem is, we don't have a reflector large enough in orbit to do it."

Doheny scraped back his chair. "We don't need an orbital reflector." Growing more and more excited, he got up and began pacing back and forth. "I haven't managed to work it all out yet, but what I have in mind is a *ground-based* reflector."

Rosen looked shocked. "Do you know how big it would have to be? On the order of three hundred meters in diameter. It would take years to build something of that size."

Suppressing a smile, Doheny said, "We already have one built. As a matter of fact, there's three of them situated in different areas around the world, each one having a diameter of a thousand feet."

Malcolm Courtland swiveled to face Doheny. "What are you talking about?" he demanded, frustrated.

"There's one at Arecibo, Puerto Rico, one on the Seward Peninsula in Alaska, and one in the Crimea."

"Radio telescopes!" cried Rosen. He threw up his hands in a wonderfully articulate gesture. "Those big dishes could be adjusted to the satellite's central frequency and reflect the power beam back at the transmitter." Rosen knew that radio telescopes acted as giant buckets to gather radio waves from astronomical objects, and were equipped with powerful amplifiers so they could detect the faint whispers from distant sources. The huge dishes also acted as reflectors. "My God," he said, "it might work."

The look in Rosen's eyes and his tone of voice reminded Doheny of a shipwrecked sailor clinging to a piece of driftwood who, after having given up all hope, suddenly sights a desert island and refuses to accept the evidence of his own eyes.

"Four years ago," related Doheny, "I used the big Seward dish to simulate the power beam's heating effects in the lower ionosphere. A NASA radar-mapping satellite in low orbit transmitted a radar beam at the dish, which then concentrated and reflected the energy at the ionosphere. The power densities and frequencies produced were much lower than the real thing, of course, but we extrapolated them using a scaling law."

He sat down, took Rosen's scratch pad, and started calculating the percentage of the microwave beam's power level that one of the big dishes could reflect back at the satellite. He factored in atmospheric attenuation as well as the amplification capability of the dish's radio receiver. It took him five minutes. "I think we can expect a thousand-foot dish to amplify and reflect approximately twenty-six percent of the beam's total power," he pronounced. "Enough to burn out the satellite's klystron tubes."

Fred Gaither puffed on his cigar and let smoke writhe out between pursed lips. "Theoretically speaking, your estimate is probably correct. However, in reality the power beam would more than likely fry the radio telescope's electronics the instant it touched the dish."

Doheny pondered a long moment before replying. "That's true, Fred, as far as the dishes positioned in temperate climates go." He got up and went to the big Mercator map. He gestured to the uppermost portion of the North American continent and slid his finger to the northwest section of Alaska, to a small peninsula jutting into the Bering Strait.

"I have in mind the big Seward dish here," he said at length. "Because it's located near the Arctic, the entire dish is covered by a protective housing that allows its surface, support structure, and electronics to be temperature-controlled to minimize deformation and breakdown in the extreme cold." He turned to face the others. "This housing can also protect the electronics from the microwaves."

Malcolm Courtland shook his head as if to clear it. "Maybe I'm particularly dense today," he said, groping for the right words, "or maybe I missed something. But how are we going to get the satellite to discharge on the radio telescope?"

"That part," Doheny said grimly, "will be easy. Remember what happened yesterday when we tried to reprogram the thing's computer? It called us 'the enemy.' Apparently our satellite is very sensitive to anything that could be interpreted as a threat to its survival. I think a properly worded message will coax Ted's defense subroutine to discharge the beam at a select target."

Courtland understood. "You're going to bait it into firing at the Seward observatory."

"Yes," Doheny said. "After the astronomers have been evacuated."

"Excuse me," interrupted Fred Gaither with a trace of sarcasm to his voice, "but if the staff is evacuated who's going to run the show? Someone has to steer the receiver, keep it aligned with the satellite right up to the time of discharge. A very dangerous job."

Doheny felt a slight rise of nausea in his stomach. At that

moment he realized who would have to man the radio telescope. As he stood there his face underwent a strange transformation. Some muscles had relaxed, others tightened. He threw Gaither an unpleasant, ironic smile. "I'm going to do it," he said quietly.

Two floors above the control room Provost Marshal Earl Clayton and three of his men were trudging up the fire escape stairwell to the second floor. Clayton was tired, angry, and frustrated. He had just finished an exhaustive inspection of the first floor, and his muscles ached from fatigue. Still they hadn't found any sign of Diane Bradford.

An hour ago, when Diane had been sighted in the ceiling crawl space, Clayton had sent an MP after her. The soldier had later reported that she had escaped through the main utility core. However, there was no way to determine if she had gone up or down the vertical core. From his set of blueprints Clayton saw that the utility core offered access to every basement and floor level in the facility. He told the MP to climb down the core and try to pick up her trail, then ordered another soldier to climb upward in case she had taken that route. Neither MP reported anything positive.

As he went up the stairs Clayton paused to rub a knee that was sore from bending and stooping. He suddenly realized he was out of shape. He blamed it on the endless daily paperwork he had to do at Fort Union.

Although he knew in the end he'd find Diane, he was also aware that his upcoming promotion was jeopardized by each passing second that she remained at large. He was thirty-seven years old and had been passed up for promotion during the past three years. He desperately wanted to make the next pay scale bracket so he could qualify for a larger pension when he retired from the army at age forty. Before he left the fort to come here he had heard through the grapevine that his superior officer would make an unannounced inspection of the plant to check on his performance. That meant his superior could show up at any moment. If the colonel discovered that a prisoner under his custody escaped he'd be passed up again.

At the top of the stairs he rubbed the back of his neck and wondered if she was receiving assistance from one of the civilians. He could think of only one man who might have the balls to do it. Clayton decided that after he had searched the second floor he would check the administrative offices on the first sublevel: particularly Doheny's office.

*   *   *

In the control room Doheny held up a hand to ward off the stream of protests from the others. "The Seward observatory has a deep basement that'll protect me from the microwaves. With a little jury-rigging the receiver controls can be operated from there. I spent six months at Seward conducting those ionospheric tests. I know the station and its instruments pretty well." He glanced at his watch. "We've got about ten hours before the satellite reaches the Arctic."

Rosen's hand clawed the air. "How are you going to get there, Mike?" he asked in frustration.

Doheny remembered Everett Nore's business jet parked on the small airstrip outside the plant. Not being a pilot himself, he'd have to persuade Nore to fly the plane. Would he do it? "I'll find a way, Professor."

He left the control room, bought two cups of hot coffee from a vending machine in the corridor, and carried them to Nore's office.

When he rapped on his employer's door a muffled voice from inside finally yelled, "Come in." The lights were off and the office was dark. A desk lamp was suddenly switched on and a small cone of light shone through the gloom, illuminating the room's occupant. The CEO of Nore Space Industries sat hunched over his desk, squinting through pouchy, red-rimmed eyes at Doheny. His face looked old, gray.

"Siddown, Mike," Nore said in a thick, tired voice.

Doheny handed him a cup of coffee, and put the second one on his desktop.

"What's this?" asked Nore, irritated. "Room service?" He sipped from the cup, grimaced, then took a gulp.

"Now listen, Everett," Doheny said, pulling up a chair. "We don't have much time." He told Nore about the satellite's commandeering of General Stratton's ASATs and of its alleged intentions of targeting the world's major cities and melting the polar ice cap. Then he explained his plan to destroy the satellite's microwave transmitter by reflecting its beam back at it.

Nore listened, his brows narrowing into an expression of alarm and surprise.

When Doheny had finished relating the details he said in a quiet voice, "I'm going to need you to fly me up there."

There was a pained expression on Nore's face. "I have no intention of making my wife a widow," he muttered. "There's some kind of high-level directive restricting us to the plant. We can't leave here.''

"You could try intimidating that provost marshal,'' suggested Doheny.

Nore sighed deeply. He tapped an impatient nervous tattoo on the desk, then flashed a deep-eyed look at Doheny. "I need some time to think.''

Doheny smiled weakly and went next door to his own office. He was rummaging through a file cabinet searching for the one on the ionospheric tests conducted at the Seward radio telescope when he was startled by a scraping sound coming from somewhere above him.

Chapter 28 *

WHEN DOHENY JERKED his head up and gazed at the ceiling he saw that one of the tiles had been removed. Framed in the opening was the face of a young woman, smudged and soiled, yet beautiful. Her long blond hair was tangled and covered with dust. Sudden recognition dawned on him. She was the reporter from Cable News Service.

"Ms. Bradford!" he sputtered. "What . . . "

Diane pressed a finger to her lips, then absently brushed the hair from her eyes.

Doheny spotted the bruise on her forehead. He grabbed a chair and put it on the floor below her, took her hand in his, and gently helped her down. With a guiding hand on her leg he was shocked to discover she was wearing only a bra and panty hose, both of which were dusty and tattered. He sat her down on the chair, then got some ice from the small refrigerator in the corner and made a cold compress with his handkerchief. He applied it gingerly to the bruise.

Diane winced slightly, caught her breath, and smiled. Embarrassed at her appearance, she started to say something about the reason for her being there but Doheny interrupted her. He had noticed the blistered burn marks on her elbow and forearm.

"There'll be plenty of time later for explanations," he said softly. "Right now we've got to take care of those burns." He pulled out a first-aid kit from his desk and dressed the wounds.

"Engineer's hands," she said admiringly.

"I didn't realize they were so rough."

"Nothing wrong with them," he said, "except they must miss the work they're used to doing."

He smiled into her questing eyes, then helped her to the bathroom cubicle in the corner of the office, where she washed up and brushed her hair. Doheny made a pot of coffee and, when she came out gave her one of his clean white lab coats from the closet. She put on the coat and inspected herself in the bathroom mirror. It hung down to her feet.

"Well," she laughed, "at least I'm decent now."

Doheny poured the coffee and the two sat down. He turned to her and said in a serious tone, "Now, Ms. Bradford, I want you to tell me what you're doing here."

When she explained he frowned and shook his head. "That's a pretty crazy stunt you pulled," he admonished. "Those soldiers mean business."

"I know," she said, rubbing her head.

"You mean one of them did that to you?" Doheny demanded. When she nodded, his scalp went back and his mouth tightened. He knew he had to get her out of the plant somehow. Her safety depended on it.

Diane took out the pen and notebook she had brought with her and pleaded with Doheny to tell her what really happened that night when the satellite malfunctioned.

Doheny got up and slowly paced around the room. He believed the public had the right to know everything about Project Sunstroke. He returned to his chair and briefly related the events that had transpired during the past three days.

In the neighboring office Everett Nore took another gulp of coffee, then rubbed his hand across his face. He was desperately trying to decide what to do, and the pounding in his head didn't help matters.

Ever since he had learned the satellite had killed that family living on the farm near the plant, he had experienced a paralyzing guilt. It was his company that had built the satellite, his firm that had benefited from one of the largest contracts ever negotiated in the aerospace industry. Worse, he had been aware of the design changes recommended by General Stratton, changes that had increased the power of the microwave beam and decreased the effectiveness of the fail-safe devices. If those modifications hadn't been implemented, perhaps that family and the people aboard the Australian jetliner wouldn't have died. He had been so haunted by the thought that it had driven him to drink in order to escape the guilt.

He slumped in his chair and thought about what Doheny had told him a few minutes ago. Something to do with a military test project that had been programmed into the satellite. The thing had gone berserk and was on its way to melt the Arctic ice cap. Armageddon. The end of the world. Doheny and the specialists had come up with a method of putting the thing out of action. Simple but brilliant. They want to use the Seward radio telescope to reflect its own beam back at it. Burn out the klystrons. But the plan hinges on flying to Alaska in time.

Nore was aware that if he helped Doheny escape from the plant and flew him to Alaska he would personally be held liable by the Washington hierarchy. If they ever needed a public scapegoat for Sunstroke he would be it. By aiding Doheny he would be moving outside the tight professional pattern of conduct he had adopted long ago. On the other hand, if the satellite melts the ice pack and floods the earth, who cares about career and business considerations? He remembered the disconnected hot line, the fact that he was now a prisoner along with the rest. To hell with Washington.

Nore felt a sense of unreal exhilaration take hold of him. He decided he was going to rebel against the masters he had served for so long. The thought made him buoyant, excited. He also realized that helping to put the satellite out of action would be his chance to make amends, to try to clear the slate.

He pulled open a desk drawer, took out a thick map book of the North American continent, and began plotting a flight path to the Seward Peninsula.

When Doheny finished recounting what had taken place during the last three days, Diane sat there, mouth open, eyes wide. It was too monstrous for her to conceive.

Doheny caught the look in her eyes, a mixture of fear, panic and resignation. "There's a chance we can stop the thing," he said encouragingly. He explained about the Seward dish and its capabilities. Afterward he said, "I've got to go to Alaska, and fast." His gaze fell across Diane. Her high-cheekboned face was tilted upward, her rich blond hair lustrous under the office lights. "You're coming with me, at least part of the way. You can't stay here, not with those goons out looking for you."

He went back to the file cabinet, found the file he had been looking for, then selected several textbooks on radio astronomy from his bookcase. He picked up the receiver on his phone and was about to call Ted Kitami in the control room when he suddenly heard the unmistakable sound of a doorknob being rattled. He instantly regretted not barricading the door, for it was flimsily constructed, with a hollow core and weak jambs. Before he could act it flew open with a loud snap amid flying splinters of wood.

Provost Marshal Earl Clayton slowly walked in, his hand resting lightly on his sidearm. For a long moment the two men stared at each other.

Clayton broke the silence. "I figured you were hiding her." He shook his head. "Dumb thing to do."

Doheny looked behind the stocky figure of the provost marshal, expecting to see a squad of MPs, but the man was alone. Apparently the other soldiers were still searching the plant.

Clayton's eyes shifted to Diane. His lips drew back and tightened against his teeth. "You've caused me a lot of trouble, Miss Bradford. But it's all over now."

Doheny came forward. He was going to try reasoning with the man. "Listen, Clayton, let's talk this over. We can make some kind of deal."

"Save your bullshit," snarled Clayton, his mouth twisted. He stepped up to Diane and grabbed her wrist. "Come on." He remembered that she had bitten one of his men. "You try sinking your teeth into me," he warned viciously, "and I'll knock 'em out." He pulled her hard. She winced.

Doheny felt the tightness in his throat. He clenched his teeth, cracking his jaw muscles. His eyelids felt hot. "Let her go, Clayton," he shouted.

The provost marshal ignored him and started yanking Diane toward the open door.

Doheny lunged forward and his hand flashed out and caught Clayton's wrist in a crushing grip. "I said *let her go*." There was a fierce intensity to his voice. The two men stood glaring at each other. Although Doheny towered over Clayton, the provost marshal was thicker, more compact.

Clayton released his hold on Diane. He looked down at Doheny's hand, which was still gripping his wrist. His nostrils widened. Then he smiled. It was a slow tightening of the small, thin lips, nothing more. But there was something inexpressibly savage about it.

This was the moment he had been waiting for since his first confrontation with Doheny. The provost marshal hated him—a hatred rooted in jealousy. In his eyes, Doheny had been given all the advantages of life: his good looks, his height, his education, and most of all, his status as one of the top aerospace engineers in the country. Clayton had seen firsthand that the plant employees

had regarded Doheny with something more than respect; they
were in awe of him. Born on a farm in Arkansas, Clayton had to
struggle to reach his present rank in the army. Doheny had
immensely succeeded in civilian life, an achievement the provost
marshal bitterly resented. And now the white-collar bastard was
jeopardizing his military career and trying to show him up in front
of this smart-assed cunt. Clayton was not about to let him get away
with it.

He wrenched his hand free, then grabbed Doheny by the throat
of his shirt and delivered three jackhammer blows to his stomach.

Doheny's breath rushed out and he doubled over, holding on to
his knees to keep from falling to the floor. He gasped and coughed
violently. A paroxysm of pain shot through his stomach. He fought
to control the rise of bile. His esophagus seemed to be clogged
with scratchy wool. His eyes watered uncontrollably.

"Mike," yelled Diane. She ran toward him but Clayton grabbed
her. She struggled uselessly. "You hurt him," she cried. "He
needs help."

Her concern for Doheny angered Clayton. A pulse throbbed
visibly in his temple and his thick neck swelled. He twisted her
arm behind her back and pushed her closer to Doheny. "Take a
good look at your protector." His voice was low and dangerous.
"Look at him," he commanded. "A *real* man would have fought
back."

To Doheny, he said, "As military commander of this installation I'm placing you under arrest for aiding and abetting a fugitive
and for interfering with police action carried out under the
National Espionage Act." He spoke slowly, confidently. "One of
the storage rooms around here can be converted into a prison cell
for the two of you," he added.

Doheny remained in his jackknifed position, trying to catch his
breath. He dried his eyes on his shirt sleeve. Through the dizzy,
swirling haze of pain he had caught the drift of Clayton's words
and knew what was about to happen. Both he and Diane would be
imprisoned, making it impossible for them to leave the plant. He
wouldn't be able to fly to the Seward radio telescope now. The
Sunstroke satellite would be free to attack the world's cities and
flood the continents. Hundreds of millions will die because of one
small-minded military policeman who had grudges and followed
orders all his life.

Doheny had met Clayton's type during his college years, when
he had frequented bars and nightclubs. They were always slow-

witted jocks, strutting their phony masculinity, always trying to
goad him into a fight because of his height. He had been in a big
man's double bind: if he hit back, he was a bully, and if he didn't
he was labeled a coward. To survive in those days he had been
forced to fight back.

But now it was different. Countless lives were at stake.
Including Diane's. She was in the hands of soldiers who were out
of control. He concentrated on this last thought and felt a hot blob
of anger rising in his body. Slowly he regained his breath and
strength. He glanced up at Clayton and saw that he was holding
Diane with one hand and unclipping his radio transceiver from his
belt with his other.

At that moment Diane wriggled free and dug her fingernails
deep into Clayton's wrist. He swore, let go of her, then back-
handed her brutally. She reeled from the blow. Her lips were split
and trickled blood.

The hot blob of intense rage inside Doheny burst. His face was
contorted with uncontrollable fury. He had only one intention
now: to beat Clayton senseless.

He sprang from his crouched position and launched himself at
Clayton. The force of the lunge knocked the startled provost
marshal off balance and threw him against the wall. His transceiver went flying and skittered across the floor. He had been
taken completely by surprise and had no time to react.

Doheny grabbed Clayton's head with both his hands and
slammed it into the wall. Then he hit him in the chest with all his
might. Clayton went rigid for a half a second, then slumped
limply. Doheny broke off his attack and stepped back, certain he
had knocked the man almost unconscious.

He barely saw Clayton's leg move, but he felt the foot drive into
his groin. Pain surged through his body. As he gasped for breath
he grabbed the foot and got a fist in the neck. He swung and
missed. Another kick sent him staggering backward. A shoulder
pinned him against a bookshelf while fingers stabbed at his
kidneys. Before he could react, the same hand made a fist, which
shot into the ribs under his heart. He felt himself growing faint,
then he dropped to the floor.

His opponent stood over him, breathing hard, with a self-
satisfied smile on his lips.

Diane grabbed the half-full coffeepot and threw it at Clayton. It
caught him in the shoulder. A scalding black stain rapidly spread
over his uniform shirt. He roared in pain and anger. Wildly

clawing at his shirt, he yelled, "I'll fix you for this, cunt." His face was flushed a dark brick red. He turned and went after her.

Grunting, Doheny propped himself up from the floor and slowly got to his feet, holding his chest. Then he saw Clayton stalking Diane. He watched as she picked up a thick physics handbook and flung it at her pursuer. He dodged it and started after her again.

Summoning all his strength, Doheny dived across the room and brought both of Clayton's ankles out from under him. The two men went down in a tangle of arms and legs, fragments of a shattered chair, and two broken coffee cups. Doheny was trying to make use of his weight and naturally strong limbs while the provost marshal relied on his speed and knowledge of hand-to-hand combat. They fought in silence, wrestling, punching, kicking. The pair rolled over the carpet amid the broken furniture and crockery. Evading the grip of the taller man's hands, Clayton twisted free and got unsteadily to his feet, his left eye cut and swollen.

Doheny took a kick in his side. He avoided the next one by a fast roll toward his desk. The shoe shot at him again but this time he caught it with his hands and twisted as hard as he could. His opponent went sprawling across the desk.

Doheny got up and charged Clayton, butting him in the stomach with his head. Then he got in close and put his shoulder muscles into a right uppercut. The other man's jaw snapped back. Doheny felt his own strength ebbing. He was tired, almost exhausted, breathing raggedly. Only his grim determination to destroy the satellite and get Diane to a safe haven kept him going. He swung again, but was too slow.

The provost marshal ducked the punch, slammed his fist into Doheny's stomach, and hammered a punishing karate blow into his face. He watched as Doheny reeled backward, blood flowing from the gash in his cheek. Then Clayton moved in for the kill, both his hands raised, his upper torso and feet in a martial-arts stance.

"Hold it right there, Clayton!" bellowed a deep, powerful male voice at the other end of the room.

The provost marshal froze, then slowly swiveled his neck toward the entrance to the office. His vision was blurry and he had to squint through puffy eyelids at the imposing figure standing in the open doorway. He was jolted when he caught sight of the officer's cap. He quickly lowered his hands. He was dead certain the figure was one of his commanding officers from Fort Union. But there was something wrong with the uniform.

Clayton blinked his eyes, finally focused them, and realized with a shock that the figure in the doorway was Everett Nore dressed in a black leather flight jacket and cap. The recognition came too late. He detected a sudden flicker of movement out of the corner of his eye just before a fist struck the side of his head. The impact stunned him; he was dazed and disoriented. His reflexes were tangled and confused by the stabbing pain in his head. His hands swiped the air blindly, missing their target.

Doheny knew he had delivered a lucky punch. He drew his right arm back again and gave a short, powerful blow to the jaw, then drove his left fist into his opponent's stomach.

Clayton bent at the waist, coughing. In a reflex action his hand went to his holster and his fingers tore at the retaining strap on his side arm.

Knowing he had to finish this now, Doheny locked his hands together, raised them above his head and brought them down with all his force on the back of the provost marshal's neck. Clayton fell to the floor in a loose-limbed sprawl.

Exhausted, battered, and bruised, Doheny collapsed in a heap on top of the prostrate body. He made one last anguished effort and yanked the nine-millimeter Beretta automatic from Clayton's holster. It felt cold and heavy in his shaking hand. He was dimly aware that Nore and Diane were at his side. He gave the gun to Nore, then rolled off Clayton. He lay there on his back, breathing heavily, his pulse racing.

Nore looked at the still form of the provost marshal and shook his head in disbelief. "I didn't think you had it in you, Mike." He and Diane helped Doheny to a chair. She applied a compress to the wound on his cheek.

Doheny jerked a thumb at Clayton's unconscious form. "He's our ticket out of here," he wheezed.

"Take it easy, Mike," said Diane gently. "You've been hurt."

"I don't think anything's broken," he protested. "Just sore." He grimaced as she sprayed disinfectant to the welts and cuts on his hands and face.

He looked at his watch. There were now nine and a half hours before the satellite reached the Arctic. He shot a glance at Nore, noting the flight jacket and cap. "Are you going to fly us out? We're running out of time."

The older man smiled wryly and nodded. "I've already drawn

up a flight plan to the Seward Peninsula. It'll take us about eight hours to get there. We'll make one stopover at Seattle to refuel and buy cold-weather gear and provisions. It's still freezing in Seward, even at this time of year.''

When Doheny saw Nore's questioning glance at Diane he said, ''She's coming with us,'' then went on to explain her predicament.

Nore nodded his assent.

Doheny pointed to the Beretta. ''Do you know how to use one of those?'' he asked quietly.

Familiar with handguns, Nore turned the automatic over in his hand and extracted the clip to make sure it was loaded, then shoved it back in. With another quick sliding action he saw there was also a bullet in the chamber.

An instant later Clayton regained consciousness and groaned.

Nore ordered the provost marshal to stand up, then jammed the barrel of the gun against the small of the man's back. Clayton winced. ''Call off your men,'' Nore ordered. ''Tell them you found Ms. Bradford and that everything's under control.'' His voice became a fierce, hoarse whisper. ''You try anything''—he prodded with the gun again—''and I'll put a bullet *right here*. I've got nothing to lose. Nothing.''

Clayton picked up his radio transceiver and did as he was told.

Five minutes later Doheny and Diane Bradford entered the control room. They were followed by Clayton and then Everett Nore, who had draped his flight jacket over the Beretta. Nore had the automatic aimed directly at Clayton's back, his finger on the trigger. There were no MPs present.

The members of the troubleshooting team and the engineers and technicians manning their stations looked up in surprise at Doheny, noting the cuts and bruises. They peered quizzically at Diane and Clayton.

Professor Aaron Rosen tugged at Doheny's sleeve. ''What happened, Mike?'' he asked, concerned. ''You look like you've been in a fight.''

Doheny shrugged off the question. ''Just a little mishap, Professor.'' He went directly to Ted Kitami and Malcolm Courtland, who were sitting at the SATSCAN computer.

Kitami held up the accordion-folded printout sheet. ''This is our message. It's sufficiently belligerent, as you requested.'' He lightly tapped the sheet with his fingertip. ''You'll be tickling the dragon's tail with this code,'' he said solemnly. ''Please exercise extreme caution.''

Then Doheny and his party hurriedly left the control room and took an elevator up to the first floor. The provost marshal told the guards at the lobby entrance that he was escorting the civilians to Fort Union. The sentries stepped aside to let them pass. The group made their way to Clayton's jeep and, with the provost marshal at the wheel, drove to the airstrip, a quarter mile to the west.

When the jeep came to a stop Doheny reached under the dashboard and pulled out the wires to the vehicle's two-way radio, then wrenched the distributor cap from the engine and threw it as far as he could. Doheny took the provost marshal's belt transceiver and jammed it into his own pocket.

Nore handed him the gun. "Keep it aimed at him. I'm going to start up the engines."

Diane scrutinized the plane. She saw the letters NSI—Nore's company logo—emblazoned on the tail section's vertical stabilizer. Then she looked at the engine pod on the left wing and spotted the black exhaust marks.

Nore saw her expression. "Don't worry, Diane. The plane's not going to burn up—not yet, anyway."

Diane looked concerned for a second, then smiled.

After helping her aboard his Gulfjet II, Nore sat down in the pilot's seat. His fingers expertly flicked dozens of switches on the crowded instrument panel as he glanced at the array of readouts, dials, and blinking lights. Within seconds the two powerful Williams International FJ-44 jet engines fired.

Outside, the air was filled with a deafening whine from the twin turbofans.

Doheny caught a glimpse of movement with his peripheral vision. He turned and in the distance saw a jeep with four MPs speeding toward them. He leaped aboard the plane and slammed the hatch shut.

"Take off!" he yelled. "*Now!* There's a jeep with soldiers coming."

Nore's right hand shoved the throttle knobs forward to their limit. Hydrazine surged through the fuel lines, burst into the combustion chambers with an animal roar, ignited, and flamed into white-hot gas. He flicked a switch and sent dozens of gallons of distilled water into the engines, where it mixed with compressed air and expanded into superheated steam. The compressor blades whirled faster. The jet whine seemed to make the ground tremble.

"Fasten your seat belts," he shouted.

Doheny made sure Diane was strapped in before fastening his own belt. They anxiously peered out the windows and saw Clayton on his feet running, pointing at the plane. The jeep was a few hundred feet behind them and closing fast.

Nore released the control yoke, grasped the steering control wheel, and let up on the pressure he had been keeping on the rudder pedal brakes. The plane began to roll down the airstrip.

Ponderously, distressingly slow and unhurried at first, the Gulfjet II accelerated steadily.

Beads of perspiration appeared on Doheny's forehead when he saw the jeep gaining on them. He could make out the determined expressions on the soldiers' faces, and he spotted the machine pistols in their hands. Then he heard the jet whine grow louder, more intense, and the jeep slipped from view.

The plane was still accelerating. More than a third of a mile of runway had already vanished behind them. Nore pulled the control yoke back slowly and the plane's nose rose slightly—about six degrees. This increased angle generated tremendous lift and the jet shot forward.

The wheels broke contact with the runway. The silver wings flexed under the increased load they were now carrying. Still gaining speed, the Gulfjet II rose swiftly above the airstrip. To the passengers it was as if the earth fell away beneath them. They were airborne. Clayton, the jeep with the MPs, and the solar power plant were now far below.

Diane looked out the window and gasped. Clearly visible in the harsh afternoon sunlight was an enormous ugly scar stretching for miles across the landscape.

"The microwave track," said Doheny, his face grim.

"It's unbelievable," cried Diane. "Just like you described."

This was also the first time that Nore had seen the track. As he scanned the swath of withered and flattened vegetation below, there wasn't a doubt in his mind that the satellite could melt the Arctic ice cap. He frowned heavily and wondered if they had a ghost of a chance in stopping a device so powerful and deadly.

Chapter 29 *

THE SEQUENCE OF events following the civilians' escape from the solar power plant moved swiftly.

One hundred miles northeast of the plant the commandant of Fort Union scowled as he listened to a report on the incident given by Clayton's commanding officer. Afterward he relayed the information to Major Thomas Linden, the control officer of the National Military Command Center at the Pentagon. Linden immediately dispatched an emergency message on the matter to the White House teletype.

After reading the contents of the EMCON message the President took a deep breath, put his hands on his waist, and paced the room, trying to decide what action he should take.

Then he picked up the phone and spoke quietly to the switchboard operator. "Put me through to General Walter Abrams, the base commander of Kirtland AFB in New Mexico." When Abrams came on the line the President informed him of the situation and issued specific orders on how it should be dealt with.

At an altitude of 24,000 feet Nore adjusted the autopilot to keep the Gulfjet II straight and level. Then he gave Doheny a searching look. "How much did you tell her, Mike?" he asked gravely.

"Everything," said Doheny. There was a defensive tone to his voice. "She earned the right to hear the whole story. Somebody has to tell it," he added.

Nore sighed and went quiet for a moment. Finally he said, "I suppose so." He turned to Diane. "Just for the record, I want you to know that my company originally proposed the Solar Satellite Project as a realistic alternative to nuclear and fossil fuels. The concept involved a new and different technology, but a clean one. The government was interested in it, but for the wrong reasons." Bitterness crept into his voice. "Yes, they wanted to turn it into the ultimate death ray, and their argument for it was basically sound. National defense. Better for us to put one up first before someone else does. The same old garbage.''

Diane raised an eyebrow. ''Why couldn't the government just come out in the open and explain this to the public?''

Nore's features twisted into an ironic expression. ''There's an old saying that politicians treat the American public the way farmers grow mushrooms: 'Keep 'em in the dark and feed 'em lots of steer manure.' ''

Diane smiled at the underlying truth to the adage.

Nore gazed out the plane's plexiglass canopy and froze when he caught sight of a glint of sunlight off beyond their right wingtip. He stared at the tiny point of brightness. With shocking suddenness the point sprouted thin wings, became cruciform, and grew larger and more menacing with its rapid approach. It was a jet closing in on them, flying a converging heading. He felt fear reaching into his chest.

''We've got company,'' Nore said to his passengers, pointing to the approaching aircraft.

Both Diane and Doheny looked out, aft of the trailing edge of the wing and saw it.

''He's coming in close,'' said Doheny, voice taut. ''And he's dropping his landing gear!''

Nore peered at the invading aircraft as it grew in size and slid alongside them. It was no more than forty yards off their wingtip. He saw the sharklike profile and the swept-back wings of a fighter-interceptor—an F-14 Tomcat. The fighter's gear and flaps were down to increase drag, trying to slow it to the speed of the Gulfjet II. The helmeted figure in the cockpit waved. Nore's gaze fell across the shrouded missiles beneath each of the jet's wings.

He slipped on his headset and hit the button on his IFF transmitter and waited. IFF stood for Identification Friend or Foe, a coded frequency beacon used to identify an aircraft as non-hostile.

A stern voice crackled in his ear. ''This is Alpha Bravo Niner to NSI aircraft. You are ordered to veer from present heading and accompany me to Kirtland Air Force Base. Acknowledge.''

''They want us to turn around and land at Kirtland,'' Nore told his passengers. He compressed his lips and flexed his hands. He was going to refuse to terminate their flight to the Seward radio telescope. Too much was at stake. He picked up the microphone.

''Alpha Bravo Niner,'' he said firmly, ''this is NSI. Negative on

course change request. We are continuing on present heading."
He paused. "Do not interfere. Repeat. *Do not interfere*." He
hoped the Tomcat's pilot hadn't received orders on how to
respond to a direct refusal.

The voice in his ear sounded harsher and more threatening than
before. "Alpha Bravo Niner to NSI. Be advised I have been
authorized to ensure you follow instructions. Veer off *now*. This is
your last chance. Acknowledge."

Nore thought it was a bluff. He didn't think the air force would
make use of illegal maneuvers to coerce him. But he was wrong.

The Tomcat was beginning to turn toward them, compelling
Nore to turn with him to avoid a collision. The turn was very slow,
but deliberate, forcing Nore to the southeast, the direction where
Kirtland AFB was located. The two aircraft kept turning slowly,
the fighter creeping closer, keeping the turn tight. Nore's compass
was now rolling through west to southwest. He fought the impulse
to make an obscene gesture to the other pilot.

"Everett, we can't give up like this!" Doheny shouted.

"I don't want to," Nore said, deep in thought as he handled the
controls.

The heading was south now, the fighter still on their wing,
racked over in the shallow turn that was forcing the Gulfjet II to
reverse course. Nore could hear the rolling thunder of the
Tomcat's engines at high power settings, barely above a stall,
mushing along to match his own speed. Nore decided to take
evasive action.

He pulled back on the throttles and gradually reduced power.
The Gulfjet II started to slow immediately, Nore holding the nose
up to stay level with the Tomcat as the airspeed bled off. The
fighter was beginning to outrun him, shifting from his wing
position to slightly ahead, still banking. Nore could see the flames
from its engines—a hard, feathery blue. Then he felt his controls
buffeting; he was right on the edge of a stall. The Tomcat shot
ahead, unable to match Nore's much slower speed.

"His engines will stall if he tries to slow down to our speed,"
Nore said as he operated the controls to return them to their
original northwest heading. "We've got him now," he murmured,
grinning. "He'll probably shoot around us for a while, get bored,
and turn back."

This was not the case. The Tomcat banked directly in front of
them, giving them a full view of the underside of its wings. Nore
saw the pyrobolts blow away from the fiberglass cone shrouds

covering the warheads of the dozen air-to-air missiles nested under its wings. Just one of those missiles could turn the Gulfjet II into a flaming tangle of ripped and twisted metal.

There was a voice in his ear ordering him to follow instructions. Then came the threat.

"He says he'll fire on us if we don't cooperate," Nore said to the startled passengers behind him. He slowly expelled his breath. "They must want us pretty badly." After a moment's hesitation he announced, "I'm going to do what he says."

Doheny eyed Nore unbelievably. "You're giving up? Just like that?"

"They've decided we're expendable," Nore replied. He pointed to the Tomcat. "I think he really will blow us out of the sky if we refuse."

Doheny's shoulders sagged slightly as Nore turned the plane around, increased speed, and came alongside the jet fighter escort. Despite their best efforts the flight to the Seward observatory had been aborted.

At Kirtland Air Force Base the three civilians were taken to the office of Major-General Walter Abrams, the base commander.

Abrams had a long, narrow face, pale blue eyes, and thinning sandy-colored hair. He sat behind a long oak desk devoid of ornamentation.

Nore angrily jabbed his forefinger at Abrams. "General," he said in a cold venomous tone, "your smart-ass jet jockey almost killed us up there!" He spat out the words. "He deliberately violated a dozen F.A.A. and air force flight regulations. If I hadn't taken evasive action we would have collided. I demand an explanation."

Abrams shook his head. "I regret the strong actions taken against you, but I have orders to detain you." He glanced at Doheny, and then at Diane, noting her lack of proper clothing. "I'm not at liberty to divulge classified information in their presence, you know that."

Nore stiffened. "Very well, General. In that case I require the use of your phone to contact my attorney."

"Your attorney?" asked Abrams, suddenly nervous. "As one of the project controlling authorities you can't—"

"The hell I can't," retorted Nore. "I'm going to use the pay phone in the lounge." He spun on his heels and headed for the door.

Abrams stood up from his desk. "Please listen to me. I'm certain the matter can be cleared up quickly."

"All right," Nore said, "but we don't have much time."

However, Abrams was still adamant in his refusal to discuss classified information in the presence of Doheny and Diane. Nore pointed out that Doheny had been project-cleared, which the general accepted. But Diane was another matter. A compromise was reached. Diane would be taken to the women's quarters on the base, where she would be given suitable clothing. Afterward she would be escorted to the private lounge outside Abrams's office. Nore agreed to this arrangement.

When Diane left, Abrams said, "Gentlemen, I believe it's only fair to inform you that the orders to intercept your plane came directly from the White House."

Both Doheny and Nore exchanged glances.

Abrams indicated a stack of papers on his desk. "This is the report I received from Fort Union on your alleged criminal acts." He eyed the two men. "Do you deny assaulting a military police officer, aiding and abetting a fugitive, and forcibly escaping from legal custody?"

"This is a waste of time," Doheny said impatiently.

Nore leaned forward, pressing his hands on the general's desk. "Those charges are false. I'll swear to that in any court of law. We left the plant on my authority."

"The satellite emergency," said Doheny, "required us to fly to the radio telescope observatory on the Seward Peninsula in Alaska."

"Why?" asked Abrams.

Doheny explained how they hoped to make use of the Seward dish to burn out the Sunstroke satellite's microwave transmitter.

"Why did you take the Bradford woman with you?"

"Because she was in danger at the plant," answered Doheny. "The MPs over there are out of control. I was afraid for her life."

"That's the absolute truth, General," confirmed Nore.

Abrams blinked. "This whole situation is highly irregular," he said awkwardly.

Doheny looked at his watch. "The satellite will be entering a polar orbit in about eight hours." He went on to explain the ramifications.

Abrams was skeptical. "I find this difficult to believe. At any rate, are you aware that within the hour Vandenberg will launch a modified Taurus at the satellite to destroy it?"

Doheny and Nore were surprised. "We had no idea," muttered Nore.

Abrams sat back in his chair and stared levelly at them. "The Taurus has been fitted with a nuclear warhead. It'll take out your satellite," he said confidently. "That's for sure."

Chapter 30 *

AT THE WHITE House, National Security Adviser Jack Conley received an update on the status of the Taurus 44E from Vandenberg. Conley took the call in the Crisis Room in the West Wing. General Wisneski informed him the countdown was proceeding on schedule with lift-off just forty minutes away.

Conley relayed the news to the President, who immediately phoned Deputy Secretary of State Alex Maguire. Kendall ordered Maguire to inform Russian ambassador Grigori Chelyuskin that in forty minutes the United States would launch a special rocket from Vandenberg Air Force Base at the solar satellite to destroy it. The President did not disclose that the supermissile was armed with a nuclear warhead. He then instructed his deputy secretary of state to tell the ambassador that President Gorodin should expect to receive a hot-line communication from the White House at the time of launch.

Kendall had decided to warn them of the Vandenberg launch so they wouldn't misinterpret it as a first strike against their country. In addition he wanted to have their end of the hot line communications system ready and waiting at the precise moment of lift-off.

The President sat back in his chair and surveyed the bank of television screens on the wall before him. They displayed a variety of scenes: the image from Cheyenne Mountain showing the Sunstroke satellite's position on the Mercator map; the tactical display of American and Russian forces dispersed across the globe; and Launch Pad 9B at Vandenberg, where the Taurus rocket was being counted down. A fourth screen, alive but blank, awaited contact with the Kremlin.

This screen was the hot line between the capitals of the two superpowers. It was linked to a nearby console containing the automatic translation system that instantly converted Russian to

English. The console was manned by two State Department linguists who had been assigned to monitor the electronic translator for errors of meaning or syntax.

Kendall felt tired, fatigued. He rubbed his neck and glanced at the others in the room. With the exception of the chairman of the Joint Chiefs of Staff, everyone was in shirtsleeves, ties askew, their disheveled hair and haggard faces indicative of the terrible strain they had been laboring under for the past three days.

Despite his weariness Kendall was excited at the prospect of finally ending the crisis. He was anxiously looking forward to receiving confirmation from Cheyenne Mountain that the Sunstroke satellite had been obliterated. This news should come approximately twenty minutes after the Taurus launch. Then he could order all U.S. military forces to a stand down, while the Russian President did the same. Afterward he would enjoy cocktails and a quiet dinner with his wife Caroline, and sleep until noon the next day.

He stared at the blank screen, the one that very shortly would show the broad face of President Nikolai Gorodin. Kendall had dealt with the head of the Russian Republic during the ICBM summits and knew he was a difficult man to deal with. Behind the genial facade he exhibited in public Gorodin was a hardened political veteran, a survivor from the Brezhnev years who had long ago mastered the art of intimidation. Kendall had learned the hard way that Gorodin was a fierce debater, possessing a steel-trap mind and an acute sense of timing.

For this reason a detailed outline of Kendall's presentation to Gorodin had been prepared. He had consulted with Dean Stratton regarding the technical aspects. Kendall would begin his speech by justifying his decision to break the 1967 Space Treaty prohibiting the use of nuclear weapons in space. He would argue that the safety of the world depended on it. Then he would do his best to obtain an admission of guilt from Gorodin that they had deliberately attacked the solar satellite with one of their stealth ASATs, causing it to go awry.

If Kendall could accomplish this it would be possible to shift the blame for the entire crisis to the Kremlin, enabling him to negotiate from a position of strength. Besides demanding a mutual stand-down of both forces at the exact instant of detonation, he would ask for a reduction of their own space-based weapons systems, particularly their kinetic-kill stealth ASATs. The fact that the United States had destroyed its own satellite would further support his position.

He shifted his gaze to the gleaming spire perched on its launchpad at Vandenberg. He realized everything hinged on the success of its mission. All our hopes, he thought, will be riding on that rocket. God help us if something goes wrong. He picked up the sheets of paper containing his speech and started studying them.

Then, at T minus 20 minutes to launch, Julie Sommers, the President's personal secretary, a handsome middle-aged woman, strode into the Crisis Room, hairbrush in hand. After making a final effort to tame the President's unruly hair, she straightened his tie and helped him put on his coat. Kendall smiled and thanked her.

Across the room the two State Department linguists hunched forward and adjusted their headsets and microphones. On the hot-line TV screen the Great Seal of the United States appeared, serving as a test pattern for the American end of the communications system. Everything was proceeding smoothly and on schedule.

Inside the concrete Launch Operations blockhouse at Vandenberg AFB General Barry Wisneski walked among the rows of consoles in the amphitheater-sized room, inspecting the myriad readout displays as well as the officers who manned them. The minutes ticked by uneventfully. There was no reason to postpone the launch.

"T minus sixty seconds and counting," said the launch director over the intercom, his voice smooth and steady.

Wisneski glanced at the big television screen on the wall. It showed the frosty, sweating Taurus 44E, puffs of vapor issuing from its sides.

"T minus forty seconds."

"RP-One fuel tanks fully pressurized," said another voice. The verbal reports picked up in frequency. "Wind from the northeast at eight knots per hour," reported the meteorologist. "Thrust vector control hydraulic fluid at one-fifty psi," said a technician.

"T minus twenty seconds."

The rapid litany of voices continued.

"Lox tanks fully pressurized."

"ACSC systems go."

"Telemetry multiplexing on."

"Lox umbilical decoupling." On-screen a thick line swung free of the rocket, dangled for a moment like an elephant's trunk, then disappeared into the tower. The vibrations dislodged a chunk of frost from high on the second stage. It spun lazily in the bright sun before it fell to the pad.

"T minus ten seconds."

Wisneski felt his body stiffen. "Retract gantry arms," he ordered, his voice taut.

Two long cranelike arms slowly swung back from the space-craft. Now only three hold-down core clamps joined the rocket to the tower.

"Flush the pad," Wisneski shouted.

A small Niagara Falls flooded the launchpad as hundreds of thousands of gallons of water poured over the metal flame deflectors directly beneath the spacecraft. The water would help dampen the intense vibrations from the engines.

"T minus five seconds. Four, three . . ."

Eight columns of white-hot flame appeared on-screen. A vibration started to build through the blockhouse.

"Ignition!" yelled the propulsion systems officer. "All eight engines." He studied the binary digits flowing across his readouts. "Throttling to seventy percent power. Eighty, ninety . . ."

The flames cascading from the rocket nozzles turned the water beneath them into billowing steam as the engines quickly built up to their full 2.7 million pounds of thrust. There was a rumble in the blockhouse, a seismic jolt that jarred bones and teeth as the spacecraft strained against its hold-down clamps.

"Release hold-downs," ordered Wisneski.

"Clamps released," came the reply. Three red shackles snapped aside from the vibrating rocket.

"Lift-off," announced the launch director. "We have lift-off at twenty-nine minutes past the hour."

The spacecraft rose maddeningly slow at first, carried aloft by an ever-lengthening orange-and-white column of flame.

"Go, go!" someone yelled.

Trailing a Promethean plume of fire and smoke, the entire twenty-three-story-high rocket cleared the umbilical tower and thundered into the clear blue sky.

In the Crisis Room at the White House the air was thick with controlled tension. Kendall watched the trail of fire arching into the sky on the TV display to his left, then shifted his gaze to the screen bearing the Great Seal of the United States.

Behind him the two State Department linguists assigned to monitor the automatic translation system sat at their consoles. An Army Signal Corps colonel adjusted the TV camera that would soon be broadcasting the President's image to Moscow.

Out of camera range sat Defense Secretary Hugh Fitzpatrick and General Willis Thompson, the chairman of the Joint Chiefs. Both men were ready to offer their advice should the President need it.

In a low voice Fitzpatrick reminded Kendall that Gorodin preferred to be addressed as "Premier," even though his official title was President of Russia. Gorodin belonged to the old line of their leadership and wished to preserve ties to the past.

Suddenly the image on the hot-line screen wavered momentarily and was replaced by the Russian flag. The connection with the Kremlin had been made. Knowing he was now being seen in Moscow, Kendall looked straight into the lens of the camera.

An instant later the colorful flag dissolved and President Nikolai Gorodin appeared, an older man in his early sixties. He had sparse gray hair, a soft, full face with a slightly ruddy complexion, and his full lips were drawn in a wintry smile. He spoke something rapidly in Russian. The autotranslator immediately cut in and a metallic synthesized voice in English filled the room.

"Good afternoon, Mr. President."

Kendall leaned closer to his microphone. "Greetings, Mr. Premier," he began. "I welcome your initiative in participating with me in this special communication, which is vital to the safety of our respective nations."

Gorodin nodded and Kendall continued. "I have requested this conference to inform you that moments ago the United States launched"—he glanced at his notes—"a modified Taurus 44E spacecraft on a northern trajectory to intercept our solar satellite, now orbiting above Canada, with the express purpose of destroying it. Please rest assured this missile will not encroach on your airspace, nor will it in any way endanger the safety of Russia or its allies."

The premier listened intently to the translation, but remained silent.

"It is with great regret," said Kendall, "that I must tell you we have chosen to temporarily circumvent the 1967 Space Treaty between our countries, due to the grave urgency of the situation."

Gorodin's eyes widened a bit. He recovered quickly and said, "Please explain." His tone was flat.

"The nose cone of the Taurus missile," said the President, "contains a small atomic warhead to be detonated upon interception of the solar satellite. The warhead possesses an infrared—"

"Excuse me, Mr. President," Gorodin interrupted hotly. "Are you telling me that you have deliberately violated *another* important treaty between the U.S. and my country?"

Damn it, Kendall thought, he's taking the offensive. "I don't understand, Mr. Premier. What other treaty are you referring to?"

"You know very well which one," Gorodin replied impatiently. "The ABM Treaty prohibiting the deployment of large-scale antiballistic missile systems in space. Such as your solar satellite."

"With all due respect, Mr. Premier," Kendall replied, "the solar satellite is merely an experimental platform deployed for the sole purpose of demonstrating an alternative energy source."

Gorodin shook his head in disgust. There was a hardened glint in his eyes. "Save your deceit for the American public," he said angrily. "Right now I want you to explain to me why you are positioning a highly dangerous 'Star Wars' weapons system in orbit above the Russian Republic, why you have placed your nuclear submarine forces on alert, and why you have launched a nuclear missile in our direction. My advisers believe you are planning a first strike against us. Is this true? Have you declared war against my country?"

The President sat back in his chair and frowned, struggling to keep his temper in check. This conference was not going the way he had planned.

The instant that SOLSAT X-1's infrared sensors detected the heat emissions from the Vandenberg missile, the self-defense subroutine directed the command computer to calculate the rocket's exact course. By analyzing the infrared signature and conducting a radar scan, the computer quickly determined the incoming missile was on an intercept course, that only seconds remained before the satellite would be destroyed.

This data automatically stimulated the subroutine to instruct the computer to engage all defenses against the onrushing attacker. The command computer immediately fired the Icarus rockets attached to the satellite's tail section. The firing sequence was brief, lasting perhaps a tenth of a second. But it was sufficient to pivot the huge satellite until its octagon-shaped microwave transmitter faced the oncoming missile head-on. The computer next sent an electrified command to the klystron tube assembly, ordering it to convert electricity into microwave radiation. The klystrons were still in an overheated state and could not respond. This prompted the computer to send a signal to the turbopump coolant valves.

The response was automatic. This time the valves opened, allowing the powerful high-speed pumps to shoot the icy liquid nitrogen through the klystron tube coolant lines. The tubes glowed a pale orange as they came to life.

The communications officer at Vandenberg Launch Operations, a pale young man with acne-scarred features, was routinely monitoring the Taurus missile's radio frequencies when suddenly a burst of shrieking static shot into his ears. He clawed his headset off and stared at it as if it had just bitten him. Simultaneously the readout screens throughout the room went blank.

"What the hell . . . ?" yelled a startled Barry Wisneski.

"There's nothing but static on all channels, sir," reported the communications officer. "We've lost all radio contact with the missile." He spun around in his seat, eyes wide. "The warhead must have gone off!"

Wisneski wondered if his junior officer was right, but one glance at the radar "scoreboard" told him otherwise. The missile blip was still on-screen, still closing in on the satellite.

Inwardly he hoped and prayed the warhead would detonate in the next few moments. But he had a bad gut feeling.

At the Space Shield command center in Cheyenne Mountain, General Stratton watched the interception on the high-resolution radar screen. The two blips were close, almost merged into one. Suddenly the large blip moved slightly, sidestepping the smaller one. Then the gap between them increased. He felt a sick hollowness in his stomach when he realized the nuclear warhead had failed to detonate.

He snatched up the console phone, called the solar power plant, and asked for a satellite status report. To his horror, Jenkins told him it was pumping coolant to the klystron array.

Keeping its microwave transmitter aimed unerringly at the missile, SOLSAT X-1 steadily discharged its tight beam of microwaves, enveloping the rocket in a flood of high-intensity radiation. The missile's second stage engines sputtered and died.

As the Taurus 44E swept by, the SOLSAT X-1 command computer probed it with a wide range of sensor scans, including infrared, Doppler, radio, magnetic anomaly, and optical television. Every electronic and electrical system aboard the missile's second stage and the warhead in its nose cone had been overloaded and burned out.

At the White House, President James Kendall made an effort to compose himself. Then he leaned toward the TV camera and addressed Gorodin.

"Mr. Premier," he said, his tone accusatory, "let me explain to you that the crisis we now face is entirely due to the unprovoked attack on my country's satellite. I have been informed that one of your stealth kinetic-kill antisatellite vehicles was deployed against it, causing the satellite to malfunction, making it impossible for our ground stations to control it."

Gorodin kept his face impassive. The voice coming from the autotranslator was harsh, but also condescending, rebuking. "This is a very serious charge, Mr. President. Do you have objective, documented proof to support your allegation?"

Kendall glared into the camera lens. "Yes, Mr. Premier, we do have the evidence, and let me say it is clear and incontrovertible." He was bluffing; all that was on record included a scant report from a CIA operative purporting that a Russian stealth ASAT had been launched, and a videotape of a "radar ghost" detected in the vicinity of the solar satellite prior to its malfunction. "Do you, Premier Gorodin, deny that the Kremlin was behind the attack on our satellite?"

The metallic voice from the autotranslator came without hesitation. "I state for the record, Mr. President, that my country did not attack your satellite, that we have committed no illegal acts against your nation. May I point out, however, that you have committed one against us by violating two important treaties between our nations, no doubt without authorization from your Congress."

Kendall felt his face flushing. He believed Gorodin was lying, and trying to cover it up by making counterallegations.

"The fact exists, sir," the President said coldly, "that your long-range Hammer bombers went on airborne alert and your ICBMs were put on line shortly after our satellite was attacked. Did you engage these strategic forces because you intend to launch a preemptive first-strike against the United States?"

A synthetic parody of a human laugh issued from the autotranslator. The strange sound unnerved Kendall.

"I assure you, Mr. President," said Gorodin, "the Republic of Russia has no intention of starting a war between our nations." He went on to explain that his Defense Ministry believed the solar satellite was a new ultimate weapon whose deployment was a threat to their republic and the entire international community. "It seems a very serious misunderstanding has developed between our two great nations due to the presence of your satellite in space. Let us take steps to resolve this crisis and restore the good relations between our countries."

Kendall stared at Gorodin's image for a moment. There appeared to be a look of sincerity in the premier's eyes. He's anxious to end this thing, Kendall thought, and so am I.

"That is an excellent analysis, sir, and I am in complete agreement with you," he said quickly. "Apparently our solar satellite has generated certain misconceptions regarding its use which have helped endanger the peace of the world. This is more than sufficient cause to justify its immediate destruction, which can only be accomplished by a nuclear explosion in space. I propose, Mr. Premier, that at the exact instant of the satellite's destruction we both simultaneously order our respective forces to stand down and return to normal peacetime status."

"I agree to your proposal," Gorodin said emphatically. "It is my most sincere wish to put an end to this unfortunate situation as soon as possible."

Kendall was pleased to have accomplished his primary objective of defusing the crisis. He was about to press Gorodin into eliminating the stealth ASAT from the Russian arsenal when one of the television screens he was facing started flashing on and off in a warning signal. He was instantly alert. This TV image originated from Cheyenne Mountain. The satellite must have blown up, he thought.

Then a message in glowing print appeared on the screen:

URGENT. SATELLITE MICROWAVE BEAM HAS RENDERED THE TAURUS MISSILE INOPERATIVE. SATELLITE IS DISCHARGING BEAM CONTINUOUSLY. REQUEST IMMEDIATE CONFERENCE.
STRATTON
USAF

Just then Jack Conley, the national security adviser, stepped up and handed Kendall a note from Vandenberg that confirmed the message. Kendall reread it, then turned to the camera lens broadcasting his image to the Kremlin. There was great physical tension and pain in his face as he informed the premier that the missile had been neutralized by the satellite.

"This has caught us all by surprise," Kendall said. "I must request a recess in our talks so that I may confer with my advisers."

Except for a slight widening of the eyes, Gorodin showed no emotion. "I also wish to consult with my staff regarding this development."

The two heads of state agreed to keep the line open. Then the premier's image dissolved into the white, blue, and red flag of the Russian Republic.

Kendall's face was slack, softened with despair. "That warhead was our last chance," he whispered to Conley. He pointed impatiently to the Cheyenne Mountain TV screen. "Put me in touch with Dean Stratton," he ordered. "I've got to know what went wrong."

A moment later General Stratton appeared on-screen, his spectacles glinting. The President listened carefully as Stratton briefly explained how the satellite was able to prevent the nuclear detonation. The general said that when it became apparent the warhead had failed to explode he had phoned the control room at the solar power plant and was informed that the satellite was now transmitting its beam continuously, without interruption. Stratton said that when he asked to speak to Doheny he was told that he was on his way to the Seward radio telescope in Alaska to stop the satellite.

"No," replied Kendall sharply. "He's in custody at Kirtland AFB. So is Everett Nore and a woman reporter. They left the plant without authorization."

"Mr. President," Stratton said, raising his voice, "the satellite could discharge its microwave beam at the earth at any moment. If Doheny has come up with a method of stopping it I think we should talk to him without delay."

"Call him," Kendall ordered.

On-screen General Stratton picked up his phone.

Kendall turned to Jack Conley. Rubbing his chin, he said, "Should we trust this Doheny? Among other things, they said he assaulted an army officer."

"You read the FBI report on him," Conley replied. "It said he was reliable, the best in his field." He frowned. "If he was on his way to that radio telescope—"

"Then we made a stupid mistake," said Kendall.

Several minutes later they saw Stratton put down the phone. "Much more is at stake then we thought," the general said gravely. He summarized what Doheny had told him regarding the satellite's reasons for entering a polar orbit.

The President stirred in his chair, his face drained of color. "Can it really do it?" he asked in a high-pitched voice.

"Yes, sir, it can," answered Stratton.

"But it's only a *machine*," protested Kendall. "It can't plot against us."

"The collision in space," Stratton said rapidly, "altered the defense program that we inserted into its computer. Somehow it blames us for the ASAT attack and for our attempt to regain control over it."

"Can we stop it in time?" Kendall demanded.

Stratton related Doheny's plan to use the Seward radio telescope to reflect the microwave beam at its klystron array. "The physics involved support his theory," Stratton said evenly. "If he can induce the satellite to discharge at the dish, the reflected radiation *will* overload the microwave transmitter. Nothing will be left to chance."

Kendall closed his eyes. He had to make a decision. Should he give the go-ahead to that engineer? The idea of using a radio telescope didn't make any sense. But Kendall realized he was no scientist.

"Can the astronomers at that observatory do the job themselves?" he asked.

Stratton shook his head. "Be advised, sir, that whoever operates the radio telescope during the discharge will be placing himself at considerable risk. We can't order those civilians to do it. They should be evacuated."

"What about someone in the air force or navy?"

"No one is more qualified than Mr. Doheny," Stratton replied. "Besides being familiar with the Seward observatory, he possesses a series of codes for manipulating the satellite."

"All right," said Kendall. "We'll let him do it." He told Jack Conley to order General Abrams at Kirtland to have Doheny flown to Alaska immediately. He also ordered Conley to see to it that the observatory was evacuated at once.

Stratton recommended that in the meantime they should keep the satellite distracted by launching every component in the Space Shield arsenal at it. This tactic could prevent it from irradiating the earth before the Seward dish was set up.

"Very well," agreed Kendall. "Proceed."

Chapter 31 *

AT KIRTLAND AFB preparations were being made for Doheny's flight to the Arctic. Jack Conley had asked General Abrams to have a hypersonic Condor recon jet, the fastest long-range plane on the base, readied for immediate takeoff. The Condor could cruise at Mach four and reach the Seward Peninsula in less than two and a half hours. A flight path was drawn up and the special equipment that Doheny had requested was being loaded aboard.

The pilot chosen for the mission was Colonel Douglas Harriman, the air force officer who had commanded Doheny's overflight of the microwave track. Harriman escorted Doheny to the pilot clothing ward and issued him a *g*-suit, boots, and a fishbowl-shaped helmet with visor.

"Time to suit up," said Harriman.

An attendant, a young freckle-faced sergeant, helped Doheny put on the strange apparel while Harriman pulled on his own suit.

"I'm afraid it's going to be a tight fit, sir," the sergeant said apologetically. "You're taller than any of our pilots."

As Doheny struggled into the silver suit Harriman's gaze fell across the bandaged cheek and bruises. "Tell me, Mr. Doheny. What hit you?"

Doheny looked up, a wry expression on his face. "Bureaucratic red tape." Both men laughed nervously.

When he had finished suiting up Doheny surveyed himself. A slight smile flickered across his lips. "I feel like a goddamned astronaut."

"You're not too wrong there," Harriman remarked. "We'll be flying close to the edge of space."

At nine minutes past four P.M. Mountain Standard Time, Mike Doheny, cradling his helmet in his hands, was led into the cavernous hangar where the airplane stood, swarming with ground technicians conducting a last check.

The plane was a radar-evasive Lockheed Aurora SR-82, nick-named the Condor because of its shape. Its bulletlike nose cone thrust upward at a shallow angle, and thin delta-shaped wings merged into the fuselage. Sleek pods at each wing tip housed Pratt and Whitney JT-15-D turbofan engines with afterburners, each one capable of generating 43,000 pounds of thrust.

Nore, Diane, and Abrams appeared beside Doheny at the hangar entrance.

Nore rubbed his hand across his face, a habitual nervous habit. "Mike," he said awkwardly, "I had hoped the two of us would tackle the thing together. I was—"

Doheny grabbed Nore's arm and led him away from the others. "Take care of Diane," he said firmly. "If something goes wrong"—his throat suddenly felt dry—"go to your cabin in the Sierra Nevadas and stay there. Take plenty of provisions. The water could rise within a couple weeks." He paused to think. "Get those charges against her dropped. And while you're at it, make them release all those people at the plant."

Nore smiled faintly. "Count on it."

"Mr. Doheny," shouted Harriman, "we're ready."

Doheny drew close to Diane, took both her hands in his, and kissed her hard on the mouth.

"Good luck," she whispered.

"Thanks. Do what Everett Nore says." Then Doheny turned and strode briskly toward the waiting plane.

Ground assistants slipped the helmet over his head, fastened it, then helped him into the narrow rear seat of the cockpit. Their hands reached in and linked the radio and life-support tubes projecting from his flight suit to the aircraft's systems. He saw Harriman lower himself into the seat in front of him and begin attaching his own systems with practiced ease. Soon the triple-plexiglass canopy was closed down on them. A hiss indicated the cockpit was now fully pressurized. Doheny breathed in the pure oxygen being pumped into his face mask. It tasted dry, rubbery.

A heavy tractor vehicle towed the plane to the runway and drove off. Harriman started the powerful engines, ran his preflight checks, then secured clearance for takeoff. The only sound inside the aircraft was a low whistling noise. Outside a thunderous roar shook the ground.

Doheny heard Harriman's voice over his radio. "It'll help if you start breathing deeply. Hold tight now."

A moment later Doheny was thrown against his molded seat with violent force. When he felt the plane leave the ground he shut his eyes and swallowed hard. It tilted back, then climbed vertically, clawing its way through the sky like a rocket.

Far below, the small knot of people gathered at the hangar entrance watched the jet's rapid ascent.

Abrams turned to Nore. "I wish we could have given him a support team of engineers and technicians," he said with regret. "But we can't spare the men. The national security adviser told me we may be going on alert at any moment. I even had to order Colonel Harriman to refuel and return immediately. We might be needing that Condor for a recon mission. The NSA said they're evacuating all personnel from the radio telescope." He paused, then said, "Doheny will be on his own up there."

"I know, General," said Nore, grim. "Heroes usually die alone."

SOLSAT X-1 continued to aim its lethal cone of radiation at the Taurus warhead, even though the missile was now almost beyond the range of its scanners.

Suddenly the satellite's infrared sensors detected the heat signature from something moving high above. It was a small metallic sphere. The heat emissions grew stronger as this new intruder descended toward the satellite by firing its thrusters, tiny pinpoints of light against the blackness. The self-defensive subroutine governing SOLSAT X-1 instructed the command computer to analyze the signature and compare it to those stored in memory. When the computer determined the infrared signature belonged to a kinetic-kill antisatellite vehicle the subroutine ordered it to engage all defenses.

With the Icarus rockets firing at its tail section, SOLSAT X-1 executed a graceful roll. As the satellite performed this maneuver its microwave beam swept wildly through space. When the desired attitude had been attained, the beam enveloped the intruder and its thrusters winked out. SOLSAT X-1's sensors began scanning for other intruders.

After receiving word that Doheny was on his way to Alaska, President Kendall sat thinking about the unexpected turn of events. He and his advisers had been certain the Vandenberg supermissile would destroy the satellite, put an end to the crisis. It didn't. The thing was still up there, firing its beam at Dean Stratton's Star Wars devices, turning the skies into a gigantic target range.

He glanced at the Russian flag on the hot-line TV screen and wondered what he would tell President Gorodin. He was conscious of harsh, whispering voices coming from behind him. He spun around and saw Defense Secretary Hugh Fitzpatrick and JCS Chairman Willis Thompson involved in a heated discussion at the conference table, their voices low and urgent. Suddenly both men stopped talking and approached the President.

Fitzpatrick's face was gray with weariness, his shoulders stooped, his white shirt rumpled as if he had slept in it. "Mr. President," he rasped, "the general and I both agree that you should persuade Gorodin to use their own ASAT arsenal against the satellite. It would give us some extra time."

General Thompson nodded. He stood erect, his huge jaw squared, his uniform crisp as ever. "It also occurred to me, sir," he said to Kendall, "that the satellite is depleting our Space Shield. In two hours or so Cheyenne Mountain will have almost exhausted its entire supply of high–earth orbiting ASATs. In the event of war this will leave our military comsats wide open to attack. It would be best if their antisatellite capability was wiped out, too."

The President nodded, his eyes bright. He ordered the Army Signal Corps officer to reestablish contact with the Kremlin.

Two thousand miles to the west Mike Doheny lay on his back, conscious of only the mounting pressure of the seat pushing against his spine as the Condor lunged toward a sky that was quickly turning from dark blue to violet, and finally to a velvety black.

Below them Salt Lake City, Utah, went by like a toy model. They continued accelerating, still climbing. At one hundred thousand feet, nearly twenty miles above the ground, Harriman cut the afterburners and leveled his flight attitude. They could not climb any farther for the atmosphere would then be too thin to support combustion inside the jet engines.

Doheny raised his head and caught a glimpse of the actual curvature of the earth. He found it to be awe-inspiring at first, then unsettling. Although he never admitted it to anyone, he had a strong aversion to flying. He stared out the cockpit canopy at the sky above; it was as black as night.

"Enjoying the view?" asked Harriman over the radio.

"Yeah," Doheny said without enthusiasm.

"We're at Mach three point nine now. It looks like all that cargo you requested hasn't added too much drag."

"Glad to hear it."

Before leaving Kirtland Doheny had asked for a supply of heavily insulated coaxial cables, a soldering kit, microwave radiation detectors, and thick insulation pads. These items as well as cold-weather clothing were stored in the plane's cargo bay. Beside him were his radio telescope textbooks, manuals, Ted Kitami's coded message, and the file on the ionospheric tests he had conducted at Seward.

He pulled the file from its fasteners and, in the eerie perfect silence of high-altitude flight, began rereading it, paying close attention to the notes he had written on the operation of the big dish.

The image of Nikolai Gorodin, leader of the Russian Republic, once again appeared on the hot-line TV screen. The expression on his face was one of worried concern.

President Kendall slowly and succinctly explained the satellite's intentions to the premier. Then he told Gorodin how the United States was delaying the inevitable by deploying all of its high–earth orbiting Space Shield components against it.

Throughout the explanation Gorodin listened in silence. Finally he glared at Kendall and spoke. The voice from the autotranslator was cold and hard. "Mr. President," he began, "your solar satellite weapon is about to deliver a mortal blow not only to my country and yours, but to the very planet itself. Maybe, just maybe, there is a slight hope that this horrible peril can be removed. I am prepared to take the necessary steps that may save us from this insanity you have visited upon us."

The sharp words stung Kendall. His mouth tightened. He was about to accuse Gorodin of causing the problem when he suddenly realized that by doing so he would be jeopardizing a potential alliance with the Russians.

"Mr. Premier," he said in a reasonable tone, "you mentioned you are prepared to take steps to remove the menace. Do I take it you are willing to cooperate with us in our efforts to destroy the satellite?"

Gorodin nodded. "That is correct."

"I am glad to hear it, sir," Kendall said, relieved.

"Do you have a concrete strategy, Mr. President?" Gorodin asked sharply.

"Yes." Kendall put forth his proposal in which both nations would deploy their ASAT arsenals to keep the satellite occupied for as long as possible. Then he leaned closer to the hot-line microphone in front of him. "Mr. Premier," he said in a calm, steady voice, "at this very moment an aerospace engineer is flying to our radio telescope facility at Seward, Alaska. He is a civilian employed by a private corporation. He intends to set up the telescope so that it will act as a giant mirror to reflect the microwave beam back at the satellite. My advisers have assured me that this will destroy the microwave transmitter."

Gorodin silently regarded the President for a moment, then asked, "Who is this American engineer?"

"His name is Michael Doheny," Kendall said. "He designed and built the solar satellite. I have been told he is a brilliant and dedicated scientist."

"Then it will be poetic justice if he succeeds in his mission," remarked Gorodin.

"Mr. Premier," Kendall said urgently, "we must give Doheny the time he needs. It is imperative that you deploy your ASAT devices against the satellite, just as we have done."

Gorodin nodded thoughtfully. "We have been monitoring the activities of your Space Shield. It appears you are making a genuine effort to distract your satellite." He stopped talking and gazed beyond the camera, his eyes fixed on nothing. The silence drew out, went past a normal break in conversation, and seemingly became a contest of wills. Then he looked into the Moscow camera. "We will engage your satellite with our space-based weapons systems as you have requested."

Kendall nodded. "I will instruct Cheyenne Mountain to coordinate this with your people at Tyuratam." He knew that Cheyenne Mountain and Tyuratam, the Russian antisatellite site in the Dzezkazgan Province, were connected through a series of comsat relays in the event of a global emergency.

Gorodin gazed closely into the monitor, and a sorrowful look appeared in his eyes. "Before we break this connection, Mr. President," he warned, "I must inform you that should your satellite discharge anywhere on our territory or that of our allies we will have no alternative but to consider this an act of war. I promise you we will retaliate promptly in a manner appropriate to such an act of aggression and provocation."

Kendall was taken aback. "I thought we—"

He was interrupted by Gorodin. "I have no choice in this matter. If your satellite attacks my country we will be *forced* to retaliate."

The hot-line conference ended on this note of grim finality.

As President Kendall ordered General Stratton to coordinate the assault on the Sunstroke satellite with Tyuratam, he had no idea that the senior communications officer for that facility was about to drop a different kind of bombshell—one that would expose treason.

Lieutenant Colonel Leonid Brusavitch, his face lined with sadness and concern, was walking briskly up the long flight of steps leading to the central Kremlin building in Moscow. He was accompanied by the minister of defense, a dour-looking man in a drab brown suit, and four others. The minister had reviewed Brusavitch's incriminating evidence against General-Lieutenant Erik Rybinsk, the head of Tyuratam, and was determined to bring him to trial on charges of treason. But first he needed President Gorodin to authorize Rybinsk's arrest.

Far to the northeast, one hundred thousand feet in the sky, Colonel Harriman announced they had just passed the midpoint of their flight. The Condor was now above the Canadian island of Queen Charlotte, the last land they would see until they reached the Alaskan frontier. Below them the currents of the cruel, icy cold North Pacific swirled and eddied.

In the rear seat Doheny's face was lit by an unnatural light streaming in through the plexiglass canopy. The satellite, enormous and bright, was now overhead and would remain so for the rest of the flight.

Inside the Space Shield command center Dean Stratton sat down at his master control console and activated the Multilateral Military Communications Network to put him in contact with General-Lieutenant Rybinsk at Tyuratam.

After the link had been established Stratton grasped his console microphone, looked up at the projection TV screen bearing his counterpart's image, and said, "General Stratton of the U.S. Space Defense Command, Colorado, here."

Static came over the speaker for an instant, then a synthetic, metallic-sounding voice said in perfect English, "Greetings. This is General-Lieutenant Rybinsk, Russian Air and Space Command, Tyuratam." He smiled coolly. "I have been expecting to hear from you, General."

Stratton was about to begin outlining his strategy for the assault when suddenly he saw two soldiers appear on either side of a startled Rybinsk. The TV screen went blank for a moment, then flashed back on. An unfamiliar officer peered into the camera.

"Please excuse the interruption, General," the officer said, his face expressionless. "It is with great regret that I must inform you General-Lieutenant Rybinsk has become seriously ill. I am Colonel Sergei Chirchik, his second in command. I am now in charge."

Stratton assumed Rybinsk had somehow fallen into disfavor. "I understand," he said, keeping his voice even.

The awkwardness quickly passed, and the two military men applied their expertise to the technical problems of deploying both nations' space arsenals in a concerted effort to divert the satellite's attention.

A swarm of small kinetic-kill vehicles were orbiting in a region of space high above earth designated Geostationary Sector VIII-IV-N-2. This area was out of range of SOLSAT X-1's sensor scans. Every few minutes Cheyenne Mountain's Space Shield controllers would deorbit one of these ASATs and direct it at the huge satellite. The moment SOLSAT X-1's command computer detected one of the devices it would unleash a torrent of microwaves at it.

An hour passed. The computer calculated that the frequency of the intruders' attacks began to diminish. It continued to keep the satellite's microwave transmitter aimed at the region where they appeared, sweeping the area with its power beam. The enemy's supply of orbiting weapons was dwindling.

Without warning a small explosion erupted near SOLSAT X-1, hurtling shrapnel at the midsection of its hull. Then the satellite's sensors detected a salvo of tiny spearlike missiles bearing down on it from a region of space exactly opposite to the zone where the earlier attacks originated. The self-defensive subroutine driving the command computer correctly surmised the battle had been joined by another earth-based enemy.

Chapter 32 *

AFTER FLYING ABOVE a deep aching blue inlet of frigid water called the Norton Sound, the Condor finally reached the Seward Peninsula, an irregularly shaped jog of land two hundred miles long and forty miles wide jutting into the Bering Sea. The peninsula was a sparsely populated land of remote military bases and observation posts. It was named after the American statesman William Henry Seward, who secured the purchase of Alaska from Russia in 1867 for $7.2 million. At the time, this acquisition was disparagingly referred to as Seward's Folly.

Their destination, the National Astronomy and Ionospheric Radio Telescope Center, lay in the heart of the peninsula, seventy miles to the southwest of McMurdo Air Force Base. Colonel Harriman reduced speed and altitude. To Doheny it felt as if the plane went into a screaming dive. The plane shook violently as it tore through the white sheets of water vapor composing a cumulo-stratus layer. Then a vast, flat expanse of tundra spread before them. The treeless plain was covered by a late-summer frost, which gave it a soft pinkish purple hue.

As the Condor started banking Doheny caught sight of the observatory. His eyes were immediately drawn to the immense reflector, a dish one thousand feet in diameter, by far the most prominent feature of the installation. It was eighteen and a half acres in area, larger than a sports arena, and sheathed in a white formfitting covering of Nomex insulation panels, 40,000 in all, for protection against the severe winter temperatures.

Hanging in midair 200 feet above the center of the dish was the triangular-shaped radio receiver, a spindly white-paneled structure 150 feet across. The receiver was suspended on cables anchored to four massive steel towers positioned around the perimeter of the dish. Access to the receiver was provided by a ski lift–type cable car rigged to one of the towers.

A cluster of long, semicylindrical concrete buildings resembling Quonset huts was situated several hundred yards from the big dish. In the midst of these buildings was the large domelike structure that housed the control room. It was encircled by a forest of radio antennas. Nearby was a blockhouse containing an enormous diesel generator for use during power failures. It was obvious the facility had been evacuated; there were no cars parked among the buildings.

The plane skidded on the ice-laden runway, its engines screaming in protest as Harriman reversed thrust and applied brakes. After radioing a message to General Abrams via McMurdon AFB, Harriman lifted the cockpit canopy on its hydraulic struts and both men climbed out. They were about a quarter mile from the observatory.

The air was biting cold, a frigid twenty-four degrees Fahrenheit. Doheny felt and heard the ice crunch beneath his boots. Harriman opened the jet's cargo bay door and the two men grabbed heavy parkas and yanked them on over their flight suits. They exhaled drafts of steam. Fortunately there was no wind.

Doheny gazed up at the gigantic piece of steel sculpture, white and stark against the gray overcast sky. Functioning like an enormous ear, the Seward dish had listened to the faint radio whispers from the fading echo of the Big Bang that created the universe. It had tuned in to peaceful-looking galaxies and discovered they were actually sites of horrific explosions. The dish also had been used to study bodies within the solar system by projecting high-frequency radio waves at them and analyzing their echoes. Comets, meteors, asteroids, and the cloud-shrouded surface of Venus had yielded their secrets to this enormous instrument.

It was strangely silent and still at the radio telescope site. The only sound was the steady hum of electricity coursing through the massive installation. There was no sign of birds or other wildlife.

They unloaded the equipment from the plane onto a dolly and took turns pulling it across the frozen runway.

Harriman's eyes roamed over the bleak landscape. "Sure lonely," he remarked. "Wouldn't want to live out here."

"It's not so bad in the early summer," said Doheny. "When the ice melts"—he swept his arm in a wide arc—"this whole land becomes a swamp with hundreds of lakes and ponds. The tundra turns green, and the caribou come out to forage. You wouldn't recognize the place." During his six-month stay at the radio telescope he had hiked and fished with some of the technicians who shared his love of the outdoors.

They soon reached the control dome, a concrete structure fifteen feet high and forty feet in diameter. For insulatory purposes most of the building lay beneath the ground. It had a domed roof to allow the snow to slide off rather than accumulate. The building also contained a basement, which served as a supply room. The entire structure was built on a six-foot layer of packed gravel and concrete. This type of foundation was an absolute necessity because ordinary concrete slabs didn't work well in the Arctic. In winter the water from the tundra would freeze solid and heave up the slabs. Years ago this phenomenon had caused unpleasant problems when the first cemeteries were dug in the area.

The entry hatch to the dome was like a heavy refrigerator door but designed to keep the cold air out, not in. Upon entering they passed through an insulated air space, another thick door, then down a short flight of steps leading to the control room.

The room was circular, with curved banks of consoles lining the walls. A large triple-paned window offered a view of the sprawling dish outside. A sheen of greenish light reflected off the room's shiny metal surfaces. There were panels of softly lit dials set in gleaming chrome steel casings and an impressive layout of buttons and switches and red-and-black knobs with white calibrated markings. There were also teletypes, a satellite communications terminal, high- and low-frequency radios, and racks of binders containing procedures for astronomical observations.

Doheny surveyed the curved instrument banks, then went to the main receiver console and inspected the panels. A twelve-inch liquid crystal display mounted above them had markings on it like the cross hairs of a rifle scope. Knowing the satellite was passing overhead, he consulted notes on the operational procedure for the receiver. His hand hovered above the control panel, decided, and touched numbered square white buttons. The instruments whirred and digital readouts flickered. He peered out the window and saw the triangular-shaped receiver slowly, majestically sliding along its cables above the dish, tilting upward as it scanned the sky.

Without warning the entire panel lit up and became a fairyland of multicolored lights. Competing buzzes sounded and quickly died. The receiver outside stopped moving. Simultaneously a loud crackling hiss came over the loudspeakers—the electronic voice of the satellite.

Doheny shot a glance at the liquid crystal display. A round, soft-blurred image had appeared between the cross hairs. The receiver was now locked onto the Sunstroke satellite. Doheny knew he would have to manually steer the receiver in this manner from time to time until the last moment because of the satellite's seemingly erratic evasive maneuvering. For this reason the receiver's automatic tracking system was of no use.

During this operation Colonel Harriman had brought in the equipment from the dolly and neatly stacked it on the floor. There was a pile of black rubbery insulation pads, coils of thick coaxial cables, a soldering kit, electrical switches, an old oscilloscope, and a couple of small microwave radiation detectors that air force technicians clipped to their shirt pockets when in close proximity to functioning radar dishes.

"Do you need anything else?" Harriman asked. "There's some spare tools aboard the plane."

Doheny shook his head. "I've got everything I need here."

"How much time do I have before the satellite discharges on this place?" Harriman asked, concerned.

"I'd say about an hour."

Harriman nodded. "My orders are to refuel at McMurdon and then fly back to Kirtland. By the way," he said, grinning, "when you're through here we're going to want all this stuff back. Best of luck to you."

Doheny smiled and shook hands with the colonel. "Thanks for the ride."

"Anytime, Mr. Doheny," Harriman said with a casual salute. He turned and left the control dome. Doheny spotted him through the observation window. The colonel nervously glanced up at the sky more than once as he walked across the icy runway.

Doheny thought about him for a moment. In a way it had all started with Harriman and his helicopter overflight above the New Mexico microwave track. They had seen firsthand the death and destruction caused by the satellite's power beam. The bodies of those innocent children more than anything else had convinced Doheny the satellite had to be destroyed, the reason why he had come here.

He suddenly realized he was the only one left at the isolated site. Harriman had told him that everyone within a fifty-mile radius from the observatory had been evacuated. He would have to battle the satellite alone, without help. A chill shot up his spine. For an instant he had the crazy idea that he had come to the Arctic to die. He dismissed the thought as being ridiculous, and went to work sorting through the stacks of supplies and equipment.

In space high above Alaska, unmanned U.S. and Russian spacecraft were maneuvered into position to engage SOLSAT X-1. This advanced space armada consisted of orbital particle-beam weapons, missile launchers, space mines, and kinetic-kill vehicles.

Suddenly small detonations lit up the space around the satellite like a fierce fireworks display. Shrapnel dug small pits along the length of its hull. Its infrared sensors scanned the heavens and found another attack force descending along a wide arc. SOLSAT X-1 expended a considerable amount of precious fuel as it changed attitude and swept its beam across them. Some of the intruders managed to launch their tiny missiles again before being neutralized. They exploded, shooting more shrapnel into its hull.

During this intense battle a small spherical ASAT designated Cosmos 3209 was carefully deorbited from its geosynchronous position above the Arctic Circle by ground controllers at the antisatellite center at Tyuratam. This particular ASAT was a stealth kinetic-kill device whose contours and special anechoic coating rendered it nearly invisible to radar systems. While SOLSAT X-1's sensors were occupied by the frontal assault the stealth ASAT dropped behind its target.

The satellite detected a sudden rush of heat coming from the rear. Its command computer swiveled the multifaceted infrared sensors in their gimbals and scanned the area behind it. The IR sensors registered the hazy thermal image of a single intruder, tiny and spherical, paralleling its own course. The computer maneuvered the satellite until its power beam engulfed the attacker.

After neutralizing the other intruders SOLSAT X-1 detected several pinpoints of light in fixed positions above. Its parabolic antenna picked up a cacophony of chattering electronic voices emanating from them. The lights were a string of military communications satellites in geosynchronous orbit. Under the direction of the self-defensive subroutine the computer analyzed these signals and determined some of them were transmitting slaving commands to the attack force while others were relaying communications between various points on the ground. After several microseconds of processing data stored in its memory the computer determined that it could halt the attacks by disrupting the enemy's communications.

*   *   *

At the White House Dean Stratton's image appeared on the TV screen. President Kendall and his advisers listened in restrained silence as the general informed them that the joint U.S.-Russian ASAT missions against the satellite were keeping the thing at bay. Before he signed off Stratton told Kendall an interesting bit of information.

"Sir, Tyuratam's commander told me they were deploying their stealth kinetic-kill vehicle against the satellite during the last run," Stratton said. "It appeared on our scopes as a 'radar ghost,' similar to what we saw two days ago when the satellite was first attacked. Colonel Chirchik said they had built only one, and wanted to deploy it in the hope of inflicting serious damage. Unfortunately it was caught in the microwave beam and was lost. I thought you'd like to know."

This revelation struck Kendall like a thunderclap. He knew from CIA reports that the Russians did indeed only possess one of this type of advanced ASAT. He was stunned.

Minutes later the Russian flag on the hot-line screen dissolved to black and was replaced by Nikolai Gorodin's broad face. Greetings were briefly exchanged before President Kendall said, "Mr. Premier, please extend my gratitude to your people at Tyuratam for their superb deployment of your antisatellite forces."

Gorodin's thick features widened into a smile. "I will extend your compliments to them personally," said the mechanical parody of his voice coming from the autotranslator, "once your satellite has been deactivated."

"I have been informed," Kendall began, "that our engineer has landed in Alaska and is setting up the radio telescope. We won't have long to wait. I propose that we issue our stand-down orders to our respective military forces the instant the satellite is rendered inoperative." Gorodin nodded, and he continued. "Mr. Premier, I have just learned from Cheyenne Mountain that Tyuratam lost its stealth ASAT a short time ago."

"That is correct," Gorodin replied. "As you undoubtedly know, we possessed only one in our arsenal." In a softer tone he said, "This fact should indisputably prove that we did not sabotage your satellite as you have claimed."

To Gorodin, Kendall said plaintively and defensively, "If you didn't sabotage it, then who did?"

"That is a very good question," said the premier. "There are several nations outside of yours and mine that possess a sophisticated space capability.'' He riffled through a stack of papers on the desk before him, selected one, and scanned it. ''For instance, as I'm certain you are aware of, an *Ariane* satellite carrier was launched from French Guiana the same day your satellite malfunctioned. The payload was purported to be a weather satellite, but my intelligence people have reason to believe it was something else entirely.'' He dropped the sheet onto the stack and looked into the camera. ''Perhaps your satellite was attacked by those who would have the most to lose should it have become functional and successfully generated inexpensive electricity to your cities. I am thinking about the Arab oil cartel.''

My God, Kendall thought, he could be right. We blamed the Russians because we were certain the thing threatened their strategic military positions in space and on earth. We completely overlooked the other possibilities. He made a mental note to have Russ Tanner at Langley investigate that French Guiana *Ariane* launch.

''Mr. Premier,'' Kendall said sincerely, ''please accept my apologies. We were mistaken.''

Gorodin's eyes misted over, but his reply was drowned out by an urgent buzzing sound coming from the Cheyenne Mountain TV display.

Dean Stratton appeared on-screen, wearing a headset and a worried expression. ''Sir, we just lost contact with our ASATs.'' The audio signal was out of synchronization, making his voice sound as if it were coming from underwater. ''The satellite is discharging at . . .'' The image began to roll as his voice faded in and out. ''. . . communications breakdown . . . Westpac comsat is—''

Kendall watched speechlessly as the image turned to snow. He glanced at the hot-line screen and saw Gorodin talking earnestly to an aide. The premier turned sharply and glared accusingly into the Moscow TV camera.

''Mr. President!'' The voice coming over the autotranslator simulated raw anger. Gorodin's face was livid. ''Our ASATs no longer respond to our commands.'' His image started rolling from top to bottom and the synthetic voice developed an echo. ''My defense people tell . . . satellite is responsible. Have you been deceiving—'' The last word of his unfinished question echoed throughout the room in duplicate, triplicate. With a loud crackle the screen disintegrated into static.

Kendall sat there, shocked. He quickly recovered and frantically shouted to the Army Signal Corps officer manning the hot line to reestablish contact with the Kremlin. The officer said they'd lost the transmission signal and couldn't get through.

The tactical display screen showing the positions of America's armed forces throughout the world rolled, sputtered, and turned to snow.

JCS Chairman Willis Thompson covered the mouthpiece of his red phone. "All military communications channels are breaking down fast, sir," he reported to Kendall. "Our comsats up there are going down like dominoes."

Kendall shut his eyes for an instant and tried to think. Wet stains slowly spread across the armpits of his shirt. Then he reached for the ordinary white telephone on the conference table before him and called the White House switchboard. His fingers trembled as they held the receiver.

"This is the President," he told the operator, his voice barely under control. "Put me through to Moscow, to Mr. Gorodin's office in the Kremlin. This is an emergency."

"Yes, sir, one moment, Mr. President," the operator said quickly. "I'm placing your call now."

There was a long pause punctuated by loud furious snaps that sounded like explosions in the President's ear. He grasped the phone in a clawlike grip. He prayed he would reach Gorodin in time.

The snaps increased in succession, stopped abruptly, and the operator came on again. "I'm sorry, sir, but we're experiencing a disruption of all overseas communications."

Chapter 33 *

IN THE LIMITLESS reaches of space high above Alaska SOLSAT X-1's parabolic antenna received the final electronic whisper from the last of the communications satellites that were within range of its power beam. All of its robot companions in orbit were now silent and would never again fill the void with their chattering. Every spacecraft in a stationary orbit for thousands of miles in each direction was now a worthless, burned-out chunk of space debris.

At this time the command computer aboard SOLSAT X-1 assessed the damage the satellite had sustained from its recent battles. The sensors placed at strategic points throughout the spacecraft registered that the cylindrical hull had been penetrated by shrapnel along its entire length. Its parabolic antenna had been punctured in a multitude of places, and several of the solar panels in its wings had been blown out. However, the most serious damage had been inflicted at the forward end of the microwave transmitter housing where a huge oval-shaped hole had been blasted by a space mine.

The discovery of this rupture immediately caused another subroutine to switch on, replacing the former self-defensive one. This new subroutine was offensive in nature and contained the instructions for identifying and attacking enemy targets on the ground. It also possessed the capability of directing the command computer to determine the origin of the space mine that had come close to jeopardizing SOLSAT X-1's primary mission.

The computer screened the vast number of signal transmissions from the ground that it had recorded during the attack. Next, it scanned a visual record of the battle made by SOLSAT X-1's TV cameras. Then it matched each ground transmission to its corresponding antisatellite vehicle by correlating the signal's instructions with the videotaped ASAT response. In this manner the

computer identified the exact radio signal that had directed the
space mine. It analyzed this signal, comparing it with those now
being broadcast from the military installations below to the dead
ASATs still in orbit.

From its vantage point high in polar orbit SOLSAT X-1's
computer scanned the earth with its radio directional finder. The
planet was spinning slowly on its axis, and various sprawling
cities flowed into view. Directly below were Anchorage and
Fairbanks. To the west lay Moscow, and to the southwest Peking
and Tokyo. Montreal and Washington lay to the southeast.

The computer traced the signal's origin to a site deep within the
Dzezkazgan Province, several hundred miles southeast of Moscow. This facility was Tyuratam, Russia's main antisatellite
installation. When the source of the signal was established the
attack subroutine ordered the computer to change the satellite's
attitude in space to direct the microwave beam at Tyuratam.

Once this singular target had been irradiated, the attack subroutine would be superseded by another set of instructions: the
program for carrying out a test of the microwave beam's capability
of melting a portion of the Arctic ice cap. The test had been
planned to be conducted on a small scale, involving the irradiation
of only one square kilometer of surface ice. However, once the
satellite began discharging at the ice cap, the microwave beam
would transmit continuously, for there was no way of shutting
down the klystrons. Their phase-control circuitry had been destroyed during the collision with the enemy ASAT two days
before. They would not overheat because of the liquid nitrogen
coolant. Within three weeks the earth would be inundated by tidal
waves greater than those generated at the end of the last ice age.

Presently the command computer executed the attack subroutine's orders and maneuvered SOLSAT X-1 to face the Dzezkazgan Province, where the Tyuratam installation lay. The satellite's microwave power beam swept through space in a lazy arc as
it headed for its target.

Just as the microwave beam was about to plunge through the
atmosphere and strike the Russian ASAT facility the satellite's
parabolic antenna received a strong radio message in binary code.

The message ordered the SOLSAT X-1 command computer to
submit to reprogramming. The computer was informed that if it
failed to comply the ground station broadcasting this message
would direct another attack against it. Finally it was told that all

previous attacks had originated from this same station. The message was repeated over and over again.

The attack subroutine ordered the computer to freeze all activity, to shut down the Icarus rocket engines, and analyze the incoming binary transmission. When the engines ceased firing, the edge of the microwave beam was grazing the uppermost region of the earth's atmosphere above Siberia.

With the radio directional finder the command computer traced the transmission to a ground station on a strip of Alaska jutting into the Bering Strait. The computer scanned this area with the infrared sensors. As the thermal image of the Arctic wilderness leaped into focus the computer detected the reddish glow from the ground station. The facility was large and circular in shape, obviously an installation of considerable size and power. The sensors also registered a much smaller station to the west.

The computer compared the configuration of the large disk-shaped structure to the digitized thermal images in its memory but could find no correlation. It scanned the smaller station to the west and recognized the unmistakable signature of an electrical substation. A digital description of this type of installation had been fed into its memory for military targeting purposes.

Under instructions from the attack subroutine the command computer calculated that if the substation was neutralized all electrical power would be cut off to the enemy's primary installation, rendering it susceptible to attack.

At precisely 6:58 P.M. local time the microwave power beam touched down a few hundred yards south of the Seward Gas and Electric Company's unmanned relay substation. The three-acre site was designated NE-PRX-76109 and consisted of a half dozen huge, black drum-shaped transformers mounted on hollow steel poles. It was the type of installation found on the outskirts of every major city in the country. Four underground cables the thickness of a man's arm, each one carrying tens of thousands of volts from the Ulmak generating plant in Nome, snaked up through the center of the poles to the transformers, where their voltage was altered and increased.

When the power beam swept over the site the thin layer of ice coating the substation rapidly melted and evaporated into steam. Several seconds passed. Then the transformers blew up, erupting into cascading showers of sparks like the Fourth of July.

*   *   *

Four miles to the east Mike Doheny stepped back from the
satellite communications terminal inside the Seward observatory's
control dome. On top of the console lay the folded accordion
printout sheet containing Ted Kitami's coded message. Doheny
had typed it on the terminal keyboard, recorded it on a spool of
magnetic tape, then pressed the transmit button. This terminal was
normally used by the radio astronomers to communicate with the
astronomical satellites in orbit.

Kitami's message was being broadcast continuously to the
Sunstroke satellite. Doheny knew the thing would zero in on the
transmission like the pilot of a plane homing in on a radar beacon.
He recalled that Kitami had said the message was "sufficiently
belligerent," that he'd "be tickling the dragon's tail" with it.

He took a last look around the control room, his lips compressed
into a hard line as he inspected his handiwork. Earlier he had
soldered two black coaxial cables to the electrical connections
atop the main console that controlled the radio telescope receiver
outside. One of the coaxial cables was attached to two simple
on-off switches. The other cable had been fastened to the old
battered Sperry oscilloscope that Harriman had given him. It
resembled a portable TV set. He had set up these makeshift
instruments in the basement, where he would use them to remotely
steer the telescope's receiver to keep it aligned on the satellite
during the discharge.

Then he had piled the rubberized insulation pads from Kirtland
on top of the consoles to protect them from the barrage of
microwaves. Each pad was three feet wide, six feet in length, and
an inch and a half thick.

Presently he clipped one of Harriman's microwave radiation
detectors to his shirt pocket. The device was the size of a pack of
cigarettes and had a metered readout. Then he went down to the
basement, slamming the door shut behind him.

At one end of the basement were a couple cots, a stereo with an
assortment of CDs, and in one corner a small desk and lab bench.
The curved walls were decorated with clipped *Playboy* center-
folds. Modest creature comforts for the radio astronomers who
spent lonely all-night vigils in the dome.

Doheny went to the lab bench and sat down, his eyes riveted to
the glowing central pulse on the oscilloscope screen before him.
He saw the green peak start to drop, indicating the radio telescope
receiver was beginning to lose track of the moving satellite. He
worked his two electrical switches until the central pulse climbed

back up the screen. Once again the receiver outside was locked on to the satellite.

His nerves were taut, his stomach muscles clenched. He checked the time. 6:58 P.M. Then he shot a glance at his portable microwave counter. The needle was still at zero. The thing should have discharged by now, he thought. What's taking it so long? He was aware the waiting game and the isolation of this place were starting to get to him. The silence of the wilderness outside overwhelmed and enveloped him like a shroud.

The green pulse on the oscilloscope shrank to a dot and vanished. The screen went blank and the basement was plunged into darkness. A power failure. Instinctively he knew the microwave beam had struck the electrical substation to the west, and not by mere coincidence. The thing wasn't taking any chances. Now he would have to leave the relative safety of the basement and go upstairs to start the generator.

He got up from the lab bench too quickly and hit his head on the overhanging shelf above it. He rubbed the sore spot and carefully made his way to the steps leading up to the control dome. He pulled open the basement door and raced to the observation window. Craning his neck, he looked for any sign of the power beam. He didn't see anything, and assumed it was still striking the SG and E substation.

With the light from the window illuminating his way, he ran across the room, past the silent consoles to the emergency generator panel, pulled off the insulation pad he had put there earlier, and read the instruction plate. He flipped switches and punched buttons according to the directions. The panel indicators lit up and he heard an intermittent whining sound coming from the steel-reinforced concrete bunker outside. The diesel generator strained and sputtered, and for a moment he thought it wouldn't turn over. The whine grew in pitch, steadied, and the overhead lights in the dome came on. The consoles around him started humming and buzzing again as the generator worked up to full power. He checked the fuel gauge and saw that the underground tanks were full. They would last perhaps four hours.

He covered the panel and was about to return to the basement when a nearby console sounded an alarm. He tore off its insulation pad and spotted a flashing warning light on the panel that monitored the radio telescope's electrical systems. He queried the console computer and it displayed the circuit diagrams for the reflector dish and the receiver on its screen. Below the schematics the computer printed out a short message summarizing the problem.

Doheny felt his heart jolt sickeningly. The message said that one of the condensers for the receiver's electric motor-driven carriage had burned out, that the receiver was now immobile. It was a common type-3C 125-amperage condenser used in most heavy-duty circuitry, including the consoles in this room. There was a supply of them in the basement storage locker. The computer showed the location of the blown condenser on the circuit diagram.

He slammed the top of the panel with the palm of his hand in frustration. Now that the receiver could no longer track the satellite, his plan to deactivate the thing had been stopped cold. And all because of a fifty-cent condenser. He surmised it had been burned out from the power surge during the generator start-up. But there was a possibility the computer was wrong. He ran down to the basement and checked the oscilloscope. The pulse had dropped. He operated his black switches but there was no response. He slumped down in the chair.

He realized he had two choices. He could forget all about the radio telescope receiver and barricade himself in the basement until the satellite's orbit carried it elsewhere. But the thought of abandoning his scheme at this point was crushing. He had been close, so close.

The alternative was to replace the burned-out condenser. To do this he would have to go outside, walk across the tundra to one of the two-hundred-foot towers supporting the cable system for the receiver, and ride an elevator to the top. From there he would have to take an open-air cable car to reach the receiver's motor carriage and then install the new condenser. He had no misconceptions about the dangers involved. Once he left the dome he would be exposing himself to the satellite for many minutes. It would be suicide to climb the tower now that the microwave beam was no doubt heading this way. There was a good chance the thing would fry him before he could return to the dome to realign the receiver. He broke out in a cold sweat. He had never anticipated something like this, had never intended to risk his life to that extent. It was too much to ask.

Then he felt a sharp pang stabbing at his mind, his heart, and maybe even his soul. The thing up there was his handiwork, his creation, and ultimately his responsibility. He had brought this monstrosity into existence, and had to share the blame for the nearly three hundred people who had died so far. Now the thing was poised in orbit, ready to destroy all human life on earth. And he was the only one in a position to prevent it.

His breathing became shallow, and he had to clasp his hands together to steady them. He stared across the room at the storage locker containing tools and a supply of electrical components. He knew with an awful certainty what he had to do.

He went to the metal supply cabinet and tried the door. It was locked. He kicked it, again and again, until the sheet steel door caved in and broke free from the latch. Grabbing the top and side of the battered door, he pulled with all his strength and wrenched it open.

Inside there was a rack filled with hand tools, and shelves stocked with an assortment of electrical parts, all labeled. He took two type-3C condensers, each one the size and shape of a standard flashlight battery, and stuck them into his pants pockets. He found a tool belt, fastened it around his waist, and shoved a power-driven Phillips screwdriver, a pair of pliers, and a wrench kit into the belt loops. He spotted a plastic hard hat and put it on. A crowbar was hanging from a bracket on the far wall. He grabbed that, too, knowing he would need it to pry open the locked gate to the fence surrounding the radio telescope site. He didn't have time to look for the keys. Then he climbed the basement steps.

Upstairs he cut off the flow of electricity to the radio telescope receiver by throwing a switch on the control panel atop the main console. He walked across the room to the satellite communications terminal. It was still broadcasting Kitami's message that had been recorded on its spool of magnetic tape. He was unsure whether he should let it run or shut it off.

The message had been broadcasting continuously, except during the brief interval of time between when the power had gone out and the generator had started up. He surmised that because the thing continued to receive the radio transmission it thought it hadn't disrupted all power to the observatory yet, and was still flooding the SG and E substation with microwaves. If this was the case, then how long would it be before the thing got wise, realized the observatory had its own independent power supply, and decided to attack? Five, ten, maybe twenty minutes? Then it would home in on the transmission, use it as a guiding beacon, and aim its beam unerringly at the reflector dish and receiver, probably while he was up in the tower completely exposed. On the other hand, if he shut it off now the thing might think it had neutralized the power to the observatory and attack immediately. He wouldn't even have a chance to replace the condenser.

He saw there were a little more than eighteen minutes left in the spool feeding the take-up reel. He'd have that much time before the message stopped broadcasting. At the end of the eighteen minutes the thing would most likely discharge at the radio telescope, but the beam wouldn't be guided by the transmission. The thing would have to aim by sight alone from a distance of some 20,000 miles. Logically the beam would miss initially, perhaps giving him time to get back to the dome. He knew he couldn't count on it: he had tried to second-guess the satellite for the past three days and had struck out miserably. Maybe this time he'd be lucky.

He pulled on his parka, clipped his microwave detector to the front pocket, and checked the transmit timer on the satellite terminal. He heard the tape counter ticking. A slight wave of panic came over him; the sound reminded him of the timer on a bomb. He entered the dome's insulated air lock, pushed open the big heavy exterior door, and stepped out into the frigid cold, his heart beating rapidly.

It was like entering an industrial walk-in freezer. The chilled air bit deep into his bones and teeth. He left the thick outer door ajar in case he had to make a hasty retreat back to the dome. Then he walked a few feet away from the building and surveyed the area.

He startled a raven that had been pecking around a nearby garbage dumpster. It flew up and cawed derisively at him as it swept away on stiff black outstretched wings. Ravens were one of the few scavengers active in the Arctic this time of year. They lived on refuse and carrion.

The closest support tower for the radio telescope receiver lay one hundred yards to the south. The structure was about the same size and configuration as an electrical transmission tower, or a large oil drilling derrick. Two hundred feet high, quadrilateral, with a latticework of steel girders. There were four of them positioned equidistantly around the one-thousand-foot-diameter reflector dish. The towers supported two eight-inch-thick steel cables, one running north to south above the dish, the other east to west. The cables were anchored to the crossbar atop each tower. The massive triangular-shaped receiver was suspended from these cables above the center of the dish.

Doheny gazed up at the overcast sky to see if he could spot the satellite, but the gray cloud cover kept him from seeing it. But he knew it was up there. He pressed his hard hat down on his head and sprinted across the tundra to the nearest tower. The frozen ground cracked and splintered beneath his boots.

He used his crowbar to force open the gate to the fence surrounding the site and went inside. The tower before him rose twenty stories above his head. He looked up and felt a rush of dizziness. "I'd better hurry up and get this over with," he muttered. Three minutes had elapsed since he left the dome. He had fifteen minutes before the tape with Kitami's message stopped broadcasting.

Without warning a gust of wind slammed against him with great force. He staggered back. It was a wind that sobbed and whined alternately as it blew through the tower's framework. He immediately knew what it was. To the west the cold air was being unnaturally heated by the satellite's power beam, causing an explosive air-pressure expansion toward the east that overcame the usual geostrophic effects. The air was hot, as if blown from a blast furnace.

A metal-runged ladder stretched from ground level all the way up the tower latticework to the top. It was for use in case of an elevator malfunction. The rungs were encrusted with icicles. He walked past it and made his way to the elevator cage inside the tower. He stepped in and pressed the ascent button. The front grating slid shut and the cage rumbled to life and started climbing swiftly upward along its rails. He peered through the bars and saw the frozen ground below rapidly shrinking. The view was disquieting.

He remembered what Everett Nore used to tell him whenever he had stressed the negative aspects of a difficult spacecraft design. "Do you always have to look down when you're climbing a mountain, Mike?" The expression was never more appropriate.

Moments later the cage came to a halt at the top. The grating slid open and he cautiously stepped out onto the twelve-foot-long catwalk leading to the cable car. The wind was heavier up here, buffeting him with terrific force. He did not look down.

The cable car was open-air like a ski lift, consisting of little more than a seat with a tool rack behind it. He climbed in and sat down, his legs dangling. He pushed the start lever and heard the overhead winch groaning in protest. The car began moving, slowly at first, and then picked up speed. It swayed back and forth in the wind. The sensation of falling was inescapable.

Below him the rim of the reflector dish reared above the

surrounding terrain, obscuring much of the Arctic wilderness. It was like being in an abstract land of precise geometrical shapes.

The cable car came to a stop alongside a steel platform below the garage-sized motor carriage beneath the receiver. He spotted a sign in red that said Access Door. He climbed out and saw that the letters were stenciled on a small hinged panel sealed shut by four dozen Phillips-type screws. He went to work with his screwdriver, removed the panel, and replaced the blown condenser.

SOLSAT X-1's command computer steadily scanned its target on the earth below. It had been irradiating the electrical substation for many minutes now, but still hadn't cut off power to the large enemy facility. The satellite's parabolic antenna was still receiving the same radio message ordering it to submit to reprogramming.

Suddenly the transmission stopped. The attack subroutine directing the computer instructed it to scan the circular-shaped installation to the east with maximum infrared resolution. It detected motion above the dish: a small vehicle suspended on a thin filament. The IR sensors picked up the body heat emanating from a human being inside the vehicle. Having been programmed to identify hostile ground troop activity, the computer correlated the movements of the human below with those of an enemy soldier.

To Doheny the cable car was moving agonizingly slowly as it headed back to the tower. The car was swaying violently in the wind, threatening to dislodge its pulleys from the cable. He shifted his weight as best he could to try to check the motion. He glanced nervously at the microwave detector on his parka. Thankfully the needle was stationary. He wondered briefly if the satellite had lost interest in the observatory, if it had decided to move on.

When the car was fifty feet from the tower a sudden movement in the sky above caught his eye. Something was happening to the clouds. They slithered, started to break up, and then seemed to magically recombine and reform before his eyes. An enormous patch directly above began swirling around and around like a gigantic whirlpool. It spun faster and faster until the clouds were pulled too tightly and shattered into wispy puffs that quickly disappeared. Now a huge hole was forming. The clouds opened up like a great cyclopean eye. At its center was a light that shone with a fierce brilliance against a deep blue sky.

Doheny was transfixed by this frightening, awesome apparition.

It was an image of the end of the world, an image that he would carry in his mind for as long as he lived. Nothing in his experience had prepared him for the sight that now filled his gaze. His eyes did not blink, his mouth hung open, his chest rose and fell heavily. He started trembling violently and shouted at the top of his voice, cursing and swearing at the thing in the sky. Primal instinct had taken over and he was venting his fear, frustration, and hatred of the thing.

He was suddenly aware the cable car had come to a stop at the tower. Breathing hard, he clambered out onto the steel catwalk. He swept his eyes over the ground below and immediately saw where the microwave beam had touched down. Billowing clouds of steam were rising from a circular area about two miles south of the radio telescope. The beam had missed, just as he had hoped. Because of the satellite's trajectory it was headed toward him. He estimated the beam was traveling at ten miles an hour. He still had a chance.

He looked up and shook his fist at the apparition. "I'm going to kill you!" he bellowed. "I'm going to kill you!" For a half second he stood there at the top of the tower, a big man with his fist raised against the sky, resolute and defiant.

He turned and ran to the elevator cage, leaped inside, and punched the down button. The grating slid shut and the cage started its long descent.

He looked down through the bars and saw a low white mist about three feet above the ground drifting menacingly across the tundra like a phantom sea, enveloping the trunks of the stunted willow trees. His microwave detector began ticking. He glanced at the metered dial and saw the needle swinging upward. It reached the eighty milliwatts per square centimeter mark, hovered there for an instant, and started climbing. He felt his skin tingle, and his hair seemed to be standing on end. He realized the fringe of the beam had reached him already. Apparently he had miscalculated.

The elevator was halfway down the tower when he heard a harsh squeal of metal on metal. The cage bucked and dropped a few inches, then jerked to a halt. He punched the down button again and again without result. The microwaves had neutralized the elevator's electric motor. He was trapped one hundred feet above the ground.

Chapter 34 *

ONE THOUGHT, NUCLEAR war, hung heavy in the air inside the bomb shelter beneath the White House. The President and his advisers had evacuated to the subterranean bunker moments after their attempts to reestablish contact with Moscow had failed.

Kendall leaned back in his chair and glanced around the small conference table. Jack Conley's face was drawn taut with anxiety. Hugh Fitzpatrick sat hunched, his mouth opening and closing as if he were gasping for air. General Thompson stood stiffly beside a bank of communications equipment, speaking urgently into a red trunk-line phone to Cheyenne Mountain. Because these special phone lines were buried far underground they were safe from the satellite's devastating microwave beam.

Thompson cradled the phone and turned to the others, his voice anxious. "General Stratton reports the satellite is discharging steadily at the Arctic. But he says it could turn its beam on the Russians at any second. It'll be another twenty minutes or so before we can patch an open link to Moscow," he added. "That's the best we can do."

"In twenty minutes," said Kendall, "they can launch an ICBM and detonate it over New York." He rubbed his temples and closed his eyes. "Can you get through to that engineer in Alaska?"

"No, sir," Thompson replied. "We've tried raising him on every frequency but there's only static."

"His plan didn't work," Kendall said with grim finality. "He's failed." He swept his gaze across the men in the room. "Gentlemen, nuclear war with Russia is now very likely. We're going to State Orange." He watched silently as Thompson executed the order.

The President knew that his State Orange alert command was

now traveling at the speed of light through the buried military trunk-lines to the many air bases scattered throughout the country, that it penetrated into hardened missile silos, and was sent by the underground ELF transmitter to the dark bottoms of the oceans where U.S. submarines silently lurked.

While the enormous military power of the United States was being mobilized, Mike Doheny stood motionless inside the elevator cage, feeling the panic well up within him.

He knew his death up here would be meaningless. There was no one to operate his makeshift controls. In a few minutes the only chance to destroy the satellite would be lost, possibly forever. After killing him, the thing would be free to flash-cook every major city and drown anyone left alive by melting the Arctic ice cap.

He had to do something, and fast. His eyes swept wildly around the cage, desperately looking for some means of escape. He spotted the ladder through the gaps in the bars. It was the same metal-runged ladder he had seen before making his ascent. At the time he had thought it inconceivable that anyone would actually use it to climb either up or down the two-hundred-foot tower. Now it was his only salvation. But first he had to get out of the cage.

At that moment the ticking from his microwave detector increased. The meter said 160 milliwatts per square centimeter. He was beginning to feel warm. The Arctic cold had miraculously vanished. He looked down and saw an eerie low fog swirling around the tower's concrete pads. A mile and a half to the south, huge columns of steam rose from the ground where the center of the beam was melting the tundra and permafrost. The irradiated area had become a boiling lake that was slowly moving toward him. There were only a few minutes left before it would reach the tower.

He tried to open the cage door but it was frozen shut. The microwaves had jammed the electric motor. Blind fury seized him. His self-control suddenly snapped. Before he knew what he was doing he had grabbed hold of the bars above him for support and was lashing out at the grating with his boots, his legs working like pistons. Despite his repeated efforts the door held firm.

The physical exertion cleared his mind and he was able to think more coherently. He took out his crowbar and rammed the straight end between the bars of the grating nearest the jamb. He manipulated the crowbar so that he could use it as a lever, with the jamb acting as a fulcrum.

He strained with all his might against that crowbar until the veins stood out on his forehead. Something had to give. There was a screech of gears being forced. The grating slid open a fraction of an inch. Encouraged by the gap, he pushed and pushed with every ounce of strength he had. The gears screamed in protest again and the grating begrudgingly slid along its rails. He stopped pushing when the gap was barely wide enough for him to get through.

There was no time to rest. He had to move quickly. With his mouth set in a firm line he squeezed through the gap, swung himself onto the ladder, and started climbing down. The rungs were caked with brown icicles that cut into his hands. He ignored the pain and climbed quickly, hand under hand, down the rungs. The wind whipped about his head, tugged at his hard hat and tore at his clothes. He was breathing hard from exertion and emotion.

With each step the three-foot-long steel crowbar and other tools dangling from his belt slapped against his body and clanged against the metal rungs. He paused just long enough to unfasten his tool belt and let it drop. It shot to the ground and disappeared in the low fog. There was a silence for what seemed like a long time. Then he heard a sharp pinging sound as the tools bounced off one of the concrete pads supporting the tower, and a thud as they landed on the tundra. He continued his descent, confident that he'd make it back to the dome safely. Keeping his gaze level with the ladder before him, he concentrated on the placement of his hands and boots. He ignored the ground below and the frightening thing in the sky above.

As he climbed down he became aware that the sunlight was rapidly fading. The sun would be setting in a few minutes. He knew this represented another crucial time factor. Once the Seward Peninsula was plunged into darkness the satellite would also enter the earth's shadow, and its solar-powered systems would shut down. He assumed the thing would fire Stratton's Icarus rockets to maneuver back into the sunlight before it crossed the terminator. If that were the case, then he might never be able to bait the thing back to this radio telescope again.

He checked his watch. It had stopped running. Unlike his portable microwave counter, it was unshielded. He was glad he had found the plastic hard hat. It helped protect his head against the microwaves raining down from the sky. Although he was growing uncomfortably warm from climbing he didn't dare

discard his parka: the garment's insulated layers also offered some
protection from the radiation.

Twice he despaired of ever making it to the bottom. Each
foothold brought a moment's anxiety, lest he should slip and fall,
and always in the back of his mind was the haunting fear of the
thing hovering in the sky.

He was midway down the ladder now, with another fifty feet to
go. Perspiration traced little patterns down his face. The counter
registered two hundred milliwatts per square centimeter. His
hands and boots slipped on the rungs as if they had been greased.
Then he realized that the brown ice encrusting the ladder was
melting. He had a bad moment when his right boot slipped off the
rung and he felt himself falling. His left arm shot out, found a
handhold, and wrenched him back to the ladder. The slippery
rungs impeded his progress, but he could not slow down.

The center of the beam was still some distance away, but
steadily approaching. He heard the sizzling roar from thousands of
tons of ice being melted and turned to steam. It sounded like
molten lava oozing into the ocean. He resisted the impulse to look
down at it.

The going was rough. He slipped again and barely caught
himself in time. Cursing, he scrambled for a secure foothold and
continued his descent. The bruised area of his chest where Provost
Marshal Clayton had hit him ached with every step. His arms and
legs felt heavy, as if he had been climbing for hours.

He pictured himself inside the control dome basement, manipulating his black switches until the green pulse on the oscilloscope
rose to its proper height. He imagined the radio telescope receiver
sliding along its cables and then coming to a full stop as it locked
onto the satellite. In his mind's eye he saw the center of the power
beam sweep across the sprawling reflector dish. He could see the
dish and receiver glowing from the microwave radiation. He
envisioned the receiver alternately converting the incident radiation into electrical impulses and then back into microwaves,
amplifying them into a coherent beam and then transmitting them
at the satellite. He imagined the klystron tubes inside the thing's
microwave transmitter shattering as they overloaded and burned
out. Finally he pictured the satellite dead in space, trapped in polar
orbit.

These thoughts were far more than an idle daydream. They kept
him going throughout his physical ordeal.

It was getting hotter. He was sweating profusely; his shirt clung to him like a second skin. The radiation counter chattered furiously. He felt a prickly, smarting sensation, as if his skin were being bathed in a weak acidic solution. The air itself tasted tart and coppery. The beam was coming closer. The roar from the approaching inferno drowned out the sound of his labored breathing, the rush of wind, and the noise from his microwave counter.

There was less than thirty feet to go now. He increased his pace. Suddenly he felt isolated drops of water pelting him from above. For a moment he thought it was raining. Then it dawned on him that all the ice coating the tower was melting and dripping. The drops felt warm. They came down steadily, first in a light shower, then in a deluge.

The wind whipped the rain into his eyes. He blinked, and at that instant his boot slipped off the rung. He scrambled for a handhold, wasn't fast enough, and fell twenty-three feet to the fog-shrouded ground below. His right foot impacted hard onto the concrete pad. His knees buckled and he collapsed into a heap.

Doheny lay facedown on the hard surface, the hot air rasping at his lungs, his breathing harsh and deep as his clamoring heart strove to supply his system with the oxygen it desperately needed. He was blanketed in thick fog, dark and strangely warm, enveloping him in fine beads of moisture. When he tried to get up excruciating pain shot through his right ankle, and he fell down again. He quickly discovered that his leg could not support his weight. He glanced at his right foot and saw that it was slightly askew. His throat constricted with horror, and his heart began to beat unnaturally loud when he realized he had broken his ankle. There was no doubt: the protruding bone was bulging out the side of his boot.

Then his fear gave voice in a deafening yell, a despairing prayer. "*Please God, no!*" he shouted. "*Not like this!*"

Now there was no hope of outrunning the power beam and making it back to the control dome. He knew with a paralyzing terror that he was going to die.

High above, SOLSAT X-1 was tracking the enemy below with its infrared sensors. The command computer determined its human target lay motionless at the base of the disk-shaped structure. It was apparent the human would soon be neutralized by the fiery splotch rapidly closing in on it. The computer calculated that the focal point of the satellite's power beam would reach the enemy in precisely three minutes, forty-eight seconds.

The satellite's sensors also registered the enormous black shadow now creeping across the peninsula below like a great ink stain. The sun was drawing nearer to the horizon with each passing second. The computer had been programmed to avoid crossing the terminator into the dark side of the world, where its solar-powered systems would shut down. As it monitored the progress of the microwave beam the command computer began calculating an orbital maneuver that would allow SOLSAT X-1 to follow the sun.

It felt like being in a steam bath with the temperature set at a dangerously high level. The heat came in waves. His radiation counter registered four hundred milliwatts per square centimeter. Doheny put his hands to his temples and felt the blood pulsing beneath his fingertips. He heard an angry roar from somewhere nearby. It all seemed so oddly unreal.

A kaleidoscope of familiar faces swam through his brain: the governor of New Mexico, the control room crew at the power plant, Nore, Harriman, Stratton, Rosen and the troubleshooting team, and Diane. They were going to die, too. The world was becoming gray before his eyes. A deadly, dreamy torpor was pushing him down and down onto the hard concrete. It would be easy to just lie there and slip into blissful unconsciousness.

No. This single thought reverberated through every fiber of his being, and penetrated the haze rapidly overtaking him. He could not give up. Not while there was still breath in his body.

He snapped his eyes open and sat up. The acute pain from this movement helped clear his head. He felt his scalp tingling as if an electric current were passing through it, and realized he had lost his protective hard hat. He had to reach the control dome, but how? He couldn't even stand up, let alone run. Then he remembered the crowbar he had dropped. It was long enough to use as a cane. He peered into the thick low fog, straining his eyes, but couldn't see it. He had a dim recollection that it had ricocheted off the concrete and hit the tundra. It had to have landed somewhere nearby.

He rolled off the cement onto the wet spongy ground. The tundra had turned into a steaming bog and hot water soaked into his clothes. He was crawling through the dense fog now, hugging the mud beneath him, desperately groping with his free hand, hoping that the crowbar hadn't sunk. He slithered around the circumference of the concrete pad, his hand clawing at the mud and slimy vegetation. He was aware that the pain and weakness caused by his broken ankle was slowly spreading through his entire body. He expected to go into shock at any moment.

He was about to give up his search when his hand suddenly struck something black and hard sticking up from the quagmire. He had found it! A surge of adrenaline shot through him. It took all his willpower to calm himself, to clench and unclench his fists, to breathe deeply and slowly.

He wrenched the crowbar free, grabbed hold of the curved end, and shoved the tip deep into the wet ground. Clenching his teeth from the pain, he pulled himself to his feet, careful not to put his weight on the broken ankle. As he stood up his head rose above the low fog. He turned his head and through the tower framework saw the boiling inferno closing in on him. He sighted on the control dome a hundred yards away and started limping toward it as fast as he could.

He was deaf and blind to the surroundings. He willed himself forward, heedless of the hot wind that stung his eyes, conscious only of the need to lean heavily on that crowbar and keep moving toward the dome, step after anguished step. He drew on a reserve of physical stamina he didn't know he possessed.

Behind him the wet area where he had found the crowbar suddenly came to a boil, spewing plumes of steam into the air.

The land was becoming a swamp beneath his feet, a nightmarish version of the spring thaw. Ponds were forming everywhere. The water was up to the top of his boots. The heated air about him was incredibly intense, and he felt the steaming breath from the center of the power beam searing his back.

Each step was agony, as if his leg pumped liquid fire with every limping stride. He felt sick and faint, but somehow he kept going, stumbling across the hellish landscape, dragging his bad leg. His boot made a sucking noise each time he lifted it from the mud.

A gnarled willow tree that he had passed by a minute ago swelled and burst apart, shooting sap in every direction.

When he was just seventy feet from the control dome he stepped into a thick patch of sticky slime that clutched at his foot. He was caught off balance and fell flat on his face into the bog. He propped himself up on his elbows and realized with a sickening fear that his crowbar had sunk into the mud without a trace. He clawed the slime with his hands but couldn't find it. He gave up the attempt and began crawling on his elbows and knees toward the dome.

In the sky above, SOLSAT X-1's command computer determined the earth's shadow was rapidly approaching. The instant its target had been neutralized it would fire the Icarus rockets at the satellite's aft section and boost it into a higher orbit, one that would be continuously exposed to the sun.

The computer detected the movement of the human figure below as it slowly made its way across the stark, barren landscape. The brilliant splotch of the microwave beam was just moments away from enveloping the figure moving near the disk-shaped structure. The infrared sensors registered bright tendrils of microwave radiation slowly wrapping around the human below.

Doheny's breath involuntarily rasped out in a hoarse shout when his bad foot caught on a submerged rock. He gritted his teeth against the pain and continued crawling.

The pointer on the dial of his microwave counter slammed hard against its pin, and stayed there. He was receiving over six hundred milliwatts of radiation. He experienced a needle bath of tormented nerve ends all over his body. His face and hands felt as if he had plunged them into a blast furnace. He heard a strange clicking coming from inside his head and at once realized the sound was being produced by thermal expansion of his brain tissues. He knew that he couldn't last much longer, that time had run out.

He was exhausted beyond belief when he finally reached the steps to the control dome. He felt a growing weakness, a weariness that brought him to the verge of unconsciousness. The heat was unbearable. It came in waves, one after another, which beat at him mercilessly. He had the insane thought that the fluids in his body were slowly coming to a boil.

He pushed the big heavy door open with his hands and crawled inside. Without pausing to rest he made his way along the floor to the main console, pulled himself up so he could reach the control panel, then threw the switch to restore electrical power to the radio telescope receiver. The ceiling lights dimmed for a moment, then brightened.

His radiation counter chattered away. The microwaves relentlessly streaming down from space were pouring into the control dome through the open door, the ventilation grilles, and the settling cracks in the walls. With each passing second they became ever more intense, reflecting and ricocheting off the metallic surfaces in a wild frenzy. The insulation Doheny had covered the consoles with kept their electronics from jamming.

There was no time to shut the door, no time to think. He had to make it to the basement now or die trying.

The clicking sound in his head became small explosions steadily pounding away at his brain. All the nerve endings of his body felt raw, flayed. He experienced a heightened sense awareness of the physical surroundings about him. He saw the scratches, grooves and seams in the floor beneath him with startling clarity. He felt his fingernails digging into the vinyl. He saw the heated air around him trembling delicately like inside a hot oven.

Then blackness began closing in on him. He shook his head and willed himself to stay conscious. He scrambled across the floor to the entrance to the basement and shoved the door open. When he tried to clamber down the stairs he accidentally put his weight on the wrong foot. He rolled and tumbled down the steps and hit the floor. He lay there, bruised and in great pain.

Summoning the last residue of his strength, he started crawling toward the lab bench with the oscilloscope and switches perched atop it. The bench seemed to be miles away, beyond hope. The oscilloscope screen glowed tantalizingly, beckoning him forward. He pressed against the floor, propelling himself across it with his elbows. Every muscle in his body ached as he slid inch by inch along the smooth surface. The pounding in his head was synchronized with the thudding of his heart.

After what seemed to be an eternity he finally reached the chair beside the bench. He used it to pull himself up and sat down heavily, gasping for breath.

With his eyes riveted to the oscilloscope screen he frantically tried to work the two black switches. His hands shook so violently he could barely flick the studs on them. When at last he saw the green pulse rise to its full height he was scarcely able to believe his eyes.

At that moment he heard the speakers upstairs hissing with the electronic noise from the satellite's on-board systems. There was no doubt the receiver was locked onto the thing.

"You're going to die now," he wheezed, keeping his eyes glued to the screen. "*You're going to die!*"

Outside the control dome the boiling, roaring cloud of thick steam came to a standstill at the perimeter of the steel reflector dish, then dissipated as the center of the power beam leaped from the tundra onto the radio telescope. The dish instantly collected the microwaves and focused them onto the millions of dipoles embedded in the underside of the massive triangular-shaped receiver suspended above. A low throbbing sound came from the receiver as it converted the invisible radiation into electrical impulses. This electricity was then transformed back into microwaves, which were amplified into a multi-megawatt pulse aimed at the satellite.

The throbbing sound grew in amplitude until the very ground seemed to vibrate. A faint bluish purple halo surrounded the receiver as the air in the immediate vicinity became ionized. The halo danced and shimmered like the aurora borealis.

Inside the control dome basement Doheny's vision blurred, and the green tracing on the oscilloscope screen swam before his eyes. His throat felt unbelievably parched, and he had a raging thirst. But somehow he managed to operate his switches to keep the receiver locked onto the moving satellite.

Suddenly he heard howling static screaming from the upstairs speakers.

SOLSAT X-1 was under attack. The radiation sensors throughout its hull registered a dangerously high level of microwaves that was increasing with each passing moment. The onslaught began the instant the center of its power beam swept onto the circular ground station below.

The microwave intensity grew steadily. Then, one by one, the command computer began to lose control of the on-board systems. The thousands of sensors monitoring their status stopped transmitting data to the computer. The satellite's parabolic antenna was swamped by loud crackling static. The computer tried to fire the Icarus rocket engines but they did not respond. The gyroscopes maintaining the satellite's orientation in the weightlessness of space suddenly jammed. A second passed and the thermal images from the infrared sensors started rolling, turned to snow, then blackness. The computer's superconducting microchip circuitry began overloading.

Without warning one of the lit klystron tubes near the rupture in the microwave transmitter housing succumbed to the flood of intense microwaves streaming in. The tube experienced a rapid heating of its pressurized argon gas. The liquid nitrogen coolant could not compensate for this sudden temperature rise. The gas expanded too fast and the tube silently exploded into shards of blackened crystal. Another klystron tube burst, then another. Soon entire rows of klystrons were detonating like sticks of dynamite strung together.

The power beam emanating from the microwave transmitter faded, dwindled to a faint trickle, then disappeared completely as the last of the klystron tubes blew up.

For a second or so the few remaining circuits in the command computer tried to send an activation signal to the Icarus rockets, and then went inert. The flow of electricity from the satellite's twin solar wings to the computer had weakened and stopped.

The zone of darkness was reaching up from the horizon below, spreading across the bright sunlit space like a cold, impenetrable black mist. The blazing disk of the sun was dropping behind the earth, bringing about the end of another day.

Every detail of SOLSAT X-1's hull was revealed by the slanting rays of the dying sun. All the shadowed cracks and hollows were pools of ink, while the vast expanse of gleaming skin seemed to be on fire. The spectacle would last for a brief moment, and then be extinguished forever by the rapidly advancing shadow.

Far below, the bluish purple halo around the Seward observatory's radio telescope receiver had vanished the instant the satellite's power beam stopped transmitting. The reflector dish itself was an island of steel amid a steaming lake. The water had ceased boiling and was now cooling down as the air temperature in the area returned to normal. The first minute needles of frost formed on the upper reaches of the receiver support towers surrounding the dish. The lake beneath was rose pink in the light from the setting sun.

The gale-force wind had decreased to a mild breeze and finally to a mere whisper. An overpowering silence descended upon the ravaged land.

In the sky above, the great hole in the overcast was quickly shrinking as the clouds re-formed and recombined. At its center the solar satellite glinted in the last bit of sunlight, flashed a brilliant crimson, and then winked out just before the hole closed up.

The sun was below the horizon now, and the long Arctic twilight began to fall.

In the basement below the observatory's control dome Mike

Doheny suddenly realized the howling static from the upstairs speakers had stopped, and the sound inside his head was gone. He knew at that moment the thing was dead. A great wave of exultation and joy swept through him, a lump rose in his throat, and tears filled his eyes. He had fought against impossible odds and won.

Then his vision of the room around him turned red and there was only a rushing blackness into which he was falling.

Thirty-one hundred miles to the south, at the solar power plant near Albuquerque, guidance engineer Carl Jenkins nervously stroked his beard as he scanned the blank microwave systems console before him. Moments earlier he and the others inside the control room had watched anxiously as the temperature indicator for the satellite's klystron array climbed into the danger zone. Then the readout lights across the board flashed red, dimmed, and went out. Simultaneously every telemetry indicator throughout the room had died.

"Mike killed it," Jenkins announced. "The whole thing is burned out."

Somewhere in the control room a voice cheered and was instantly joined by a dozen others. The entire room echoed with wild shouts of triumph.

Jenkins felt a nervous twinge in his stomach. He had been given instructions by General Stratton to report any change in the satellite's status to the Pentagon via the reconnected trunk line. He went to the red scrambler phone, picked up the receiver, and spoke to Major Thomas Linden at the NMCC.

Major Linden immediately transmitted Jenkins's report to the teletype in the White House bomb shelter.

An anguished President Kendall tore off the printout, read it once, then shouted to General Thompson to broadcast a Condition Blue message ordering America's armed forces to stand down, to go to peacetime status.

Four minutes later contact with Moscow was established. President Gorodin told Kendall that the Russian military had stepped down from its strategic alert stage an instant after the United States. Because the hot-line autotranslator system was still inoperative, the two heads of state had to speak through interpreters. Their phone conversation was awkward and brief. Afterward the President smiled genuinely for the first time in three days.

*   *   *

Carl Jenkins's report was also relayed to Cheyenne Mountain and Kirtland Air Force Base.

Although General Dean Stratton was glad it was all over he still felt a slight pang of regret. For a long time he had thought that Sunstroke would be the high point of his career, a spectacular military achievement. He remembered the glorious multiple launches from the Cape, and the awe-inspiring space-based deployment. Now all he had to look forward to was an early retirement.

At Kirtland General Walter Abrams handed Everett Nore the printout from the teletype machine in the corner of his office.

Nore read it quickly. He grinned, and the wrinkles fanned out from his eyes. "Hallelujah!" he yelled. "Mike did it. The thing is dead."

He left the room and went to the lounge outside. He saw Diane Bradford sitting on a sofa, writing in her notebook. Across from her sat an air policeman.

Diane looked up, surprised. "Everett . . . ?"

Nore approached her and smiled in a lopsided way. "It's all over. He stopped the thing."

Her eyes widened and her lips parted. "Thank God."

"If you'll excuse me," Nore said, "I'm going to call Mike and congratulate him." He went to the phone near the door, turned his back to the others in the room, and pulled out a flask of Scotch from his flight jacket. He took a long swallow and then made the call.

Inside the basement of the Seward observatory's control dome Mike Doheny was jolted awake by the phone on the lab bench. He lay on the floor beneath, unable to summon the strength to pull himself up. The phone rang thirty-six times before he managed to yank its cord. It clattered to the floor just before he plunged back into a feverish unconsciousness. He had a dream in which Nore was standing on a distant mountain shouting to him.

Ten minutes passed. A half hour. Somewhere in the distance a planed droned. He stirred and moaned from the pain. His lips formed silent words. The drone grew nearer and lower, building into a steady roar of propellers that sounded across the tundra.